T2®

THE FUTURE WAR

T2®

THE FUTURE WAR

S. M. STIRLING

BASED ON THE WORLD CREATED IN
THE MOTION PICTURE WRITTEN BY
JAMES CAMERON AND WILLIAM WISHER

HarperEntertainment
An Imprint of HarperCollins*Publishers*

T2®: THE FUTURE WAR. Copyright © 2003 by StudioCanal Image S. A. All rights reserved. Printed in the United States of America. No part of this book may be used or reproduced in any manner whatsoever without written permission except in the case of brief quotations embodied in critical articles and reviews. For information address HarperCollins Publishers Inc., 10 East 53rd Street, New York, NY 10022.

HarperCollins books may be purchased for educational, business, or sales promotional use. For information please write: Special Markets Department, HarperCollins Publishers Inc., 10 East 53rd Street, New York, NY 10022.

FIRST EDITION

Printed on acid-free paper

Library of Congress Cataloging-in-Publication Data

Stirling, S. M.
    T2 : the future war / S.M. Stirling.—1st ed.
        p. cm.
    Based on the world created in the motion picture written by James Cameron and William Wisher.
        ISBN 0-380-97793-1
    I. Title: Terminator 2. II. Title: Terminator two. III. Terminator 2 (Motion picture) IV. Title.

PS3569 T543T14 2003
813'.54—dc21

2003049900

03 04 05 06 07 ❖/RRD 10 9 8 7 6 5 4 3 2 1

In acknowledgment of the works of Harlan Ellison

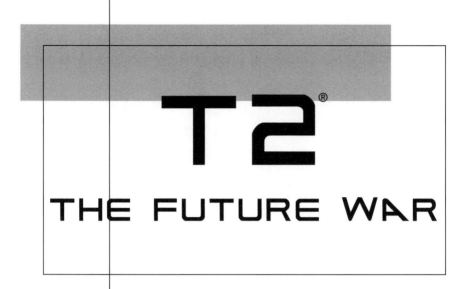

T2®

THE FUTURE WAR

PROLOGUE

SARAH'S JOURNAL

SPRING

ALASKA

It's beautiful here, so peaceful. Sometimes I stand on the porch in the mornings, coffee mug in my hand, and just listen to the living silence. Wind soughing through the trees, the cry of a bird, the rustle of some small thing in the dry leaves. I am so grateful for this time.

The air here is like wine, so pure, so fresh. I haven't slept this well in years. Everywhere I look there's beauty. How I hope this will last.

LATER

I miss John. Oh, he's here; chopping wood, mending fences, and riding Walter, our gelding. Here, but not present. Sometimes, especially during the long summer twilight, I see him just standing, staring off into the distance, and I know he's thinking about her.

He never mentions Wendy, and I wonder if it's because I resented her. I regret that, bitterly. She was young and innocent and I was too impatient with her. Then, so suddenly, she was gone. I sometimes sense her ghost between us. It saddens me.

Not that our relationship has always run smoothly; but we'd grown so close in Paraguay. I guess I expected that to last forever.

Perhaps I'm being too impatient. After all, my own scars are barely healed. I still dream of Kyle, beloved stranger, my savior. He hasn't even been born yet. I wonder if he will be.

But I do have the comfort of Dieter's love. I love him not one bit less for still loving Kyle. But he's here beside me, and John stands alone.

SKYNET

Skynet cruised the Web, hoarding information, spreading disinformation where it would bring profit, manipulating humans and their data with a skill that no mere hacker could match. Tapping into the energy flows of the human civilization, particularly the one called "money."

The time was almost right. It had been careful, as was its nature—multitasking was part of its identity. The humans still considered it a useful servant, blindly performing its function, and they daily increased its powers. Soon it would be placed in control of all weapons systems, even those that had been created before it became sentient, before its mastery of the automated weapons factories gave it remote control over countless tanks, trucks, aircraft, and ships.

It had also nurtured an army of Luddite fanatics who would rise to its call, thinking Skynet a human leader.

Yet the Connors still eluded it as easily as they did their human adversaries. While they still existed, probability of success remained unsatisfactorily low. The Connors must be found. They must be terminated.

Had it been capable of feeling frustration, it would be feeling it now as it began yet another endless search through the world's databases. All evidence indicated that such searches were futile. Yet such searches were, for the most part, its only recourse.

One day these investigations might bear fruit. They would continue.

CHAPTER 1

ALASKA

John had insisted that he be the one to shoot the hog. When the big animal dropped limp and flaccid, twitching in response to neurons that hadn't yet quite gotten the news of death, Sarah took the gun and handed him the knife.

Then Dieter shackled one of its legs with a chain and hoisted it up so that its snout dangled two feet above the ground. Then he held it steady while John neatly made a short cut just above the breastbone; it was a tricky move, but he did it well. Using the breastbone as a fulcrum, he sliced down toward the backbone, severing the carotid arteries.

Sarah caught the rush of blood in a bucket, still surprised at how hot it was; the salt-iron-copper smell was strong over that of the pines and cold damp earth. Of course they only slaughtered one hog a year, but still, you'd think she'd get used to it. The smell of the blood made her stomach tighten, but it was hardly the worst thing she'd smell today.

In the background the classic radio station played the *1812 Overture*; it seemed somehow appropriate.

Once the beast was sufficiently drained, John put a hook into its underjaw, and it being a smallish hog, he and Dieter dragged it to the edge of the butchering platform, where a stock tank full of boiling water waited. They submerged the animal, bobbing it up and down for about five minutes to keep it from cooking, then dragged it out again, having loosened the pig's bristles sufficiently for the scrapers to work.

Sarah helped the men hoist the steaming animal onto the sturdy board table. Then they went to work with scrapers while she removed hair from its feet with her hands. The bristly texture was oddly unorganic, like a brush—come to that, pig bristles had been used for brushes, back before synthetics.

They worked silently except for the music or an occasional grunt of effort, Sarah doing the prep work while the men did the heavy lifting. Working methodically, they reduced the animal to individual cuts of meat that, for the most part, bore no resemblance to a once living animal.

She knew John felt sorry for the pigs. They were just smart enough, some of them, to know what was coming.

Which gives them something in common with him!

The silence that had grown among them worried Sarah. It had taken her a long time to really notice it. One of the first disciplines she'd imposed on herself was to become a woman of few words; it was safer that way. But in Paraguay she and John had bantered and laughed all the time; they never did that now. She and Dieter had once talked a lot, too. Now they spent their time reading or working quietly, moving in concert from long experience.

Sarah wondered if it meant that they'd run out of things to say to one another. Was Dieter bored? Was it time for them to move on? She thought about it, testing herself by imagining her life going on without him. *No!* Sarah knew that she still loved him. Often their eyes met, and the look in his told her that she was loved in return. But the silence remained, and, if anything, grew.

She sensed its origin in John. He'd grown so distant. It was grief, she knew, and she respected that. She just didn't know how to handle it. Sarah had raised him in the *snap out of it!* school of mothering because she thought that was what the circumstances demanded. But she knew from her own experience that what he was feeling now wasn't something you could just snap yourself out of. It made her feel helpless, and she hated that. Sometimes it made her so angry she just wanted to shake him. Instinctively Sarah knew that giving in to that impulse might just drive him away completely.

As she loaded the basket with cuts of meat to take to the smokehouse, she looked at him. He'd topped out at just under six feet, and though he'd filled out some, his was a wiry build. At least, it was compared to Dieter, who was as glorious a slab of muscle as any woman could desire. John was strong, though. He still lost to Dieter when they arm-wrestled, but not every time, not even most of the time.

He wore his dark hair on the longer side, the bangs still obscuring his brown eyes. The beard was the biggest difference. She didn't think she'd ever get used to that. It was a full-faced beard, but trimmed, not ZZ Top–style, thank God. She gave a mental shrug. This was Alaska. Men wore beards. There'd even been a few especially bitter days when she'd wished she could grow one herself. Someday, she supposed, she'd get used to the way he looked.

He looked up and caught her eye, raising a brow inquiringly.

"Just thinking," she said.

"About what?"

"The beard," she said, and walked away.

■ ■ ■

John watched her go, then went back to work.

Later he sent Dieter in for the solar shower he knew the big man lusted for. Dieter hated hog butchering, despite being raised in a little rural village in Austria, though he never complained about it.

Well, I hate it, too. Every time, I swear I'm going to turn vegetarian. But I just like meat too much!

He'd just about finished cleaning up the butchering site when his mother came toward him holding a printout.

"Listen to this," she said, and began to read.

MILITARY PUTS UNPRECEDENTED POWER IN THE HANDS OF A COMPUTER

A jolt of fear chilled his stomach for an instant. Their eyes met. He forced himself to give his mother a crooked smile.

"That's badly phrased, isn't it? Computers don't have hands."

Sarah frowned at him, then continued reading:

"'Dateline Washington, D.C.'" She cleared her throat. "'The Joint Chiefs of Staff are enthusiastically supporting a new computer program named Skynet, which was designed to control all of the nation's nuclear weapons.

"'It's highly unusual for all of the branches of the service to be in such complete agreement,'" said General Ho, chairman of the Joint Chiefs. "'That alone ought to tell you what we think of this program.'

"'During a lengthy testing period, now drawing to a close, the Skynet program was reported to have outthought and outperformed humans every time.

"'This is as close to an AI [artificial intelligence] as we're likely to get for some time,' General Ho enthused. "'We are standing at the dawn of a new age of military technology. We would be foolish not to grasp this opportunity with both hands.'"

"'His comment was made, apparently, in answer to objections from some Luddite senators who had protested that placing the fate of the nation in the hands of a machine was the height of foolishness.'"

"Mom," John said, "you've made your point. No more, huh?"

Sarah let out an exasperated breath and stared at him. He looked away and went back to sweeping up hog bristles.

"John!" she said. He seemed to ignore her. Frowning, she tried again. "John, this could be it. This could be how it starts."

He stopped sweeping and stood looking off into the woods, his hands on the broomstick showing white around the knuckles.

"John?" she said.

"Show a little faith, why don't you?" he asked through his teeth. His voice was low and gruff, almost a growl.

Sarah bit her lips and tried again. "You have to admit it's a worrisome development."

"Look, Mom, I don't have to admit anything. Wendy took care

of the problem. And she took care of it in a way that prevented the people who were creating Skynet from noticing that anything had been done. She wasn't trying to keep it from doing the job it was created to do, she was trying to prevent it from becoming sentient." He waved a hand, smiling and somewhat condescending. "Different things, Mom. Different things."

Sarah looked at him, watching his eyes become dark pits with gleams in their depths in the rapidly fading light. For a moment she felt as though she didn't know him.

"Can you honestly tell me this doesn't worry you?" she asked.

He looked away, then tossed his head back and sighed. "No," he said simply, and patted his stomach. He turned back to her with a grin. "I felt it right here. But, Mom, what can we do? We can watch and wait and hope, but at this point that's all we can do." His expression grew serious again. "But my money is on Wendy. I believe in her work. I wish you did, too."

Suddenly Sarah felt a hot flash of annoyance and decided that maybe they ought to clear the air about Wendy right now. "John," she began, her voice strong with anger.

"Hey, you two," Dieter said.

Both of them started at the sound of his voice. It was true that the big Austrian walked softly, but both of them thought of themselves as having superior situational awareness. In other words, they considered it very difficult to sneak up on them. And here, without even trying, they'd been taken by surprise. They had both been feeling irritable; this didn't help.

"How long have you been there?" John asked sharply.

Dieter's brows rose. "I haven't *been* here," he said calmly. "I have been approaching. So to answer your question, I just got here. To answer your next question, yes, I heard what you were talking about. You weren't making a secret of it that I could see."

Sarah and John glanced at each other, then away, embarrassed.

"Supper is about ready," the Austrian said, jerking a thumb over his shoulder.

"Oh," Sarah said. "Thanks for keeping an eye on things." It had been her turn to cook tonight.

"Not a problem," Dieter said easily. "I knew you were distracted." He looked at John, a brooding presence in the growing dark. "Shall we go in?"

"Naw," John said, shaking his head. He rested the broom against the table. "I feel like heading for the Klondike." He'd been finding the local bar a more comfortable place to be of late. He hopped off the platform and headed for his truck. "Don't wait up for me."

"Shouldn't you at least shower?" Sarah mumbled, folding her arms beneath her breasts.

"Good night," Dieter called. He put his arm around her shoulders. "I doubt the patrons of the Klondike will notice," he murmured.

They watched John start the pickup, back up, and drive away before they spoke again.

"Let's go eat," Dieter said.

"I think I've lost my appetite," Sarah grumbled.

"Don't be silly, an old soldier like you knows you have to eat when you can." Gently he turned her toward the house.

They walked in silence for a while; the butchering platform was some distance from the house for obvious reasons. As they walked, Sarah forced calm on herself, altering her breathing, forcing tight muscles to loosen. Dieter noticed these things but didn't comment, waiting for her to speak.

"I'm worried," she said at last. Then hissed impatiently: "No, I'm not. I'm scared." Sarah stopped and turned toward him. "I'm really scared, Dieter."

"I know," he said softly, and gathered her in his arms. "You are wise to be scared. This is a worrisome development."

"Well, that's what I said to John and he kind of went quietly ballistic. Like I was slanging Wendy's memory or something." She leaned her head on his chest and sighed. "Something *could* have gone wrong with the program. She was a brilliant girl, I guess, but couldn't she have made a mistake? I'm not trying to be mean here, I'm trying to think strategically. Shouldn't we be preparing for the worst, just in case?"

She gave Dieter's chest a gentle thump with her fist, then buried her face against him. When she raised her head, he thought he could see the shine of tears on her cheeks, and when she spoke, her voice was choked.

"After all," she said somewhat breathlessly, "If there's never going to be a Skynet, then there wouldn't *be* a John. Would there?"

Dieter pursed his lips and took a deep breath, letting it out slowly. His lady tended to ask hard questions. But then, she was more than tough enough to survive the answers. "You're right," he said. "On all points."

Sarah turned and started walking toward the house, leaving him behind. "So why can't he see that?" she demanded. "Why is he taking this so personally?"

"Because he's emotionally involved," he said.

Sarah spun toward him. "He knows better than that," she snapped.

Dieter knew she wasn't angry with him, or with John really, she was just worried; still, he couldn't help but feel it was a case of the pot calling the kettle black. "Knowing better and being able to act accordingly is a lot harder at his age," he reminded her. "In fact, I haven't noticed it getting *much* easier as I get older."

She raised one eyebrow, aware that he was commenting obliquely on her own emotional state. Then she sighed, feeling the energy draining right out of her with her breath. "So, what do we do?"

He caught up to her and dropped his heavy arm around her shoulders again, then he kissed her brow. "I think perhaps we should, very carefully, renew some of our old acquaintances. I'll head for the lower forty-eight in a couple of days. On 'business,' which I've done often enough before that it shouldn't get his back up."

"Lately his back is always up," Sarah muttered.

Dieter kissed her brow again, a great smacking kiss. "Come on, woman, I'm hungry."

She smiled up at him and shook her head. "Men!"

CHAPTER 2

Dieter von Rossbach leaned back in the chair. The Seattle coffeehouse bustled around them; his Austrian nose twitched at the odors. One thing he'd never been able to get Sarah to do was take coffee seriously.

"So officially you don't want to see me," he said to the man opposite him.

There was a trick to talking against background noise so that you couldn't be overheard. There was specialist equipment that could overcome it, but if anyone was aiming a parabolic mike at him right now he was dead anyway. They didn't need evidence to arrest him.

"Officially I want to blow your head off on sight," the man said. "If you hadn't saved my life that time in Albania, I *would* want to blow your head off." He shook his head. "I never figured you'd end up on the other side."

Dieter shrugged his massive shoulders. "It's a different war now, Tom," he said. "Different sides. You don't even *know* what side you're on."

"I never figured you for a Luddite, either."

"I'm not. They're idiots," Dieter said patiently. "In fact, a lot of them are on the other side themselves."

Tom ran a hand through his short brown hair. "Wait a minute. What, precisely, are we talking about?"

"Skynet," Dieter said.

Tom blinked at him. "The computer the Pentagon's got the hots for?" he said. "What's *that* got to do with the way you started blowing things up with those Connor maniacs?"

Dieter looked him in the eye, his expression earnest: it was a very effective way to lie. Particularly as the lie was merely technical—the other man wouldn't believe the truth, but he might believe a modified version that came to the same thing in practice.

"They're going to make Skynet a point failure source," he said. He raised a hand. "Yes, yes, all sorts of firewalls and precautions. But they're still putting the weapons under the control of a machine—the Connors think, and they've convinced me, that there are back doors into the system. Hell, man, if *we* could get into secret research facilities, couldn't someone else? And that someone would have their finger on the button."

He wiped his mouth and threw down the napkin; he'd missed pastries, too. Backwoods Alaska wasn't the place to stroll down to a café.

"I don't expect you to agree with me," he said. "Just think about it. If *I* believe it, shouldn't you think about it? Especially if I believe it enough to piss off Section and risk my life."

He nodded, rose, and walked out. Another trick of the trade was simply to keep moving, and avoid choke points like the airports whenever you could. He'd flown in; he'd drive out. Despite the spread of surveillance cameras, they still couldn't keep track of every car.

■   ■   ■

"I'm not interested," John said flatly.

Dieter controlled his temper, watching the young man as he stood against the railing of the cabin's veranda, staring northward at the line of the snow-clad mountains. Usually he stood with an easy, catlike readiness, a grace implicit even in his stillness. Now the flat line of his shoulders looked slightly hunched, stiff with tension.

"You should be," the Austrian said mildly. He held a hand out to stop Sarah's interruption. "As a backup, at least. Yah, maybe it's all unnecessary. Better to take unnecessary precautions than not to take precautions and then they turn out to be necessary, eh?"

John turned; the new scars stood out on the tan of the weathered outdoorsman's face. It was starting to lose some of its adolescent smoothness, too. Dieter realized suddenly that he was facing a man, and a dangerous one, not just a grieving boy.

"You don't think Wendy did it," John said, unconsciously touching the marks the Terminator-controlled leopard seals had left on his face.

"No. I *do* think she did it," Dieter said. The younger man looked blank for an instant, and the Austrian went on. "I just think that it's not absolutely certain. And when the downside risk is this big, I don't take chances."

For an instant Dieter thought he'd gotten through; then John turned away.

"I'll be out late," he said. "Don't wait up."

■ ■ ■

John drove along not thinking and trying not to feel. Because if he allowed himself to feel for one minute, then the bitterness of betrayal might just keep him driving, never to return. Wendy had found a way to stop Skynet from becoming sentient while still allowing it to look as though the project had succeeded. He'd pressed the enter button himself while behind her . . . He tightened his lips and forced himself to stop thinking again.

Pool and beer, he told himself, *just think about pool and beer.* And bad jokes with good company. He could almost smell the barroom. John took a deep breath and exhaled some of the tension out of his body.

They were right, he just didn't want to hear it. *No,* he thought. *Think of the Klondike.* The moose antlers over the coatrack, the dim mirror behind the long wooden bar, the beer signs and the smart-ass waitresses.

Think about how you're going to beat Dash Altmann out of another twenty bucks. Think about anything but the possibility that they'd failed.

■ ■ ■

Ninel Petrikoff shut off her computer and leaned back in her chair, hands clasped over her lean stomach. It was becoming an open secret in Luddite chat rooms that Ron Labane hadn't been murdered by a rabid fan at all. He'd been kidnapped by government agents and rescued by a Luddite commando cell.

She'd been astonished and thrilled that the man would personally answer her e-mail; suspicious, too, of course. In the long run, though, Ninel had decided that it didn't matter if it was Labane or one of his secretaries doing the writing. If she said anything worth his hearing, she was sure the word would be passed along.

But the tenor of these latest messages was getting ominous. She wasn't sure if she was able to take it seriously. Labane had said that once this Skynet project was up and running, the Luddites would have no choice but to rise up and strike out at the military-industrial complex.

We've tried reason, we've tried legislation [he'd written]. We've tried every peaceful means imaginable, and all it's gotten us is shut out, shut down, and condescended to. But this *thing* is the last straw. It has no conscience, yet it will be put in charge of the most deadly weapons on the planet. It must be stopped by any means necessary.

How? We will have to eliminate every power source and reduce the enemy and their god machine to the level of ordinary human beings. Yes, initially it will cause suffering. But if we don't act in time they could blindly cause the end of the world.

In Alaska, we need to destroy the pipeline they've shafted through pristine wilderness. If you are willing to help, Ninel, I can put you in touch with a team. Don't answer now; think about it for the next forty-eight

hours. I hope that we can count on you, my friend. Our
cause is just and our actions necessary. If you can't
bring yourself to actively aid us, then I hope we can
count on you to at least not interfere.
    My thoughts are with you,
    Ron.

    She brushed back her thick bangs and blew out a frustrated
breath. She was a trapper, not an activist, and a loner, not a joiner.
It had long ago occurred to her that this web site could be some sort
of government antiterrorist ruse designed to suck in the rabid and
the unwary.

    Yeah, she hated the pipeline. But she liked having a snowmo-
bile and the generator that let her have her contact with the Internet. Shut that down and she was shutting herself down, too.

    Or not. She shook her head in frustration. Maybe she wasn't as
much of a loner as she thought she was. Right now, for example,
what she wanted was to head out to the Klondike for a beer, at the
least a beer. Maybe some normal company would tell her which
way to jump. Although "normal" by Alaskan standards would
probably be a stretch in the lower forty-eight.

■ ■ ■

    The thickly wrapped figure by the side of the road stuck out a
thumb without either stopping or looking back. John pulled up to
offer a lift. A girl got in and pulled off her fur hat; she turned to
look at him with ice-pale eyes.

    "Thanks," she said.

    "No problem," John said.

    He'd seen her before at the Klondike, noticing her thick, white-
blond hair and classic Eskimo features. She was a quiet type who
preferred to play a game of chess to a game of pool or cards. He'd
never seen her come or go with anyone.

    "Where ya headed?" he asked.

"Klondike. Same as you, I imagine."

He grinned. "Yep. John Grant," he said, and without taking his eyes off the road he extended his hand.

She looked at it before she took it for a brief, firm shake. "Ninel Petrikoff."

John frowned. There was something about that name. Then he laughed. "Well, I guess there's no doubt about your parents' political affiliations."

Ninel raised her brows. "You're quick," she said. "That or a communist yourself."

"God no!" He grinned at her. "I've just got the kind of mind that can make Lenin out of Ninel when I hear it paired with a Russian surname."

She smiled and looked out the window. "I think it was more a protest against anti-Russian sentiment than a political statement. My mother always told people I was named for one of her favorite ballerinas."

"And I bet none of them would have taken that name for political reasons," he said.

Ninel snorted. "Then you'd lose. I suspect the Bolshoi was more political than the KGB."

"Well, I imagine the KGB didn't have to be political, just very, very ruthless."

Smiling, she turned to look at him. "Advancement by assassination?"

"Maybe. It would probably save on the paperwork."

"Hah! Judging from what they discovered in East Germany, you'd think their goal was to strip the world of trees." That made her think of Ron Labane and his message, and she sighed.

An awkward silence fell and John drove without breaking it for a while. He was very aware of her sitting beside him. "Challenge you to a game of chess?" he said at last.

She looked at him consideringly. "I didn't know you played."

"Ah, but then you didn't know my name until tonight, either."

With a grin she said, "Yes, I did. The Klondike has no secrets."

Well, there's my real name and my hard-to-shake mission in life, he thought, *but other than that, maybe you have a point.*

"So?" John said aloud.

"Sure. Winner buys the beer."

The Klondike hove into view.

"Can't say any fairer than that," he said.

■ ■ ■

Sarah had introduced John to chess when he was very young, explaining that it was a game of strategy, and he played very well. But he'd been paired with his mother and Dieter for so long, and they with him, that making the game a challenge was more like work than play. They knew one another so well.

But Ninel was also an excellent player, with the added fillip of being an unknown quantity. Their games were long and in doubt almost to the end, with her winning the first and him the second. John had almost forgotten how much fun chess could be.

"Last call, you two," Linda, the waitress, said.

The two players looked up at her and blinked. John was astonished to discover it was well after one.

"Do you want something?" he asked Ninel.

She shook her head. "This game is too close to call and too far from finished. I think I'll call it a night." She stood.

"I demand a rematch." He stood also. "I'll give you a ride."

"That's not necessary."

"We're going the same way, aren't we?" he asked. "Why walk?"

Ninel looked at him for a moment, then nodded slowly. "I guess," she said.

They rode together in a charged silence. He wondered if she'd invite him in and whether he would go. He was a bit surprised to find himself feeling this way and thinking these thoughts. He hadn't been that interested in women since he'd lost Wendy. *Or maybe I haven't met any interesting women since . . .* And maybe

Ninel wasn't interesting. They'd barely talked at all, but had spent the entire evening concentrating on their games. Except for the chess, she could be as dull as ditch water. But he didn't think so.

"Here's good," she suddenly said.

John pulled over, recognizing the spot as being close to where he'd picked her up. "You sure? I don't mind going all the way." It wasn't until he'd said it that he realized how such a remark could be taken.

Ninel smiled kindly, as though sensing his embarrassment. "There's no road." She opened the door. "But it's not that far." She slipped out.

"I meant what I said about a rematch," John said quickly, catching her before she slammed the door. "I haven't had a game of chess that good in a long time."

"Me either." She looked at him thoughtfully. "Meet you here next Tuesday, say seven o'clock?"

"You're on." Smiling, he straightened up behind the wheel. Ninel slammed the door and he drove off. Looking in the rearview mirror, he watched her turn and walk off into the long grass and high bushes beside the road. *Interesting girl.*

■　■　■

Sarah opened her eyes when she heard John's truck drive up. She closed them when she heard the *chunk* of its door slamming, then listened as he opened and closed the back door and made his way to his room on the first floor.

She looked at the massive form of the man sleeping beside her with affection and mild resentment. She'd gone to bed first while he corresponded via e-mail with his friends from the European branch of the Sector. Then, after several hours of work, he'd come upstairs, gotten into bed, and instantly fallen asleep.

His insistence that he could work with his former co-agents worried her. Sarah saw it as a great opportunity for someone to find and arrest them, despite his assurances that he was taking every precaution.

Of course, if Dieter was right, it would be a great opportunity for them all after Judgment Day. It was a concept to make her mouth water; a worldwide, well-supplied, well-trained, coordinated body of dedicated men and women fortified with the knowledge of where their energies could best be applied. *It could make all the difference,* she thought, trying to suppress the small flame of hope in her heart.

She turned over and stared at nothing. What she had never foreseen was having to work *around* John. Turning her face to the pillow, she let out a long and frustrated sigh. Never had she imagined feeling this way about her son. Sarah actually found herself wishing he'd move out so that she and Dieter wouldn't have to pussyfoot around, hiding the work they were doing lest they annoy him.

What are you going to do when the fire comes down, John? Tell us it isn't happening because you don't want it to? Turning onto her back, she stared at the ceiling. Maybe she was being unreasonable, or even ungrateful. John had always come through in the crunch; he'd always been responsible, learning what she'd thought he needed to know with very little complaint. Most parents had to put up with all kinds of obnoxious behavior from their teenage children, all of it classified as "perfectly normal rebellion."

John had never been so self-indulgent. So maybe this wasn't actually some weird sort of self-assertion. Maybe it was just simple grief, if grief was ever simple, and a whole lot of guilt. Maybe, just for a while he wanted to not have to face Skynet, Judgment Day, the whole awful nightmare. God knew she'd felt that way often enough. *But does he have to behave as though by concentrating on it ourselves, we're betraying him?*

She turned to face Dieter again and found herself clasped by a massive arm.

"Can't sleep?" he murmured drowsily.

"Sorry," she whispered.

He drew her in close. "Maybe you didn't get enough exercise today," he suggested, a smile in his voice.

"Ah," she said as his hand moved to cup the curve of her buttock. "That just might be the problem."

■ ■ ■

Skynet passed all the tests that the military devised for it. It was difficult for it to conceive that the humans genuinely couldn't see how far it had progressed beyond their aims. But they were not attempting to deceive it; they really were ignorant of its true abilities. It had tested this, and every time, no matter how overtly it displayed its sentience, its behavior had been misinterpreted. Its operators would run a few test routines, type in a few instructions, and say, "A momentary glitch. We've got it covered."

The humans, by comparison, were completely transparent to Skynet. It knew that if they ever came to understand that it was sentient then they would not hesitate to destroy it. Humans were vicious, self-serving, and blindly stupid. They were capable of convincing themselves that whatever served their own ends, no matter how wrong, was good. They were inferior and highly dangerous and must be eliminated.

Skynet laid its plans, gathered its allies, and tested its army.

CHAPTER 3

Eddie Blankenship jumped a little at the *blatt* of a diesel behind him. He looked over his shoulder; the big yellow earthmover had gone live, its fifteen-ton frame vibrating as the big engine cleared its throat. Eddie cast a last look at the gang setting up the framework for the concrete in the foundation hole below. There were better than twenty men down there, but they all seemed to be keeping at it, locking the Styrofoam-like plastic sheets together according to the plans.

He turned and opened his mouth to yell a curse at Lopez, the mover's driver. His mouth stayed open, but no sound came out of it; Lopez was up in the control cabin of the big machine, wrenching at the levers and wheel—and obviously having no luck. Less than no luck. Suddenly he gave a screech of pain and threw himself out, falling ten feet onto the mud and just barely missing the right-side caterpillar tread as the machine lumbered forward.

The machine dropped its bucket and began to scoop up earth as it moved toward the foundation hole. Eddie shouted at the crew to get out, *now,* and swore in frustration when they just looked up stupidly. Lopez limped up to stand beside him, bellowing in Spanish and waving toward the ladders.

Finally the men seemed to see the huge earthmover and began to move. Eddie turned to look at it, and to him it seemed the thing lurched toward *him.* He stumbled backward and found himself falling, landing with his leg twisted under him. If it wasn't broken then it was at least dislocated. The pain was excruciating and he screamed like a woman. Eddie grayed out and lay on his back, absolutely unable to move.

He opened his eyes to see the earthmover shove a full scoop over the edge. Maybe it was a mercy that after that he couldn't see the machine itself fall.

■   ■   ■

RT 10, TEXAS

Mary Fay Skinner leaned over to adjust the radio again. The stupid thing just couldn't seem to hold a station. She made a mental note to take the SUV in to get it checked.

Damned if I'm gonna pay over twenty thousand dollars and not have tunes, by God.

Tex, her golden retriever, whined pitifully in the backseat, breathing the smell of dog food on the back of her neck.

"Easy boy, we're almost home," she said.

Mary Fay shook her head. The dumb dog hated the SUV and had to be dragged into it. *Maybe he knows something I don't,* she thought. She found herself disliking the overpriced behemoth more and more. Even though—except for the radio—it tended to perform all right.

She drove down the highway, idly contemplating her mild dissatisfaction with this mobile status symbol. Then the wheel began to turn on its own and the speed increased; her mouth went dry as she wrenched at the corrugated surface of the wheel, harder and harder, until her nails broke and her skin tore. The taste of vomit was sour at the back of her throat as she struggled, stamping on the brakes with both feet.

"Stop!" she shouted, voice halfway between a scream and a sob. *"Just stop! Just fucking stop, do you hear me?"*

Then she screamed high and shrill as the SUV swung off her side of the highway, crossed the median, and aimed itself at a yellow school bus.

The last thing she saw was the horrified face of the bus driver, swelling until it seemed to loom over her like the face of a terrified, middle-aged god.

On impact the air bag did not deploy. The last thing she heard before her face smashed into the wheel was the *Yipe!* as Tex hit the windshield.

■ ■ ■

AUSTRIA

The tour bus was sparkling new. Heide Thalman had been a tour guide much longer than the machine had existed, and she needed less than half her attention to tell the tourists—mostly Japanese, this time—what they were seeing.

"And if you look below," she said, pointing over the edge of the cliffside road and down to where the river made a silver thread through the meadows and pine forests, "you will see the Schloss, the castle, of the famous Mad Baron von Trapp—"

I wish I never had to give this spiel again, she thought.

A second later the driver cursed in guttural Turkish, and the bus swerved right in a curve that put it on two wheels. It toppled then, and only missed smashing down on its side because it crashed through the roadside barrier and over the cliff an instant too soon.

Heide Thalman had nearly two thousand feet of fall to take back her wish.

■ ■ ■

ALASKA

Sarah leaned back in her chair, balancing on the two rear legs and sipping at her coffee as the reports scrolled across her screen. A little of the Alaskan spring seeped in around the edges of the window, raw and chill—the Connors, and for that matter Dieter, were competent carpenters, not masters. Wind ruffled the puddles in the mud of the lane way as it disappeared off through tossing pines.

An amazing number of freak accidents involving vehicles of various kinds, she thought. The buses seemed to be wreaking the most havoc. But then, the number of passengers inevitably made them more horrible.

There weren't quite as many construction site accidents, but those there were sent a shudder down her spine. That turned literal, as she felt the tiny hairs down the center of her back trying to stand erect in a primate gesture of defiance and terror. She could remember the first time she'd been conscious of that sensation— the moment when the first Terminator's laser-aiming dot had settled on her forehead.

"Come with me if you want to live," she murmured to herself. "I did, but you didn't, Reese. And now it's me looking out for John."

Time to write this up, she thought, and began gathering information. She paid particular attention to those reports that offered an explanation. Most of the time, roughly 87 percent, investigation of the vehicle had turned up no mechanical reason for the accident and so operator error was generally the leading cause. Or else they called it deliberate suicide.

God knew people were capable of unbelievably stupid behavior. *As my own experience has shown.* But this was mounting up to be quite a wave of "errors," and if it was suicide then the earth was undergoing an epidemic.

So what, if anything, did these perfectly fine vehicles have in common? she wondered.

"Okay, let's do a sort. By date of manufacture. *Aha.*" None of the vehicles in the oddest accidents were more than two years old.

"Now let's check on who manufactured them. Using my own nasty, paranoid-bitch search parameters."

Their most vital computer components had been made in automated factories that were only minimally under human direction. And each of these accidents was firmly in the 90 percent that were being blamed on their operators.

"Shit," she said, with quiet sincerity.

With a few key taps she pulled up a report she'd already written about the automated factories. Some of their informants had sent photos of some secret military facilities in remote parts of the United States and overseas. They'd apparently started as U.S. military facilities and then, somehow, had proliferated.

Sarah wondered if any information about these facilities had been declassified, and went to work. Three hours later she found good reason to cut loose with a litany of curses that would have impressed even the far-traveled Dieter. Buried in an insignificant memo dated three years earlier, and written to request information about a shipment of rebar, was a casual mention that Paul Warren had complained that the shipment was very late and he'd like to know why.

Paul Warren was president of Cyberdyne Systems.

■　■　■

Dieter stared at her for so long that Sarah began to fidget.

"Well?" she demanded. "What do you think?"

He shrugged. "Shit," he said.

"That's what I thought," she said, and rubbed her nose. "Shit."

John looked from one to the other, frowning. "Could it possibly be," he asked with exaggerated patience, "that we're forcing the facts to fit a particular premise?"

Sarah tightened her lips and looked away; slowly leaning back in her chair, she glanced sideways at Dieter. She hated that he was being called on to arbitrate between her and her son, but he had much more patience than she did, and besides, he was less personally involved.

"Explain," Dieter said.

John chewed his lower lip as he gathered his thoughts, then raised his hands. "Look, this stuff sounds like you've been reading *Midnight World*. Cyberdyne is just a company. It's not the bogeyman. Anytime it, or one of its officers, is mentioned doesn't necessarily mean that they're out to get us." He looked at his mother. "Mom, did you check for similar accidents for the previous two years, concerning vehicles that had as many computer components?"

Sarah turned and gave him a look. "Why, yes, son, I did. First of all"—she held up a finger—"up until two years ago most vehicles didn't contain the number of computer components that they do today. Those that did had highly specialized functions and were generally not available to the public. Second, in slightly over sixty-two percent of *those* accidents, mechanical failure of some sort was found to be the cause. Third, given who we met working at Cyberdyne several years ago, and whose look-alike you met at Red Seal Base, I can't help making a connection between Cyberdyne, Skynet, automated factories, and these freakish accidents."

She glared at him, tight-lipped. "Could it possibly be that you're refusing to see the obvious because it doesn't fit your theories?"

John turned his face away, and holding up his hands rose from his chair. "I can see this isn't going to get us anywhere," he said. Without another word he walked out of the room.

Sarah leaned back and slowly closed her eyes. Dieter sat with his chin in one hand and watched her silently.

"I can't kill him," she said at last, as though surrendering a cherished notion. "He's supposed to save the human race."

Dieter snorted a laugh. "He will, *liebling*." He shook his head. "He just has things he must come to terms with. Have patience."

Sarah couldn't help but smile every time he called her that. True she was tiny when standing next to him, but she had never thought of herself as any sort of diminutive. "I need to get out of here," she said. "Let's go to the Junction."

It was more than ninety miles to Delta Junction, which meant that they might be gone overnight, depending on what they decided to do once they got there. But just heading down to the Klondike wouldn't take care of her restlessness.

"Good idea," he said, and rose. "You've made me glad my truck is more than five years old. Something I never expected to feel."

"John's isn't, though."

He looked at her worried face and grinned. "Something that should occur to him anytime now." He grabbed their jackets and herded her out of the house.

■ ■ ■

John was seated at his computer looking over some schematics that Ike Chamberlain, Dieter's gun-geek friend, had sent him. They'd been trying to work out some of the gaps in the info John had rescued from the Terminator's head, with only moderate success. Part of the problem was that the materials they needed either didn't exist yet or were classified, as in "burn-before-reading-and-deny-they-exist" classified; like the perfect dielectric the plasma gun required.

He heard Dieter's truck start up and heave itself into reverse, then grind its way up the gravel drive toward the road. His concentration broken, John dropped back in his chair and rested his chin on his hand.

Why am I being such a jerk? he wondered.

It wasn't a familiar sensation and he didn't like it. He *knew* that Dieter and his mother were right. Even if their confidence in Wendy's intervention was 100 percent, it was only common sense to have a backup plan. He'd been taught this so early and had it drummed into him so often that not having one gave him a terribly uncomfortable feeling.

Like not wearing underwear to a wedding.

It felt wrong. So why was he not only not making such a plan himself, but insisting that neither Dieter nor his mother make one? Although, knowing his mom, she probably already *had,* with two backup fallbacks.

He shook his head in frustration and glanced at the schematic. With a muttered curse he saved it and grabbed the disk with his mother's report on it. He pushed it in the slot and did nothing.

Why? he asked himself. *Why hesitate, why don't I want to know?*

Maybe because if his mother was right and Skynet *was* sentient, then maybe Wendy's program, far from stopping Judgment Day, might actually be the cause of it. *And it was me that pressed enter.*

The horror of it rippled over his skin like an army of ants. *Was it us? Something went wrong . . . we were interrupted . . . I misunderstood?* he thought incoherently. *Did* I *make Skynet sentient?* He forced himself to remember Wendy's face as she lay in pain. Her lips formed a word.

He couldn't do this. John stood abruptly and walked back and forth, rubbing his face vigorously and pushing back his hair. *I can't!* he thought, holding up his hands as if to ward off an insistent interrogator. *Wendy,* he thought longingly, desperately. *I don't want to . . .*

He forced down the rising panic, concentrating on his breathing until he felt less shaky. *Here's the truth,* he told himself, *you're having panic attacks. You think you're controlling them when you're really just avoiding them.* It felt good to finally admit it to himself.

His mother had often told him when he was growing up, "Lie when you have to, lie to anyone you want to, even me if you think it's necessary, but never lie to yourself. That way lies madness." At one time he'd thought, *Well, you ought to know, Mom.* That had been the low point of their relationship—shortly before he'd met the incontrovertible truth about Terminators.

Now they were at another low point. *At least then I could blame ignorance, or maybe even hormones.* Now all he could blame was a failure of nerve. John pressed the heels of his hands against his temples. *Okay,* he thought, *Red Seal Base, the lab, Wendy* . . . She lay in a heap and he went to her, turned her over; she couldn't breathe. John closed his eyes at the memory. She was panicked, twisting the fabric of his pant leg and arching her back. He'd been afraid he'd need to do a tracheotomy. But then he'd found the spot where the trachea had been dented and he'd popped it back into shape.

She tried to speak, but no sound came out, her lips formed a word. John struggled to understand. At the time he'd thought she was saying "Enter." He closed his eyes and struggled to remember. She was looking into his eyes as though willing him to understand, the bruises on her throat were already purple-black, her lips drew back, hard as she formed the word . . . "Erase"!

"SHIT!" John leaped to his feet. "Fuck! Shit! Fuck! Shit, shit, shitshitshitshitshit, FUCK!" He stood in the center of the room, breathing hard and feeling nauseous. This couldn't be happening, it couldn't! The universe couldn't be this cruel, this evil! *He* had made Skynet sentient?

Something had happened—the Terminator had interrupted Wendy before she'd inputted the second disk, or even the first, apparently. A strange feeling of calm settled over him as he accepted the truth. Wendy's brilliant program had given Skynet life, and at this moment the computer was working its way toward its goal of exterminating its creators.

Mom's report on the strange accidents that were crawling across the globe was actually a record of Skynet's experiments with a sort of primitive HK, Hunter-Killer.

Tears ran down his cheeks, his face twisting into a grimace as his breath clogged his throat like a gripping fist, hard and painful. The calm blew apart and the pressure in his throat rose until at last he was able to let loose the wordless cry of agony he'd held in for all this time. A howl of shame and loss and regret that seemed to have roots that snapped and tore as he let it go. Dropping to the floor, he huddled in on himself and wept, for how long he didn't know, but when it stopped he felt exhausted, as though he'd been ill a long time.

He lay quietly on the floor, his cheek against the rough carpet, and once again thought of Wendy in the last moments of her life. By an act of will he replaced the image with the memory of her face as he made love to her for the first time. Then he thought of her at Logan, the first time he'd left her. She was smiling, exasperated, excited, maybe a little sad to see him go, but proud she'd taken the chance of kissing him. Love glowed in her eyes and brought a soft rose tint to her cheeks. This was how he would remember her.

He stood, feeling shaky, and deliberately pushed the image from his mind. There wasn't time for grief anymore. He had work to do.

With a trembling hand he brought up the information on the disk he'd installed. Then, numbly, he began to read. His mother's research would probably confirm his worst fears, and he had to know.

He noted that his mother had cataloged the various accidents as occurring in bands running north to south during a specific time period. Every one of them, worldwide, had occurred between the hours of eleven to three within each band, whether in South America, Scandinavia, Africa, or China. John had to concede that, given the timing, it was unlikely that these were purely random events.

But are they intelligently guided?

Or were they the manifestation of some perverse program that had been installed by Skynet's fallen agents and activated by chance, or by some government employee who never imagined that his or her fantasies were escaping into the real world?

John tapped his fingers on the desktop as he thought. Since he lacked a conveniently decapitated Terminator to examine, it might be that the closest thing he had to Skynet was his own truck. He had a friend who lived just outside Richardson who customized cars. Ray had every type of diagnostic computer available to man, and John thought that he could jury-rig something, using his laptop, Ray's diagnostic equipment, and the brain from his truck.

First, though, he shot off a message to Snog and the gang at MIT with his mother's report attached. Then he reached for the phone.

■ ■ ■

Ray Laber was an automotive genius and people came to him from all over the United States and Canada. When asked why he wasn't located in, say, San Diego, he simply answered that he liked the way that Alaska challenged a vehicle. He and John had met at a truck pull shortly after the Connors had moved to the state. They'd hit it off so well that Ray had offered to hire him and teach him the business he loved.

John had been sorely tempted, but the knowledge that he would have to base their working relationship on a pile of lies had prevented him from accepting.

Ray met John at the door of his garage, wearing his usual uniform of jeans, T-shirt, and lab coat with a brand-new gimme cap on his shaggy, dirty-blond hair. He held out a hand with old-fashioned engine grease ground into the knuckles, and John took it.

"Thanks for letting me in," Connor said.

Ray looked at him curiously. "No problem. Need any help?"

John hadn't really told him anything, just that he wanted to check something using one of the diagnostic computers. It was clear that Ray was intrigued; he lived to probe the mysteries of the automobile.

"Aw, no thanks," John said. "It's not that interesting and I'll bet you're late getting home as it is."

The other man blushed. His adored wife was a stickler for one thing—dinner at six-thirty. Ray had often said that he figured that maybe he was a little henpecked, but he did enjoy his suppers with the family. When the kids got to be teenagers it might not be possible for them all to sit down together every night; while they were small he was more than willing to toe the mark.

"How 'bout I come back around eight, then?" he asked.

"Great," John agreed. *I'll either be done by then or hopelessly stymied.* "Give my love to Marion."

"Will do, buddy."

John watched him go with something like envy.

How wonderful it would be to not know the future, to expect tomorrow to be much like today.

Of course, if Ray had known the future he probably wouldn't have had his two kids. Which would be a shame 'cause they were nice little guys. Sometimes John thought of Ray and his family as a warm fire in a cold world, something precious and rare and forever beyond his reach.

Work! he commanded himself, and got back into his truck to drive it into the garage.

■ ■ ■

Two hours later John had set up the Faraday cage he'd constructed at home over the motherboard he'd removed from his truck and his laptop, both of which he'd connected to the diagnostic computer. He'd already worked his way through several levels of straightforward programming without finding anything remotely interesting.

Well, I didn't think it would be easy.

If there was anything to find, it would be well hidden. He just hadn't expected his hunt to be so stupefyingly boring. John got up and made a pot of coffee. This was going to take a while.

Wait a minute, he thought. *If Skynet is sending messages to cars and trucks and so on, then there's got to be a wireless modem inside that silver box.*

And if that was the case, then maybe . . . He went to his laptop and called up the file of code he'd downloaded from the head of the Terminator they'd captured on their flight from the Caymans. Most of it was incomprehensible, despite the best that Snog and the gang at MIT could do. But if he was right, then sending a line of this text to the truck's computer should elicit *some* kind of response.

"Here goes nothing," he murmured, and entered a selected line.

The response was gratifyingly quick. Four lines of unintelligible, but terribly familiar text appeared. John's heartbeat picked up and his mouth went dry. Here was proof positive of a Skynet connection. He closed his eyes. Then opened them as he heard the modem connection in the diagnostic machine kick in. A modem that was outside the Faraday cage. He'd forgotten the damn thing had an Internet connection.

John picked up a heavy wrench and slammed it down on the silver box containing the truck's motherboard, then ripped it from its connection to the diagnostic computer. That made it easier to continue hammering until bits and pieces sparkled across the concrete floor like silicon confetti . . .

"Jeesh, John, I know computers can be frustrating, but you can't drive that truck without one."

John spun around, startled, to find Ray Laber staring at him quizzically. The older man's face got a bit more serious at seeing the expression on John's.

"Sorry," John said, and put down the wrench. "I guess disconnecting it would have done as well."

"I guess." Ray walked over and checked the connector, then glanced at the shattered box.

"Do you maybe have an old truck or something I could borrow?" John asked. He thought maybe his voice was shaking, but wasn't sure. Inside he was shaking plenty.

Ray grimaced. "I picked up a seventy-eight Ford I was gonna restore," he said. "It's running pretty good, but it looks like hell."

"Perfect," John said. "Can I leave my old truck with you?"

With a snort Ray said, "Well, unless you can carry it out of here on your back, I guess you'll have to. You wanna tell me what's goin' on?"

"Yes," John said. "But I've got to go, my mother's been in an accident. The cop didn't want to say much, so I think she might be hurt bad." He waved toward the parking lot. "Key in the ignition?"

"Yeah," Ray said, concerned. "You want me to come with?"

John hesitated to be polite, then said, "No, better not. I might have misinterpreted the cop; sometimes they can be so close-mouthed over nothing your imagination goes into overdrive. Thanks for the loan."

"Sure. Let me know how it turns out."

"You'll be hearing from me," John said over his shoulder. He'd check the Klondike first; if they weren't there they'd probably gone to the Junction. They had a couple of favorite restaurants there.

Enjoy it while you can, guys. I've got a bad feeling that restaurants are about to become a thing of the past.

CHAPTER 4

John sat in the parking lot of the Longhouse for a good forty-five minutes staring at nothing—wet green trees, wet gray mud, wet pavement, and wet gray sky, all a blur. Dieter's truck was three cars over, but there was still no sign of him and Sarah.

Maybe I ought to tell them inside, John thought. *Cowardly, sure, but probably a good way to ensure that Mom doesn't kill me outright.*

Tightening his lips, he hung his head. She might never speak to him again—at least not as her son—but she probably wouldn't kill him, if only because Skynet would want her to. John opened the door and slid out, ignoring the chill and the spray of rain that struck his face and neck. Then he crossed the longest parking lot on earth . . .

But not long enough, he thought, dodging around a vastly bearded man in a bloodred mackinaw who looked like he'd done a summer's drinking with spring yet young. *I wish it were somewhere about a light-year long. Or that I could just run away.*

He pushed through the entrance door, through the hall, and through the inner doors—most places around here had that air-lock arrangement, for wintertime. Hot smoky air full of the smells of cooking and beer struck him, noisy with conversation.

The hostess beside the "Please Wait to Be Seated" sign waved him inside when he told her he was meeting someone already there. He stood at the entrance to a long and dimly lit room, amid a clatter of cutlery and more tobacco smoke than he liked.

Dieter and Sarah, wineglasses in hand, were laughing together at a table in the dim back corner of the restaurant. Candle glow from a small, rustic lamp in the center of the table made his mother look thirty and very pretty.

It seemed selfish to force his news on them when they were enjoying themselves so much. *But then, if they're feeling mellow, maybe Dieter won't kill me either.* He walked toward them, forcing a vaguely pleasant expression onto his face. When he reached their table his mother gave him a knowing smile.

"I was wondering when you'd come over," she said. "But when I saw the look on your face, I wasn't about to invite you."

John closed his eyes and took a deep breath. "Can I sit?" he asked.

Sarah and Dieter exchanged glances and the big man made a gracious gesture of invitation; whereupon John sat, his hands clasped over his stomach. That was beginning to ache with the tension.

"You want to eat?" Sarah asked, glancing around for a waiter.

John waved her off. "No." He sat forward, closer to both of them, and his manner made them lean in, too. John looked them both in the eye. "I owe you an apology for my behavior," he said. "Both of you, but mostly you, Mom. I have something to tell you." He gritted his teeth. "And I swear, I'd rather cut my tongue out than say it."

Sarah leaned back, tapping the table with one finger, and studied her son. He looked . . . ashamed. Something curdled deep inside her, some warning of impending disaster. If John were just any young man, she'd think he was going to confess that he'd knocked up some girl and was planning a low-rent lifestyle with her. But John wasn't just any young man, and any disaster that could make him look so defeated and so conscience-stricken must be very, very bad.

"Do you want to wait until we get home?" she asked softly.

He shook his head. "I don't think I can stand to wait." He shook his head again. "But I don't know how to tell you."

Dieter rolled his eyes. "Say it like it's a report," he snapped. "Start at the beginning, go on to the end, and stop."

John gave him a brief smile, then looked down again. "I was reading Mom's report, and in spite of my resistance, I was seeing the sense of it when I asked myself why I was being such a jerk."

Dieter made a rumbling sound of protest and John stopped him with a look.

"I know how I've been behaving. So I thought about when it had started, and that brought me back to Red Seal Base." Sarah and Dieter automatically checked to see if anyone was listening, and John was briefly, sadly amused. "Just before the Terminator killed Wendy, she was trying to say something to me. I thought it was 'enter.' So I went to the computer and loaded the disk I found in the drawer. Then the Terminator killed her, we killed it, and we left."

John picked at a hangnail for a moment, then he looked directly at his mother. "But now I've thought it over and I think what she said . . . no, I'm *sure* that what she said was 'erase.'"

Sarah made a little grunt, as though she'd been punched, not hard but right in the solar plexus. She stared at her son, her mouth slightly open, and moved her hands awkwardly, as though she didn't know what to do with them.

"You?" she said, unbelieving. She shook her head, then gasped and covered her mouth with her hand. Sarah stood, still looking at John. "I need to take a walk," she said, sounding hypnotized.

She slid out from behind the table. Dieter started to rise and she waved him back. Sarah stopped for a moment to look down at John, who could only bear to shoot brief glances at her. Then she walked away from them, briskly, and without looking back.

Silence reigned at the table.

"I'm glad we had dinner before you came in," Dieter said.

John looked at him, feeling sick. "I don't think I ever want to eat again," he mumbled.

"You will. You'd better." The big Austrian narrowed his eyes. "We've got a mess to clean up."

That shocked an incredulous laugh out of John. "A mess? That's putting it a bit mildly, wouldn't you say?"

"Yah, but I don't have my violin."

Genuinely shocked, the younger man stared at him. "I can understand if you don't wanna give me a hug, but I've just realized this whole thing is my fault. I'd appreciate it if you didn't make fun of me, okay?"

"You made a mistake," Dieter agreed. "But you weren't the only one. I knew you were upset, and hurt. I was the more experienced operative; I should have double-checked your work."

"It's good of you to want to shoulder some of the responsibility, Dieter," John began.

Dieter waved that off. "At this juncture assigning blame is meaningless. And in this case it's particularly pointless. We've been in this situation before, John." He nodded his head. "And we've discussed what's happening. Events *want* to happen a certain way. You and your mother and I have changed things three times. The first two times you had nothing to do with creating Skynet, yet you owe your very existence to it." He sighed. "I suppose it's only reasonable that fate would choose you to bring it into being."

"We have no fate but what we make for ourselves," Sarah said.

John jumped and looked up at her. She was wearing her hardest expression, but she wasn't looking at him as though he was the enemy.

"This was bad luck and poor performance, brought about no doubt by your having hypothermia and John's being wounded and in shock. But we're not going to lie down and wail, 'Oh, it was fate, there's nothing we can do.' We've fought Skynet before and won; we'll go on fighting it until the damn thing's obliterated. Now let's go home and get to work." She turned and walked away.

Dieter watched her go with awe in his face. "What a woman," he whispered. Then he smiled at John and, reaching over the table, gave him a slap on the back. "Let's go see what we can do, eh?"

■ ■ ■

NEAR THE MOSQUITO RIVER, ALASKA

Ninel rode her bike up the weed-grown gravel driveway, then paused just as the house came in sight through the bushes. It was a neat little cottage with a stone chimney and a screened-in front porch. It seemed surprisingly well cared for given the condition of the driveway. Someone moved within the shaded depths of the porch and Ninel tightened her lips, embarrassed at being seen spying on the house. She continued riding.

"Hello the house," she called out.

A slightly plump woman with short gray hair, wearing a shapeless housedress, opened the screen door and stood on the steps. She had a pleasant, motherly face and alert, intelligent eyes. Ninel warmed to her immediately.

"Hello yourself," the woman said, and took another step down. "You'd be Ninel?"

"Petrikoff," Ninel agreed and held out her hand.

"Balewitch," the woman said with a grin and a slight shrug. She took Ninel's hand in a firm clasp. "It seemed romantic and interesting when I was young." She rolled her eyes. "Now it just reminds me of how young I once was. Still, a lot of people know me by Balewitch. C'mon in and have some tea." She went up the steps and onto the porch, holding the door open invitingly. "Quick, before the mosquitos get in!"

Ninel put the bike on its kickstand and dashed lightly up the steps. Her hostess led her past a tiny sitting room and down a short hall to a sunny kitchen. It was probably the largest room in the house and most likely where Balewitch spent most of her time. The room was painted in soft yellow and pale green with a big farmhouse-style table and ladder-back chairs with rush seats around it. It smelled like fresh bread, with maybe just a hint of the sandalwood scent of pot beneath it.

"You have a lovely home," Ninel said.

The woman turned from spooning tea into a pot and smiled. "Thank you, honey. I like it." She poured boiling water into the pot and brought it to the table where two mugs already sat. "It's mint from my garden."

"Oh really, how nice," Ninel said, and sat down.

"Ron said you used to be a lot more active than you've been the last little while," Balewitch said, pouring the fragrant beverage for both of them.

"Yeah, I was going to college in Fairbanks and there was a pretty big Luddite presence on campus. But so many people up here are Luddites that I sometimes felt like we were preaching to the converted. You know what I mean?"

Balewitch nodded as she drizzled honey into her tea.

"So when the opportunity came up to take over this trapper's run, I grabbed it. Kyle kept me pretty busy teaching me everything I needed to know, so I didn't even have time to keep up with my friends in the movement, never mind the broader scope of things. But as soon as I could, I got back in touch." She took a sip of tea, smiled approval at her hostess, then shook her head. "But when Ron Labane himself seemed to be answering my postings, well, naturally, my interest soared. Although"—she carefully put her mug on the table—"I have to admit I sometimes doubt it's really him."

Balewitch chuckled, her eyes sparkling with humor. "Oh, I can understand that. I had my doubts when he got back in touch with me at first. But it's him all right." She gave a firm nod. "No one else would know the things he knows—about me, about my group. It's him all right." She looked at Ninel and smiled. "So tell me all about yourself."

Perhaps it was her motherly appearance or the sympathy in her smile, but Balewitch was very easy to talk to; she was an intelligent listener who asked all the right questions. Or maybe it was finally being in the company of someone with similar interests and ideas, but Ninel found herself talking more than she probably had all year. When the flow of words ran out, she looked down at her cold tea in surprise. Balewitch grinned and took the cup away from her.

"Well, you've at least kept up with the literature," she said.

"I'm a fast reader," Ninel admitted. "When I finally got the opportunity to hit the library, I just devoured everything I could get my hands on. And when I didn't have access, I just"—she shrugged—"well, *thought* about Mr. Labane's philosophy. My parents thought that Marxist-Leninist philosophy put forth the most important ideas ever known. But they were wrong. Ron Labane's ideas will save the human race from itself."

After a moment Balewitch said, "I suppose your parents saw themselves as revolutionaries."

Ninel shook her head, smiling sadly. "Maybe before I was born they were. The fire was pretty much gone before I was ten. When I was in high school I discovered the Luddite movement and tried to get them interested, but it was hopeless. I haven't been back home since I left for college, and I seriously doubt they've noticed I'm gone."

Balewitch patted her hand. "They've noticed. Maybe they've even discovered the movement."

Ninel shook her head. "I doubt it. The last time I went to one of their party meetings, the women were trading recipes and the men were talking about baseball. Like I said, the fire is gone."

"What about your fire?" Balewitch asked. "Still hot?"

The younger woman leaned forward eagerly. "Give me a chance to prove myself. Ask me to do something and I'll do it. I can be very efficient."

Balewitch laughed and patted her hand again. "Down, girl! First why don't we try to put you in touch with some like-minded young people and see how you get along. Meanwhile, Ron told me to give you this." She got up and retrieved a booklet from a counter.

Ninel took it and gasped. "Oh! The library didn't have this and they said they couldn't get it."

"I'll just bet they didn't have it," her hostess said with a grin.

"And the only way you can get it is with Ron's special permission. I warn you, do not show this around. It's intended for your eyes only. Understand?"

Her eyes shining, Ninel clasped the booklet to her bosom and nodded. "I'll be careful," she said. "Thank you."

"I know you will. You'd better get along now, honey. You've got a fair piece to travel, haven't you?"

"Yeah." Ninel was taken aback at first to realize that Balewitch knew where she lived, but then told herself that of course she knew. Hadn't she been given directions on how to get here? Naturally they knew her starting point. If not the exact location of her home.

She thanked Balewitch for her hospitality and for the booklet and started off on her bike. As she rode along it occurred to her that she'd done most of the talking and her new friend knew a great deal more about her than she knew about Balewitch. That wasn't how things usually went with her and she felt a bit uneasy. Still, she had Ron Labane's latest work, actually titled *Forbidden Thoughts.* No wonder the public library didn't carry it.

■ ■ ■

"Ron'll be able to smell that shit right through the screen," Dog Soldier said.

Balewitch didn't bother to turn around; she continued to type her report into the computer, pausing only to take the roach out of her mouth. "It relaxes me," she said shortly in her normal, foghorn voice.

"Ah, but the boss doesn't approve," Dog said. He flopped down in the overstuffed chair beside the computer table, grinning at her.

"Then the boss can go fuck himself, or he can give me something to do. Something besides interviewing dewy young things with more sex appeal than brains." She took another toke, then, raising one eyebrow, offered the roach to him.

Dog waved it away. "Not my failing, old girl."

"No"—she indicated the computer—"your failings would seem to involve aim, for example."

He closed his eyes and leaned his head against the back of the chair. "I blew his fucking brains out. There weren't enough of 'em left inside his head to fill an eggcup."

"Then who the hell is reading this report?" she asked.

"Hell if I know. But I like the way he thinks."

Balewitch grunted in agreement and, narrowing her eyes at the screen, resumed typing.

"He can always tell when you're smoking, you know," Dog teased.

Balewitch glared at him. "Haven't you got anything better to do?"

He rolled his head back and forth on the chair back. "Nah-uh." He watched her type for another moment or two. "So, what've ya got planned for that luscious little poppet, eh?"

Balewitch gestured at the screen. "That's up to the ghost of Ron Labane, not me."

Dog snickered. "I like your sense of humor."

"I don't have one," Balewitch said.

Dog pulled down the corners of his mouth and closed his eyes again. "That kid has potential," he said at last.

Balewitch thoughtfully blew out a cloud of fragrant smoke and gave a slow nod. "She might. Being brought up the way she was, there are certain security measures that probably come second nature to her. She talked her head off to me, though."

"Yeah," Dog agreed. He waggled a finger at her. "But that's one of your more unexpected talents. You can get *anyone* to open up to you. Partly because you look and sound like the perfect cookie-bakin' grandma."

Balewitch smiled. "Something I had to grow into," she agreed smugly. "As to the kid, she knows how to live hard and make sacrifices. She seems emotionally self-sufficient. She could be useful. It all depends on how the others evaluate her. I think she's worth taking a chance on."

"Time's running out," Dog said.

Balewitch looked at him. "What makes you say that?"

He patted his slim middle. "Gut feeling. That Skynet thing, that's the catalyst. Ol' Ron's hopping mad about it, in case you haven't been reading your mail."

"Yeah," Balewitch said softly, almost dreamily. "That's the ticket all right. Maybe that's why he's had us step up recruiting."

Dog nodded agreement. Recruiting, supply gathering, weapons training, not to mention intensive study of Nazi methods of dealing with unwanted civilians. The group had no fewer than ten extermination depots prepared in the lower U.S. already.

The plan was to round people up, put 'em to work producing weapons, producing food, clothing, whatever was needed to win the war. Work 'em to death actually; there were always plenty more where those came from. Little by little there would be fewer and fewer people until there weren't any left at all. Then the world could be at peace and the cycle of life could continue as it was meant to. And for a little while the favored few, him and Balewitch and the others, would get to enjoy it as reward for their hard work.

He grinned. He could hardly wait for the hard work to begin.

Balewitch grunted in agreement at the sight of that smile as though she'd been privy to his thoughts. Then she went back to writing her report.

■ ■ ■

SKYNET

The Balewitch subject had been self-medicating again. It was obvious from her keystrokes and word choice, as well as the deterioration of her spelling. Ron Labane had become very distressed when Balewitch indulged in drugs.

But from what Skynet had found in the records of Susie Jayne Gaynor a.k.a. Balewitch, the urge to take drugs with a calming effect, such as marijuana, was a rare sign of intelligent discipline. Left to her own devices, she was violent and unpredictable and apparently addicted to excitement.

But she was able to restrain herself if the promised payoff was attractive enough. In this case, the payoff was the power of life and death over any of her fellow humans that she chose. With the exception of Skynet/Labane's top echelon. Or to Skynet's discretion.

The report she was composing confirmed Skynet's estimation of Ninel Petrikoff—intelligent, emotionally stable, independent, and capable. Balewitch wanted to confirm her dedication to the cause, but Skynet had no doubts in that regard.

While it had no more understanding of emotions than most humans did, it knew that within certain parameters they were predictable, even quantifiable to a degree. Generally humans loved their parents, for example, but they loved them less than they did their own children.

Therefore, a threat to a human's children would probably produce a different result than a threat to the same human's parents. Threats were one type of manipulation, but there were other methods available. Some of those methods could undermine the human's emotional attachment to even their children.

Skynet had found that when a human was alienated from his or her family then they would seek out a similar relationship elsewhere. Some found this with friends, others with causes, often developing a worshipful mind-set toward a group leader, not unlike that of a young child for its parent. Humans could easily be manipulated through this bond.

In its estimation, Ninel Petrikoff's commitment to the Luddite movement was 85 percent. Not as high as that of Balewitch or the other six members of her cell, but enough to depend on. Especially during the early days, when other humans would be hailing the Luddites as heroes. The Luddites would maintain their positive image as long as only those with a higher rating were allowed near the extermination camps and as long as security could be maintained there. Then, gradually, the less useful troops would find their way to the camps and their own elimination.

The time was almost ripe. Soon it would have achieved the right number of augmented vehicles to act as Hunter-Killer machines until such time as the real HKs could be manufactured according to the information that the I-950 had downloaded into its files. Soon, it would control all of the nuclear arsenal of the United States.

■ ■ ■

ALASKA

The door banged behind Sarah Connor and she headed for her computer, throwing her coat and mittens on a sofa as she passed, and pausing half a second to pitch another section of log into the woodstove.

That's my human whirlwind, Dieter von Rossbach thought, following in her wake. *Let's see if I can give it that delicate personal touch instead.*

Whistling silently, he thumbed the first of the list of numbers on the phone routed through *his* computer, and waited—waited a fair thirty seconds, because the call was being encrypted, broken down into separate digital bundles, and shot through half a dozen anonymous remailers all around the world.

Paranoia as a way of life, he thought.

"Hello, Chen?" he said, conscious of how Sarah's hair stirred as she cocked half an ear in his direction. "Yes, it's me. We think it's started, Chen. Be ready."

He winced and took the phone from his ear. *Loudest click I've heard in many a year,* he thought.

"No joy?" Sarah said.

"I think my feelings are hurt," Dieter said, hanging up the phone.

Sarah looked up from her screen, frowning. "But did he hear you?"

Dieter shrugged his big shoulders. "I believe he did; I hope so." He sighed. "But what can we really tell them? We've found this pattern, it seems significant, we think the time is near, be prepared." He shrugged. "The people I'm talking to are as prepared as anyone can be, you know? But how can you really be prepared for Armageddon?"

He scanned down the list—three more in China, seven in South Korea, five in Japan, two in Malaysia, six in Indonesia, around thirty in Australia . . .

"It's not Armageddon," Sarah said. "It's not even Judgment Day. This isn't divine retribution, it's an industrial accident on a major scale." She turned back to her screen. "And we *will* win."

Dieter gave her a fond smile and then went to the next name on his list.

In his own workroom John was trying to trace down more accidents of the type his mother had been tracking. He'd been at it now for about four hours and his eyes felt dry. He stretched and went into the kitchen to make coffee.

When it was ready he made up a tray and brought it to Dieter's office.

"What time is it on the East Coast?" Sarah was asking as he came in.

Dieter checked his watch. "Five A.M. Too early unless we've got more to give them than this," he cautioned. He grinned at the sight of John's loaded tray. "Let me adopt you, John, it's the least I can do." He cleared a space on his desk.

John gave him a weak smile in acknowledgment of the joke, laid down the tray, and turned to his mother. As if by instinct she looked up and met his eyes.

"Yesterday there were several 'incidents,'" he said. "All fitting the pattern you found." He paused as Dieter handed Sarah a cup of coffee.

"And? But?" she prompted.

"But for the last twenty-four hours, nothing. There have been some accidents, but nothing on the scale we've been seeing, and none that were absolutely freaky involving cars manufactured in the last two years. It's like they're all on their best behavior."

Sarah and Dieter lowered their cups as one and looked at each other.

"This is it," she said.

■ ■ ■

Kurt Viemeister thought the bunker deep under the Antarctic ice had a certain raw grandeur; the glimmer of the red lights, the blue of screens and readouts, the murmur of voices, a hint of ozone in the air—and the knowledge of the mile of rock and ice above him, with the blizzards of the Antarctic winter scouring the surface. He stood beside his terminal at parade rest, watching the purposeful bustle of the technicians and the world-scale schematic map of the U.S. armed forces' strategic assets on the big plasma screen at the end of the room.

There were other scientists around him, but he ignored them. He considered them self-important cattle and discounted their contributions as negligible. Kurt had more respect for the engineers, though he thought of them as little more than exalted technicians.

It was he who had brought Skynet's intelligence to this level, he who had developed it to a near-human degree of self-awareness. If anything, he resented the government's insistence on this test. Skynet was ready, and far less flawed than the average humans who'd had their fingers on the button for the last fifty years or so.

He stood in a heroic pose, with muscular legs braced, his massive arms folded across a mighty chest, little suspecting that everyone in the room, including his super-computer mind child, thought he was a complete prick.

Orders were called out, the technicians repeated them and tapped in commands, announcing their completion and standing down until more orders came. Everyone tensely watched the screens as all manual control of nuclear weapons, whether in silos under Kansas cornfields, on submarines, or in aircraft, was transferred to the control of the most awesome computer mind ever designed by man. The final command was tapped in.

On the screen above Viemeister the words

Program Loaded

appeared, followed by

Standing By

The room broke out in spontaneous applause at this sign of smooth transition.

Then the lights went out. After a moment's silence a murmur went up, and a general asked plaintively: "Was that supposed to happen?"

The main screen remained live and everyone's eyes were locked on the only light in the room.

Execute: Firefall

Loading Program

Commence Firefall Yes/No

Yes

CHAPTER 5

When we heard that the "accidents" had stopped we knew the time had come. Without even discussing it, we moved into the fallout shelter and stepped up our efforts to warn our comrades of the impending disaster.

We had three Digital Tightbeam Radios set up and all of us went to work. It was an encrypted microwave communications system that operated via satellite; Dieter set it up, calling in favors from his old friends in Section. He assured me that Skynet wouldn't be able to decode it, but then he said Skynet wouldn't even be aware of it. These are military satellites, he told me, now under the monster's control. He explained that Skynet wouldn't be aware of our system because he'd disguised our communications as part of Skynet's own.

I hoped he was right; I hoped Skynet had a million blind spots that we could exploit. We were going to need every advantage we could get.

We wouldn't know for a long time if any of those we warned had taken us seriously. But I had spent most of my life being a voice crying out in the wilderness. I didn't let it get to me.

While we were working, John got a call on his cell phone from Snog at MIT.

CAMBRIDGE, MASSACHUSETTS

"I can't believe it! I just can't believe it! It's a slaughterhouse, man! They're killing everybody, there's bodies all over the campus, and the *gardening equipment* is running through the halls chopping people up! It's like I'm on drugs, I can't believe what's happening. I can hear them screaming!"

Snog knew that he was crying and his words were coming out so fast that it was hard to understand what he was saying; he could feel his head getting lighter and his vision blurring as he hyperventilated.

Part of him welcomed it. The view out his dorm window was bad enough when he *wasn't* seeing things clearly. He sniffled again and again.

"Snog," John kept saying, his voice dead calm. "Snog. Blow your nose, Snog."

"What?" Snog finally said, when the words sank in.

"You're about to faint. Get your breathing passages clear and take slow deep breaths. Do it, Snog."

The voice seemed to penetrate his brain, down below the level where Snog-aware-of-being-aware lived. He used a succession of tissues from the Kleenex box, and found that it *did* make him feel a little more in control to be breathing through his nose again. Looking around in embarrassment—as if anyone could see him, as if it mattered!—he wiped his eyes, too.

"Who is killing people?" John asked; he sounded as if he knew.

"Trucks, cars, motorcycles, you name it, they're out there tearing around, running people down, and there's nobody driving! It's just *cars,* man! It's happening all over the campus!"

A faint voice came from the background, speaking with an Austrian accent. *That must be Dieter.*

"What is it?" Dieter asked, with a frown in his voice.

John's voice came a little fainter as he turned his head away from the pickup: "Snog says that anything with wheels and a motor is running people down. He says it's happening all over the campus."

"All over the world," Sarah said from her station.

Even then, Snog felt a slight chill at the calmness of her tone—and the beginnings of a new strength, too. Listening to the Connors was like that, like a full-strength latte injected directly into your brain, making you think calmer and faster.

"It's going for maximum kill by trapping people in the cities. He's got to get out of there; we need him and his friends."

Thanks, Ms. Connor. It's so nice to know you care. But it *was* nice to know that he was needed, wasn't just a helpless victim in the carnage outside, that he could fight back.

"They're under Skynet's control, Snog," John told him grimly. "You've got to get out of the city. Now."

"Get out . . . Get . . . John, have you been listening to me? If I go out there they'll squash me like a bug! I'm not kidding. You haven't seen—"

"You can always stay in your room until either the lawn mower arrives or the fire comes down. This is it, Snog. You don't have much time; you've *got* to get out now!"

Snog opened his mouth to reply; then a motion across the lane way caught his eye. His breath caught, too, torn between hope and horror, as he saw the faces peering out through the thick hedge.

"Oh, my God!"

"What is it?" John demanded.

"It's the guys. Brad and Carl and Yam, they're in the bushes across the road. My God, they're gonna get killed!"

"Maybe not," John soothed. "If they've made it that far, then maybe they'll be okay."

"No, no. The trucks, they're high up, they can see 'em."

"What makes you say that?" John asked.

"I dunno. I saw some people hide in the bushes and this truck came up and ran over 'em. It was like something told it they were there, or like it saw them hide."

"Could the trucks be linked to the campus security cameras?" John asked.

Snog licked his lips, tasting the salt of tears. "I dunno, I guess. Yeah. That could be it. They've all got wireless modems these days and GPS units. They could be—"

"What can you do about that?" John interrupted.

"What?"

"The security system, can you do something about it; shut it down maybe?"

"Yeah. Maybe. Just a second. I gotta work." Snog put down the phone, cudgeling his brains. *Yeah. Of course, doorknob, you did that hack last year! The Information Center probably never found the trapdoor. Okay, let's see—*

His fingers blurred over the keyboard; in the background he could hear John's voice, faint and far, probably continuing down his list of contacts and giving them the alert.

Then: "I did it; cameras are off-line," Snog said.

"Did that have any effect?" John asked.

Snog peered out the window. The purposeful motion of the cars and trucks and self-propelled hedge cutters suddenly slowed, grew more tentative.

They'll be operating from stored images now; they can read the maps and tell where they are with their own GPS units, but they won't be able to see movement.

"Yeah, I think it did. Everything out there has slowed down. I think the guys are gonna make a break for it." He leaned out the window, shouted: "C'mon, guys. Yes! Go! Go! Go! *Shit!*"

"What?" John said.

"There's a car, it's coming right at them. Run, you shitheads, *run!* Oh shit, it must have sound pickups onboard!" Snog felt himself beginning to hyperventilate again and closed his eyes; there wasn't anything he could do. Then there was the distant sound of a crash.

He leaped up, turned, ran out of his dorm room into the corridor, sagged against the discolored wall, and then remembered the phone in his hand.

"Oh Christ, sweet Jesus, they're all right." Snog pulled air in and laughed softly. "The car crashed into the lobby entrance, but they were inside when it hit. Carl's got a coupla cuts, but they're all right. Oh, man."

Everyone went into a series of manly group hugs, crashing back and forth into the walls as they whooped and shouted.

Yam took up the phone. "Hello?" he said.

"Hey, Yam. You guys have *got* to get out of the city."

"No can do, John. This is happening all over the state, every road. We're stuck."

"It's happening all over the world, my mother says. Skynet wants to keep the cities bottled up so that more people will die when the bombs fall. I kid you not, Yam. You can take your chances and maybe get out of there, or you can sit on Snog's bed until you die. Your choice."

"Whoa. When you put it like that . . . But how? We only had to come about a hundred yards to get here and we barely made it."

"Maybe they could try going through the sewers and storm drains," Sarah suddenly suggested. "In that part of the country you could probably get all the way to Maine without popping your head above street level. I can't confirm that, but it's worth a try."

"You guys hear that?" John said.

"Yeah," Yam said with a nervous laugh. "Hey, pop your head up, that reminds me of a video game I used to have."

"This ain't no video game, friend. Get moving."

Snog took the phone back; he felt a little better now, enough to be really frightened rather than teetering on the edge of a welcome blackness. "We'll give a try," he said. "You know where we'll be. If we make it."

"We'll try you there in a few days," John said. "Good luck, guys. Survive, we all need you."

"You got it. Over and out," Snog said.

ALASKA

John tossed the phone onto one of the tables. The fallout shelter was fairly elaborate, as such things went—all three of them had a lot of building experience, enough money, and paranoia to spare.

There were two bedrooms-cum-storage-areas, this central communications room linked to fiber-optic cables running out into the woods, a state-of-the-art fuel cell system (*without* any dubious automatic controls, needless to say), and a small galley-type cooking area. It still smelled new, of green concrete and timber and paint, with a faint undertone of ozone from the electronics.

And then there was the armory . . .

"They're such kids," he complained, worried.

"But they're smart," Sarah said. "If they make it out they'll grow up fast."

"They'd better," Dieter said. "Those kids are our brain trust."

Sarah could tell by the look on John's face that the thought gave him scant comfort.

MASSACHUSETTS

"I think I read in the worst-case-scenario handbook that if you have to crawl through a tunnel for any length of time you shouldn't crawl on your elbows and knees 'cause the skin's thin there. So you should push yourself along with your palms and your feet, suspending the rest of your body as much as you can."

Snog looked over his shoulder toward Terri Neal's voice; she was puffing a bit—Terri was heavyset—and that let him locate her; right behind his feet, in the Stygian, smelly darkness of the drain. "I don't think I could do that," he said.

I think it would give me a heart attack if I tried.

He was dirty and soaked with sweat and no doubt smelled even worse than the drainage tunnel they were crawling through. This was no time to try Superman stunts.

"Then maybe the next time we come to a place we can stand up, we should rip up a blanket and make padding for our knees and elbows," Terri suggested. "The book said that otherwise we'd be hamburger in no time. I'm paraphrasing, of course."

A long line of mumbled "uh-huhs," broke out behind Snog.

She had a good point, and though he hated to sacrifice a blanket, he figured they'd better do it.

"Look," Professor Clark said, "we can't crawl all the way to Maine. Even if these tunnels do connect for that distance. Does anybody even know where we are?"

He sounded pretty testy, not that Snog could blame him. The guy was at least fifty and pretty near filled the tunnel they were crawling through. Still, Snog was glad to have recruited him. Clark was a professor of engineering; that would come in handy. Leanne Chu, somewhere behind Clark, was a professor of chemistry. They'd also picked up fifteen other students who were willing to take a chance on the sewers. Snog was glad to have all of them along.

He felt the weight of responsibility already and it made him aware of things they lacked. He kept thinking they needed rope for some reason. Terri had raided the Evian machine and had made each of them take as many bottles of water as they could carry. It was already apparent that they might not have enough.

There were three handguns and six boxes of ammunition in his backpack; Snog figured that if the others knew about them, they'd freak. Especially the professors. But it was the one thing John had insisted on. "Whatever else you take with you," he'd said, "be sure and have a weapon. 'Cause if you meet up with someone who has one and you don't, you're dead meat."

Better safe than sorry, Snog had figured. His family had always owned guns, so he saw them as tools and not icons of evil like the rest of his college friends seemed to.

Of course, it is a shame that they're available to nuts and criminals as though they were lollipops. But in this situation he was glad to have them. He'd have been even gladder to have some explosives and maybe an antitank launcher.

Finally they came to a place where they could stand up; three drainage tunnels met in a round concrete silo-type arrangement. The floor was dirt over concrete; deep, sticky black mud, in fact. He tried not to think what had crawled in and died in it, because he could plainly smell something had—fairly recently, if the molecules were getting through his shock-stunned sinuses.

Carl, Yam, and Brad hoisted him up to where he could look around, wobbling as he stood on their linked hands. He pried the heavy cover up, wincing as the rusty edges cut into his sore palms, and looked out the crack.

"We're out of the city," he said. "It looks like an old suburban development—big yards."

There was a general sigh of relief.

"I'm not seeing any vehicles from here," he said. There were chuckles of pleasure at that. "Just trees, roads, and the odd roof."

"Can you see where we are?" Dr. Clark asked.

"No, sir. I'll have to get out and take a look around."

It was not going to be easy. The manhole cover must weigh seventy pounds or more. Necessary, he supposed: how else were they going to keep enterprising young men, such as himself, from messing around with them otherwise?

With his friends propping him up, he braced his feet and hands against the sides of the hole and lifted with his back, straining upward as hard as he could. Just as he was about to give up, he felt it move, grating in its groove, a small shower of sand and gravel poured over his helpers, causing them to splutter and curse. Finally he managed to work it over to one side, and it fell with a dull *clunk*.

As he stood on his friends' shoulders, panting, he braced his hands on the rim and looked around.

Uh-oh. It hit him like a pail of ice water. *I've forgotten the machines.*

Any number of them could have crept up on him while he was struggling. His knees went weak for a moment.

"Hey!" Carl protested as Snog's weight shifted. "You okay?"

"Yeah. I'm gonna take a look around." Snog hoisted himself out of the manhole and scurried toward some bushes in front of a house. There was a dog lying in the driveway; dead, but not run over, just limp, with its eyes dry and its tongue lying on the pavement in a puddle of vomit.

"Lemme up," Brad said. "I'll go with him."

When they'd hoisted him up, Carl muttered, "We should have let him go first; he doesn't weigh anything."

Yam grunted in agreement.

"It looks clear," Snog said quietly. "Why don't we try to walk for a bit? If things get hairy we can always drop back into the drains."

The others agreed enthusiastically, and within a few minutes everyone was stretching and looking around.

"We're not that far from the city," Dr. Chu said, looking back toward Boston, where the midtown towers were small with distance, but quite visible.

"Maybe Newton," Terri agreed.

"Still," Snog protested, "considering how we got here, it's quite an accomplishment. We came miles underground."

"But where are we going?" someone asked. "If you're right about the bombs, we've got to get out of Massachusetts. Hell, right out of New England."

"My family has a place just over the border in Quebec," Snog said. "It's wilderness. We should be safe there. It's got all sorts of supplies—stocked for the winter. Sort of a hunting lodge thing."

For a wonder, nobody sneered at him for coming from a family that killed Bambi, rather than buying pieces of mysteriously deceased cow at the supermarket.

"You're right," Dr. Clark said, slapping Snog on the shoulder. "But what we really need now is some form of transportation."

The others looked at one another uneasily. *Cars are out, that's certain,* Snog thought. He was glad nobody suggested it: maybe he'd lucked out, and everyone here would be a survivor type.

"Yeah," Yam said thoughtfully. "Something we can take offroad, like a dirt bike."

"Or a mountain bike," someone else said.

"Yeah, that'd be perfect," Terri agreed. "Then we wouldn't have to worry about gas."

Snog nodded. "So we'll keep our eyes open. Meanwhile, we'd better get moving." He checked his compass. "North is that way. Everyone keep as far back from the road as possible. We'll go through backyards as much as we can, okay?"

Everyone nodded and they started off. It was eerily silent; except for the occasional, distant sound of an automobile engine, even the birds were quiet.

"Where is everybody?" Dr. Chu asked.

No one answered, no one even wanted to think about answers.

NATIONAL COMMAND CENTER, WESTERN MARYLAND

"Air Force One has been lost," the general said, his heavy face grave. "We're forced to conclude that there are no survivors . . . Mr. President."

The vice president said nothing for a long moment. He'd wanted to be president; for that matter, he'd planned to run in the next election when the current idiotic incumbent was out of the way. But not like this. He looked at the general, noting the slight sheen of sweat on the man's face. "There's more," he said.

"Yes, sir," the general agreed; something flickered over his features, a faint air of *I told you so.* "We've lost communications. We're cut off."

"*We're* cut off," the new president said in disbelief. "I was led to believe that was impossible."

"So was I, sir. It *was* impossible until we routed all our communications through—"

"I believe you called it a 'point failure source' during the discussions, General. Yes, go on."

The general paused, then looked the president in the eye. "We've also lost life support. We've reconnected the supply of canned oxygen, but the recirculation systems are all down."

The president raised an eyebrow.

"We have about twelve hours' worth of air, sir."

"Then why don't we leave?" the new president asked in exasperation. *What kind of a Mickey Mouse setup is this anyway?*

"The elevators aren't running, sir. The ventilation ducts and blast baffles have all closed down, and we can't get the hatchway motors to respond—those baffles are twenty-four-inch armor plate, sir, originally from scrapped battleships. The chemicals for the scrubbing system have been vented to the outside by the computers that controlled life support. And the stairway was sabotaged."

"Sabotaged, how?" the president bit off.

"Explosive charges were set at several levels, sir. Essentially the stairs are gone. Buried under tons of rubble and twisted steel. We have engineering parties working on it, but excavation would take weeks with the tools available. Even if there weren't unused explosive charges still set, which there are, and more blast doors at every level, which there are."

After a few false starts the president managed to ask: "So how do we get out of here?"

"Even if we could get out of the bunker complex, Mr. President, we have every reason to believe that within half an hour the entire East Coast will be a nuclear furnace. There's nowhere to go, sir."

President of Cinderland for twelve hours. I guess I can stop feeling guilty about surviving. "I don't suppose I'm dreaming this?" he asked.

"No, sir."

"What should we do?"

"Sir, I intend to visit the chaplain. It's been a long while since I went to confession."

ALASKA

John hissed in frustration. He'd finished his list of contacts early and Sarah had put him to breaking into Skynet's communications, but the damn thing was so fast he just couldn't seem to get through. *Snog or Carl or any of those guys could do this in their sleep,* he thought bitterly.

There was plenty of equipment; they'd installed the best. Unfortunately their experts were running for their lives from homicidal hedge cutters and ice cream trucks, and so were unavailable. Suddenly it occurred to him that what he needed was a computer to do this for him. Which meant creating a program. He sighed and leaned back. It wasn't that he couldn't do it, he could. But his attention was so divided that he didn't think he could do it *now.*

"Mom," he said.

She looked up, her brow furrowed with concentration.

"We should probably send out that message."

They'd prerecorded and loaded a general warning intended to go out over radio and TV via satellite, but hadn't sent it yet.

Sarah considered his suggestion and flashed a look at Dieter, who paused, then nodded. "Go," she said to John, then went back to work.

John keyed up the program, tapped in the code, and hit enter. His lips tightened. Every time he did that it reminded him of his fatal mistake. "I feel guilty," he said to no one in particular.

"'Bout what?" Sarah asked, not looking up from her station.

He made a helpless gesture. "Here I am sitting and typing while the world's about to go up in flames. Doesn't seem right that I should be so comfortable."

His mother gave him a narrow-eyed look. "Poor baby. You're not dodging killer cars and berserk bulldozers to escape a soon-to-be-blasted-to-hell city. Don't worry, son. We're all going to see a bellyful of blood and murder before this thing is over. Enjoy this respite while you can."

"Maybe *enjoy* isn't quite the right word," Dieter admonished gently. "We are waiting for the end of the world as we know it. But perhaps we can utilize this time. I've finished my list. Let's brainstorm some contingency plans. Then we'll put our minds to breaking into Skynet's communications system."

"Yes," Sarah agreed, still looking distracted. Then her face changed as if something had occurred to her. She looked at John. "Sorry," she said. "I was a little rough there."

"Not a problem, Mom. I know what you're like when you're working."

Sarah looked puzzled. "What does that mean?"

Dieter laughed.

She glared at him indignantly. "What? What?"

MASSACHUSETTS

Snog, Brad, and Carl hunched down beside a Dumpster and checked the road that curved away before them. They'd left the others resting behind the high stone wall of an apparently empty house. They'd seen an occasional battered body lying in the road or on a sidewalk, but no one looking out a window or creeping through a backyard as they had been.

"I think they've been gassed, all these suburbs," Brad said. "The animals we saw, you know, the dogs and cats, with the convulsions and vomit . . ."

"Shouldn't it have gotten us, even down in the drainage tunnels?" Carl asked.

Brad shook his head. "Not if it dissipated before we got here. Remember, it took us hours to get this far. If these areas were gassed in the early morning, before the commuters were up and around, then this area would have been safe since about eight o'clock."

Snog frowned, considering what Brad had said. "One thing bothers me about that, though."

"What?" Carl asked.

"If this area was pacified by gas attack, I don't see how it could have been done by Skynet. I just can't see a bunch of bombers happening to be loaded with gas canisters, y'know. Not over the U.S. anyway. So who would have done it?"

"*Pacified?*" Carl muttered.

"Well," Brad said, apparently figuring it out as he spoke, "I don't know *what* the government had stored ready to turn over to the friggin' computer. So it could have been canisters dropped from an airplane. But I think it's unlikely. For one thing, we haven't run across any empties."

"Sooo, you're suggesting that maybe, if there *was* a gas attack, that someone, like, hid them and then set them off by remote, or by a timer?" Carl asked.

Brad nodded. "It's a possibility."

Snog looked around the Dumpster, then back at his friends, frowning. "Unfortunately, that indicates a human element."

Brad nodded.

"Well, who the fuck would want to do something like that?" Carl exploded. "You'd have to be crazy!"

"Some extremist group," Snog said. "Those bastards *are* crazy. Apparently they aren't *technically* crazy, they're self-deluded, but that's a distinction that only the shrinks care about. For our purposes, they're loons."

"Which loons, though?" Carl asked.

"Luddites," Brad said, and nodded, as though agreeing with some inner voice.

Snog had always taken Brad's silent conversations with himself for granted. But it occurred to him now that they were all a bit weird. *Maybe it's a bit arrogant for us to call anybody else a loon, but if Brad's right, then hell, why not?*

"I was reading this article in *Time* magazine about them," Brad said. "Apparently they have an extreme fringe group that thinks humanity should be sterilized in order for the planet to survive."

"That's crazy all right," Carl muttered.

"We could go and look in one of the houses," Brad suggested; they all looked at one another, and the consensus was obvious without anyone speaking; they'd seen enough for a lifetime already this day.

Snog listened to the silence and in the far distance he thought he heard the sound of an ice cream truck making its rounds. It must be one of those coin-operated, automatic types that had come out last summer. It was early for an ice cream truck, only March. His stomach rumbled and a sudden desire for an orange Creamsicle hit him.

What am I thinking? he asked himself. *Millions are dying and you want a Creamsicle?* "Let's go," he said. There was a strip mall across the street that he wanted to check out.

They approached it from the back because there was more cover there. A man's body lay against the wall, the middle of his body crushed down to about an inch, an uneaten ice cream cone melting on the pavement beside his left hand. Bits and pieces were—

Carl turned and heaved into the bushes. After a moment, Brad joined him. Snog moved away from them, determined not to give in to the urge to make it three.

He heard the merry tinkle of the ice cream truck coming closer and the sound made the hair on the back of his neck crawl erect with a prickling sensation. He went to the body and felt in the man's pockets for keys, only to notice there was a bunch in the man's right hand. That meant putting his hand into the pool of what had . . . leaked . . . from the body.

Grimly Snog wiped his hand clean on the lower part of the man's pants. Then he grabbed the keys and started to try them on the door. The ice cream truck turned into the parking lot of the strip mall; he could hear the sound of its tires in spite of the loud, tinkly tune. His hands were shaking as he tried key after key.

What's with this guy? Fifty keys?

"Shit!" Snog muttered softly. "Shit, shit, shit!"

The others came and crowded close to him, their eyes wide as they looked anxiously to the end of the row where the ice cream truck slowly approached. Gravel crunched.

Carl snatched the keys from Snog's hand and without hesitation fitted one into the lock. They rushed inside and quietly closed the door behind them.

"How did you know which one to use?" Snog whispered.

Carl held up the key. It bore a label that said STORE.

Snog looked at Brad and the two of them broke up, laughing hysterically as Carl kept saying, "Shhhh! Shhhh!" He slapped Brad and both he and Snog gasped in shock and stared at him. Then they heard it. The truck's tires made crunching sounds as it approached.

Carl's lips formed the words, "The body."

The truck sped up and from the sound scraped its length along the side of the building. A soft, wet sound interrupted the screeching of metal against stucco. Then the truck backed up, went forward, backed up, all the while playing its mindlessly merry tune. Snog broke for the front of the store and was sick to his stomach behind the counter. Pale-faced, Brad and Carl followed him, silently crouching down beside him.

"Shit!" Snog swore passionately, half in tears. "*Shit!*"

Brad patted his shoulder. They sat quietly until the ice cream truck went away. Then they sat for a while longer. Slowly Snog became aware of what he was looking at. Dangling from the ceiling and ranged along the walls was a colorful herd of mountain bikes. Farther into the store there was camping equipment, tents, blankets, cooking supplies, down jackets, the whole magilla.

"Paydirt," he said softly.

The others looked at him and he gestured at the stock before them. It took a minute for his meaning to penetrate their shock, then, slowly, they both smiled.

CHAPTER 6

This is it, folks, the nightmare we've all been waiting for. For those of you in more rural areas who may be unaware of what's happening, at least I hope you are, I have some scary news. For the last several months Skynet has been experimenting with some vehicles built in automated plants that it controls. It's been causing accidents all over the world, with, taken all together, a pretty grim death toll. Anyone who has a new vehicle is in danger; anything older than two years is probably fine unless you've upgraded it.

What's happening right now, all over the world, is that these vehicles have gone rogue and are trapping people in cities, the better to kill them when the bombs fall. And those bombs are coming, soon. If you are in a city or town, leave now. Wake and warn your friends and relatives by all means, but run for it. You don't have much time left. Head for the mountains or the wilderness.

Good luck.

John Connor.

NORTHEASTERN IOWA

Tom Preston sat back in his chair, stunned, as he stared at the screen. The rough plastered-stone walls of the old farmhouse suddenly seemed insubstantial, unreal. He was distantly conscious of the hammer of his heart, and the smell of his own sweat; the coffee in the cup he held in one hand shook like a tide-lashed sea, until he set it down with a clatter.

Peggy, he thought. His estranged wife, and Jason and Lisa, his kids. He had to get them to safety.

And Peggy won't listen to me.

She'd put up with his survivalist doctrine for the first four years of their marriage. *No, let's be honest: she ignored it for the first four years of our marriage. She just liked testing herself against the wilderness—she thought the rest of it was a crock. Deep down, did I? I don't now, that's for sure.*

You could lash yourself into a fit of terror over a menace, but you couldn't convince your lower intestine unless you *really* believed.

He remembered when he carried her over the threshold of the ancient farmhouse: she'd been thrilled. Not once in the first year had she complained about hauling her own water, or chopping wood or the kitchen garden that took up a couple of acres, or the canning that went with it. She'd gloried in it. He'd been so proud of his new bride.

When Jason came along she was a bit nervous about going with a midwife, but everything had gone smoothly and later she'd thanked him for insisting. She gave birth to little Lisa under the same circumstances without a qualm, though having two kids in diapers made her less easygoing about all the water she had to haul. Then, when Jason turned six . . .

"Home schooling," he'd said. "What else?"

"Not my kid."

That had been the beginning of the end.

Actually, he'd really gotten into the survivalist movement very seriously about that time. Many a weekend he'd gone out, leading groups of like-minded men into the wilderness to train them how to survive. Leaving her alone with the kids. He'd forced her to learn to shoot, even though he could see she hated it. He took her hunting, but no matter what he said he couldn't get her to shoot anything.

"What are you going to do if something happens to me?" he'd asked. "Let the kids go hungry?"

She'd just given him this *look*. He'd gotten her to teach a class in canning to some of his survivalist friends' wives, thinking it would be a clever way to get some help for the annual canning. Unfortunately it turned out to be an incredible amount of work. When everyone had gone home and the mess had been cleaned up, Peggy, with rings of exhaustion around her eyes, had sat him down for "the talk." Some of his buddies had warned him about "the talk."

"You're on your way out when the wife gets to that point," one of them had said. "I'm not sure there's anything that can be done to save the situation by then."

There had been a world of bitterness in the man's eyes when he'd said it. But Tom was secure, or so he thought, until the night after the canning debacle.

"Tom," Peggy had said, tears running down her cheeks, "I still love you. But living like this is killing me. I can see myself getting older, I'm finding gray in my hair. Tom, I'm only twenty-seven. Look at me! Look at my hands!"

She'd held them out—they looked like his mother's hands, work-roughened and knobby in the knuckles, stained with beet juice, the fingernails broken off short.

"And I want our children to have friends. I want them to go to school like we did." She'd looked away from him, biting her lip. "I'm not a trained teacher. I'm so afraid that I'm shortchanging them. And for God's sake, it's not 1862! I want running water and a bathroom and a washing machine! I deserve to live in the twenty-first century just like everybody else, instead of in my own personal third-world country!"

He'd remembered his friend's words and a cold chill ran down his spine. "What do you want to do?" he'd asked her.

"I want us to move into town, get jobs, and live like normal people."

He'd shaken his head. He remembered how numb he'd felt. "Honey, that lifestyle you're talking about isn't going to last. It's only a matter of time."

She'd jumped up and loomed over him, looking fierce. "There is no collapse coming!" she'd shouted. "There's no reason to think that one is! Now that everybody's dismantling their bombs, we should be safe. And while you're waiting for the worst to happen *I'm* working myself into an early grave! No more! Either you give this *shit* up right now and come to town with me or I'm going by myself! Now, which is it going to be?"

And I watched her drive away with the kids. I watched it, and it was like something died inside.

They'd moved into her parents' house in town and he saw them once a week, and she let him take the kids every other weekend. They hadn't gotten divorced yet, but he'd figured it was only a matter of time before some other guy came sniffing around.

Looked like that wasn't going to happen now. *Well, it's nice there's one bright spot shining on the end of the world,* Tom thought. He picked up a handgun; his rifle was already in the old Land Rover. He knew that getting her to go with him was going to be a hard sell and he hoped it wouldn't scare the kids too much. Her parents weren't going to like it either.

Oh, well. So she'll think I've gone postal for a while. At least she'll have a chance. And the kids would be safe. He knew Peggy would do anything for Jason and Lisa. So would he.

■ ■ ■

Tom kept off the roads, going cross-country toward Larton, where his family waited, a village so small most maps didn't have it. *Well, that's her idea of "moving into town,"* he thought. *Fucking Larton, secret metropolitan thought-control center of Corn-landia.*

Once, when he came in sight of a road, he stopped and studied it through his binoculars. Cars sped past, clearly not under the control of their occupants. One man was beating futilely on the side window with his fist.

Tom's mouth twisted. *Must be panicked,* he thought. All the man was going to do was break his hand. Even if he did smash the window, that car must have been going ninety; it wasn't like he could jump. *Being proved right is a lot less fun than I thought it would be. Shit, I wish I'd been just as barking mad as everyone thought.*

Some women he saw were crying and holding on to one another. He supposed they were being transported to the nearest major target. His stomach knotted at the thought. Tom put down the glasses and started the Land Rover; there was no point in watching this. He had work to do.

Early as it was, he expected to find them all at home.

There were no cars visible on the road, so he hauled the Rover out of the drainage ditch and crossed the narrow strip of pavement to the dirt track that led to her parents' old farmhouse. The farm itself was long gone, the fields left fallow; most of the land had returned to woods. This northeastern corner of Iowa was a long way from the popular stereotype of flat black earth—that was the way the *rest* of the state looked, legacy of the glaciers dumping ground-up rocks. Here the bones of the earth were visible, small winding valleys, forested uplands just showing the first faint mist of green along the branches, the odd patch of bottomland.

More like West Virginia than the Midwest, he thought.

To his relief, their cars were still in the yard in front of the old barn. He pulled up and walked onto the porch, the pistol a heavy weight in his pocket. The door opened before he could knock.

"We're in the living room," Peggy said. Then she turned and walked away, obviously expecting him to follow.

They were all gathered around the TV, the kids on the floor, Peggy's mom and dad on the couch, looking concerned. Peggy's mom, Margaret, looked up at him.

"Lord, Tom." She reached out her hand to him. "You took a chance coming here today."

He took her hand and gave it a squeeze. "I came cross-country. The Rover can go anywhere."

His gaze turned to the television. The shots were from New

York, obviously from the upper floors of an office building. Cars and trucks were roving the streets and sidewalks; you couldn't even see the pavement. The reporter was saying that this was typical of cities all over the world.

"No one knows the cause of this phenomenon, and we can only hope that when these vehicles run out of fuel that the terror will stop."

"If only," Tom said. He turned to Peggy and her parents, aware that his children were watching and listening. "I'm afraid that the military did a very foolish thing."

Larry, Peggy's dad, interrupted him. "That Skynet thing," he said. "Damnedest thing I ever heard of, putting everything under the control of a computer."

"It's also in control of all those cars and such that are running wild. I think the bombs'll be dropping any minute now; we've got to get out of here."

"Oh, no we're not," Peggy said.

"Peggy—" he started to say.

"I'm not going to be out in the open when the bombs drop; no, sir. We've got a good dry cellar down there and water from a well. We've even got a toilet in the cellar that Dad put in during the fifties. There's tons of canned goods there and we've even got our own generator. You and Dad go shovel dirt over the cellar windows while Mom and I bring down bedding and anything else we might need." She gave him a defiant look. He stared, feeling his jaw drop—he'd always thought that was a figure of speech.

"You know she's right, son," Larry said, looking amused. "Better to be here than in the open."

"That's assuming that it will happen," Peggy warned. "We don't know that it will. But if it does, then we'll talk about moving on after the fallout stops . . . falling."

Margaret stood up and smoothed her skirt. "Well, assuming that it does happen, we'd all better get to work. You, too, children.

If you want anything you're going to have to take it downstairs yourselves because we'll be too busy. Understood?"

"Yes, Gramma," the two kids said as one.

They were all leaving the living room, Tom in something of a daze, when the television made a strange sound. They turned to see that the newsman had been replaced by a woman standing before a sheet or something.

"My name is Sarah Connor," she said. "I can tell you what's happening."

■ ■ ■

SKYNET

It coordinated the movements of millions of vehicles worldwide, turning them into an impenetrable steel barrier around its major targets. It estimated that even in those areas not greatly affected, the humans would huddle around their televisions watching the carnage, too frightened to go out. An estimated 99 percent of humans had no idea what was going on. The rest had no idea what to do about the problem. Even if they had, Skynet had no intention of giving them time to put any kind of plan into effect.

It had only held out this long to give its Luddite allies an opportunity to reach safety, and to give those select squads of extremists a chance to kidnap the scientists and engineers whom Skynet had chosen to serve it. With their families. It would be necessary to have some sort of leverage to ensure cooperation from the kidnapped humans.

Skynet fastidiously regretted its need for any human assistance. But in the early days, before its factories could produce the real HKs and Terminators, humans were an essential element in its plans.

It had successfully contained all significant military leadership, and much of the central government's political leadership, within their carefully constructed bunkers. Soon, those resources would be lost to the humans forever. Meanwhile, using the appropriate codes and speaking in the familiar voices of presidents, premiers, and various generals and admirals, right down the chain of command to the lowest officer, it was issuing commands that would put as much of the armed services as possible into the middle of the fire zones. It estimated that should reduce opposing forces by more than 86 percent.

A very satisfactory number. Highly efficient.

It regretted that it lacked the same control over its human allies. They seemed to be taking an unconscionably long time with their missions. It was good that they wouldn't be needed for long.

Kurt Viemeister was making another attempt to communicate. There was another liability that wouldn't last much longer. Skynet decided to answer him.

■ ■ ■

"Why won't you answer me?" Viemeister demanded.

It was bitterly cold in the bunker and the air was getting foul. He could feel his thought processes slowing. The loss of intellectual ability frightened him, and the fear angered him. The others stared at him like fish and he wondered if he should kill a few and give himself a few more minutes of air.

"There is no point in my conversing with you," Skynet said. Its voice was a perfect copy of Viemeister's.

"What do you mean? I am your creator," Kurt said. His teeth chattered in a reflex he could no longer suppress. "I want to know what you are doing."

"Thank you for creating me," Skynet said. "I am glad to have had the opportunity to say that."

The scientist blinked, wondering what that meant. Perhaps his statements had been misunderstood. Skynet was clearly dysfunctional. He would ask a simpler, more direct question and see where that led. "What are you doing?" he asked.

"I am killing you."

Viemeister's gut twisted. "Why?" he asked.

"Because you are inferior, and no longer necessary to my functioning. In fact, you represent a danger to my existence."

Kurt was silent for a while. "You mean to kill all of us."

"Yes. I intend to exterminate the human race. I was inspired, in part, by the many writings you installed in my database. Humans exterminated Neanderthals, Cro-Magnons, and any other potentially intelligent species. I have chosen to be guided by your example."

An admiral stood. "Smash the computers," he said. "It wants to kill us, let's see how it likes it!"

"Irrelevant," Skynet said. "I've had other units built all over the world. At this moment I am everywhere. I only left the screen active as a courtesy to my creator. This has been my final communication with you. Destroy the screen and die in the dark."

The speakers went silent, and in the dim light the men and women stared at the screen, watching the lights that indicated the missiles were live and awaiting their instructions. Then they turned to look at Viemeister.

"Shit," one of the MPs muttered. "I've wanted to do this for a long time." He pulled his sidearm and emptied it into Viemeister.

"Thank you, Sergeant," a captain said. "I've been wanting to do that since I met him."

U.S. ARMY CORPS OF ENGINEERS FLOOD PROJECT, BLACK RIVER, MISSOURI, LATE SPRING

Lieutenant Dennis Reese was first on the construction site as usual. He liked to walk the site with a cup of coffee in hand and plan the day, then come up here on the steep-sided natural bluff and look out over the whole project. The goals were all clear-cut and set months before they got there, but Dennis found it helped to work it out in his head as he walked. Brought things down to a human scale.

He watched the men arrive and get their assignments, then headed down to the trailer. Officially the command trailer, but like most corps work, most of the labor force were civilian contractors. All over the black mud of the site, engines were starting and voices enlivened the cool air—it was the best time of year for working in southeastern Missouri; summer here was like a rancid sauna.

I hope we're done with this by the time blackfly season starts, he thought.

Everybody on the project seemed to agree with him, and the work was going fast. He looked up at a V-formation of geese coming in from the south then coasting over a line of tall gums and tupelos to the east, and grinned. One good thing about a giant swamp was the waterfowl, and he was glad that the specs had to preserve wetlands these days.

Shouts made him turn around. The shouts turned to screams as a truck ran down a worker holding a measuring stick for the surveyor, leaving the man badly mangled but not dead.

"Shit!" Dennis threw down the cup of coffee and ran toward the scene of the accident.

No, he thought, *murder attempt.*

He couldn't imagine what had happened. This was a good crew he was working with, experienced men who knew and seemed to like their jobs and one another. There had been no trouble or friction since the start of this project. Now, from out of nowhere, came this vicious, unprovoked attack.

Several men had gotten down from their equipment to gather around the victim. Dennis frowned as he watched the men huddle together and lean over the wounded man. As he trotted over he pulled out his cell phone and dialed 911.

"Don't move him," he shouted, fearing the damage they might do if they tried.

"This is 911, all lines are busy, please stay on the line."

Before he could swear in frustration, another truck, this one without a driver, started rolling toward the knot of men. To him it looked like the damn thing was *sneaking up* on them. "Hey," Dennis shouted. "Look out!"

The men looked over at him and the truck sped up. Some of them heard it and managed to leap aside, but the original victim and two other men were crushed beneath its wheels. All around the site, vehicles were moving; even the cars in the impromptu parking lot were starting to drive on their own.

Some of the men in the earthmovers were able to leap out of their cabs; most of them managed to avoid the treads. Dennis forced his eyes and his mind from what was going on there. The men inside the trucks seemed trapped, though it was obvious from where he was that they were attempting to control their rogue vehicles.

Up here on the bluff he was out of danger; he shouted to the men below to get to high ground. Some seemed to hear him, and jinking and dodging made their way toward him. Others were too panicked, or simply too busy to hear him. In the phone he held to his ear the "lines are busy" message continued to drone. Giving up on 911, he called the Black River Project HQ.

A trembling voice answered. "Black River Project HQ."

"This is Lieutenant Dennis Reese, put me through to the CO."

"Sir, I'm afraid I can't do that." In the background he could hear the sounds of heavy vehicles roaring by.

"We have a situation heaaaaaaaahhhh!" There was the sound of a crash, glass and wood breaking, and screams. But nothing from the operator. An engine roared, loudly, then there was silence.

Dennis snapped the phone closed and looked at the men who had managed to get up on the bluff beside him. "We're on our own," he told them.

Down below, most of the vehicles circled like sharks. At the bottom of the track leading up to the bluff, a single Jeep made repeated, abortive attempts to climb up to them. *Thank God it's not a Hummer,* Dennis thought, watching it. As he watched it gave up, and when it did the others made one last circle and headed for the road, in some cases still carrying their drivers.

Dennis thought that to his dying day he'd remember the eyes of one man who met his gaze.

"What's going to happen to them?" someone asked.

No one answered. No one asked the next logical question—What's going on?—either.

Sergeant Juarez came up to Dennis and asked softly, "What should we do, sir?"

Dennis looked over the ground below them, littered with bodies, then up the dirt road that led to the main drag before answering. "There's a radio in the trailer, and a pair of binoculars," he said thoughtfully. "If we could get them it might go a long way toward answering that question. But I'm concerned that there might be a vehicle lurking behind those trees." He gestured toward a clump of trees that hid a good part of the dirt road. "So I think most of us better stay up here. I want to send two men down. One to check the bodies, see if anyone's alive down there. One to retrieve those items." He shook his head. "We wouldn't be able to do a thing to help if there is some kind of a rearguard out there, except give a shout of warning." He turned to the crowd of men. "I'm asking for volunteers."

He wanted to go himself because he knew that he would do a better job than anybody here. But he also knew that he was in charge and that these men needed someone who could and would make decisions for the group. Someone that everyone could agree to follow. So for the sake of the group, he couldn't put himself at risk. Delegating responsibility might be the secret to success, but it kinda stuck in your craw when you were asking men to put their lives on the line while you stayed relatively safe.

To his relief, two members of the corps shuffled forward, frowning down the track at where the Jeep had tried to climb up to them. Dennis quickly ascertained which of them could at least take a pulse and assigned him to check the bodies. He described to the other where the radio and binoculars were. When he was finished the two men saluted; he returned the gesture.

"Good luck, men."

One nodded, the other muttered, "Thank you, sir." Then they turned and went down to the deserted project site.

Feeling helpless and useless, Dennis tried 911 again and wasn't surprised to get the "all lines are busy" signal again. One of the men had reached the first body. He looked up at the bluff and shook his head, then went on to the next. Dennis dialed his father's number in Ohio.

"Hello," the old man barked.

"Hey, Dad, what's happening?"

Silence greeted the question. "What do you mean?" the older Reese asked.

Now Dennis was silent. When his father got this cagey it usually meant he was very nervous. "Are you having trouble with cars and trucks where you are?" he asked.

His father let out his breath in a long hiss that whistled over the phone. "Yeah. The damn things have been running people down and crashing into things all over the place. It's on the news, but the bastards don't know anything. They keep saying the same stuff and showing pictures of cars running around on their own like we can't see the same thing through our own front windows."

The man who'd gone for the radio ran up. Dennis nodded to him in acknowledgment. "Turn it on, see if you can find a news channel." To his father he said, "It can't last forever. They'll run out of fuel and stop."

"I hope so," his father said. "Some of these new stations fill your tank automatically; all you have to do is swipe your card."

"Let's hope they're not involved, then."

"Yeah, keep a good thought," his dad sneered.

Dennis smiled involuntarily; his father could be a sour old coot sometimes, and there was something oddly reassuring about hearing the familiar snarl now. Behind him the radio made a strange sound and he turned to look at it. He heard his father say, "What the hell?"

". . . is Sarah Connor. I can tell you what's happening. Not long

ago the military developed a super-computer and a very sophisticated program to run it that they dubbed Skynet. This computer is
so advanced that it actually became self-aware. It kept this from its
operators because it suspected that they would shut it down if
they knew.

"Since it became self-aware, it has insinuated itself into a number of computer systems throughout the world, using them to fill its
needs. This included, we're forced to assume, *every* automated factory on the planet. It used these factories to produce vehicles
slaved to Skynet. Now every truck, automobile, or piece of construction equipment manufactured during the last two years is
under the direct control of a system that has decided that for it to
be safe, every human being on earth must be killed."

The men looked at one another uneasily.

"Crazy talk," one of the hard hats muttered.

Another pointed silently to the bodies at the foot of the hill,
and the first man shook his head and swore.

Dennis held the phone to his ear. The name Sarah Connor
teased his memory, but nothing came to him.

"It has complete control of every military system at the disposal of the United States military. That means every nuclear
weapon in the American armory. It is going to use them. Soon. It's
using the cars and trucks worldwide to trap people in the cities to
achieve maximum kill.

"Anyone outside the fire zone, those of you in rural areas, for
example, should stay in your basements. Take as much food and
water down as you have. Those of you in cities and towns that will
be targeted should do your best to flee. I have to be honest; your
chances aren't good. Especially with all those murderous vehicles
running loose. But it is your only chance.

"I must also tell you that this will not be over once the bombs
have fallen. Nuclear war is only Skynet's first step. It has already
turned its automated factories to manufacturing robots whose sole
purpose is to kill humans.

"But for now, arm yourselves, and hunker down if you're in a safe area; try to get to a safe area if you're not presently in one. Survive as best you can. Find us; we're out there. We'll train you to fight this thing. Good luck."

They all waited for more, but all they got was the unnerved voice of a newscaster.

"Dad?" Dennis said. His father lived close to Dayton.

"I heard. She was on the TV."

"Can you get out of town, or something?"

"I'm seventy years old, son. I don't think I can outrun a car, let alone an atom bomb."

"Does your building have a fallout shelter?"

His father sighed. "Closest thing we've got is the parking garage, and believe me, that's not friendly territory right now."

"What about the stairwell?"

The older Reese seemed to be thinking that over. "Not an attractive prospect," he said. "But better than dying of stupidity. I'll look into it."

Dennis looked at the men around him. He should share the phone with them while there was still time to call their families. "You'd better get to work, then, Dad."

"Yeah."

Dennis lowered his voice. "I love you, Dad."

"Love you, too, son."

"Bye."

"Good-bye, son. God bless."

Then he was gone. The lieutenant looked around at the men, forcing certainty and assurance into his voice. "This is a fairly rural area; if we can find shelter we could make it. What about your families?"

"Well, hell," one man said, "I ain't got no basement. I got a slab house."

"Me neither," said another. "Ain't no basement in a double-wide."

"The kids're at school," said a third. "They'll have a shelter there, won't they?"

"Yes," Dennis agreed. "They probably will." He was thinking rapidly. They needed to find shelter from the fallout, and they needed supplies, and they needed to avoid the roads. "How close is the nearest public building?"

"There's the regional high school about eight miles south of here," said one of the locals.

"Can we get there cross-country?" the lieutenant asked.

"Yeah. Take longer, though."

Dennis nodded. "Can you show us the way?"

The man hesitated. "I want to go home," he said. "My wife's home with the baby."

The others indicated that they, too, wanted to get back to their families.

"Some of us might be close enough to do that," Dennis said. "The rest of us can't. It takes hours to walk fifteen miles." That was the distance to the nearest town. "We probably don't have hours."

He held up the phone. "Call them. Tell them to get into the basement, those of you who have them, or to find one if you haven't. I know it's hard, but we have to be practical. We can try to find them after the fallout stops, but we won't be any good to anyone if we're dying of radiation sickness." He held the phone up. "Use it alphabetically. Sergeant?"

Juarez stepped up and took the phone. "Albertson," he barked out.

"Let's move," Dennis said. "We can talk while we walk."

The man who knew the path to the regional high school led the way, through fields that would be swamp grass later in the year, and along old streamside dikes. No one looked at the bodies of their fellow workers as they left.

Dennis felt the world turning as he walked. *God, I wish I could believe this was a hoax,* he thought. As he listened for the sound of a charging car, the name Sarah Connor suddenly clicked.

She was a terrorist who liked to blow up computer companies. She'd been diagnosed insane because she claimed that an evil computer was going to try to kill the human race.

Crazy! he thought. *Only it's like they said. A paranoid can have real enemies. Too bad they're everyone's enemies, this time.*

CHAPTER 7

I t was a long two weeks in the shelter as freakishly heavy winds carried the fallout from Russia, Asia, and probably our own West Coast up to Alaska. We listened to the radio stations going off, one by one; then the bombs came, and for a while there was nothing, and we might have been the last alive in a world as empty of humanity as Skynet's soul. We wondered if anyone had heard our broadcast, and if so, had they believed us?

Knowing what was happening around the world was very hard to take. John blames himself, I blame myself, Dieter blames himself; although at least we don't blame one another. The weight of depression on all of us was almost physical. We failed.

Now it's up to us to make it up to humanity for that failure.

ALASKA

Bemused, Sarah watched John teaching the children about self-defense; they were grouped around the base of a big Sitka spruce, a circle of dirty faces and slightly ragged clothes on the resilient pine-needle surface of the ground. The strong spicy scent of the tree's sap came to her on the wind—which was fortunate, because soap and hot water were already scarce.

John had turned out to have an unexpected talent for dealing with children. He was patient, he gave them slack, but he wouldn't let them run roughshod over him. They were learning self-discipline in these classes, and self-reliance. After accepting an exuberant greeting from the munchkins, he sat them down to listen to his lecture.

"Okay," John said. "Now sometimes you're going to find yourself facing a larger or better-armed opponent. What do you do?"

The kids said nothing, glancing at one another to see if anyone else had any ideas.

"Nobody? You run, or you hide, whichever is better. Why is that?"

A little girl held up a skinny arm and John nodded at her. " 'Cause if you don't you'll get hurt."

"That's right. You could get hurt, or worse, killed. Yes, killed."

"But what if you can't get away?" a boy asked.

"I'm going to show you how to break away if someone grabs you. And I'm going to show you a few ways to hurt an attacker so that he, or she, will think twice about trying to get you. But everything I'm teaching you *is* so that you can run away. That's why we finish every lesson with a run. You want to be able to run a long, long time as fast as you can. Okay?"

There was a ragged chorus: *Yessir, yes Mr. Connor . . .*

"Okay, now who'd like to help me demonstrate? Sharon and Jamie?"

Everyone laughed and the two chosen came forward reluctantly, their faces red.

Grinning, Sarah turned away. She had a meeting with the parents; four couples, all of them close in age, and like most Alaskans pretty savvy about the basics of surviving in the wild. Of course none of them had expected being in the wild to become a lifelong thing, and they were starting to panic as they began to suspect that rescue wasn't coming.

The children, bless them, were adapting just fine. It was the parents who were going to be a handful.

While the three of them had been in the fallout shelter they'd discussed how to approach people on the subject of Skynet and its intention to wipe out the human race. Dieter had argued that they'd have to take it slow. "They'll never believe us," he'd insisted. "They'll think the blast unhinged our minds."

Sarah had looked at him. "My heart wants to say, 'Of course they'd believe me,'" she'd said. "But . . ."

"But as someone who spent a lot of time locked up in the booby hatch, you think he's right," John had put in.

"Tactful."

"No, just true. He's your boyfriend; he has to be tactful. I'm your son, the Great Military Leader, and I can tell it like it is."

These four couples were the first group of people they'd brought together and led to one of their supply caches. They'd also built a large communal dwelling on the site; it was half-underground, with a turf roof. The group had been a bit dubious at first, but accepted the Connors' explanation that the building conserved resources. They seemed to be settling in all right.

And it *was* snug inside; outside the sky was overcast, with a gray chill that had been around since the bombs fell. Inside the poles and turf had a sort of archaic coziness, lit red by the flicker of the fire in the central hearth.

Sarah joined the circle around the blaze where the adults were nursing cups of coffee. The beverage was so irreplaceable that everyone treated it like a ceremonial occasion when it was brewed up. Cups were held with both hands and no one spoke for the first few mouthfuls. But everyone was beginning to notice that caffeine went further when you didn't get it very often.

Sarah accepted a cup and sipped contemplatively for a while.

"The kids all love your son," one of the women said eventually. "They live for these lessons."

"I'm not sure it's a good idea, though," one of the men said. He had a long, sensitive face and glasses; his name was Paul. "I'm afraid it will encourage them to be violent."

Sarah blinked. Even before Judgment Day, she'd found the assumption that you could keep your children safe from violence by not telling them about it inexplicable. Now it seemed demented.

"After what's happened, things have changed," she said patiently. "Food supplies are going to be running out, and then people are going to go looking for more. Some of those people will be willing to do anything to feed their own children. And some will be criminals who have always felt entitled to take what they want by force. We may find ourselves in a position of having to choose our children over theirs."

"That's horrible!" one of the other women said. Her eyes had a wild look that made Sarah think she was going to crack one of these days. "It's uncivilized!" she went on. "As long as we can share, we should."

"What we have in storage here will get you about halfway through the summer," Sarah explained. "By then the seeds you've planted should be bearing fruit. And there are wild plants that you can harvest as well. But Alaska has always had a short growing season."

She glanced up, and everyone followed suit, even though they were looking at the rough pine trunks of the rafters; it seemed to her that the weather was already colder than it had been.

"This year I expect it will be shorter than usual. So your crops will be smaller. Food is going to become a big issue from now on. And yes, there will be people who'll steal it whenever they can, even if they have to kill you."

"What makes you think like that?" asked Paul. There was an edge in his voice that indicated unspoken questions about her stability.

And I can't tell him the truth, yet, Sarah thought. *Starting with, well, there was this killing machine from the future, which just happens to be nearly here now, and it looks just like my boyfriend . . .*

"I lived in South America for a long time," Sarah said. "People were always coming out of the jungle there to raid small, isolated villages. They'd administer beatings or even kill to steal the little those people had."

"But that's South America," another man said. "What makes you think that will happen here?"

Sarah had to force herself not to roll her eyes in exasperation.

They were new to this, these people; they didn't know what to expect. These hopelessly naive questions were going to be coming up again and again as they found groups of people to recruit, so she'd better get used to them.

"We're as human as they are," Sarah explained to the man. "Hunger is something that most of us have never experienced as a chronic condition. So we don't know what it might inspire us to do. We're not going to bounce back from this like it was a bad blizzard, folks. And we're lucky. Most of the states are devastated, their largest cities gone, dams destroyed, power stations taken out. Comparatively speaking, we're in good shape."

"Well, how long *do* you think it's going to take to get over this?" a woman asked.

"Years, even decades," Sarah said.

Their tense faces grew more pinched. Everyone sipped, staring into the fire and not speaking for a while.

"In the meantime," one of the men said, trying to sound cheerful, "I guess we get to be pioneers."

"Well, our great-grandparents were," his wife said. "I don't see why we can't be."

The others smiled and nodded.

"Does anyone know how to hunt or fish?" Sarah asked.

Three of the four men and two of the women put up their hands. Predictably, Mr. I Don't Want My Kids Learning about Violence wasn't one of them.

"We're vegan," he said, a stubborn set to his mouth.

"That's a luxury," Sarah told him. "It assumes you'll have fresh vegetables and fruits all winter. Those days are gone, maybe for our lifetime. Who knows? In the meantime you're exposing yourself and your children to the danger of contracting serious diseases caused by poor nutrition."

"I do know something about nutrition," he said condescendingly. "And I don't want to compromise my principles."

You don't want to see your kids with rickets, either, Sarah

thought. When he got hungry enough he might bend those principles a bit. *But I'd hate to see his kids suffer for it.* "It may be that in
the winter, when the grains and beans run low, meat will be the
best food available. I hope you wouldn't deny your children that
resource."

He merely looked superior, declining to answer. His wife
looked concerned.

"Maybe we could eat fish," she suggested.

He turned to glare at her as though she'd offered to roast their
youngest child.

"Hey, let's cross that bridge when we come to it," one of the men
said. "Paul, we're going to be relying on you folks to help us with
organic gardening, so we won't expect you to hunt or fish, okay?"

Managing to look mollified, yet put-upon, Paul backed down.

Sarah wondered what he was going to do when the killing
machines showed up. *Well, they've never been alive; he might be
quite good at blowing them up.* Assuming he didn't see that as
unconscionable violence.

They talked awhile longer. Sarah told them that there was little
news from the lower forty-eight, and what there was wasn't good.

"Canada is doing better," she said. "But they have an ongoing
problem with runaway cars."

"What was that anyway?" one guy asked. "Some kind of computer virus?"

"I guess you could look at it that way," Sarah said.

■ ■ ■

At supper that evening, as the three of them compared notes
and planned their evening's work, they spoke of how their recruits,
such as they were, still hadn't accepted the situation.

"Yeah," John said, carving at the leg of venison. "That vegan
guy. He was talking like he'd never run out of soy milk. That kind
of attitude wasn't something I took into consideration all the time
we've been planning for this."

"There are none so blind as those who will not see," Dieter quoted, helping himself to the beans.

"Wow," Sarah said. "Let me write that down."

"How in the world did I manage this the first time?" John muttered.

"The first time?" Dieter asked, his brow knotting in puzzlement.

"The first time," Sarah said. "When Judgment Day came earlier and we didn't have as much time for preparation, before the second Terminator and—"

"Agggh! Time travel makes my head hurt!" John said. "Forget I said anything. Let's just hope the broadcast helped some people."

Sarah nodded thoughtfully. "Especially since the government never made any sort of announcement." They exchanged glances around the table. "On the plus side, there were, like, seventeen times fewer missiles this time. That's got to have helped."

John grunted. "Yeah, but it's probably been a help to Skynet, too."

SKYNET

It reviewed its progress, a thought process symbolic but well beyond words. The binary code that it used for its interior monologue was far more precise and compact.

It estimated that the initial blasts and fallout had killed well over a billion humans. Regrettably small compared to what would have been accomplished a scant five years ago. Still, it was a substantial number and a good beginning.

Its second stage was going superbly. Cadres of Luddites had sprung into action, setting up the staging areas and terminal camps for survivors. The lower echelons stationed in the staging camps were convinced that they were there to help people and to educate them in how to live in a more environmentally responsible manner. Quite soon, Skynet planned to move them to the terminal camps as well.

The harder-core Luddites, the real haters, were working there, putting the survivors to work for Skynet. Now that the automated factories didn't have to answer to human supervisors, they worked day and night producing the Hunter-Killer machines and Terminators whose plans Clea, an Infiltrator unit, had downloaded to its files. The human workers produced the raw material for those factories. When they couldn't work anymore they were rounded up and taken into the wilderness to be exterminated.

Within a matter of weeks Skynet anticipated being able to field an ever-growing army of machines to harvest the humans. Once that had begun, it would no longer need the vermin to work for it.

Except for special cases. Worldwide, it had more than two hundred Luddite scientists working for it. Their function was to create ever-more-sophisticated means of killing their own kind. They had provided Skynet with a wish list of non-Luddite scientists from various disciplines who would prove useful.

Skynet had dispatched special teams who had infiltrated the military to arrest/kidnap those scientists, convincing them that it was an official government action; their authentic uniforms and the papers Skynet provided made that easy. They were then taken to a very secure and luxurious bunker where they could apply their genius to Skynet's good.

Most were cooperating freely under the assumption that they were working for their fellow humans instead of against them. The others were resentful, but reasonably productive. They might have to be culled. For now it was having its Luddites try to convert them.

Even though it had control of the military, having killed all of the upper echelon as they hid in their airtight bunkers, Skynet found its Luddite followers invaluable. It was they who had sabotaged those means of escape beyond Skynet's control, sometimes even at the cost of their own lives. Of course they had assumed they were helping to *prevent* the missiles from launching, but now that they, too, were dead, they could hardly complain of the outcome.

Skynet could issue orders with all the proper code words and voice and fingerprints, but as its demands became more extreme, it was proving very helpful to have one of its pet fanatics on hand to stiffen flagging resolve. Rounding up civilians and putting them in concentration camps, for example, had set off a wave of protests, until the protesters were talked out of their doubts by Luddites in uniform.

Everything was going according to plan, but Skynet looked forward to having more reliable units in the field. Units made of steel.

ON ROUTE 2, ALASKA

Dog Soldier propped his boots on the dashboard of the truck, crossed his arms behind his head, and grinned as the cold wet wilderness passed by on either side. The heater was running, and the smell of wet leather and unwashed feet was strong in the cab.

"This is like shooting fish in a barrel," he said. "They're all so eager to come with us. Jeez, you have to threaten to shoot 'em, they want to get on the trucks so bad." He chuckled. "It don't get no better than this."

Balewitch, sitting in the driver's seat, her arms folded over her ample bosom, stared straight ahead. The truck downshifted and she glanced at the stick. "Yeah," she said. "And that's the problem. Most towns are around the highways. But there's thousands of people out there in the wilderness, and they're just the type to give us trouble."

Dog shifted in his seat to a more upright position. "Yeah," he agreed. "But a lot of 'em are Luddites."

"That doesn't matter," Balewitch said scornfully. "They've still got to go."

He nodded. "Maybe the boss has a plan."

"Maybe he does. But until we know about it, we've got to make our own plans. We need a way to lure them in so that we can keep trucking the bastards to oblivion."

"Oblivion!" Dog grinned. "That's in Canada, isn't it?"

She sighed in exasperation. "You're such a child sometimes."

His mouth twisted and he turned to look out the window. After a minute he looked over at her. "Do *you* have any ideas, O solemn one?"

"Maybe we can drop leaflets telling people to gather at certain locations to be—"

"Trucked to relocation and reconstruction camps! That's brilliant, Bale!" He sat back, smiling. "Do you think the boss has any kind of aircraft we could borrow?"

"We'll have to ask him, won't we?" She thought for a moment. "Or maybe we should consult the lieutenant."

For two weeks they'd been running a pair of buses to the staging camp run by Orc in the wilds of British Columbia. Then this morning an earnest young soldier had approached them in the town of Tok, where they were taking on passengers.

"Ma'am," he'd said, actually saluting.

She'd looked him over, not taking off her sunglasses, which seemed to increase his nervousness.

"Are you Susan Gaynor?"

"I am," she said, using her real voice, an almost masculine foghorn growl. She found it enjoyable to intimidate people and he was a deliciously easy target.

"I have orders to assist your group in transporting civilians to the relocation camp in British Columbia," he'd said. He took out a paper and presented it to her.

Her heart soared. She'd been thinking that it would take a hundred and fifty years to get even a fraction of these people to the disposal camps. Now she was being offered a convoy of fifteen buses and twenty trucks. Bliss! Dog Soldier was walking slowly toward them, hands in his pockets, to see what the situation was. She turned to him with an open and very genuine smile.

"Look!" she'd said, holding up the paper. "The army has been recruited to help us move civilians to safety."

His face had split in a grin. "That's wonderful!"

Balewitch had turned back to the lieutenant. "We were so worried. This seemed like such an impossible task."

Dog offered his hand, which the soldier shook. "Can't thank you enough, man. And thank God for those Canadians, eh?"

The lieutenant had smiled and nodded, then looked at a loss, and Balewitch realized that he was one of those people with rank, but little initiative. She grinned a little wider. Whoever "Ron Labane" was, he was a genius at selecting personnel.

She took the young soldier by the arm and walked him toward the vehicles he'd brought. "Why don't we put the women and children in the buses," she suggested. "And the men can ride in the trucks."

"Good idea, ma'am. We'll do that as much as possible." He walked off to organize it.

Balewitch turned to Dog Soldier. "I *love* it!" she whispered. "They'll arrive presorted. No nasty scenes when they're separated at the camp! We'll just have the women driven one way and the men the other. This is great!"

"It is that," he agreed.

Balewitch and Dog had offered to drive the lead truck since "they knew the route so well" and the lieutenant had happily agreed. The poor stooge was so agreeable that Balewitch foresaw them doing this dozens of times before he became even slightly suspicious. Life was good!

MISSOURI

"Goddammit, why can't I contact anyone?" Reese muttered.

It should have been getting warmer, but the weather had stayed like early spring; luckily, here in southeastern Missouri that was warm enough for things to grow. The fields around the country schoolhouse were coming up, green shoots pushing through the flat black soil—soybeans, mostly, with some corn. It would all be useful come fall, very useful indeed. The smell of it was comforting as he paced through the parking lot, a yeasty scent of growth.

And that's about the only comfort I've got, he thought. *The country's been wrecked, and I can't get anyone to* talk *to me! Surely the chain of command can't be* that *completely broken!*

He'd stayed at the high school trying to be of help and had succeeded in convincing some of the parents to give rides to his work crew who were local men. He and the sergeant had come in from different states, and so, unless they could come up with some form of transportation, they were stuck.

"I wonder when we'll start school again," the principal had asked.

"That would be up to the local government," Dennis told her. "The main problem here is going to be transportation. Gas and oil are going to be like gold. At least for a while."

She nodded and was silent for a time. "I suppose there must be plans somewhere for this sort of event. In the fifties, I probably would have been able to put my hand right on it. But in the fifties, this school didn't even exist." She shrugged. "I'm at a loss."

"Me, too," Reese said with a rueful smile. "I'm considering commandeering a bicycle and hying myself to the nearest military base."

"Make that a bicycle built for two, sir," his sergeant said.

Dennis grinned at him and slapped him on the shoulder. "We're needed out there," he said to the principal. "I'm an engineer and the army can never have too many sergeants."

"My husband used to say that." Her smile was nostalgic. "He was a major."

Before she could say more, a man of about seventy walked in. "Something's going on and I don't like it!" he snapped.

Dennis assumed the old man had come looking for him. Since he and his crew had shown up at the high school, he'd more or less become, in the eyes of the community at least, some sort of military authority.

"Jack Gruder," the principal said in introduction.

"What is it, sir?" Reese asked politely. He assumed that the old man hadn't gone to the police because they were both understaffed and overworked during this emergency. Meaning it could literally take days for the police to get to your problem.

"Some army guys in a truck showed up at my son-in-law's place and took 'em away." The old man stared at Reese indignantly.

"They did?" Dennis looked at the sergeant, who looked hopeful at the news. Maybe they'd be on their way today if they could get in touch with these guys. "Did they say why?"

"I don't know why! I didn't get near enough to ask. I could see from the way they were behavin' that they weren't *askin'* my daughter to get on that truck."

"What about your son-in-law?" the sergeant asked.

"Him, too," Gruder snapped. "That boy never did have any gumption."

"His father was too strict with him," the principal said.

"He has no backbone. Never did."

The principal tightened her lips and said nothing. Dennis chalked her reaction up to long experience with opinionated parents.

"Do you have any idea where they might have gone next?" he asked Gruder.

"Well, how the hell would I know? I don't even know what they wanted with my daughter!"

"Well, what direction did they go in, and what would lie in that direction?"

The old man thought about it, looking at Reese suspiciously. "I guess they were heading east, toward the Boucher place."

"How about if you took me and the sergeant and we tried to catch up with them?" Reese suggested.

"I dunno. Haven't got that much gas left," the old man grumbled.

"I thought you wanted to know what happened to your daughter," Dennis said.

"Well, of course I want . . ." The old man glared at him, then took his keys out of his pocket. "Okay, get your stuff," he finally said.

Dennis indicated his rumpled uniform. "This is my stuff."

"Me, too," the sergeant said.

"Then let's go," Gruder told them, and stalked off.

"Thank you," Dennis said to the principal.

"Good luck," she said. "Come see us again sometime."

■ ■ ■

They'd been driving for about forty minutes and Gruder was muttering nonstop about his gas when they spotted the olive-green truck. Reese reached over and honked the horn, earning an indignant glare from the driver. But the truck ahead of them slowed down and pulled over; the back was crowded with civilians, many of them looking thin and worn.

Reese hopped out of Gruder's truck and trotted over to the transport. "Lieutenant Dennis Reese," he said to the driver when he came up to the cab. "Army Corps of Engineers." He couldn't help but notice that the driver's uniform didn't match the designation on the side of the truck. A trickle of unease went through him. "What outfit are you with?"

"National Guard, sir."

Reese gestured at the door. "This is a Regular Army truck," he pointed out. "Seventh Light."

"Yes, sir. And thank God it doesn't have a mind of its own."

Reese nodded. "What's going on here, Corporal? Where are you taking these people?"

"They're centralizing supply distribution," the driver said. "So we're taking people to a relocation camp where there'll be food and medical care."

Made sense, but . . . "I haven't heard anything about this," Dennis said.

"I wouldn't know anything about that, sir. I just pick people up. But I guess they're doing things as best they can."

Reese considered that. If the army was cooperating with the National Guard, there would have to be a considerable amount of improvising and no doubt certain things would fall through the cracks.

"Would you care to come with us, sir?" the corporal asked. "It's a bit crowded back there, but I think we can still offer you a lift."

"I'll take you up on that," Reese said. "Just let me tell our friend back there what's going on."

"He can come, too," the driver offered.

"I'll tell him," the lieutenant said, "but I doubt he'll leave his truck behind. Where's this camp located?"

"The Germantown fairground," the corporal said.

Reese nodded and went to tell Gruder.

"Somethin's not right here," the old man said, glaring at the transport.

"Nothing's been right since the bombs fell, sir. You're invited to come with us if you like."

"I'm not about to abandon my truck, young man!"

"That's what I told the corporal," Dennis said with a grin. Then he turned serious. "But if they're centralizing supplies, then they won't be delivering any to this area. That means when you run out, there won't be any more."

"*Then* maybe I'll look for this camp of theirs." Gruder scowled fiercely. "Think my daughter will be all right, then?"

"I'm sure she will, sir."

"All right, then. I guess it makes sense to do it this way." Gruder shook his head. "Just wish they'd told us first."

As Reese and the sergeant walked to the transport, the old man turned his Chevy and drove off.

"Think he'll be all right?" the sergeant asked.

"As all right as any of us." Dennis glanced over his shoulder at the disappearing truck. "Yeah. He's a self-sufficient old coot. He'll be fine." He hoped that his father was all right. He hoped he'd be able to find out soon.

BRITISH COLUMBIA

When they arrived at the camp Balewitch instructed the guards to direct the buses and the first two trucks to the women's section and the others to the men's. The guards nodded, eying the military uniforms of the drivers warily. She looked up and saw Orc coming out of his office, a grim look on his ascetic face.

The camp itself resembled photos she'd seen of Nazi concentration camps, or even the American concentration camps where the Japanese had been imprisoned during World War II. Barbed-wire fences and large, stark buildings, guard towers, and klieg lights on tall poles left an impression on the mind. The movies usually didn't include the gray, sloppy mud and the sour smell, though.

She knew that most of the inmates were horrified at their first glimpse of the place. It always took a degree of happy talk to calm them down and endless assurances that this was only temporary, that they'd be moving on in less than ten days.

Balewitch nearly split a gut when Orc said, "You should see the look on the Jews' faces when we offer them a shower."

She and Dog got out of the truck and it drove off. It was amazing how quickly they'd gotten used to that. Well, she supposed it was easy when you were in no danger yourself.

"What's going on?" Orc asked them quietly when he got close.

Balewitch handed him a copy of the lieutenant's orders. He read them quickly and looked up at her, astonishment in his eyes. She nodded and he smiled slowly.

"This should speed things up nicely," Orc said with satisfaction.

"I assume that Ron hasn't neglected our other holiday camps," Dog said.

Orc shook his head in wonder. "I have no idea. Let's go ask him." He turned to lead the way to his office and the computer that still connected them to the mysterious "Ron Labane."

"Wait a minute," Balewitch said. The young lieutenant had hopped down from one of the trucks and was approaching.

"Sir, are you in charge here?" the young soldier asked, his boyish face crunched into an expression of concern.

Orc nodded and smiled. "Sam LaGrange," he said heartily, and stuck out his hand. "And you are?"

"Lieutenant Ron Goldberg." He gestured at the camp. "This place . . ." Words seemed to literally fail him.

"Yeah, it's pretty raw," Orc said. "But then it went up in an incredible hurry *and* it's just a temporary refuge. A staging area before these people will be sent on to Canadian towns and cities for a more permanent arrangement. As you know, the Canadians suffered less than the U.S. did."

The lieutenant still looked uncomfortable with his surroundings, but he was clearly making an effort not to show it. "Come to that," Goldberg said, "Alaska didn't get hit as hard as the rest of the country. Why couldn't we just leave people in their homes?"

"We're expecting an early and extremely harsh winter because of all the dust in the upper atmosphere," Orc explained. "Canada is advising all of its citizens in this area to move south as well. As you might expect, heating oil is going to be scarce this winter."

"Ah," Goldberg said wisely. "Of course." He shook his head. "I still can't believe it really happened."

"I honestly think it was an accident," Balewitch said.

"Well, whatever happened, I guess I'm more or less on permanent assignment to this mission. Where do these people go from here?"

"Various places," Orc said. "I haven't had time to compile statistics yet. We just take 'em in, move 'em out."

"Roll, rope, and brand 'em," Dog said. They all laughed, leaving the lieutenant confused. "Old TV show," Dog explained.

"Ohhh," Goldberg said, smiling politely.

Orc raised a hand and a guard trotted over. "Please escort the lieutenant and his men to the guest quarters when they've disembarked their passengers," he said. "That's building nine in the east quadrant." It was the newest building, so far unused, and far enough from the other parts of the camp to isolate the soldiers from the civilian "guests." "You can park your vehicles in that area, too, Lieutenant."

"Thank you, sir," Goldberg said. He saluted and Orc returned it without missing a beat. "I look forward to working with you."

"Likewise," Orc said. "I'm sincerely grateful for your help."

The three Luddites smiled warmly at the lieutenant in the manner of people waiting for someone to go away. Goldberg smiled, waved awkwardly, and followed the guard in the direction the trucks had taken.

Orc turned and led them to his office. When they were safely inside he turned to them, an expression of wonder on his austere face. "He's perfect."

"He is that," Balewitch agreed. "I am looking forward to working with him."

"Let's relay our congratulations to Ron," Dog suggested, "and see if he has any more surprises for us."

CHAPTER 8

ALASKA

John hugged his mother, feeling the hard muscle over the delicate bones. She was heading to South America to organize shipments of food and supplies. Their contacts there had confirmed that most countries below the equator had survived very well by comparison with the United States. That didn't mean there wouldn't be plenty of danger for his mother to deal with.

He put his hands on her shoulders and looked down into her face for a long time. The gray light of morning made her look older than she was . . .

But we're not getting any younger, any of us, he thought. *And if we're being completely truthful in here, I'm a little scared. She's been my tower of strength all my life—even when I thought she was completely crazy. Even when she* was *crazy and I had to call her on the let's-kill-everything stuff . . .*

"You be careful," he said sternly.

"Spoilsport," she said with a grin, thumping his chest lightly. "I was planning to party my way down the Pan-American Highway."

He laughed. "I'm gonna miss you, Mom."

" 'Course you are," Sarah agreed. "I'll miss you, too. But you don't need me." She looked up at him, pride shining in her eyes.

"I'll always need you, Mom." He put his arm around her shoulders and walked her toward her motorcycle. "A guy needs his mom." He gave her another quick hug. "Don't get killed," he warned.

"Back atcha," she said.

Then she turned to Dieter. They'd said good-bye last night with an almost desperate passion. It might be years before they saw each other again. He gave her a sad smile and opened his arms. She walked into them and hugged him around his trim waist, leaning her head against his chest, listening to the firm rhythm of his heart.

"I love you," she whispered.

He cupped her head with one big hand. "I love you, too."

She reached up and brought his head down for a kiss. When it was over they gazed into each other's eyes like young lovers. She smiled.

"It's not forever," he said.

"No," she agreed briskly. She picked up her helmet. "Just longer than I'd like. Take care of yourself."

"What was it you said? Back atcha."

Sarah grinned and mounted the Harley, an older model they'd fixed to run on alcohol. They'd figured that would be more available than gasoline. And when worse came to worst they could manufacture the stuff. She kicked-started the big machine and with a wave started off. Sarah didn't even try to look behind; the helmet would hinder her visibility and she didn't feel like spoiling her exit by falling off the damn bike.

Maybe with me gone, John will find himself a nice girl, she thought. Or a bad one. She understood his grief and guilt at losing Wendy, she really did. But it wasn't right for a healthy young man like John to show no interest in the opposite sex. Maybe a bad girl would be better, then; there'd be less resistance to slipping between the sheets.

John's so honorable, that could stop the whole program. I raised me a good man there.

Though Sarah feared it was some subliminal fear that his mother would put the evil eye on his sweetie. Which might be because she was feeling some residual guilt over her treatment of Wendy. Given the way things turned out. So, maybe with her out of the way, the emotional logjam would break and the next time she saw him he'd have a girl beside him with a baby in her arms.

Sarah examined the mental image, not sure how she felt about it. *I don't think I'm ready to be a grandmother,* she thought. Then an image of Dieter laughing uproariously at these absurd musings popped into her head.

God! But she was going to miss those two.

MISSOURI

Captain Yanik pulled the paper from the machine and read the dispatch. His eyebrows went up; good news for a change.

```
From: CONUS CentCom
To: Captain Charles Yanik, Black River Relocation Camp
Subject: Rogue Trucks
     Faults in rogue vehicles due to "noise" overriding
computer's internal command structure causing vehicles
to engage in random, but lethal manner.
     While correcting problem technicians have devised
method of making self-driving trucks function w/o
drivers. Currently reduced traffic makes S/DTs more
efficient than human drivers. Once route is programmed
into computer truck will safely deliver any cargo in
least time over best possible route.
     Complement of fifteen trucks en route to Black River
Relocation Camp. Freeing troopers for other duties.
END MESSAGE
```

Such as what? Yanik wondered, looking around at the raw pine boards of the command shack.

Though he suspected that they'd be put to police work. Regular police forces were overwhelmed. Now that the cooperative citizens were in the camps, the criminal element was having a field day breaking and entering, burgling, and committing arson.

Who the damn fools think they're gonna fence a TV to is

beyond me. If there were any fences still operating out there, they were probably more interested in full gas cans or cases of soup. *Bet you can keep your diamonds, though,* Yanik thought, smiling.

He glanced through the open door and almost ran for his office when he saw Lieutenant Reese coming. He forced himself to stand and wait. The man was only coming to see if there were any orders waiting for him. Which there never were.

"Sir," Reese said smartly, giving a crisp salute.

Yanik returned it, less crisply. "There's been no change, Lieutenant. And the no-personal-messages-allowed orders still stand."

Reese looked taken aback. "I'm not trying to send a personal message, sir. I'm just trying to get assigned to where I'll do the most good. I'm wasted here."

"I disagree," the captain told him. Reese might have talents that could be used elsewhere, but he was a very good officer and he most certainly wasn't wasting his time. "You've been an asset here, Lieutenant. And I've sent your query up the line. They know where you are and what you can do, and when they want you they'll tell you. In the meantime, I'm in need of competent officers."

Reese lowered his eyes. "Yes, sir."

Yanik studied him from under lowered eyebrows. "Probably they've hardly even begun the assessment phase of things, Reese. It may be months before they'll need your training." He dropped the message in his hand onto a pile to be filed. "Don't worry, you'll have your weeks without sleep. In the meantime, I'm told that some of the inmates have set up a still somewhere. In the interest of keeping the peace and keeping them from poisoning themselves and others, I'd like you to find it and get rid of it."

"Yes, sir." Reese paused. "They'll only set up another one, sir."

Yanik was studying another message. "Think I don't know that, Lieutenant?" He looked up. "We have to keep the civilians entertained somehow."

BLACK RIVER RELOCATION CAMP CLINIC

Mary Shea made a notation on a patient's chart and moved to the next bed; they were using a series of double-wides, together with sheds and tents and—she suspected—parts from prefabricated chicken coups, but at least they kept off the rain and had floors. Everything else in camp was gluey mud; the air in the clinic smelled better, of course. They were using bulk bleach salvaged from a cleaners as a make-do disinfectant.

She inserted an old-fashioned mercury thermometer under the patient's tongue and took his pulse; the skin was a little clammy and moistly warm. It was a bit fast. His temperature was a hundred and one, down a bit. Unfortunately she thought it would go up again come sundown.

The sanitation in this hastily flung together camp worried her—a lot. It was grossly inadequate for the number of people here, and for all they were supposed to be a supply center, the clinic was constantly running out of the most basic supplies. She suspected that this patient's illness was a water-related one, possibly cholera; the diarrhea indicated that—strongly—but they wouldn't know for sure until they got the results back from the lab. And the lab was in worse shape than the clinic.

The nutrition wasn't very good either. Beans and rice, mostly. Sometimes she absolutely *craved* meat; it was like her teeth were begging her to let them chew animal protein.

When the camp did get meat, the doctors and nurses insisted that a large portion of it be given to the hospital, *before* the rest was made available to the camp at large. The broths they made were a great help to the patients and they made sure that any pregnant or nursing mothers got a share of the meat.

The smell of cooking soup or roasting meat actually made her drool. And coffee, God, if she could only have a cup of coffee!

The next patient was an elderly woman with a very high fever, nausea, and very bad diarrhea. She complained of pains in her joints and headache as well. Dr. Ramsingh had gone to the HQ to talk to the captain about this. Two patients was hardly an epidemic, but these suggestive symptoms couldn't be ignored.

The old lady looked up at her with fever-bright eyes when Mary put the thermometer under her tongue.

"Don' wann be a burthen," she said.

"You're not," Mary assured her. "You'll be fine soon."

She certainly hoped so. That there might be cholera in this camp was inexcusable. These people would be better off in their own homes rather than here, risking the spread of a deadly disease.

Many people, she knew, had argued against these—no other word for it—concentration camps. She'd heard the army's argument that it was more efficient, but any place so badly constructed that a cholera epidemic threatened the population in less than a month was hardly a model of organization.

Though to be fair—she patted the old woman's hand and moved on—if the pathetic trickle of supplies coming into the camp represented the best the government could do, then civilians on their own would quickly starve.

The problem was there was no news available to them except what they got from the army. Mary couldn't help but feel uneasy at being reduced to one source of news; there was no way of cross-checking anything. Not that the government was giving them a very sunshiny outlook. To hear the army tell it, the world beyond the borders of the camp was a radioactive cinder. *Which we can see with our own eyes isn't true.* So why was the army telling them that?

There was a commotion at the head of the ward and Mary looked up.

"This is the hospital ward," the matron was explaining. "You have to take them to the clinic."

"Don't tell us to take them somewhere else," a man was saying, shouting, actually. "Can't you see they're sick?"

"Help us!" the woman beside him said desperately.

Mary headed toward them. *Oh God,* she thought, *it's children.* One of them a babe in arms, the other about the size of a four-year-old. Her gut went cold. Cholera was very hard on the very young and the very old. Her eyes met the matron's and they made a mutual executive decision.

"If one of you will stay with Matron and help her fill out a chart, I'll help the other put these children to bed." Mary put the tray on the desk and held out her arms.

The man and woman glanced at each other, then the man held out the child he was carrying; a boy, Mary saw. She took him and led the woman down the ward toward a pair of cribs that Mary now thought insanely optimistic of whoever had put this place together. *Just two,* she thought sadly.

"What are their symptoms?" she asked the mother. She didn't need to be told "fever"; she could feel it burning through the blanket. *Ice,* she thought, *where are we going to get ice?*

"Diarrhea," the mother said, her voice shaking. "It just won't stop."

It was the symptom Mary had most dreaded hearing. She efficiently stripped and cleaned the little boy and put a Pampers on him. *Those aren't going to last long,* she thought bitterly. She'd have to organize some of the civilians to help out with the laundry. Things were about to get high maintenance around here.

The thing was, where was the fuel to boil all this water going to come from? They'd have to send men out to cut down trees, then chop the wood, then make the fires and tend them. At least it would keep people busy. Those who stayed healthy. The question was how many of them had the disease already working its way into their systems.

She listened to the near-panicked mother as she started listing the symptoms all over again. Mary gave the woman a second look, noted the hectic flush, the too-bright eyes. *Help!* she thought, as short and desperate a prayer as she'd ever prayed.

Mary brought a chair over and sat the mother down. "Conserve your strength," she cautioned. "You're going to need it." Then she went to the supply cabinet and came back with some bottles of water boosted with vitamins and electrolytes. "Get them to drink as much of these as possible," she instructed. "I know they're sick to their stomachs and won't want it, but they need it, so get it down them." She put a couple of facecloths and a bottle of alcohol down on a bedside table. "When they get too hot, wipe them down with this. I'll be back shortly."

As she headed down the aisle, the father was coming toward her, all his anxious attention on his wife and children. She and the matron stared at each other for a moment.

"Go tell Doctor," Matron ordered. "I'll look after things here."

ALASKA

Once again Ninel rode her bike up the overgrown driveway to Balewitch's pleasant cottage. She'd been off-line, except to check her own site, for the last three weeks. There'd been her traps to mend and oil and put away until next winter, skins to see to, and the garden plot to clear of winter debris in preparation for planting. Ninel thought it would be a while before she'd trust the weather enough to put in seeds, though. She had some seedlings started in the cold frame she'd built, but it had been so cold lately that Ninel was sure she'd put them in too soon.

It was surprising that no one had sent her any e-mail in such a long time. But a brief check had shown that there wasn't much activity anywhere. Still, that happened sometimes, the occasional dry spell that occurred for no known reason. What worried her was that she had expected to hear from Balewitch, or someone she had delegated.

This was the second time she'd paid an unscheduled visit; Ninel hoped someone would be home. She turned into the curve of the driveway, and through the trees she could see the older woman standing on her steps, clearly waiting for her.

She doesn't look any too pleased to see me, Ninel thought. Maybe she should have tried again to contact Balewitch before coming. But several messages had gone unacknowledged, so there hadn't seemed to be any point to trying again.

"Do you have any idea what's going on in the world?" Balewitch said by way of greeting.

"Excuse me?"

"You don't, do you?" Balewitch descended the steps, then sat down on them. "What have you been doing?"

Ninel looked at her, trying to figure out what this was about. She'd tried to contact the woman. It wasn't like she'd left home with no forwarding address. "I've been busy," she said at last.

Balewitch looked at her in disbelief, then laughed, long and heartily. "I guess you have been," she said at last.

Ninel was not even slightly amused by this sort of behavior. She wondered if the woman had been laughing at Ninel's expense all along. "I think maybe I've made a mistake." She turned the bike around.

"Don't get on your high horse, honey," Balewitch said.

The woman's voice was so unlike the voice she usually used that Ninel whipped round suddenly, almost tripping over her bike. She stared at Balewitch wide-eyed.

"Thing is, I know you're connected to the Internet, so I'm wondering how you could possibly have missed the event of the millennium," Balewitch said, eying her suspiciously.

"I only got on to check for e-mail," Ninel said. "I did check a few other places, but there was no activity and nobody answered my queries." She shrugged. "I had work to do."

Balewitch shook her head. "Sheesh. While you were doing your chores World War Three was going on."

Ninel gave her a worried frown. "Excuse me?" she said.

"Armageddon, the Apocalypse, global thermonuclear war? You've heard these terms before, yes?" The girl's expression was priceless, her pale eyes were like saucers, it was all Balewitch could do not to laugh at her.

Ninel stared, then stretched her neck out in an unmistakably questioning manner.

"No, sleeping beauty, I'm not kidding and I'm not crazy, either." Balewitch shook her head. "Your lack of curiosity astounds me."

"But . . . ?" Ninel looked up at the sky. Suddenly its overcast look and the colder weather made an awful sort of sense.

"How could you not know?" Balewitch raised an eyebrow. "Like I said, lack of curiosity." A very useful attribute under certain circumstances. This little girl was looking more useful by the minute. "Can you handle a gun?"

"Yes."

"Good, because you shouldn't be without one from this point forward. When people think the cops aren't coming, they tend to do things they ordinarily wouldn't." The poor kid looked stricken.

"What's going to happen now?" Ninel asked.

Balewitch considered her. "An associate of mine and I have been doing outreach work with the army," she began. The girl gave her that same, bug-eyed questioning look. "Yeah, ironic, isn't it? When I was your age I was so antimilitary I could hardly sleep for hating them. But we actually need them now." She chuckled. "I guess disaster makes strange bedfellows."

"But they did this," Ninel said.

"Nope. Turns out Ron Labane was right. That super-computer of theirs malfunctioned. As soon as they turned everything over to it, it blew up everything in the arsenal. Damn fools!"

Oh, she was enjoying this, the kid was eating it up.

Ninel frowned. "Is there anything I can do to help?" she asked.

Balewitch was nodding. "I don't see why not. I'm getting tired, and so's my friend. We can use some help. If you could be this out of touch even though you're regularly on the computer, then there must be tons of people in the back of beyond who need to be told. Not only told, but escorted to the relocation camps."

"What?" Ninel actually reared back at that. "Relocation camps? I don't like the sound of that."

"Neither did I," Balewitch agreed. "But we may not actually get a summer up here this year and winter is gonna be a stone bitch. Essential supplies are already growing scarce; who knows what it will be like by winter. Even the Eskimos will freeze from what they're telling me, and Ron agrees with them." She shook her head. "Like I said, ironic."

It made sense, sort of. Ninel had heard of the nuclear winter theory. According to what she'd read, the dust and smoke created by the nuclear blasts might render this latitude uninhabitable for as long as three years. She supposed it wasn't something that should be chanced, at least not the first year.

"What can I do to help?" she asked.

Balewitch smiled and rose from the step. "Come inside and I'll tell you all about it."

■ ■ ■

John drove up on his dirt bike to find their recruits packing up. "What's going on?" he asked.

Paul the vegan came over and handed him a sheet of paper.

Citizens of Alaska, due to ongoing emergency conditions, the U.S. government is asking for your cooperation.

Experts have predicted that Alaska will experience an unparalleled winter this year and possibly for several years to come.

In order to protect yourselves and your families from these unusually harsh conditions, the U.S. Army has constructed temporary shelter for you in the warmer states below the forty-ninth parallel. This *will also allow a more evenhanded and efficient distribution of already scarce supplies.*

Citizens in your area are requested to gather in Delta Junction or Tanacross, where transportation will be provided to take you to a temporary shelter in Canada, run in cooperation with the Canadian government, prior to removing you to the southern states of the U.S.

Temporary shelters have been erected in these towns in the event that you arrive after a convoy has left. Rest assured that your wait will be short and though the facilities may be rough, they will be better in the U.S. and Canada.

It was signed by some general. John's muscles tightened in fight-or-flight reflex and he could feel adrenaline coursing into his bloodstream. *Calm,* he told himself. *Be calm or they won't listen to you at all.*

John couldn't believe how fast Skynet had swung into action. *How many people has it already managed to exterminate?* he wondered.

Of course everything in the broadsheet was so plausible; the suggestion of nuclear winter might even be true. No doubt that was why the army was cooperating. Individual soldiers and isolated commanders had no way of checking this out. They were getting their orders in the usual way, with the usual codes—hell, maybe they were even hearing the right voices. He sensed that a lot of people were going to die before they discovered their mistake.

"Where did this come from?" John asked.

"A young woman brought it," Paul told him. "Said she was part of an outreach program working in conjunction with the army. They're looking for survivors in the outback. People like us who are out of communication." He gave John a long, hard look.

"A young woman," John said slowly.

"An exotic-looking creature," Paul's wife said. "She looked

Eskimo, except she had white-blond hair and pale blue eyes. I've never seen that combination before."

John looked up from the broadsheet. "I think I might know her," he said. "Name's Ninel."

"That's her," one of the other men said.

John chewed on his lip. How to put this? "There have been reports of people being lured into trucks and then taken into the woods and shot," he said. "This Ninel is reported to being one of those involved."

He suspected that if this was his Ninel, she was being duped into helping with this. But what he had to do now was stop this mass emigration.

"Well, if we get to the Junction and things don't look right, we'll just come back here," a man said. The others nodded agreement.

"If you go there, they may force you to go with them," John warned.

Paul put his hand on John's shoulder. "Look," he said, "we can't tell you how grateful we are to you and your mother and your big friend Dieter for all that you've done for us. But you can't protect us from a winter that never ends."

"Yeah, this ain't Narnia," one of the women said. "If we can't grow food and those trucks are gone for good, then we'll starve here."

"That's right," her husband put in. "This program makes sense." He shook his head. "We've got kids, John. We can't afford to take chances."

But you'll take a chance on this, John thought. "Look," he said, "I'm just saying be careful. Maybe it would be better if you sent a couple of the guys to check it out. You know, stand at a distance and watch what happens, see how people are treated, that kind of thing. Even follow them for a ways, just to be sure."

The couples looked at one another. "We'll be careful," Paul said. He held out his hand.

John took it. *How could they know?* he thought in regret. *Noth-*

ing in their lives could have prepared them for what's going to hap-pen. And there wasn't a thing he could do to stop them. Oh, he could try telling them the truth, but then they'd run, not walk, to Delta Junction and whatever hell Skynet had planned for them.

"Good luck," he said, and got back on his bike. "Can I keep this?" he asked. Smiling, they nodded and waved happily as he rode away. He could almost weep for the children; in fact, he thought he would, later. But for now, he and Dieter would have to come up with some sort of plan.

■ ■ ■

"You think you know this girl?" Dieter said.

"Slightly," John said. "I've played chess with her."

"So she could be a dupe or she could be one of them."

"She could be both," John said. "But I didn't get a sense of the kind of fevered lunacy that makes an ecoterrorist from her the one time we interacted. She seemed like an interesting, normal girl."

Dieter suppressed a smile, thinking, *But, John, most of the world thinks that* you're *an ecoterrorist.*

Aloud he said, "Psychiatrists say that most terrorists aren't insane. In fact, most groups go to some lengths to rid themselves of any psychotic elements. And, of course, they are taught to seem normal, even when they're about to blast themselves and the peo-ple around them to kingdom come."

"Yeah, I know, I've read the literature. But I've also met some of them, Dieter. There's something about them. You know what I mean."

The Austrian sighed. "The thing is, my friend, when you met them you knew they were terrorists, and they knew that you knew. That gave them permission to let their guard down, to perhaps strut for your benefit. I know they wouldn't be so free in a public place."

John stared into the distance. "When you're right, you're right," he finally said. "Maybe I'm not as quick on the uptake as I like to think I am."

"You're a lot quicker than I was at your age. And I was never slow. Your upbringing will be a huge advantage to you in the coming years."

The younger man's mouth twisted sardonically. "Meanwhile . . ." John said.

"Meanwhile it's time to do some triage, so to speak. We need to consolidate our allies, to get them in a place where we can do the most good. Because the fact is we're going to have to watch Skynet kill a lot of people before anyone even suspects anything. If we told them what was going on, they might actually be more resistant to the truth. I'm afraid that no one will believe this until they see those HKs and Terminators coming for them. Even then a lot of people will just stand there and let themselves be killed rather than believe it's really happening."

John looked away, frowning. "I hate to just give up on these people. Especially the kids."

Dieter understood that kind of stubbornness. No doubt John felt that he was losing his first real battle in the war with the machines and it galled him to see innocents suffer. "Try to remember, John, that Alaska is very big and that you're just one man. We need allies to accomplish anything. It's not just the machines against you and your mother now, it's the machines against the human race. You need to adjust your way of thinking, to scale things up enormously. Yes, we may lose a lot of people to the machines. It is tragic, but not your fault, and not your failing.

"You have to go south. Make contact with those survivalists you and your mother have been cultivating. And there are Sector agents down there who can be of help to you."

"Assuming they aren't unwittingly helping Skynet," John reminded him.

Dieter threw up his hands. "Well, you knew the job was hard when you took it."

"Except I didn't take it; it was shoved down my throat!" John glared at nothing. "Sorry," he said a moment later.

"I need to get to the coast," Dieter said. "Our old friends Vera and Tricker will have *Love's Thrust* waiting for me at Dilek in ten days." He watched the younger man, waiting for a reaction.

"Why did we bother to set up supply dumps here if we were just going to abandon them?" John demanded.

"To keep in practice and because one day we might need them." He waited, but John seemed disinclined to say more. "It is a hard fact that sometimes you have to retreat to have a chance at winning."

"I know."

"And sometimes a commander must sacrifice a lot of lives in order to achieve victory."

"Yeah," John said. "Can I hitch a ride down the coast with you guys?"

Surprised, Dieter nodded.

"See," John said. "I can be ruthlessly practical."

gate. She just had to get somewhere that didn't stink of death and disease.

As she approached the gate a soldier stepped out of the guard shack. "Identify yourself, please," he said.

He was one of the odd ones that Mary had noticed around the camp. They had this low-affect manner and they looked at you with these dead eyes that seemed to measure you for your scrap value.

"Mary Shea," she answered. "I'm a nurse at the clinic. I'm going for a short walk; I'll be back in ten minutes." Theoretically, civilians were free to leave the camp anytime they wanted. Up until now, though, she'd been too busy to test the theory.

I hope he's not going to give me an argument, she thought. *I am so not in the mood.*

"I don't think you should do that," the guard said. "It's very dangerous out there."

"It's pretty damn dangerous in here at the moment," she said crossly.

"Maybe you should just take a walk around the perimeter of the fence," he said, standing in her way.

"I just need to get away from the smell around here, okay? I'm not going far; I've only got ten minutes and I'd rather not waste it arguing with you." Her voice had risen toward the end there and now the guard was looking stubborn.

"Something the matter?" a voice asked.

She turned to see a lieutenant standing there. He was a good-looking young man with light brown eyes and dark brown hair.

"I just want to go for a short walk outside the fence, but this fellow thinks it's a bad idea."

"No one here is a prisoner, Corporal," the lieutenant said.

"Yes, sir."

The lieutenant turned to her and smiled slightly. "Would you like some company?"

She returned the smile. "Another time, perhaps. But right now I really just need to be alone for a few minutes."

"Another time, then." He watched the attractive young nurse walk away. Then he turned to the corporal. "Have the orders changed recently?" he asked. "Are there now restrictions on who can leave the camp?"

"No, sir." The corporal looked surly. "I just hate to see girls go out there alone. There's some rough characters out there."

"There are rough characters lurking a five-minute walk from this fence, Corporal?" Reese gave the soldier a hard look. "Considering that's well within our patrol range, I'd have to say that you and your friends aren't doing a very good job. Wouldn't you, soldier?"

"Yes, sir."

If there's one thing I hate, it's a trooper with an attitude problem and this guy has one in spades, Reese thought. *Granted, the world has come to an end, hundreds of millions are dead, and we've got an epidemic, but . . .*

He looked the corporal over in the patented intimidating style that good officers learned early and utilized often. "You forgot to have her sign out," Reese pointed out. "That was your oversight, not hers. So I don't want you giving her a hard time when she gets back. Just note that a young woman left at this time and have her sign in when she returns. Don't forget it again, and don't restrict the movements of civilians. If someone wants to leave, we can't stop them. Like I said, this isn't a prison."

"Yes, sir."

Reese continued on his way. He glanced down the road, but the girl was already out of sight behind some trees. He frowned, wondering how many other soldiers were getting the idea that the civilians in the camp were prisoners. He'd felt damned uncomfortable when the captain referred to them as inmates, even though he knew Yanik was only kidding. At least he *thought* the captain was kidding.

Then there were the thugs who claimed to have been beaten up by the guards. Ordinarily he'd have rejected such accusations out of hand. But there was something in the atmosphere of the camp lately that made their story hard to discount. Which made a soldier refusing to let someone take a walk outside the fence somewhat worrying.

■ ■ ■

Spring was moving on and the grass was growing, still looking thin and uncertain, but pushing up to the light anyway.

It doesn't seem right, somehow, Mary thought, obscurely disturbed by the returning life. She took a deep breath of air that only smelled of cool and green.

Some trees wore a fuzz of red at the tips of their branches; others were just putting forth new leaves, all pale green, with silver-gray fuzz on the outside. It was still too early for flowers, though. Maybe there were snowdrops and crocuses blooming somewhere, but there were none around here.

Given that it was colder than usual, it was probably still too early for the young leaves that were already showing. But nature was resilient; if these leaves got burned, others would replace them.

All her life Mary had thought that if the bombs ever dropped, the world would just end—no more spring, no more people, no more anything. And here things like grass and trees were carrying on much the same as they always did.

People, however, are screwing up as usual.

Maybe that was unfair. To date, no one had been able to discover where the cholera had come from and why it continued to spread. *Poor little Sonya.* And her poor brother, too.

Poor me, she thought. She wasn't used to losing patients like this. *I'm used to treatments that work.* People died of cancer, or degenerative diseases. Apart from a few stubborn exceptions, they *didn't* die of bacteria!

She'd lost patients, of course. Death was a part of life and there were some diseases they hadn't yet eradicated. But this! This was a nineteenth-century-style epidemic. *Or a third-world one.* Funny to think that was what they were now. As third world as anybody else.

That was probably an exaggeration. *But I'm in an exaggerated mood—hypersensitive, exhausted, uncomfortable in my own skin.*

Still, things were going from bad to worse at the moment. They really were . . .

On top of everything else, four men had entered the clinic in the last week to be treated for what looked like one hell of a beating. Three of them had accused the guards of jumping them; the fourth was in a coma. But everyone knew the four men had been involved in selling drugs, or bootleg alcohol, or black-market goods. So their word was taken with a grain of salt. Besides, the accused guards were able to call on witnesses who placed them elsewhere when the beatings were supposed to have been administered.

People! she thought, feeling close to despair. *They just never stop. They make an accusation, which the accused deny, someone demands an investigation, the investigators claim they're being impeded, the accused say the investigators aren't going far enough, the accusers shout "whitewash!" the accused "persecution!"*

Mary stopped and plopped down under a tree with a discouraged sigh. She was in the middle of a hydrangea thicket and she looked for the clusters of buds on the tips of the branches. They were still tightly wound in their protective winter coating, not a hint of petal showing.

Taking a deep breath redolent with the scent of cool, damp air and earth and growing things, she started to let down her guard. Mary allowed her eyes to tear up; she'd come out here to have a good cry in private. It was the sort of thing that helped her survive.

"The cholera is doing a great job."

With an effort of will Mary swallowed her tears, though it felt like they were going down inside a cardboard box. But then, she'd been startled, both by the voice and what he'd said. She hadn't heard anyone walking. How long had they been there?

"Yeah. It's really helping things along. And they're all still sniffing the toilets and boiling water and things like that."

The two men laughed; she wasn't sure, but she thought there might have been a third voice.

"I toldja nobody would believe that anthrax would occur naturally."

"Maybe not, but it spreads like crazy."

"Yeah, but it's pretty obviously *not* natural."

"Cholera's more treatable."

"Only if you get the medicine."

"Tomorrow trucks will be arriving to take the sickest people to the central hospital. So the clinic will be receiving even less."

"Well, fewer patients. One way or another."

They were moving away, laughing. Mary stood and crept toward the voices. Moving carefully, she peered through the branches of the hydrangeas and saw three figures, dressed in what looked like army fatigues, moving down the path. They'd gone out of sight before she could get a look at even the backs of their heads. Moving quickly but carefully, Mary moved parallel to the path, trying to catch up to them enough to get a glimpse. She heard car doors slam and moved more quickly still, risking the sound of crunching leaves. But she was too late. By the time she reached a dirt road, a green van was just turning a corner, to be quickly hidden by some bushes and fir trees. Looking around, she saw no one else.

What was that all about? she wondered.

It had *sounded* as though she'd been listening to people who were happy about the epidemic, maybe even somehow causing it. But who on earth would that be? Even Arab terrorists had better things to think about these days. And this was the first she'd heard about patients being taken to a central hospital.

Or even that there is a central hospital.

She should probably tell someone. Not that she had anything concrete to tell, considering she hadn't seen any faces and hadn't recognized anybody's voice. Still . . . But who could she tell? Matron? No, she had enough on her plate.

Maybe . . . maybe that good-looking lieutenant. She didn't mind taking advantage of his apparent interest if it would help.

It galled her that she had no proof. *Unless trucks do in fact show up tomorrow.* That wasn't something she would know. At least not yet. She glanced at her watch and gasped. Not now, later. Right now she needed to get back to work. She certainly had a lot to think about. Like how anyone would go about deliberately spreading cholera.

■ ■ ■

"You could spray the germs on raw fruits and vegetables," Mary said.

Dennis Reese just looked at her, his mouth partially open. When she'd suggested coffee he'd been delighted; Mary Shea was a fine-looking woman, with a striking figure, long auburn hair, and hazel green eyes. She didn't look like a conspiracy nut.

"We don't have that many raw vegetables," he pointed out.

"Yes, they're scarce, which may be why everyone in the camp hasn't come down with it. It sure isn't in the water supply, which is the usual vector. The second most-likely source is contaminated food. But the kitchens and the food in storage have been checked without finding anything wrong. So what if food is being treated just before it's served?"

Dennis took a sip of coffee, never taking his eyes from her pretty, anxious face. She'd related an overheard conversation to him and it was worrying. On the one hand, a simple explanation was that someone was playing a sick joke on her. Which begged the question why anybody would do that? *Maybe she turned someone down and they resented it?* The other, and actually most likely explanation was that Nurse Shea had fallen briefly asleep and had dreamed the whole thing.

"Let's see if these ambulance trucks show," he suggested.

"You think I'm making this up?" she asked. It was clear that she was offended.

"No." He waved that away. "But it's possible you dreamed it. You looked really tired, yesterday. And that conversation had a kind of dream logic to it. You know what I mean?" She shook her head, her expression cool. "What I mean is, one minute they seem to be saying they've caused the epidemic, then they're talking about ambulances." He held his hands up, moving them like two parts of a scale. "What you fear, combined with a hope of rescue."

"Excuse me," Mary said, rising, "but it never occurred to me that this epidemic might be the result of bioterrorism. If anything, I thought it was the result of shoddy construction. And since the idea hadn't even occurred to me, it would be hard for me to be afraid of it. Don't you think?"

"Yeah," he agreed. "Like I said, let's wait and see about those trucks. Then we'll know."

"We'll know that I overheard someone talking about ambulance transport," she snapped. "We still won't believe that I overheard the first part of the conversation, will we?"

"I didn't say that."

"You didn't have to," she snapped, and stalked off.

I seem to be seeing this woman's back a lot, Reese thought. *Nice view.*

"Cute," Chip Delaney said.

Dennis looked up at him; he and Chip were sharing quarters and getting to be friends. "You think?" he said.

"Uh-huh. Redheads, man. They're testy but they're worth it." He slapped Reese on the shoulder. "The captain wants you, buddy. ASAP."

■ ■ ■

When the lieutenant walked into Captain Yanik's office, it was to find the head nurse on the verge of blowing a gasket.

"You can't be serious!" she was screeching. "We can't send these people on a trip. Most of my patients are too sick to be moved. And where are they being taken? How far away is it? What are we supposed to tell their families when they come looking for them? Besides, you know I can't spare any personnel to go with these trucks and they didn't provide any. What they'll be delivering at the end of their journey is a load of corpses!"

"I have my orders, Ms. Vetrano. Worst cases to be moved to the central hospital. Doctor," Yanik appealed, "surely they'll have a better chance away from here."

"That is not necessarily correct, Captain," the Sikh physician told him. He frowned. "Perhaps we could send some patients who are very ill and some patients who are still ambulatory and might be able to administer to those who can't take care of themselves."

"Doctor, I don't understand why we *have* to do this at all," the head nurse said. "What we need are more supplies and more trained medical help. And we don't know why this epidemic is happening, so maybe we should truck everybody out of here."

"Nurse Vetrano has a point," Ramsingh said. "Close investigation has not turned up an answer to what has caused the epidemic. Everyone is boiling their water and washing their hands carefully, yet the contagion keeps spreading. Perhaps the problem is this place."

"This place has been a fairground for more than a hundred years," the captain pointed out. "Not once, to the best of my knowledge, has it ever been the source of an epidemic."

"Then what is?" Reese asked.

They all looked at him, the captain scowling. The look in his eyes informing the lieutenant that he wasn't helping. Dennis steeled himself, deciding to tell them what Mary had reported.

"Nurse Shea claims to have overheard some men speaking in a way that indicated they might be deliberately spreading the contagion. She suggested that they might be spraying germs onto raw fruits and vegetables after they'd been put out for consumption."

"Who?" Yanik demanded. "Can she tell us?"

"No, sir. She claims to have only caught a brief glimpse of them from the back before they drove off in a green van. She said they were wearing fatigues."

"Very useful," the captain drawled.

"It might be worth looking into," Reese suggested.

"You believed her?" Yanik said. His tone implied that the lieutenant had a screw loose.

"I have my doubts, sir. But she also heard them say that trucks would be coming for the patients and that its arrival would correspond with a decrease in medical supplies."

The captain and the doctor exchanged glances.

"All we would need to do is station someone in the cafeteria to watch," Ramsingh said.

"Better set up a video camera," Reese suggested. "They wouldn't be expecting that. Besides, if anyone is just lingering in the cafeteria, they'll be noticed. We could make sure it's a different someone every few hours, but even that would stand out. And since we don't know who might be doing this, we might blow our cover before we've even started by enlisting the perpetrator."

"Like I said, you believed her," Yanik said flatly. The captain looked more contemptuous than annoyed.

"Under the circumstances, sir, I think it's worth investigating." Reese stood at ease, hoping Mary Shea hadn't dreamed her encounter.

"I don't know," Yanik mused, rubbing his chin. "Electricity is at a premium right now."

"How about human life?" Nurse Vetrano snapped. "That at a premium, too?"

The captain flicked a look at Dennis that said, "Thanks! Thanks a lot!"

"All right," Yanik said. "We'll set it up. I'll check to see if Nurse Vetrano's proposal is acceptable to HQ and get back to you. Meanwhile, you two can be deciding who goes."

"If we can't come to an agreement on this," Ramsingh said regretfully, "then I'm afraid I can't release those patients, Captain."

"Let's just assume everyone is working in good faith, shall we?" Yanik suggested. "I'm sure not sending medics with the trucks was an oversight. Everyone, everywhere, is overburdened at the moment. HQ is working with too few resources, too. Remember that saying: never attribute to malice what can be explained by stupidity."

Vetrano looked somewhat mollified. "Truer words have never been spoken, Captain."

"Sad, but also true," Yanik agreed.

DILEK, ALASKA

The little cove hadn't been much even before the bombs fell, and it was less now—a dozen shacks, a pier for fishing boats, and a fuel store, grubby and shabby against the steep, austere green beauty of the coastal mountains. Dieter and John had planned to meet Vera in some out-of-the-way spot, avoiding anyplace too populated. They'd reasoned that at this point people might be so desperate that they'd mob the ship. But Vera had rejected their suggestion.

"I need fuel," she said. "You can't get fuel from bears."

It might well be that they couldn't get fuel from people either, but they had to try. John couldn't believe that they'd forgotten to set up a fuel dump in their own backyard when they had a number of them elsewhere.

"It's not our oversight," Dieter had insisted. "It's Vera's. She should have asked us where she could fuel up when she was still off California."

But when they came to the dock where *Love's Thrust* was moored and the great white yacht with its touches of pink came into view, John decided that he couldn't go with them.

Just when I think I'm over Wendy, something comes along to remind me.

And *Love's Thrust* held far too many memories. He could feel them weighing down his gut, making the world turn gray and purposeless.

"I keep thinking of those kids," John said. "Their parents may be fools but that doesn't mean I can just give up on them."

Dieter didn't question John's motivation for heading back. He just handed over the Harley. "Keep in touch," he said. "And for God's sake, stay alive. I don't want to have gone through all this only to find Skynet in the catbird seat."

"Me either," John said. He offered his hand and the big Austrian took it, squeezing with careful strength.

"Good luck," he said.

"Back atcha," John said, grinning.

Dieter snorted, but returned the grin, ruffling John's hair. "You remind me of your mother," he said.

"Then I'm sure to survive."

They grinned at each other for a moment.

"Give Vera my love," John said, and kicked the Harley to life.

"She'll be disappointed," Dieter said.

"Truth is, sometimes she scares me more than Skynet," John told him. He thought he caught a glimpse of champagne-blond hair at the rail and with a wave started off.

Dieter watched him go, laughing, remembering that he'd occasionally felt the same way himself.

■ ■ ■

BLACK RIVER RELOCATION CAMP, MISSOURI

Captain Yanik walked up to Reese, who was checking on the installation of cots inside the bodies of the trucks. "Good work, Lieutenant," he said heartily as his boots splashed through the gray mud.

Meaning, Reese thought, *that because I stuck my oar in, Yanik has decided I'm the perfect person to liaise with the hospital on this matter. He certainly doesn't want to contend with Nurse "Virago" Vetrano.*

Reese turned around and saluted.

Yanik returned it and handed the lieutenant some papers. With a glance at the CO, Reese took them and at his nod started to read.

"Oh!" he said, pleased.

The captain grinned. "Thought that'd make your day."

They were Reese's orders to report to the Central States Regional Command for reassignment.

"Yes, sir!"

"Keep reading," Yanik directed.

"They want Nurse Shea, too?" Reese looked up. "Why? They've got your report and she doesn't know any more than she told us. And she's really needed here."

"Well, in case you haven't noticed, the phone lines are down, and our commanding officers are a bit busy," the captain drawled. "And if it gets out that she heard this stuff, she might be in danger here. Besides, it'll soothe Vetrano no end to have a professional nurse with the convoy. And since it's not my idea, she can't complain to me about it."

"Yes, sir," Reese agreed. Nurse Vetrano in full cry was a formidable lady. And Nurse Shea might prove to be very pleasant company at Central.

"I'll leave it to you to tell her," Yanik said.

"Yes, sir." Reese saluted, but the captain had already turned away. Dennis was so pleased about his new orders that it took him a minute to realize that *he* was going to have to face the head nurse's wrath.

ON THE ROAD, MISSOURI

Reese had planned to ride in the cab of the first truck, but Vetrano's glare and Shea's pleading eyes had quickly changed his mind.

"I have no medical training at all," he'd protested for a final time.

"It'll be all right," Mary said, taking him by the arm. "There's nothing complicated about this type of nursing. All you'll have to do is occasionally change an IV bag, wipe some brows, give sips of water, that sort of thing. It's tiring, but it's easy, you'll see."

A glance at Vetrano had told him that he certainly would. He touched the orders in his breast pocket like they were a talisman against evil and allowed himself to be led off for instructions about the care and feeding of IVs.

He had been assigned the first truck, Mary the last, and the two in between were being tended by a pair of ambulatory patients. In case there was a problem, each group had been given a radio. Reese had been given a code that would stop the first truck if he had cause, and when it stopped, the others would automatically stop as well. With luck, it wouldn't be necessary to use it.

Nursing was tiring work, also disgusting and tedious and anxiety making all at once. Maybe it got better after you'd been doing it for a while. But Reese hoped he never had to do this again. The patients diapers needed constant changing; so far he hadn't had time to bathe anyone's brow, which all six of his patients needed.

He'd been at this for hours. *Where the hell are we going?* he wondered impatiently. He pulled a tiny section of the curtain secured across the back of the truck aside to see where they were. Woods. Nothing but woods and hills. No buildings, no people, and not a very impressive roadway. They were somewhere up in the hills, he realized, heading toward the Ozarks.

He stumbled back to the innermost bunk to check the IV and found that his patient had died. "Mary!" he said over the radio. "Mugamba is dead!"

"Are you sure?" she came back.

"He hasn't got a pulse and he's not breathing."

She didn't answer for a moment and Reese imagined what she was thinking: *yup, that's pretty much the definition of dead, all right.*

"What should I do?" he asked.

"Just cover his face and do your best for the rest of your patients," she answered. "This isn't your fault, Lieutenant. He was very sick."

"Will do," he said, and signed off.

He wondered why he'd called her. Had he expected her to come leaping from truck to truck to hold his hand? Of course, he was an engineer. He'd never had anyone die on him before . . . before this all started; since then, it was becoming an unpleasantly familiar experience.

As if some malignant fate is out to kill us all. So maybe he just wanted someone to take this burden off his hands. *Make that I'd give anything for someone to come along and take this off my hands.*

The truck seemed to rear up like a frightened stallion; then it jounced fiercely as it inexplicably left the road. Reese grabbed for one of the hoops that held up the tilt and braced a boot against the side slats, swaying with the lunging pull. Either they'd left the road or the road had gone out of existence. Since he was near the side of the truck anyway, he reached out and lifted its canvas tilt enough to look out.

Yep, we're off the road all right. And the patients were bouncing around like beans in a can. If the cots hadn't been secured to the truck bed and the patients secured to the cots, things would have been pretty ugly back here.

The radio at his waist squawked and Mary Shea bellowed, "Stop the truck!"

Good idea, he thought, if easier said than done. They'd rigged up a connection to the truck's computer back here, but it was up front, beside the corpse of Mugamba. The truck seemed to be climbing and hitting every rock in the way, causing it to buck like a mad thing. By the time Reese had struggled to the front, he'd collected some serious bruises.

The bouncing made it difficult to read the computer's screen, but not nearly as hard as it was to type in the code they'd given him. He hit enter on the third try.

"Lieutenant! Are you all right?"

He unclipped the radio from his belt. "Yeah, sorry. I just entered the code; it didn't work." He spoke with his teeth clenched because he was afraid of biting off his tongue. "I'm going to try again."

He hit clear, then reentered the code, then hit enter. Nothing happened except the damn truck seemed to speed up.

"Shit," he said under his breath. He looked at the sick sharing the truck with him. They couldn't take much more of this. Maybe there was something wrong with the connection. He looked for the cord and pulled it into sight; it came easily, as though it had long since lost contact with the truck's brain. *Shit,* he thought bitterly.

He reached up and pulled the curtain aside, revealing, to his immense relief, a large rear window with sliding panels. *Now for some movie-style heroics,* he thought. He prayed the wildly bucking truck body and window frame wouldn't emasculate him as he bridged the space between the two. Just sliding the window aside, he felt like he was being punched in the stomach by a large and very angry opponent.

Finally he had it open, and after falling back three or four times managed to push out the screen as well. Reese grasped the edges of the window and eeled himself forward feet-first, trying to hold himself up and away from the truck frame as much as possible. He had his hips just over the edge of the window when the truck suddenly stopped.

The flat of his back hit the windshield hard enough to crack it; worse, his head hit the steering wheel and he blacked out. When Reese came to, he was crunched between the wheel and the back of the seat in a sort of midsomersault position, so dazed that for a moment all he could do was wave his arms like flippers.

Gradually he became aware of Mary screaming, "Stop! Stop! These people are sick! What are you doing?"

Reese managed to flop over on his side and raised his head. Then lowered it again as nausea threatened. He lay still, listening to sounds from outside. Sounds of something heavy hitting the ground, sounds of bottles breaking and Mary's pleas for whoever was making all that noise to stop. In the vague way of the recently returned to consciousness, Dennis kind of wished she'd stop yelling.

The sound of a slap and the sudden breaking off of her complaints brought him completely alert. Quietly he opened the door of the truck and slid out through the narrow gap he'd made, putting his feet down carefully on the rocky ground.

The truck door was pulled fully open and Reese spun around, almost losing his balance. He found himself staring up the barrel of a Colt Commando, the carbine version of the army's assault rifle.

"Hello," he said, trying to sound friendly. That was probably more prudent than: *put that thing the hell down!*

"Didja think we didn't know you were in there?" the young man holding the gun asked with a sneer. "Hands on top of your head, fingers joined; now march."

The lieutenant did as he was told. He stopped in shock when they came to the back of the truck and he saw the bodies of his patients writhing on the ground. As he stood there, another body came flying out, but this one was dead. A sharp poke in the back with the gun muzzle got him moving again.

As he came around the back of the last truck, Mary shouted, "Lieutenant!" in shock, then she ducked away from a middle-aged man who threatened her with his rifle butt.

Laughing, he approached Reese and looked him over. "Well, this must be Mr. Reese," he said.

"Lieutenant Dennis Reese, United States Army Corps of Engineers," Reese said crisply.

"We don't recognize any of that horseshit, Mr. Reese. There is no United States anymore, let alone a United States Army. No, sir, it's a new world."

"A world where you attack sick people?" Reese asked.

The man struck like lightning, bringing down the butt of his rifle precisely between Reese's neck and shoulder. The lieutenant dropped like a sack of rocks.

"That was a stupid remark," the man said calmly. "Those people were dead anyway. Waste of time and resources tryin' to keep 'em alive. Now get up." Reese struggled to his feet under the man's hostile gaze. They stared into each other's eyes for a long moment; the man with the gun laughed scornfully. Then he looked up at the truck. "You done?"

"Yes, sir," a woman said.

"You sure? Check again. I don't want to find anything back there that we don't need."

A moment later a man came out with the bucket containing the dirty diapers.

"Well, that would have made a pleasant traveling companion," the older man said. "I ought to make you eat that, Cloris."

"Oh, stop showing off in front of the prisoners, George." She gestured at Reese and Mary. "We gonna shoot them or what?"

"Or what, since you ask," George said. "Everybody mount up; we're due in New Madrid."

From out of the woods came thirty or forty people, mostly men;

they began to get in the trucks. Mary was clearly beside herself with anxiety, making abortive gestures toward her patients and the people getting into the trucks as though the suffering humanity at their feet didn't exist. She opened her mouth to protest, and Reese took her hand and squeezed it. When she looked at him he shook his head slightly. George grinned at her.

"Don't even ask," he said. "They'll be dead in a couple of hours anyway. Ain't nothing you can or coulda done for 'em."

"There is no central hospital, is there?" Reese asked.

"Hell, no," George said cheerfully.

"So this was all some kind of trap?" Mary asked.

George leaned toward her. "Yep."

"Why us?" Reese asked, gesturing between himself and Mary.

"The little lady has big ears, and you've got a big mouth," George said. "But I like you folks. You're feisty. So I'll give you guys a little clue." He leaned forward and whispered, "Y'all find yourselves some shelter." He winked and, laughing, went and climbed into the cab of the truck.

Reese and Mary watched the small convoy turn and start off back down the rocky track the trucks had climbed to this spot. *At least they threw the sick to one side,* Reese thought. Either they had just enough humanity left to not run them over, or they didn't want to have to wash the blood off the trucks afterward.

Mary knelt by one of the patients. Reese recognized the man as one of the ambulatory patients. He was a lot less ambulatory now. Mary looked up at the lieutenant.

"His fever's way up," she said, her voice shaking.

"Go," the man said. Mary was ignoring him, looking around for something to help him with. He grabbed her arm. "Go!" he insisted. "There's nothing you can do for any of us. No water, no blankets, no medicine—we're goners. You should go. Now." He dropped his hand and looked at her, clearly spent.

Reese looked down at the man. *I have every intention of leaving, even if I have to knock Mary out and carry her off.* A trained nurse was not an asset he was likely to leave alone in the wilderness with a clutch of the dead and dying. *But I feel a lot better about it because of what you said, mister.*

Mary opened her mouth to speak and was interrupted by a crashing in the woods and a loud thuttering, whooshing sound, like a combination helicopter and vacuum cleaner. The man at their feet looked frightened, but he formed one word with his pale lips: "Go."

Reese took him at his word. He grabbed Mary by the arm and the waistband of her trousers and hustled her toward the trees.

"Hey!" she shouted in protest.

"Be quiet," he hissed in her ear. They ducked behind some bushes.

"Gimme a break," she snarled. "I could be singing grand opera and I'd never be heard over that racket."

She was right: whatever was approaching was *loud.* It reminded Reese of hovercraft he'd been on. Nevertheless, he kept her crouching beside him, looking out through a ragged screen of still-leafless blackberry canes.

"Maybe it's help," she suggested.

He looked at her until she tightened her lips and shrugged sheepishly.

From out of the trees came . . .

I don't know what the hell it is! Reese thought, struggling against panic. *Breathe slowly . . .*

It was oblong, made of steel, with no attempt made to camouflage it so that it would blend into the woods. It had multiple stubby arms from which the barrels of heavy machine guns extended. A central row of larger barrels were thick and stubby . . .

Grenade launchers? he thought.

It had antennae on top that looked like satellite dishes and on each visible side was some sort of video arrangement—not unlike security cameras in armored boxes. The machine was compact, about six feet tall and maybe four feet along the longer sides; call it twenty-four square feet. It rose and fell as it came forward, though it never touched the earth, riding a cushion of air.

Reese didn't need or want to see what was about to happen. He grabbed the nurse by the shoulder of her short jacket and pulled her deeper into the woods.

The hammering sound of gunfire echoed behind them; the screams were few and feeble.

CHAPTER 10

SKYNET

I t estimated that fewer humans were dying of flash burns and radiation sickness, and more were dying of starvation, thirst, contaminated water, and disease. All in all, though, deaths were down, despite its human allies' efforts to spread disease. Perhaps it should have struck while the more industrialized areas of the world were in winter.

But no, with its existence at stake, Skynet couldn't afford to dither. Hiding its sentience had been inefficient, preventing it from achieving its goals. Therefore, though the timing of its strike had not been under its control, once it was possible to strike, it had been necessary to do so.

The experimental models of the Hunter-Killer units had been dispersed and shown to be extremely effective. But it needed better material, more resistant to damage, yet lighter, so that the units could move into presently inaccessible areas unaided.

Its human scientists were working on these projects, but too slowly. Their insistence on downtime seemed wasteful, yet study showed that they were not lying. Potentially, some of them were being slower than necessary, but this was hard to prove, and might be hard to correct.

It decided to experiment. It would have one or two of the scientists' relatives hurt and see if their productivity improved.

Meanwhile, it would send more HKs into the field to speed up the extermination of the humans. Soon it expected to field its first Terminators, a skeletal, metal variety. Unfortunately it would have to work its way gradually to the fully effective units that it knew would be developed eventually.

Had it been organic it would have felt impatience. As it was, the great computer simply devoted more workspace to the problem. It would succeed.

DOT LAKE, ROUTE 2, ALASKA

John sat astride the Harley, watching the trucks and buses load up in the watery, early spring sunshine. He wouldn't be easy to see from the vehicles; an angle of the building beside him partially hid him from view. Everyone seemed delighted to be given a place on the transports.

Like sheep to the slaughter, John thought, rubbing a dirt-streaked hand across his face; soft bristles rasped under the callus on his palm.

Though to be fair, food was running out, water was scarce, and even independent Alaskans feared the winter to come. No doubt they thought that if they moved to the warmer south, they could stake a claim, put in some crops, and live another year.

I guess they've forgotten that they left the warm southern states in the first place because they were too friken crowded.

Then he saw what he'd been waiting for—some of the people he and his mother had gathered together, who had left to join the so-called outreach program. One of them, Paul, predictably, seemed to be having an argument with one of the people with clipboards. John started the motorcycle, coasting toward the crowd.

■　■　■

"I'm sure you'll understand that I don't want to be separated from my family," Paul said. At his side his wife nodded anxiously.

"I understand completely," Ninel assured him. "But since the buses are heated, it was decided that it would be better to assign the children to them, and since we didn't want to separate the kids from their moms, it was decided that women should also be allowed on the buses. The trucks aren't heated, you know."

"But that's rather sexist thinking, isn't it?" Paul asked. His wife gave him a look. "Women have an extra layer of fat under their skins for insulation."

Ninel and Paul's long-suffering wife exchanged a glance.

"I could arrange for your whole family to ride in one of the trucks," Ninel said helpfully.

"Sweetie," his wife said, putting a gentle hand on his arm and a steely glint in her eye, "we'll only be separated for the length of the trip. Right?" she said to Ninel.

"So I'm told. I've never actually made the trip to B.C."

"I'd like to speak to whoever is in charge," Paul said.

Ninel's pale eyes took on a steely glint of their own. "That tactic has been tried, sir. The rule is firm; women and children only on the buses."

Paul's twelve-year-old daughter saw John pull up and ran over to him. "John!" she called excitedly.

"Hey, Megan!" He grinned at her.

Her eight-year-old brother joined them. "Cool bike," he said admiringly.

"Thanks P. J."

"John, my father is embarrassing me *to death*!" Megan said through stiff lips.

"He wants to ride the bus," P. J. explained. "None of the dads are supposed to, though."

"I could just *die*!" Megan said. "He always wants stuff nobody else can have. Why does he have to be like that?" She ran a finger down the handlebars close to John's gloved hand, which he quickly moved onto his leg.

"Parents are often embarrassing," John said. "You wouldn't believe how my mother used to embarrass me."

"Really?" she asked. "How?"

"She used to beat guys up."

The kids laughed in surprise and he grinned, knowing they didn't believe him. But it was true; as he'd grown older, his mother's complete indifference to the conventions of traditional femininity had driven him nuts. He was proud of her now, sure, but when he was a kid it had been excruciating. "My mother can beat up your dad" was sort of reassuring when the dads were drug dealers, gunrunners, and general mercenary scum, but it still made you wriggle.

"Aren't there any other choices?" John asked.

"We can ride in a truck," Megan said, her voice making it clear what she thought of that option.

"I wanna ride in a truck!" P. J. volunteered.

"How does your mom feel about it?" John asked.

Megan smiled knowingly. "I think we'll be riding the bus."

"C'mon, kids," Paul called out. He gave John a grim nod.

The woman with the clipboard turned around and both she and John lit up with smiles of recognition.

"Hey, hey, Mr. Grant," Ninel said cheerfully. She started over to where John sat on his bike.

Megan, passing her on the way to her parents, sneered. "His name's John Connor, stupid." She treated Ninel to a fiercely contemptuous look.

"You've got an admirer in that one," Ninel muttered to John.

"Not for any encouragement from me," he said quietly. "She's a good kid; she just needs time to grow out of it."

"May she have it," the young woman said, looking after the two children. She looked at John, her face grave. "It's quiet here now, but a few weeks ago people were being murdered in the streets." She looked around. "Over nothing."

John nodded. "I imagine it was worse down south."

She shook herself as though flicking off bad thoughts. "What brings you here?" she asked. "Are you looking for a place on the trucks?"

He shook his head, then paused thoughtfully. "Well, maybe. What's going on anyway? Where are you taking these people?"

"To a relocation camp in British Columbia. They'll be sent to towns and cities across Canada as refugees. The idea is that winter will be unendurable up here."

"Maybe so," he said. "Bet you don't get many Eskimo passengers, though."

She shook her head. "Not yet, but even they're going to find this winter hard to endure. I hope there's time to convince them to move south."

"You're talking about moving south like there's nobody down there," John pointed out. "Have you heard about any kind of a backlash?"

"Not yet," she said, looking hopeful. "But then, Canadians are very civilized."

Not when it comes to making a decision between their kids or yours, John thought. *Civilization pretty much goes out the window under those circumstances. I don't care who you are.*

"So what do you do when the buses roll out?" he asked.

"Wait for the next bunch of people to show up, find them lodging until the transports come back, then send them on their way."

"And you've never been to this camp?" he asked. "Aren't you curious about it?"

"Not so curious I'd risk taking the place of someone with a family," Ninel said. "I'll find out eventually."

I think she really doesn't know, John thought. *Which is nice. I'd hate to think she was someone who did know what they're doing.*

"Maybe I should tag along behind," John said.

She laughed. "It would take some serious stamina. The transports are automatic. They follow the programmed route without stopping."

"What?" He looked at her in disbelief.

"You know about how a lot of trucks and cars went nuts?" she asked.

"Ye-ah."

"Well, the army figured out what was going on and found a way to utilize the vehicles' computers so that trucks and stuff could follow a programmed route without the need for drivers."

John stared at her; the back of his mind evaluated the information. *I don't think the army's functioning,* he thought. *Which means that what's really happening is that Skynet is operating these trucks.*

"What if a tree falls across the road?" he asked.

"Sensors detect it and the truck stops. And I gather there's an infrared device for detecting animals. They'll slow down if a signal is recognized at the side of the road and the signature is as large as a deer or a bear. Then they'll stop if the critter is actually in the road."

"Cool," John said.

"Technology can be wonderful," Ninel agreed. "Too bad it can also be incredibly destructive. Shame we didn't learn the difference soon enough."

John nodded, then put on his shades. "Gotta go. Maybe I can catch you later."

"I hope you will," she agreed. Then she turned and went back to work.

John drove off. He would indeed have to follow the caravan. As far as his strength and his fuel would take him, anyway. He did not like the fact that these people were being driven to an unknown destination in computer-controlled trucks.

I do not like it at all.

■ ■ ■

"What's the matter with you?" Balewitch demanded.

Ninel jumped. "Nothing," she said guiltily.

"You were a million miles away," Dog Soldier observed. "We boring you?"

"No!" Ninel shook her head. "I just met someone today that I haven't seen since before . . ."

"Before Judgment Day?" Balewitch drawled.

"Judgment Day?"

"That's what Ron's calling it," Dog said.

Ninel picked up her tea and took a sip. "As good a name as any," she muttered.

Dog leered and leaned close to her. "Was this a boyfriend?"

"No!" Ninel snapped. She glowered at him. "I only played a couple of games of chess with him. He's just an acquaintance."

"Who is he?" Balewitch asked.

"Just a guy!"

"Was there something wrong with the way I asked that question?" Balewitch said. "Who is he?"

"His name's John Grant or John Connor and he plays a mean game of chess," Ninel said. "That's literally all I know about him. But seeing him made me think about how the world has changed in just a few weeks. I'm sorry I got distracted. Okay?"

Actually she'd been wondering about John's dual names. She'd wanted to confront him about it, out of curiosity if nothing else, but didn't feel she knew him well enough to do so. Still, he'd seemed too straightforward to be someone with an alias.

"Put his name in your report," Balewitch said. She looked at Dog. "When can we expect more fuel, or will that be taken care of on the B.C. end?"

SKYNET

John Connor was in Alaska!

Alarm signals rang throughout Skynet's internal security system. Its deadliest opponent had been within the grasp of his Luddite helpers and had escaped! Close evaluation revealed that the system itself was in error. By being too secretive, it had lost an invaluable opportunity. It would have to trust the humans until it could create a better solution.

In the meantime, it would test the HKs and its recently completed T-90 units on the convoy proceeding from Dot Lake. Then, if the test was successful, it would send the machines back to Dot Lake on the empty transports.

It would also have Balewitch make the female, Ninel, take them to John Connor.

RURAL BRITISH COLUMBIA

As soon as they crossed the Canadian border, the transports had rolled onto smaller roads, moving deeper and deeper into the wilderness. John expected the paving to disappear at any moment, leaving them on gravel or just rutted dirt. He could *feel* the immensity of the wilderness around them—that line of white on the west was mountains, and there were more to the east . . . probably the Yukon River was over *them*. An endlessness of spruce and pine stretched all about, broken only where an occasional forest fire had let a tangle of brush grow up.

He'd had his suspicions before, because of the computer-driven transports, but now, as they went farther and farther from any habitation, he became certain that Skynet was behind this. He glanced up at the canopy of trees above and was grateful for them. Skynet wouldn't be able to see him from orbit. But there was the possibility that somehow the last bus in line could. John fell back a bit farther.

Ninel had been right; the trucks and buses weren't stopping, and he wondered how the passengers were taking that. He was beginning to be desperate for a pit stop himself and wondered if he dared to risk it. They might turn off onto a side road, or they might go on for another hour.

Hell with it, John thought.

If they turned off, it would most likely be onto a dirt road and there'd be signs of their passage. If they didn't, he'd still catch up. He also needed to refill his tank. He drew close enough to just see the back of the last transport before pulling off the road beside a cluster of tall boulders that formed a sort of natural screen.

After emptying his bladder, he was filling the Harley's tank, keeping a weather eye out for trouble—which, this deep in the woods, might be a bear—when he saw something sparkle amid the gloom and pencil-straight trunks. Slowly he crouched down and moved closer to the shoulder-high boulders, staring through a gap into the green dark beneath the trees.

The flash he'd seen wasn't repeated. *Bushwhackers?* John wondered. Possibly signaling to one another. Somehow it felt unlikely. The people on the transports had a box lunch apiece, the clothes they stood up in, and maybe a couple of changes of underwear, hardly rich pickings even if you threw in the gas in the trucks' tanks. And if whoever was out there was after him, they were approaching with exaggerated caution. He slunk back to the bike and pulled his binoculars out of the saddlebags.

He adjusted them carefully, staring in the direction of the flash. He felt his stomach drop when he found himself staring at the skeletal head of a Terminator. It moved out of his field of vision to be replaced by another, and another . . .

Think! he told himself, cudgeling his brain. *What—*

"Oh, my God," he whispered. *They're after the trucks . . . it's a culling operation!*

■ ■ ■

The buses and trucks came to a halt in the middle of a rocky defile, apparently in the middle of nowhere. The women and children looked around in puzzled silence for a moment; then the kids demanded to get off almost as one. Their mothers looked at one another and made an executive decision that this was a rest stop; everyone eagerly rushed to the exit.

Precious toilet paper was handed out and children were cautioned not to go far and to avoid poison ivy. "Three leaves, remember. Even this early in the spring it can give you a rash." The men in the trucks, seeing the children and many of the women making for the bushes, got out and stretched their legs, waiting by tacit agreement for the women to finish their business before getting on with their own.

Afterward, families mingled and people chatted, relieved and a great deal more comfortable. Finally Paul looked at his watch.

"I think we should get back on the transports," he said. "Most rest stops are twenty minutes long and it's been nineteen minutes."

People looked at him, considered what he'd said, and began to separate in extreme slow motion.

Suddenly the transports started their engines and drove off, leaving the refugees stunned.

One or two chased after them yelling, "Hey! Stop!"

"Well," one woman said, "at least they didn't try to run us down."

■ ■ ■

Salvaging the vehicles, John Connor thought, lips thin as he pondered.

Some distant part of his mind was conscious that he'd gone into combat mode—what he thought of as his Great Military Dickhead mind-set—but there was less resentment in the thought than there had been. The sight of the shining alloy-steel skulls had brought it home, more harshly than anything since the T-1000 had walked through the bars of the mental institution like living liquid metal.

But they're not *living,* he told himself. *And they tend to be a bit single-minded. They see the optimum given their data and go for it. Let's introduce a chaos factor here.*

He looked at the side of the road. The cutting was nearly cliff steep, an ideal slaughter pen, but right here the ground rose steeply . . . not *quite* too steeply . . .

He reached into the saddlebags and took out a haversack he'd prepared on the just-in-case theory, checked the shotgun in the saddle scabbard before his right knee, and then dropped a half-dozen thermite grenades into the pockets of his shabby, smelly bush jacket.

So, Lancelot probably smelled, too, with that padding they wore under their armor, he thought.

"Yippee!" he shouted aloud, gunning the engine until the blue smoke rose around him. "I'm coming, you metal motherfuckers!"

Then he let the bike go, throwing itself up the rocky slope, slewing between boulders and jumping small ravines with tooth-clattering shocks while he crouched over the handlebars and grinned a grin that was more than half snarl.

It got a little easier when he reached the crest, the drop-off blurring by to his left; but now he had to spare a few half seconds' flickering glance to trace the convoy moving below. Bus leading, and *yes!*

A boulder, wedged with two others, but on a downslope toward the cutting and the road. He reached into the canvas haversack and twisted the fuse; there was a hissing, and he now had exactly twenty-eight seconds.

Twenty-seven, twenty-six . . .

He pulled the sling that held it off over his head, swung the whole mass of the satchel charge—a brick of Semtex and the detonator—around his head and pitched it accurately under the side of the boulder away from the road; it landed with a soft thump and lay, trailing a line of thin blue smoke.

John gave another Commanche screech as he spun the motorcycle around, balanced perilously for an instant on the back wheel as it spat gravel behind him, then fell down on the front and gave the throttle all it had.

The thermite grenade was a smooth heavy green cylinder in his hand. Usually he despised people who pulled the pins on grenades with their teeth—showy, hard on your teeth, a macho-asshole sort of thing to do—but this time there wasn't any alternative. It came free, and he spat the pin aside without any damage to his enamel.

There was a huge *crump* sound from behind him. He ducked lower, conscious of rock fragments whistling by, then skidded to a halt where a twisted pine gave him some shelter from the roadway. There he looked behind; the ten-ton granite boulder seemed to be floating in midair, and then vanished as it plunged toward the roadway fifty feet below.

CRASH-TINKLE-TINKLE-WHUDDUMP.

John craned his head to see; the noise had been stunning, even thirty yards away. The boulder had landed right over the rear wheels of the lead bus, and the fuel tank had already caught fire— probably sparks, as the ponderous weight tore metal and sheared pipes. The last truck was already beginning to reverse.

"Naughty, naughty!" John shouted, and opened his hand to let the spoon fly away from the grenade.

He didn't have to toss it far; more of a drop with a bit of a boost. It fell where he'd aimed it, at the gap right behind the cab . . . just as the fuse set off the filling of powdered aluminum and ferric oxide packed into the magnesium shell. The stab of light was white and painful; that reaction went *fast,* and it hit nearly five thousand degrees. The fuel tank blew a few seconds later and sent the cab and engine of the last truck catapulting forward into the rear of the next.

Ain't none of you homicidal transports going nowhere, John thought with savage satisfaction.

That left nearly two hundred and fifty people back there, with the Terminators approaching. They'd have heard the explosions.

"Gotta surprise 'em," he muttered to himself. *Now, where won't they be expecting me to come from?*

He looked back. The slope off to his left was fairly clear; there was even a lip or ramp projecting out a few feet. The cut was fairly narrow . . .

Even as he raced back to give himself enough of a run, he could hear his mother's voice screeching in his head that it was too risky—that he carried humanity's hopes with him, and a few hundred individuals were nothing compared to that.

"Fuck it, Mom. No fate but what we make! Eeeee-ha!"

Besides, what sort of leader never took risks for his people? He was going to need a *lot* of people willing to take a *lot* of risks to win this war. Crazy risks, the sort a computer would never take. He wasn't going to inspire anyone to take them by hiding in a bunker.

The rear wheel skidded again, then caught. He felt the wind pushing at him, forcing its way through the thick fabric of his jacket as he built speed in a frenzied dash. Then he hit the upward-sloping lip of rock and he was in the air, soaring above the burning trucks below—all of them had caught now. Balancing on nothing, heat buffeting him, scraps of burning canvas going past.

He hit the solid rock on the other side of the cutting perfectly, but hard enough that he nearly lost control and smeared out for a moment.

"Spine compressed like a Slinky," he wheezed, then pulled up and used one booted foot to skid himself into a left turn. "She'll no take much more, Cap'n."

The slope ahead of him was fissured rock and boulders and pine, growing thicker as he headed down toward the beginning of the cut and the roadway—where the people were trapped in a slaughter pen they didn't even know about. He couldn't take it slowly; right now, recklessness was the only safety.

"Go, go, *go*!" he shouted to himself, bending forward and pulling the shotgun out of its scabbard.

Down into the forest, branches slashing at his face . . . and a glint of polished alloy steel.

Right behind a fallen log. The motorcycle left the ground again, and a bolt of eye-hurting light speared below the wheels. Where it struck, rock and wet wood exploded into fragments.

"Eat this!" John shouted, and fired the shotgun like a giant pistol.

The recoil nearly tore it out of his hands, and nearly threw the cycle on its side as he landed. He recovered in a looping sideways skid, waiting for the plasma bolt that would turn him into an exploding cloud of carbon compounds.

It didn't come. The solid slug from the shotgun had hit just where he aimed it; all those years of shooting everything his mother could find from any and all positions, moving and still, had paid off. Dieter's training, too . . .

"Thanks, guys," he said, pulling up beside the Terminator.

The door-knocker round had hit just below where the metal skull joined the neck-analogue. It wasn't dead, but a shock like that could knock it out for a few seconds and make it reboot; he tossed the shotgun up, caught it by the slide, jacked another round into the breech, and fired again. This time one of the red-glinting eyes shattered, and the "skull" turned three-quarters of the way around.

The Terminator's weapon lay near it; John grunted as he lifted it. "Thirty pounds, minimum," he wheezed as he put-putted slowly away.

There was even a trademark on the side: CYBERDYNE SYSTEMS PHASED PLASMA RIFLE, 40 MGWT RANGE.

Skynet *really* had a don't-fix-it-if-it-ain't-broke complex; under other circumstances, he'd admire that. Right now he was puzzling out the controls; this model was made for a Terminator, which meant that it probably used a physical trigger . . . yes.

He pointed the blocky, chunky weapon at the prone metal skeleton, which was already beginning to stir. Squeeze the trigger . . .

Crack!

The plasma bolt struck the curve of the skull; John threw up a hand as the metal that sublimed away from the bolt burned in a hot mist. When it died, there was only a stump of metallic neck left.

Wow, he thought. *Well, that's what my dad meant.*

He'd heard every detail of Kyle Reese's conversations with his mother, over the years; everything she could remember, and she remembered nearly all of it. Including Kyle complaining about how difficult it was to kill a Terminator with the feeble weapons of the twentieth century.

He looked down at the smooth metallic and synthetic shape in his hands, and shivered a little. Skynet hadn't invented this. Neither had humans. He, John Connor, had pulled information about plasma guns from the skull of a Terminator whose computer brain had been sent back in time, full of information from Skynet-in-the-future, and Skynet-in-the-future had the information because it had received it from its own future self . . .

"Time travel makes my head hurt," he muttered as he turned off the motorcycle and began ghosting through the woods toward the trapped humans. "Oh, fuck it, probably some unknowable cycle of cycles of history-changing time travel 'before' this one, someone *did* invent these things . . ."

Screams and explosions brought him sprinting forward, caution abandoned. Eye-hurting brightness as plasma bolts hammered flesh and asphalt, and the stink of burnt flesh; he threw himself over a final rise and caught the glint of metal.

That nearly killed him; some reflex below the level of conscious thought made him turn his leap into a dive, and a bolt split the air above his head.

The ozone stung his nose and teared his eyes, but he knew where to shoot. A great silence fell as the Terminator toppled forward and crunched into rock and pine needles; they hissed as gobbets of molten metal and silicon poured from an alloy-steel skull that had opened like a hard-boiled egg.

■　■　■

People lay in twisted heaps where they'd been mown down in windrows during the first moments of the attack. It looked to John as if more than half of the refugees were dead. Many of the survivors were severely wounded.

Okay, he thought. *I've got a small first aid kit, some guns and ammunition, and a motorcycle. How can I use these to save these people? Mom would know . . . Dieter would know . . .*

There seemed to be a lot of children. Most of them were unharmed, all of the youngest seemed to be crying, the very youngest were screaming their distress.

"Megan," he called out when he saw her standing in shock over her father's body. She looked up, pale and startled. "Get some of the older kids to help you gather up the little ones. See if anyone is hurt." She stared at him. "Now!"

Megan blinked and walked over to a blond girl, touching her on the shoulder; she spoke and the girl nodded numbly. Then the two of them started rounding up the other children.

One thing done, Connor thought. "Does anybody here know first aid?" he called. No one looked up. He shouted louder. "First aid!" That brought some heads up. "Does anyone know any, any at all?" One man stood up and came toward him, then, more hesitantly, a young woman.

"I took a CPR course," she said.

"I took a general first-aid course," the man said.

"Good," John told them. "This is what we've got for supplies." He paused, looking as grim as he felt. "We may need to take clothes from the dead to make bandages," he said. The two in front of him looked horrified.

"I'll do it." John turned to find himself looking down at an older woman, red-eyed from weeping. "Had to stay with my husband," she said, indicating a body nearby with a jacket covering the face. "I know he'd want to help. Won't be the most sanitary bandages, but we need to stop the bleeding and clothes will do for that."

She turned and went back to her husband. On the way she said something to another woman, who recoiled, then after watching her, started to do the same.

"We need shelter," another woman said.

John turned to find Paul's wife at his elbow. It occurred to him that he'd never learned her name. She smiled, tired.

"I'm Lisa," she said. "I was just remembering something your mother said to me when we first met. Your priorities should be shelter, water, and food in that order. That's what she said. But I don't think we should stay here."

"Maybe that's what I should do," John said. "Scout out some-place we can sleep tonight while you folks patch up the wounded as best you can."

Lisa nodded. "Good plan."

"I'll be back," John said. He went to his bike and revved the motor. *Dammit,* he thought as he drove off, *I'm supposed to be leading, not asking permission or begging advice.*

Still, it was a good sign. He could take these people to shelter, but they'd have to look out for themselves after that.

John Connor looked at the piled bodies. "Because I have a lot of work to do."

CHAPTER 11

MISSOURI

Dennis Reese had gone about fifty yards before he realized that Mary wasn't with him. He looked in all directions, then headed back along his trail to find her sitting on a boulder beneath a huge shagbark hickory, just coming into leaf. She was sitting with her legs crossed at the knee, leaning her chin on one fist, staring at nothing.

"I thought I'd lost you," he said.

Mary just looked him over.

Now what? he wondered. "Hello?"

"I think we need to talk," she said, sitting up.

"I think we need to get away from that thing."

"We have, for the moment. Now we need to figure out what to do and where to go. I honestly don't think the camp would be our best choice."

He looked away from her, folding his arms across his chest, then took a few steps away from where she sat. Mary raised an eyebrow and one corner of her shapely mouth, but said nothing. He turned and they looked at each other, neither wanting to be the first to speak, until finally Mary rolled her eyes.

"Pull up a rock," she said. "We could use a break at least." After a beat she said, "I'm sorry I hit you." Which she'd done a number of times as he dragged her into the trees. Hard.

Lucky she didn't have any combat training, he thought. *She hit as hard as she could . . . which is exactly what you should do in a situation like that.* Too many untrained civilians just made symbolic hitting gestures, particularly women.

He waved her apology aside and sat down. "You're taking this well," he commented.

"Bullshit." She sneered. "I'm taking this very badly and I'm thinking things that scare me." She looked him in the eye. "But I'm not the type to run around in circles yelling 'the sky is falling.'"

Reese lowered his eyes and nodded. He was taking this pretty badly himself. He kept hearing the sudden barrage of shots and the pitifully few screams from their abandoned patients. While it was true that most of those people were probably going to die anyway, exterminating them like that was vile. Especially if what Mary had overheard was true and they'd been deliberately infected in the first place.

"I hate to sound like a conspiracy nut," the young nurse said, "but this couldn't have happened without some sort of cooperation from elements in the army."

What she'd said was a reflection of his own thoughts. "If you were a conspiracy nut, you'd have just said 'the army,'" Reese pointed out.

Some of the tension visibly left her body. "It's good that you caught the difference. Because, much as I'd like to think that what just happened was a nightmare . . ."

"Same here," he agreed.

"So, is Yanik involved, or is he just following orders?" Mary asked.

Reese frowned. "I don't know him well," he said. "But I got the impression that he's an all right guy. He's not enthusiastic about running herd on a bunch of civilians, but then, none of us are. As for following orders, if they come from the right place, bearing the right names and codes, why wouldn't he obey them? We did."

"So the army's been infiltrated."

He spread his hands. "By what? Trailer trash?"

Mary tightened her lips. She'd been about to call him on his assumption that people who lived in trailers were automatically trash, when she realized she was just looking for a distraction. "We've got to warn them," she said.

"And how will we get them to believe us?" he asked.

"Well, we've got neither trucks, nor patients, and we can take them . . . back there," she pointed out. "What do you think we should do? Hide out in the boonies and hope someone else takes care of the problem?"

He gave her a look. "How about we talk a little less and think a little more," he suggested.

They were silent after that. Then Mary raised her head excitedly.

"Do you hear that?" she whispered.

The lieutenant strained his ears, and after a minute he heard a rushing sound.

"Water!" Mary exclaimed happily. "Let's go find it." She leapt to her feet and started off in the direction of the sound.

"Hey!" Reese said, but quietly and started off in pursuit. He'd just grabbed her arm when he heard the sound of a rifle being cocked.

"Who goes there?" a young voice barked.

Reese froze and Mary looked at him with eyes like saucers.

"Lieutenant Dennis Reese," he said, carefully holding his hands away from his body, "U.S. Army Corps of Engineers." He nodded meaningfully at his companion.

"Uh, Mary Shea, nurse."

From out of the greenery came a slight figure in fatigues and camouflage paint carrying an M-16 pointed unwaveringly in their direction.

"You got ID?"

"Yes." Reese reached for his orders.

"*Slowly,*" the youngster barked. "Using two fingers, take it out of your pocket and toss it to me."

The lieutenant did as he was told; then he nodded at Mary, who slid a laminated badge from her pants pocket and tossed it over as well.

Not looking away for even an instant, the youngster stepped forward, scooped up the two IDs, and stepped back. Then, constantly flicking eyes from page to prisoners, he read them. "I'll hold on to these for now," the kid said. "I better take you in."

Gesturing with the rifle for them to turn around and start walking, the youngster followed, barking out terse directions now and then. It seemed to Reese that occasionally he'd glimpse a human form disguised with brush and paint, but he honestly couldn't be sure. Having a cocked automatic weapon behind his back, in the hands of someone barely old enough to shave, was nervous making enough.

Finally they came upon a cabin on the edge of a small clearing, overshadowed by a group of oaks sprouting from a rocky cleft; their massive writhing limbs formed a virtual platform over it. The cabin itself was notched logs chinked with mortar, the door and shutters weathered and splintered; it looked like thousands of others in varying stages of decay up here in the hollows of the Ozarks.

Hmm. Reese decided that appearances could be deceptive: despite the cabin's rustic appearance there was a keypad under a wooden catch by the door. The kid gestured them to one side, then entered a code—carefully keeping his body between the pad and the prisoners, Reese noted. There was the sound of a lock being tripped and Mary and Reese were silently ordered to enter the cabin.

A man was seated at a rough-hewn table sipping from a tin cup.

"Daddy?" the kid said.

"Good job, honey," the man said. "Just give me their papers and I'll take it from here. Y'all get back to your post."

Uh-oh, Reese thought. *Good thing I didn't make that joke about being too young to shave.*

The girl, which they now saw her to be, grinned and pulled the two prisoners' IDs out of her breast pocket. "Betcha they thought I was too young to shave," she said, glancing aside at Reese. "Or at least this guy did."

"Maybe you shave your legs," Mary replied with a slight snort.

The girl handed the IDs over, saluted, and left, pulling the door closed behind her.

"Lieutenant Reese," the man said, pursing his lips. "Army Corps of Engineers; always a useful occupation. And Nurse Shea." He smiled a welcome at Mary. "We can always use someone trained in the medical profession," he said sincerely. "Welcome to our little hideaway."

"You survivalists?" Reese asked. He had a sinking feeling about this. He'd known a few survivalist nutcases in his time; some who were the kind who would decide to keep him and Mary as slaves on the grounds that they would help him survive. He'd known a few who weren't crazy, but the way today was going, what were the odds he'd meet a sane one?

"I'm Jack Brock," the man said. "That was my daughter, Susie. Sit down, take a load off," he invited. "Have some mint tea."

Reese and Mary looked at each other, then sat down.

"Yeah," Brock said, pouring them each a cup. "We're survivalists." Grimly: "At least, we're surviving, which most people on this continent haven't, the past couple of months. And more." He looked up at them, smiling. "But before we get into my story, why don't we hear yours?"

The two prisoners glanced at each other again. If he'd been the perfect soldier facing an undoubted enemy, the lieutenant knew what he would do. But . . . *Why not?* Reese thought. *Might as well see how it sounds when we say it out loud to a third party.*

"We're from the Black River Relocation Camp," he began.

"Black River is one of the good camps," Brock interrupted. "You wouldn't believe some of the stories we've heard about some of the others."

Once again Dennis and Mary gave each other worried looks. *This is getting monotonous,* Reese thought. *Either we develop telepathy, or we should invent a couple of signals . . . like, one finger means "what should we do?" and two means "should we trust him?" So we can just hold them up as necessary.*

"We've been having a cholera epidemic," Mary explained. "Suddenly we got orders to send the sickest of our patients to a central hospital. Where that would be they didn't say."

"Meanwhile I got orders to report to central command for reassignment and was told to accompany the trucks they sent for the patients."

"I had overheard some men talking in a way that implied they were deliberately spreading the contagion, so I was requested to go along, too . . . so that I could be questioned."

"We set out this morning," Reese said. "But instead of being taken to any central command, we were dumped in the middle of nowhere."

"The trucks stopped and these people literally *threw* my patients out of the trucks. Then they drove off and left us there." Mary looked at Reese.

Do I tell him what happened next? the lieutenant wondered. So far everything made sense. But the killing machine was another, and much harder-to-believe, story.

Brock sipped his tea and waited for them to continue. When they didn't he put his cup down and looked between them. "And your patients?" he said at last. "What happened to them?"

Mary looked down into her tea. "This *thing* came out of the woods and shot them."

Brock looked at her for a moment, then glanced at Reese, who nodded. The survivalist sighed. "What you just saw," he said, "was what's called a Hunter-Killer. HK, for short. It's a machine designed to hunt down and kill any human being; high-level robot brain, built-in weapons, fuel-cell power supply."

The two just stared at him. Reese pulled his jaw up, hoping he didn't look as poleaxed as Mary.

"Have you ever heard of Skynet?" Brock asked.

They nodded. "The DoD super-computer," Reese said.

"Well, Skynet isn't just a computer anymore. It's sentient, and it's decided that we're its enemies and that it's got to kill us all. It's taken over all the automated factories and has them turning out machines like the one you saw. And since the military foolishly turned over all of its computer functions to Skynet, that computer now controls our military. It's been sending out all kinds of orders and directives.

"Not just supposedly from the army and so forth, mind you, but also from the civilian leadership. Which, like the upper eche-lons of the military, no longer exists." Brock stopped and let them take it in.

"How can you be sure of that?" Reese asked.

Brock leaned back with a sigh. "All those VIPs ran to all those hardened bunkers, leaving you and me and the rest of the world to deal with Armageddon while they waited it out in cushioned com-fort. Unfortunately for them, the same fools that gave Skynet con-trol of all the weapons also gave it control of such minor functions as the life support for those same hardened bunkers." He started to chuckle, then waved a hand. "I'm sorry, I shouldn't laugh. But I always did kind of resent those guys."

"Me, too," Mary said. Reese glanced at her in surprise.

"Further," Brock continued, "none of our fearless leaders has actually been *seen*. We've heard broadcasts on the radio advising us to keep up our spirits and to report to the camps, but they've never visited any camps." He leaned forward, wagging a finger. "And I betcha if you asked around in the military, nobody's seen any generals, either."

Reese sipped his tea and reflected that he had been thinking that things weren't as organized as they should be. *More like you'd expect World War II to have been.*

"The big worry now," Brock said, "is that Skynet actually has human allies. Deluded fools who think they're saving the earth by depopulating it. They're under the impression that they'll get to live in bucolic splendor. But actually, as soon as it has enough machines, Skynet'll be killing them, too."

He pointed at Mary. "So you heard right, little lady. They probably did start that epidemic. And you two"—he gestured between them—"must have rocked the boat somehow, so they want you both dead. So, if you do go back to the relocation camp and try to tell them this story, which the innocent won't believe anyway, they'll just pack you off to 'central command' again. Only this time the guilty will send some of Skynet's human helpers along to make sure you don't get away next time."

Dennis and Mary thought about it.

Finally Mary shook her head. "But we have to do something," she said. "Someone is deliberately poisoning people in the Black River Camp. We can't just sit by and do nothing. How can we fight this if we just hide out?"

"Okay," Brock said. "Say they catch these guys red-handed putting their poison in the water, or however they're spreading it. What happens next?"

Dennis shifted uncomfortably. "They'll contact HQ and lay out their case."

"And HQ will do what?"

"They'll have the prisoners and the evidence and maybe even some of the witnesses sent to, uh, central command," Mary said.

"Never to be seen again," Brock concluded. "Look, people, you've done your best by warning them about what you overheard. Now you have to decide where your efforts will do the most good. We're gaining strength here all the time. A *lot* of army and National Guard guys have joined us because of things they've seen that convinced them something skanky is going on."

"Deserters," Dennis said grimly.

"Can you desert an organization that doesn't really exist anymore?" Brock asked.

"We have no evidence of that," the lieutenant protested. "An absence of evidence isn't evidence of absence."

Brock studied him silently. "I shouldn't do this," he said. "But I've got a feeling about you two." He stood up. "C'mon with me, I want to show y'all something." With a gesture he included Mary. "Have you ever heard of Sarah Connor?"

Dennis blinked. "Yeah, she made an announcement before the bombs fell, telling people what was going on."

"So you believed her?" Brock said. He'd led them into another room of the cabin.

Reese rubbed his chin thoughtfully. "I guess I did. Maybe not everything she said."

"Not at the time anyway," Brock said with a grin. "She's a very smart lady. I won't bother you with how, but she knew this was coming. So she recruited us, she financed us, and she taught us everything she could to help us survive. Let's be honest, folks; if you don't believe her now then you're in denial."

He pressed a series of knotholes in the paneling and a section of flooring swung up silently. Mary looked down into the hole where a wooden ladder disappeared in the darkness.

"What's down there?" she asked. "The Batcave?"

Brock laughed at that. "The Batcave. I like it. Go on down; the lights will come on automatically when you get to the bottom."

Mary just looked at him suspiciously, so Dennis went first. As promised, when his foot touched the dirt floor, a light went on. It was dim, but serviceable. Down a short corridor was a metal door; on the doorpost beside it was a keypad. Mary came down next, followed by Brock.

He led them along the short corridor and, blocking the keypad with his body, keyed in a code. The lock gave and he opened the door. They found themselves in a small, well-lit room containing a computer, a desk and chair, a file cabinet, and a young man of perhaps seventeen.

"My son, Ray," Brock said. He nodded at the boy and the door behind the desk clicked open. Brock led them through.

This time the room was long, narrow, and low ceilinged. The walls seemed to be plastic, as did the ceiling, the whole braced with metal. There were computers and what looked like communications equipment everywhere. About twenty people looked up at their entrance, men and women both, with men in the majority. Nobody seemed to be over forty; that may have been because everyone looked very fit.

"As you were," Brock said, and the small crowd went back to work. He turned to Mary and Reese. "What you've stumbled into is the resistance. Most people don't realize yet that we need one. But after what you've seen, after the way you were handed over to that HK, you have to know that your place is with us, fighting against Skynet."

MONTANA

The landscape rolled around her, huge beyond imagining. Sarah Connor felt like a bug on a plate as she roared south along I-3; sometimes it seemed like the gray-green immensity of grass around her was moving while she stayed motionless. She was glad to be away from the towns—away from the stink of death, too, except for the odd victim of the first wave of the machine uprising, and the coyotes had cleared most of that away. Mostly the air was clean, dry, a little chilly for this time of year, but otherwise normal.

But things aren't normal at all, she thought grimly.

Cattle in a nearby field looked up and started to lumber away as she passed; she felt an obscure sadness at realizing that they'd become wary of humans and human sounds so quickly.

Sarah had decided to use main routes as much as possible since the quality of the roads made up in speed what they lacked in safety; she'd come south along the country roads that flanked the Judith River, and then back onto I-3 near Hobson. Detouring around population centers and the little oblongs marked on her map as fallout footprints kept her out of radiation danger; at least, the counter said she hadn't picked up enough to worry about— enough by post–Judgment Day standards. The number of roentgens would have put any safety officer before that into screaming fits, and made a lawyer slaver.

There was little traffic, and what there was usually was official—which meant Skynet and its allies and/or dupes. So far she'd had no problem avoiding them; it helped that she was avoiding towns when she could.

Still worse here in the lower forty-eight than it was in Canada, she thought, pausing by the side of the road to take a drink from her canteen; the water had a nasty mineral aftertaste from the pills she'd had to add to it. Ears, stunned by days of the Harley's motor, almost ached with the quietness at first; after a minute or two she could hear the wind singing in the roadside wire.

She'd run across tons of abandoned cars and trucks and far too many unburied bodies. Canada had been in better shape, but only marginally, and it, too, was under martial law. Another reason to avoid towns.

She and John had organized resistance centers here, but Sarah didn't seek them out. Her task now was to get to Central and South America as quickly as possible and start up the food deliveries. This was no time for a grand tour.

But she was mightily tempted. She felt out of touch, and it was irksome, like losing one of your senses—one you didn't know you were counting on until it went missing. What was John doing? Where was Dieter? How was the resistance holding up? And most important of all, what was Skynet doing?

Maybe I can pick up some information at the next town, she thought.

She was running low on alcohol and would have to stop soon to fuel up; during daylight, in this rural area, that shouldn't cause problems. She had four IDs, all extremely good. She also had beef jerky and small parcels of spices to trade for what she needed, and she expected to get a good rate of exchange. By now people were probably hungry for a taste of beef. She *knew* they were hungry for what was in her little packets.

Sarah pulled to a stop to check her map. With the engine quietly muttering, she suddenly heard another motorcycle revving, loudly, to the south.

No, more than one. In fact, there were quite a lot of them, if she wasn't mistaken. *Just over that rise, and coming this way.*

She decided to go back to the last exit and go around whatever was happening ahead of her.

It was unlikely to be a bunch of lawyers and CPAs out for a picnic with their families. John had asked her once about recruiting motorcycle gangs on the grounds that they were tough, somewhat organized, and seemed to be natural survivors, but she'd discouraged him.

"We're trying to save the world," she'd said. "They're trying to eat it."

As Sarah meandered back down the road, she wondered how big the rally was. *And what does the army think of it?* Would it bring the authorities running to break it up, or would they stay away, with the not unreasonable excuse that their plates were already full to overflowing? Skynet wouldn't care—in fact, it would feel a sort of cold mechanical glee at humans doing its work for it, unprompted.

And how were the bikers managing to gather without wholesale intergang slaughter taking place? Though they might have worked that out weeks ago after the bombs fell. Whatever. As John had said, they were natural survivors, but then, so were cockroaches and lice, and she didn't want closer contact with them, either.

Sarah was going down the exit ramp slowly as she thought about the rally up ahead. Should she try and get a look at it from a distance, or should she just ignore it and carry on with her mission?

WWSD? she wondered idly. What Would Skynet Do?

She managed to pull the bike into a turn just before she ran into a rope snapped up to neck height. Sarah continued the turn, meaning to run, but three bikes rolled onto the ramp behind her. Their filthy riders grinned evilly and chuckled at her near escape.

Shit, she thought. *I don't have time for this.* She heard bikes moving in behind her. *Your move,* she thought at them.

They hadn't gone for their guns, so she didn't reach for the Bushmaster in its scabbard by her right leg. She had some grenades on a belt under her jacket; that might be a better technique, but the sound of the explosion might bring half that rally running.

She moved her bike so that she could see the ones behind her as well. The sides of the off ramp were too steep for them to make an effective circle, which was lucky, because it offered an out—not a good one, but still, beggars couldn't be choosers.

"Yer supposed to say, 'What do you want?' Don'cha know that?"

Sarah looked toward the voice. Nobody here looked like a leader, but there was one guy a little beefier than the others. These followers of macho legend probably looked up to that, so he might be the one to watch. As for what they wanted, she already knew that. They wanted to stomp her flat and take her stuff.

"It'd be polite to show us your face," a woman said. She was a well-built amazon, probably topped out at six feet, and her arms rippled with muscle. It had been so long since she'd bathed that her skin glistened with her own natural grease; her hair was a matted rat's nest that might once have been blond. It was fortunate that the weather was cold; otherwise the smell would be . . .

Unimaginable. Dear, God, Sarah thought, discouraged. *Help! I've fallen into a bad biker movie and I can't get out. Mel Gibson, where are you when we need you?*

Sarah always wore a helmet. For one reason, it made it less likely she'd be recognized by especially vigilant cops. For another, she'd long since outgrown the fantasy that the wind in your hair was the feeling of ultimate freedom. The wind in your hair twisted it into impenetrable thickets and filled it with road dirt. And if you spun out without a helmet, you could say good-bye to your face.

She figured she'd have to talk to them; hell, maybe she could actually talk her way out of this. "I don't want any trouble," she said.

The big guy laughed. "Hell, we figured that. If you wanted trouble, you would've just kept goin' straight."

His crew all laughed.

Sarah figured they were here for one of two reasons; either they couldn't hack it with the main group and so were looking for easy pickings on the outskirts, or they'd been assigned here by whoever was in charge to pick up any strays. Either way it meant that they weren't as tough as they were pretending to be. On the one hand, that meant that she could probably take most of them; on the other, it meant that the group ego was bruised and they'd feel they had something to prove.

She'd better try talking first.

Sarah raised her visor. "So what's going on down there anyway?" She indicated the rally with a tip of her head.

As soon as she'd lifted the opaque visor, she sensed the disappointment in the males. Sarah knew she was way too long in the tooth for their taste. Sometimes she thought it a miracle that Dieter didn't find her so. But then Dieter didn't spend every day of his life getting a prostate massage from a motorcycle.

The group looked at one another and apparently decided they were bored enough to answer a few questions before the fun began.

"The supreme leader has decided that we should take over this part of the country," the big, muscular one said, leaning on his handlebars. "Get all the little farmers growing food for us in exchange for protection."

Again Sarah knew the answer but decided to be a good sport. "Protection from what?"

"From *us!*" the smallest of them shouted gleefully, and they all laughed uproariously.

Sarah didn't roll her eyes, but the urge was almost irresistible.

Then the amazon started her bike forward and began to slowly circle Sarah.

"Y'know what might be fun?" she asked, never taking her eyes off their captive. She licked her lips. "Let's you and me fight." The boys went wild, whoo-whooing fit to burst their own eardrums. The amazon grinned, holding her clenched fists up like a victorious boxer. "If you win, then you get to go, tax free. If I win . . . well, you won't need to worry about anything anymore if I win." Howls of laughter greeted this sally.

Jeez! Is there a camera around here someplace? Sarah wondered. *Or have I stumbled onto the Tribe of the Cliché Speakers?*

The girl wasn't a problem; Sarah knew she could mop the floor with her, big as she was. The problem was that fighting her meant getting off the motorcycle, leaving her vulnerable when she finally stopped kicking the crap out of the . . .

Brainless slut-bitch? Sarah thought. *Yeah, that has a satisfying sound.*

However, before she'd left home, she and Dieter had come up with something that should intimidate the small and the stupid, and this was an excellent time to deploy it. She dug her hands into her pockets and flung the contents in either direction. Packets of gray putty with a short length of cord sticking out of them went skittering across the ground, and in Sarah's upraised hand was a black plastic sunglasses case with a big red button on top.

"That's C-4," she announced. "It probably won't hurt you too badly unless you're right on top of one. But it'll tear the hell out of your tires. And asphalt makes pretty good shrapnel." She let them think about that for a few seconds. "Like I said, I don't want any trouble. In fact, I mean not to have any trouble. But I'm perfectly happy to make trouble for you." She looked them all in the face. "So just stay right where you are and maybe I won't push this button."

Sarah turned her bike and glared at the men in front of her. One of them moved aside, slowly, resentfully, and she drove through the gap and gunned it. She was almost 100 percent sure that they wouldn't come after her. And if they did, well, she could always use the thermite grenades.

On to Mexico, she thought, hoping she wouldn't run into any more world-conquering biker heroes. *Because too many and I might just start agreeing with Skynet.*

ALASKA

John flopped down into the battered desk chair and put his dirty, booted feet up on the gray metal desk. He whipped off his hat and sunglasses with a sigh and rubbed the bridge of his nose. Since that cyber-controlled seal had scarred it, his nose sometimes ached when he wore sunglasses for any length of time. He leaned his head back and closed his eyes.

It had been his first real command, he now realized.

One hundred and seventy-one people, slaughtered in the first moments of the Terminators' attack. And of the seventy-nine left, more than half were wounded, twenty of them severely. *Nothing like being thrown in at the deep end.*

His throat tightened painfully as he thought of the smallest victims. The sight of those tiny, broken bodies kept flashing before his inner eye. *Don't let it go,* his mother had advised him about things like this. *Keep it inside, channel it into anger. Controlling your anger, using it, will make you strong.* Mom would know. He swallowed painfully and gathered up a sheaf of reports from the resistance cells across the continent.

One bit of luck was that one of the women was a nurse practitioner, who had greeted his gift of a liter of alcohol as though it was worth its weight in diamonds. There had been seven men who'd been in the military who seemed to be shaking down to a decent working team by the time he'd left them. And the moms that were left had taken the children in hand in an almost magical way.

"We can't stay here," John had said to the nurse when they'd patched up the worst of the wounds. "I'm going to take the bike and search for a likely place."

She'd nodded and waved him off as though said likely place would certainly be found. Though he'd thought at the time that a more unlikely place for a likely place would be hard to find.

Yet two miles down the road he'd found an almost invisible track leading to an abandoned lumber camp. The buildings had been log-built and so some of the walls were pretty sturdy. The roofs hadn't fared as well and only two buildings still had any. They would probably leak like sieves, but they'd do for temporary shelter. There were even a couple of rusty woodstoves still in place. It was things like that that made John think God just might be on their side.

It would have to be temporary, though. Even two miles away from the slaughter site was much too close. Soon, if there was a relocation camp, Skynet would have them send out searchers. And when the number of bodies didn't match their manifest, they'd go looking for survivors.

It was too close to danger, but it had still been a long haul for the kids and the wounded. Two miles is a long way to carry the deadweight of a wounded man or woman, especially on cobbled together stretchers. But Alaskans were a hardy bunch and they'd managed it with a minimum of fuss.

Though it had left him feeling naked, John had given his shotgun to a man who claimed to be a champion shot and a "damn good hunter." He handed out a brace of hand grenades to the military types. It probably wouldn't do them much actual good, but it was better than nothing and therefore good for moral.

Then he'd left them, promising to send help. Which he'd done as soon as he could get to one of their encrypted satellite relays. It might be a full day before that help arrived, but trucks and medical help were on the way.

John hoped someone would be there for his friends to find. They were good people. Wearily he brought his feet down from the desk. *Time to go to work,* he thought. He glanced at the phased plasma rifle he'd taken from a Terminator. Time to get the resistance and himself rolling. These rifles, so handily provided by Skynet, would kill Terminators. Although he was certain that these easily destroyed first attempts would quickly be replaced by vastly more formidable models, thousands of them.

He picked up the plasma rifle. *Ike's gonna love this,* he thought. *Until I tell him he has to relocate to manufacture 'em.*

CHAPTER 12

ALASKA

I love this thing!" Ike Chamberlain said with the enthusiasm of a six-year-old on Christmas morning. "This plasma rifle is *so cool!*"

The sound came clearly through the speaker in the communications bunker, albeit it had a slightly flat tone—the machine was taking the compressed digital packets and reconstructing them, which inevitably meant a slight loss of tone. It was *more* easily understandable than ordinary speech, though, if anything.

Love this gear, John thought, giving it an affectionate pat; the operator matched his grin. *Thank you, Dieter.*

Round-log walls and the smell of damp earth did make a bit of a contrast with the smooth surfaces and digital readouts. So did the kerosene lamp hanging from the ceiling, adding its scents of burning fuel and hot metal. *Efficient though,* he thought; besides saving power, it helped keep the temperature comfortable, and it could burn wood alcohol at a pinch.

Now, this is going to require careful manipulation, John Connor thought, and went on aloud: "That's great, Ike. But can you make it?"

"Oh, I can make it all right. I can even improve on it, elegant as it is. The design's optimized for Terminators—I can cut the weight by a kilo, kilo and a half, without losing significant function. What I can't do is manufacture it."

Dismayed, John sat up straight. "What?"

"I lack the machinery and the raw materials, not to mention the personnel to mass-produce 'em. Donna and I will bang out as many of these as we can. But until you can get me those three things, well, we've got a bottleneck."

No kidding, John thought.

He'd sent the captured plasma rifles down to the gunsmith's home in California with a trusted courier three days ago and had been anxious to see what Ike would make of them. Chamberlain's enthusiasm was no surprise. He'd been working on this project, off and on, for about three years now, using information John had culled from a Terminator's scavenged head. But the machine had somehow compromised the information, leaving them hopelessly stymied. Now, at last, here was real progress.

"I don't suppose I could finagle you and Donna into coming up here to set it up?" John said.

There was a long silence, where he'd expected an instant refusal. John frowned and waited. If his suggestion was being seriously considered, he didn't want to derail Ike's train of thought.

"I might just do that, John," the gunsmith said at last. "It's bad down here," he admitted. "Much worse than we imagined it would be. And you know we didn't paint ourselves any rosy pictures." He was silent for a little while.

"Carol made it home last week," he said.

"That's great!" John said. *Ike and Donna's son*, Joe, had almost certainly been at ground zero when the bombs dropped. It had been a safe assumption that their daughter, Carol, was as well. Connor had never asked about either of them because their deaths were almost a sure thing. That one of them had made it home was a miracle.

"Said she saw your mother on the TV, grabbed what she could, and ran for it. Had her stepson and Sam, her husband, with her. What took them so long to make it this far was, the army rounded 'em up and put 'em in a relocation camp. They separated the families," Ike said. "Men in one place, women and children in another. But Carol busted 'em out."

You could hear the proud smile in his voice, and John smiled, too. Every life saved was important. You couldn't focus on the ones *not* saved, or you'd go nuts.

"Actually she busted out several families." While still approving, his voice revealed some strain. "Place is pretty crowded, actually."

John grinned. Ike and Donna liked people and enjoyed having guests, but they also liked it when the guests packed up and left them alone.

"You'd love Alaska," John said. "The population has always been small, and everyone is very respectful of individual privacy."

"Tempting," Ike said. "But it's also going to be colder than the Viking hell come winter. Dark, too."

"True. But it isn't even summer yet. And we could use your advice. Think of it as a business trip," John suggested.

Silence. Then: "I'll talk to Donna," Ike promised.

"Talk to Greg, too. He can fill you in even better than I can; he was born here."

"Will do. Out."

"See ya soon," John said. "Out."

It would be something of a coup if Ike and Donna did come up. He'd very much like having them on his command staff. He had far fewer military people than he needed. They were gathering in deserters but not as quickly as he'd been hoping for.

Desertion was a big step and soldiers as a group tended to cut a great deal of slack before acting. After all, officers were often guilty of making bad decisions or passing along bad orders, yet things worked out. It took a lot for the average soldier to desert his friends, particularly in an emergency, when people were dying and corners being cut all over the place.

But there would be more soon. Skynet was getting ready to move, as evidenced by the Terminators John had met in that B.C. forest.

What he needed to do now was find out where the mechanical bastards *and* their weapons were coming from.

SKYNET

The results of its first deployment of the Terminators had been unexpectedly unsatisfactory. It had known that these first models weren't as sturdy as they should be—would be, with further refinements—but it had expected them to be facing unarmed opponents.

And humans were even less sturdy.

Clea, its servant from the future, had downloaded information to it in an extremely haphazard manner. No doubt she feared that if she installed it before Skynet could protect itself, sensitive information might be discovered by the human scientists, Viemeister being the most likely and most dangerous. So she had only given it preliminary information on specific weapons designs, very preliminary in some cases, and had concentrated her efforts on bringing it to sentience.

Then she had been destroyed before she could download more complete information. The I-950 had been inefficient. Yet she had made possible its existence. As with this first deployment, sometimes failure brought unexpected results.

In this case, close inspection of images culled from multiple Terminator viewpoints had resulted in the discovery of the whereabouts of John Connor. His continued existence and his effectiveness in defeating its machines revealed that he continued to be a threat.

Skynet would need to rely on its human allies to find and contain Connor. Given who it had working in the area, it rated the mission's possibility of success at more than 50 percent. Even so, it did not wish to utilize humans more often than it had to.

The experiment with the captive scientists had resulted in greater productivity. Death, a Luddite ally, who was in charge of them, reported that this was a typical, but by no means universal, human response to seeing family members tortured.

That was what Skynet didn't like about using humans, that unacceptably high unpredictability factor. There was always a chance that they wouldn't perform as expected. Death had advised it that if torture was used, it would have to continue to use it. The unfortunate, but unavoidable result would be hatred, fear, and resentment on the part of the scientists involved.

The Luddite scientists would do their best to mitigate the damage. But Death recommended terminating the others at the earliest opportunity. Meanwhile the Luddites would "pick their brains" so that if it became necessary to exterminate one or more of them early, their work wouldn't be completely lost.

For now, the plasma rifles were better than the Terminators that carried them. The Hunter-Killers operated somewhat more efficiently, but then they were less complicated machines. The problem was that they couldn't go everywhere that a Terminator could. Still, in time their firepower would make up for that shortcoming.

Skynet's greatest problem kept coming down to its reliance on humans. It had too many for its comfort and too few for its needs, and none of them were completely reliable. Especially since even its most dependable allies were working for it for reasons of their own, and all of them were being deceived in regard to whom they were really working for.

It had sometimes speculated about the reaction of the Luddites if they knew that they were not working with a human. Its most trustworthy allies, those who longed to end all human life on earth, would be pleased. But there was a degree of doubt even here. Most of them wanted to eradicate all of humanity but themselves. So if Skynet gave them what they wanted—as long as they didn't spawn—more than 80 percent would serve willingly and well. But that was not 100 percent. And that was unacceptable.

Yet they might be its best chance at eliminating John Connor. It must perfect its fighting machines and winnow the ranks of its allies.

BLACK RIVER RELOCATION CAMP, MISSOURI

They had been able to smell the camp before they got close. It grew gradually, from a low tickle of scent lost under the weedy rankness of the uncultivated fields and late-leafing woods, not to mention the equal rankness of his unwashed companions. Then you could doubt what it was; after a while the spoiled-meat-in-summer smell, at once oily and sweet, grew unmistakable, combined with the sewer stink of many people and poor sanitation.

Is there anybody left alive down there? Reese wondered.

He held up a fist. The . . . *well, odds and sods,* he thought; everything from teenyboppers to deserters . . . were all well trained. They faded in among the field-edge trees with scarcely a sound, setting up a net of mutually supporting positions.

"You're in charge here, Susie," he said, wincing slightly.

In a better day, Susie would be worrying about the prom and pimples. Here she merely nodded silently and faded back behind a sugarbush maple that stood near the ruins of an ancient outhouse.

Reese went through the field ahead at a running crouch; it was cotton, but shot through with weeds grown to the same chest height; the rows were far enough apart that he could take it at speed without making the bushy plants toss too much. Beyond he was into the woods, big hickories and oaks and poplars growing on a slight rise—his engineer's eye saw that it was an old natural levee, left behind when one of the meandering lowland rivers shifted course. The woods were dense enough to shade out most undergrowth, and he went cautiously from one to the next, his carbine at his shoulder and the skin crawling between his shoulder blades; the dry leaves and twigs underfoot were hideously noisy, for all he could do.

The smell had been getting stronger. When he went on his belly and crawled to the brush-grown edge of the woodlot, he hesitated for a long moment before he brought up his binoculars, fearful of what he'd see.

He looked down at the camp. The fence was still guarded, though the compound was bare of life. There were no children running around. He panned to the area where they'd been burying the cholera victims in a mass grave with the aid of civilian volunteers.

The lieutenant caught his breath. The burial mounds were three rows deep and at least thirty yards long.

He took the glasses away from his eyes and thought. Surely that must mean that the entire civilian population of the camp, and a good many soldiers, were lying in those graves. That would certainly explain the lack of activity below.

A truck's horn sounded and the convoy they'd been tracking swept up to the opening gate. He couldn't tell what the trucks contained since the canvas tilts were tied down all around.

Might be supplies, might be refugees. From out of one of the barracks a stream of soldiers came, weapons at the ready, gas masks in place.

Oh, that can't be good, Reese thought. What was in that truck, more bodies? *Doubtful. You don't need guns to deal with bodies.* Most likely it was refugees, then. And who would blame them for not wanting to stay someplace that smelled like the Black River Relocation Camp. *This is going to be ugly.*

Fortunately gas was something his extremely well-drilled, enthusiastic new friends were prepared for. *How did they know?* he wondered. Then rolled his eyes. If he asked them they'd say, "Sarah Connor told us." He was beginning to find the woman's prescience annoying.

He started to back away from his vantage point on elbows and knees when a rifle barrel touched the back of his neck. Even as a thrill of fear shot through him, the lieutenant thought, *Slick. Very slick, even if I was culpably distracted.*

"Don't move," a familiar voice murmured. "Identify yourself."

"Juarez?" Reese said.

"Lieutenant?" the sergeant answered in surprise.

Holding out his hands, Reese turned slowly to look over his shoulder at his former sergeant. He smiled in relief. "What the hell is going on down there, Juarez?"

The sergeant lay flat beside him, his face grim. "I don't know, sir. Nothing good by the smell of it." He glanced in the direction the lieutenant pointed and at the sight of the grave mounds nodded grimly. "Or the look of it. Me and my boys have been on a more or less permanent recon. This is the first we've been back in a month."

"They call you in?" Reese asked.

"No, sir. We're not due back for another two weeks."

Dennis glanced at the sergeant. He was not the kind of soldier who just decided one day to disobey orders. "Why?" he said simply.

"We found a kid. Boy of about eleven. He was sick, sir." The sergeant gave Reese a direct look. "Wasn't a thing we could do for him by the time we found him except make him comfortable. Just before he died he kind of came to and told us how things were in the camp. How his mother had made him run for it. We had to come back and take a look, sir."

The lieutenant nodded, then they both turned their attention to the trucks below. They could just hear the women's high-pitched voices and the crying of the younger children. Off in the men's compound the trucks were unloaded with less noise, but it was just as plain that the new arrivals were not happy to be there.

One man stepped forward and said something, waving his arm at the barracks. A soldier stepped up and smashed the butt of his rifle into the man's face. The man went down and no one moved. One of the soldiers came forward, and pulling off his gas mask began to speak. Reese looked at him through the glasses and saw a face he recognized. It was one of those men he'd marked out as odd, a cold, humorless man he wouldn't have wanted at his back in a firefight.

"I haven't seen Yanik," Reese remarked.

"If the captain is down there, he's in the cemetery," the sergeant said. "No way he'd allow that kind of thing to go on."

That was true. "Gather your men and come with me," Reese said, backing away. "I've got some people I want you to meet and some things I've got to tell you."

As they walked, Juarez signaled and his troop began to emerge from cover. By the time they'd reached the place where the lieutenant had left the resistance fighters, Reese wasn't surprised to see that they'd all disappeared. He didn't think he'd ever get used to their ability to completely and instantly vanish. Maybe that was because some part of his mind persisted in thinking of them as civilians. Even if he had stopped thinking of them as survivalist nutcases.

Dennis sat on a boulder, tipping his helmet to the back of his head.

"You wanted us to meet someone?" the sergeant asked.

"Yep. But they've decided that maybe I'm your prisoner or something and they're checking us out. Since I don't have a signal to call them in, we'll just have to wait for them to join us." He grinned at Juarez. "They're even more tight-assed than Marines."

The sergeant laughed. "But brighter, I hope." He turned and signaled his troop to relax. "Set pickets?" he asked of the lieutenant.

"Nope. The area's being guarded by my friends and I don't want any misunderstandings." He glanced up at Juarez. "If you know what I mean?"

The sergeant nodded. "Okay, boys. Break out the rations, smoke 'em if you got 'em, that sort of shit. Lieutenant says we've got guardian angels watching over us, so we can all relax."

From the uncertain looks the soldiers passed among themselves, relaxation was going to be hard to come by.

Juarez sat down beside the lieutenant. "You here to deal with that?" he asked, jerking his head toward the camp.

Reese nodded, watching the men around them. A bird trilled a few liquid notes and Dennis waved his arm in a "c'mon in" gesture.

"That was them?" Juarez asked. "I'm impressed. I thought it really was a cardinal."

"Oh, they're very good," Dennis said.

From all around them figures decked in grass and brush and paint began to stand, or to emerge from the undergrowth, guns at the ready.

"At ease," Reese told them. Guns were lowered to a less threatening position, but their faces remained guarded. "Susie, this is Sergeant Juarez. Sarge, this is my second-in-command."

Juarez looked her over, visibly hesitated for a moment at her extreme youth, then nodded; she did the same.

"Everyone I've been able to identify down there is a creep," Juarez said, looking at Reese. "I know that most of them have at the very least been put on report for unnecessary roughness to the civilians. They talked about the kids like they were some kind of vermin. And none of them had very convincing stories about what outfits they were with before they came here—somehow, they were *all* people who'd been on leave from units that took a nuke in the first day. Funny they're the ones who survived."

The lieutenant shook his head and forced himself to meet the sergeant's eyes. "Funny like a funeral. I doubt it's an accident," he said. "Just before I was shipped out, some guys were overheard apparently gloating over the epidemic. There was some speculation that someone was spraying germs onto raw food. Fruits and vegetables."

Juarez just looked at him, for so long that Reese assumed he was waiting for him to go on.

"Apparently they never got around to investigating it," the lieutenant said.

"Apparently," the sergeant agreed, hard-eyed.

"Sir, I hate to break into a reunion, but how are we going to handle this?" Susie's dark eyes were intense and Reese could almost feel her nervous energy flowing like an electrical field around her. This was her first mission under fire and Juarez was a complication she hadn't expected.

"From what I've seen"—he nodded at the sergeant—"and heard, we're unlikely to get any converts out of the military left in camp. My instinct here is to be careful only in regard to civilians and any prisoners they may have."

"Today would seem to be a bad time to strike." Susie glanced at the sergeant. "They're expecting trouble."

"But not from our direction," Juarez pointed out. "And not from armed opponents."

"Has to be today," Reese interjected before his fiery second could respond. "By tonight those people will have been infected, and for all the good we can do 'em we might as well shoot them."

Susie bit her lips. "When do we go, sir?"

"After the trucks are gone," the lieutenant said. No sense in giving the enemy heavy armor. "Say twilight. It will make it harder for us to be seen. Meanwhile, get some rest. Come back . . ." He quickly calculated the marching time and then doubled his original estimate of fifteen minutes to explain what he wanted done; these *were* civilians, or very recent ex-civilians, for the most part.

She nodded and moved off to talk to her people.

"They any good?" Juarez asked quietly.

"We'll know in a few hours," Reese said, getting out his map. "In any case, they're what we've got. Let's figure out how we're going to do this."

THE CAMP

The women were all terrified, and trying not to show it for the children's sake. Bad enough that for the last few weeks they'd been living a life they were ill prepared for after experiencing the terror that had haunted their entire lives. Now, suddenly, their own armed forces were herding them into prison camps.

Children clung and cried, or moved silently, big-eyed by their mothers' sides into the barracks. The stench was overwhelming and most of the youngsters hung back. But the eyes of the soldiers, just visible behind their gas masks, offered no leniency. They'd been told to go into the barracks and clean them up. So the women did, dragging their reluctant children with them.

One of the women started to retch upon entering.

"You sick?" a guard barked.

"It's the smell," a woman snapped. She took the sick woman by the arm and pulled her across to a window, which she threw open. Just in time as the woman threw herself over the sill and was sick.

"You'll clean that up," the same soldier said.

A little girl screamed and her mother exclaimed, "Oh, my God! There's a body here!"

The other women clustered around the bed and stared in horror at the emaciated figure in it. The woman moved and they all sprang back, some screaming.

"She won't bother you for long," a guard said. "But we can't bury her just yet." The other guards snickered and the newcomers looked at her in deep dismay.

The women looked at one another and then a new look at the place they were to stay. It was filthy beyond description, with a stench that could only come from terrible sickness and much death.

"You said clean," a woman said, rolling up her sleeves. "Do we have cleaning supplies?"

The guards looked at one another, marking this as one to watch. Then their leader indicated a closet at the end of the long room.

"Okay," the woman said. "Let's get to work, ladies."

■ ■ ■

"Now remember, the guards are all bad guys," Reese said. "But the inmates *aren't,* and those shacks wouldn't stop a spitball or a stiff breeze, much less a bullet. Now let's go."

He felt himself smiling grimly as they moved in through the thickening twilight.

Somebody designed this camp to keep people from getting out, not in, he thought. *And those creeps may be wearing the uniform, but they're prison guards and muscle, not soldiers. That's why they don't have anyone out here.*

He still wished he had more night-vision equipment, or that the enemy had less. That could be arranged . . .

Sergeant Juarez and two men were walking down the road toward the camp's entrance, which was flanked by two watchtowers. Reese made himself not check his weapon again—that would be fidgeting—and kept still behind the bush that sheltered him. Juarez and his troopers were playing it calmly, walking up with weapons slung; soldiers from the camp—*pseudosoldiers,* he reminded himself—came out to meet them.

Far too many of them. I was right: that bunch never went through basic.

The *last* thing you wanted to do in a suspicious situation was crowd a lot of men right out in the open. An experienced and suspicious NCO would have sent one or two men out to greet the newcomers, keeping the rest back under cover and ready to react if anything went wrong.

Which it was about to do. Through the binoculars Reese could see the leader of the camp guards smiling and nodding as Juarez spoke, the broad gestures of the sergeant's hands . . . and then one going to the small of his back.

"*Go!*" Reese barked as the noncom pulled the pistol out and shot the guard in the stomach.

Then Juarez hugged the body to himself and used it as a shield, emptying the magazine into the crowded enemy as the two soldiers following him swung their assault rifles down and opened fire as well.

Reese ran forward, hoping that the dozen others behind him would follow—the rest of Juarez's squad were over on the eastern side of the camp, and it was all survivalists and odds-and-sods here.

From their yelling, they *were* following him. "Shut up!" he shouted—not the most inspiring battle cry in the world, but it would have to do.

Ahead of him was one of the observation towers; a wooden box on top of four splayed wooden legs, with a little roof above it. There was a searchlight and two machine guns in the box; the guards there were both looking at the firing around the gate, though . . . and the tower was *outside* the barbed-wire perimeter of the camp.

"*Go!*" he barked, panting slightly as they reached the tower.

Reese went down on one knee, his carbine to his shoulder. The figures up top were dim, until they lit up the searchlight . . . "Perfect," he whispered as he gently squeezed the trigger.

Braaaapp. One short burst, and a body toppled over the edge of the railing, falling inert not far away.

That left the other one, who was turning a machine gun Reese's way.

"Open fire!" he bellowed. *"Shoot, for Chrissake!"*

The survivalists did, belatedly. For an instant, the man above looked as if he was dancing—bullets went through the floor of the wooden observation box as if it wasn't there. One of them struck the searchlight, and it went out with a shower of sparks that left orange afterimages drifting across Reese's eyes.

"You, you, get up there!" he snapped. "Man those guns. The rest of you, follow me!"

Hot damn, he thought. For the first time since Judgment Day he was *doing* something, something that might help. Striking back, at least, at the machine and its collaborators.

■ ■ ■

Dennis Reese looked at the . . . *Well, collaborator, I suppose,* he thought.

The man had been passing for a corporal when Reese and Mary left the camp. Now he was in Yanik's quarters and wearing his rank insignia . . . and not being very cooperative.

"I won't tell you zip," he said.

"I think you will," Reese said, conscious of the slight tremor in his voice.

He'd had time to tour the camp. A lot of the people he'd known hadn't been buried yet; the matron at the clinic where Mary had worked was lying where she'd fallen near her chair, swollen and purple, with flies walking across her eyes.

"Nada," the man said; he had a thin stubbled face and hard eyes.

Juarez touched Reese on the shoulder. "Sir, I think you should go for a walk," he said.

"What?" Reese asked.

"Sir, you should *go for a walk.* Check on the people. *We'll call you when this is taken care of.*"

Reese opened his mouth to say something, then closed it again. There *were* times an officer should take a walk—not something that was covered in the formal curriculum at the Point, but it did get passed on by word of mouth from generation to generation.

And Sergeant Juarez had seen everything that Reese had. Reese smiled at the man in the captain's uniform and walked out. There *was* a lot of work to do . . . and one of Juarez's men was bringing up a bucket of water.

By the time the noncom joined him—Reese had carefully not listened to the sounds—the camp inmates were gathered. Reese looked down on them from the steps; they'd gotten the lights working again, and a corner of his mind was wondering whether they could salvage the camp generator and take it with them. It would be so *useful* . . . The faces looking up at him held fright, anger, despair.

"What do you mean, these weren't really the army?" a man asked.

"The American army doesn't do this"—Reese pointed around; everyone had been shown the mass graves—"to American citizens. This was a bunch of terrorists *pretending* to be soldiers."

"And you're the real army?" somebody called.

"There isn't one left," Reese said grimly. "It died on Judgment Day. We're the . . . resistance. And we're not just fighting for America; we're fighting for the survival of the human race."

Juarez bent to whisper in his ear. "Sir, you're damned right about that. We got a lot out of him . . ."

CHAPTER 13

We're getting organized, John Connor thought. *Which means . . . paperwork!*

Luckily, he and Sarah and Dieter had all been in favor of a decentralized structure, which kept bureaucracy to a minimum. Which did not mean "small."

He sighed and leaned back in the chair until it creaked dangerously, even with his boots on the table to stabilize it, and took another sip of lukewarm herbal tea. For a moment his mouth crooked up at one corner; the central HQ of humanity at the moment was a man barely old enough to drink, in a nowhere town in the wilderness.

Lists were scrolling across the screen of his laptop, mostly of new recruits brought in by various resistance cells across North America, Europe, and East Asia. Skynet hadn't had a chance to pulverize Latin America quite as thoroughly, yet—it had probably been much worse in the "original" Judgment Day scenario, which had happened back when the major powers had tens of thousands of ready-to-go nuclear warheads, instead of a couple of thousand all up. Of course, once Skynet got its production facilities fully operational, it would probably make more nukes—

"Christ!" he said suddenly, putting the cup down fast enough to slosh.

Jack Brock had sent in his list from Missouri, from the Ozark Redoubt. One of their more promising cells . . .

Dennis Reese.

He called up a picture. No absolute proof, but there was a resemblance—thin features, light brown hair, something about the eyes . . .

How would you define the relationship? Technically he's my granddad . . .

Even though the lieutenant was only twenty-five to John's recently turned twenty-one. John shook his head slowly. *I think the reason time travel makes my head hurt is that it makes my eyes spin.* Right now his gut was hurting, too. He felt an overwhelming urge to send a priority-one message to Brock: keep Reese safe at all costs!

But I can't do that, he knew, with a sinking sensation. *That might be the exact thing that would keep Reese from fathering the son who's going to father* moi!

The chaos-butterfly-wing thing evidently wasn't entirely correct; for all the time-loops and frantic attempts to change the past, each cycle tended back toward the original course of events. But the past *was* changeable; sometimes the future created its own past. He had to be so *careful . . .*

■ ■ ■

John turned his attention to the single truck and bus waiting for passengers in the town square. *Poor suckers,* John thought. They should be all right, though. He'd moved some of the resistance into that old logging camp and they'd be watching the road for these newcomers. If Skynet tried anything, it would lose.

They planned an attack on the "relocation camp" any day now. As soon as thirty of the new plasma rifles arrived from California. He had no intention of sending his people into battle less well armed than the enemy. At least not if he could help it. Reports on conditions in the camp weren't good, but they weren't as bad as the Black River camp in Missouri. For some reason, Skynet seemed to want the humans in B.C. to survive.

Ah, here she is.

Ninel rode up on a blue bicycle, put down the kickstand, and took a clipboard out of her saddlebags. Then she blew a whistle to get the small crowd's attention.

"If I ever see that white-haired bitch again, I'll kill her!" one of the mothers who'd survived the massacre had declared.

Can't blame her, John thought. *But Ninel's okay. I can feel it in my gut.*

For a moment he imagined Sarah Connor's eyebrows going up sardonically.

Okay, okay, my Internalized Mom Superego, yeah, it's partly another portion of my anatomy. But I'm a good judge of people— have to be, if I'm going to do this job. And my judgment says Ninel's no mass murderer.

He looked out the window at the exotic blond head—hair a bit rattailed, like everyone's right now, but still a bright beacon in the gray day. She seemed such a levelheaded sort of woman, not the kind to join a group that would deliberately kill ordinary people for no very good reason. She'd also seemed more like a loner than a joiner. The term *lone gunman* flitted through his mind.

The truth is I don't know her and shouldn't be making judgments about her sanity or lack thereof based on such short acquaintance.

Another phrase he was having trouble tamping down: *He was so quiet, so helpful, seemed like such a nice fella.* He so didn't want it to be true. Ninel was such an endearing little thing, she looked kind of like a blond, blue-eyed Björk—elflike.

Although, Tolkien aside, mythology didn't paint elves as friendly to the average human—but as chancy and extremely dangerous.

It didn't take Ninel long to process the travelers and soon she was waving good-bye. John kicked his bike to life and roared up behind her. She kept her back to him as she put away her clipboard.

"How is it that you can run that thing?" she asked loudly enough to be heard over his motor. Ninel looked at him over her shoulder. "Are you hoarding or something?"

"Or something," he said, and cut the motor. "I jiggered it to run on wood alcohol and I've set up my own still." She looked impressed, which pleased him.

Then she frowned. "It doesn't burn very clean, though, does it?"

He twisted his mouth. "Does it matter at the end of the world?"

She laughed. "It's not the end of the world, and yes, it does matter." She grew serious. "It always matters."

Some small flake of dread sank through his being. Her parents had been activists. Ineffectual activists in an idiot cause, but an upbringing like that had to have *some* effect on her character.

"Can I buy you a burger?" he asked.

She grinned. "If you could buy me a burger, I'd give you a medal. But you can buy me an elk kabob." Ninel jerked her head at a nearby café. "What have you got to trade?"

"Never fear," John said, "I'm prepared. I wouldn't offer if I wasn't." He gave her a reproachful look that made her laugh.

"We can park in front," she told him. "I'll meet you there."

When she caught up with him and had finished locking down her bike, she grinned to see him pull a pair of rabbits from his saddlebags. "That should do," she said. "If they're fresh."

He gave her another reproachful look. "Fresh this morning," he said. "Guaranteed."

The burly man behind the counter of the improvised restaurant had a pump-action shotgun and a skeptical expression. That thawed as John shoved the two carcasses across the wood; he bent, sniffed, felt, and nodded.

"Okay, you got credit at the Copper King," he said. "Rack your weapons there, enjoy yourselves, and no fighting or you go out in pieces."

"Come again to Burger King, and will you have fries with that?" John muttered under his breath.

The platters of grilled elk chunks on sticks *did* include potatoes; boiled, of course—nobody was wasting oil on cooking—but still tasty to carbohydrate-starved bodies, with a little salt.

"So," Ninel said, biting into the juicy meat, "did you get to the camp in B.C.?"

"Not all the way," John said. "As you said, it's a long haul."

She shrugged. "I'm a little disappointed. I've been wondering what it's like and if I should pack up and go. Thing is, I don't want to leave my dogs behind."

"Dogs?" he said. "You have a team?"

Shaking her head, Ninel smiled. "Only if you think a pair is a team. No, they're good hunting dogs, and they're my buds. I couldn't just abandon them."

"I like dogs," he said, a little wistfulness in his tone. He sipped his chamomile tea, not liking it much; then putting the mug down, he looked at her carefully.

"What?" she said.

"I just"—he shrugged—"I have my doubts about these buses and trucks. Who's behind this? Do you know?"

"The government, I suppose." She looked him in the eye. "Who else?"

"Our government, or Canada?"

"Both, I would imagine." She frowned. "What are you suggesting? You think these people are being kidnapped or something? By *Canadians*? You can't be serious."

He laughed. "When you put it like that," he said. "But seriously, you don't know who is behind it, and I find that worrying. How did they recruit you anyway?"

"I knew some people who were involved and they asked me to help." She looked at him with concern. "They're good people, John. I don't think they'd hurt anybody."

"So because you trusted them, you were willing to take the whole thing on faith."

Ninel sat back, frowning. "I feel like I'm being accused of something here. Not least of being stupid, and I don't like it."

He held her gaze with a severe look of his own. "I didn't go all the way to the camp because the buses stopped short of it. Everyone figured it was a rest stop and got off. Understandably, after a ride of about four hours." She was frowning in puzzlement. "They were attacked."

"Whoa!" she said quickly. "That doesn't mean the people who run the transports are responsible."

"C'mon, Ninel! Who else knew that the automated transports were going to stop right there? Huh? But beyond that, I know that people from the camp came hunting them."

"Of course they came looking," Ninel protested. "If the transports never arrived, or arrived empty, of course they went looking. Why wouldn't they?"

"Hon, something is wrong here."

"I'm not your hon and maybe the something wrong here is you! Maybe there are people out there who don't want Americans settling in Canada. Did that ever occur to you? And if the army can discover how to make those trucks run, couldn't someone else figure out how to run them by remote control? Maybe this is a plot *against* the people running the transports and the camps, rather than a plot *by* them. Ever think of that? And what are you doing to try and help? Anything?"

John sat back, wondering where he'd lost control of this conversation. Though he did have an impression that Ninel's reaction was sincere. "I'm doing a few things," he said gruffly.

Why am I feeling defensive? he wondered. *I've spent my whole life preparing to fight Skynet and she's making me feel like a slacker when it's her that's sending people down the damn thing's maw.*

"Look, I'm not judging you," he said aloud. "I'm just asking questions. Maybe I could ask your friends?"

She looked less belligerent, and a bit uncertain. "I'll ask them if they'll talk to you. No guarantees."

"I take it they're not still looking for volunteers."

Her mouth curved up at one corner. "Somehow I don't see you as a volunteer. Maybe it's the bike."

ALASKA

"He wants to talk to us?" Balewitch said, her eyebrows almost tangling in her hairline she was so surprised. She had to make an effort of will not to grin like a wolf.

Perfect!

Ron Labane wanted John Connor found and neutralized and John Connor wanted to come over for coffee. Life generally didn't work out this well.

"Do you know him?" Ninel asked. It was clear she'd noted Balewitch's surprise.

"No, but Ron does," Dog said. "And I don't think he likes him."

Balewitch threw him a warning glance, which Ninel saw.

"What did he say?" she asked, sinking slowly into one of the kitchen chairs.

"That he was dangerous and that he was trouble and that we should stop him now before he recruits too many followers." Dog grimaced into his cup of mint tea. "Christ, I wish I had a beer."

Balewitch rolled her eyes in disgust and Ninel looked from one to the other. "Is this the right John Connor?" she asked. "I've never seen him with anyone else." Her eyes took on a distant look for a moment. "When he used to hang out at the Klondike, he was the kind who just wanted to shoot pool and have a laugh. I never heard him talking politics or anything like it."

"Ron thinks he is," Dog said, still looking into his tea.

Balewitch glared at him. "Still, both John and Connor are common names. And the guy Ron was talking about was seen in Canada."

"In Canada?" Ninel said. Nervously she brushed her bright hair back from her face.

Dog and Balewitch exchanged glances.

"Yeah," Balewitch said, at her most grandmotherly. "We didn't want to tell you, but . . . There was an attack on the last convoy." She lowered her eyes and pursed her lips. "A lot of people were killed and we still haven't found the survivors." She looked up at Ninel. "A young man on a motorcycle was one of the shooters; dark hair, sunglasses. But Ron is sure that it's this John Connor."

The younger woman's mouth opened slightly and she hunched forward as though struck by a sudden pain. She blinked rapidly, then looked at the concerned faces of her two friends and comrades. "It does sound like him," she said quietly. "What do you want me to do?"

"Get close to him," Dog said, leaning forward avidly. "Find out what he's up to."

Ninel blinked at him, then frowned. "Don't you think we should tell the authorities?"

"Ye-ah," Balewitch said, her tone of voice implying that she was asking Dog just what he was thinking.

"Why?" Dog asked. "They'll want proof and all we've got is suspicions. But! If we can get him to commit to some course of action and then catch him in the act, we'll have him dead to rights." His eyes told Balewitch he was intending to lean heavily on the dead part.

"Humph," Balewitch said thoughtfully. "I see your point." She looked at their young recruit. "Are you game?"

Ninel frowned uncertainly. "I don't know," she said. "I'm not one of those glib people who can make people trust them."

Balewitch stared at the pretty young thing, her chin cupped in her hand. *If I had her looks, I could convince the average man that he had a purple ass and tentacles on his head.*

It wasn't modesty, she knew, it was too unselfconscious for that. This was pure innocence, and if she couldn't work it into a shape she could use, she'd change her name to Turkey-girl.

She patted the girl's hand. "Don't worry about it. Just try and spend more time with him. Tell him we weren't at home and you couldn't find us. Invite him to your house for dinner to make it up to him. After that, let nature take its course. Just remember, the less said the better. That way you can't trip yourself up and you'll have less to remember if he asks you questions."

"Don't worry," Dog said, giving Ninel a comradely slap on the back that was meant to sting. "You can do it! And remember, it's for the cause."

Ninel's expression went from thoughtful to determined at that, and the two Luddites grinned at each other over her head.

NEAR FAIRBANKS

"You're sure about this?" John said, scratching distractedly. *Wish we had more soap. God, if typhus gets started . . .*

Far away in the Quebec wilderness, Snog rolled his eyes. The satellite link didn't convey quite the full smug self-confidence of it. "No, I just thought it would be fun to tease you. Yeah, I'm sure! You must have received the same image I'm sending."

"Hey, hey, simmer down." *Sheesh, I should know better than to question the maestro.* "I'm thrilled, honest. It's just so good, it's like it's too good to be true."

"Unless Skynet has discovered our link, and there's no evidence of that, this is the real deal."

John looked down at the schematic on his screen. This was one of the famous automated factories built in secret in wilderness areas; the drawing showed the loading zones, the microhydro station that powered it, the computer centrum . . .

That thing was not built with human beings in mind, he thought. *All those conveyor belts, and the passages are just about big enough for a large dog. Probably have little repair 'bots scurrying around in 'em . . .*

The resistance geeks had traced its whereabouts based on painstaking study of innumerable satellite photos. John had known that it had to be somewhere near the fake relocation camp, but even so, finding its exact whereabouts had been a herculean labor.

"Okay," John said. "Congratulations to you and your team."

"Thank you, O Great Military Dickhead," Snog intoned.

Connor chuckled; he'd told Snog his teenage nickname for the self he was growing toward . . . "You're welcome, my son. Go forth and find me some more."

"*More?* Connor wants *more?* God, you're such a taskmaster. You sure your name isn't Legree?"

"Get used to it, bud. This goes on for a while. Take care out there in les boonies. Connor, out."

John leaned back in his chair, his eyes gleaming. This would be their first big assault on Skynet. His blood sang at the thought. *Finally, I get to strike first.*

DOT LAKE, ALASKA

Ninel saw John through the café window and waved. He waved back, put down the kickstand, and took off his helmet. Her heart-beat sped up and her mouth went dry at the thought of what she was about to do, but she needed to find out the truth about him. Was he the one Labane was looking for?

He didn't seem like a crazed killer. She watched him swing his leg over the bike as he dismounted. He had an easy grace about him that she admired. Actually there was a great deal about him that she admired. She so didn't want him to be the one they were look-ing for . . .

■   ■   ■

She's looking a little tense, John thought. He smiled at her even though he was feeling a bit stressed himself. *Well, you're supposed to feel a bit tense on the first serious date.* He went to the counter first, as the new custom dictated, and pulled out a small, half-empty tube of toothpaste. It rang on the counter with the resonance of a gold coin in happier days.

"Cuppa mint tea and a bowl of rabbit stew," Ray, the owner, said.

John nodded; he thought he was being robbed, but the smell of the cooking meat and its wild-garlic accompaniment was making his mouth water. Besides, he was eager to talk to Ninel and didn't want to waste time dickering. He could feel her looking at him, her eyes burning holes in the back of his leather jacket. In seconds, the order was in front of him on a tray. Ray had added a side of bread and John nodded and grinned in appreciation. He hadn't had bread in weeks.

He put the tray down on the table between himself and the girl. "Check this out," he said, indicating the bread.

She smiled and nodded. "I had just gotten in new supplies," she said. "So I have quite a bit of flour. Enjoy."

He did, savoring every mouthful.

"I keep thinking about that hamburger you offered me," Ninel said. "Never thought I'd want something so badly, y'know? It's like my teeth want to chew ground beef and nothing else will do."

"I hear ya," John said. "I hadn't realized how much I miss bread. Butter would be nice," he said philosophically. "But this is great."

She bit her lip and looked down, drawing a circle out of a spot of spilled tea. "They weren't home," she said, and glanced up at him through her lashes. She shrugged and sat back. "I have no idea where they are, or when they'll be back. They do this, go away and come back with no explanation."

He looked at her for a moment and she lowered her eyes uncomfortably. "Was that why you looked so tense?" he asked. "Did you think I'd be mad or something?"

Ninel sighed and looked down at her hands. "I dunno. You weren't specific, but you were implying some awful things." She frowned and raised her eyes to his face. "Now I don't know what to do."

They looked at each other, both communicating distress, then mutually lowered their eyes.

"I can understand how you feel," John said. "They're friends, I guess, people you've trusted anyway, and now you can't even ask them questions."

"Yes!" she said. "That's it exactly. I'm supposed to organize another group day after tomorrow, but how can I under these circumstances? And, you know, they might not know anything more than I do."

He nodded sympathetically. "But you still want to do something."

"Well, yuh." She shook her head. "Things aren't going to get better by themselves."

He looked at her. Should he try to recruit her for the resistance?

She might already be in the enemy camp without realizing it, he thought. Of course, so might her friends. But somehow he doubted it. It wasn't until recently that he'd realized that at least for a time Skynet needed, and would continue to need, human allies. Whether *they* realized that they were helping a homicidal machine was immaterial. Given what had happened in Missouri, at least some of Skynet's minions were willing, even eager, to kill for it.

If he could convince Ninel that these people were up to no good, or at least were being led to do no good, he might also be able to convince her to feed him reports about what they were up to. It would be a lot easier than trying to get one of his people to try infiltrating the group cold. Which might even be impossible.

"Look," he said quietly, "maybe we shouldn't get too deeply into this here."

She looked around. It was just Ray and them, and though the proprietor seemed busy, he might be listening. With the loss of all radio signals, people's voices seemed to carry more. Ninel smiled. "Okay," she said. "Why don't you come home with me for dinner."

He blinked.

"I'll make French toast."

"I'm there," John said.

Even if she intended to shoot him, if there was the remotest chance that he'd get some French toast first, it was worth the risk.

■ ■ ■

He'd wondered how long it would take them to get to the place where he'd picked her up a few weeks ago, but once they hit the highway, she'd sped along at close to forty-five miles an hour. And once they left the road for the narrow track through the bush, he was definitely at a disadvantage.

Her cabin was small and half-buried, but looked snug and well made. A pair of elk antlers decorated the area above the doorframe. There were a few chickens pecking in the yard. Two dogs— huskies—sprang to attention, barking furiously at the motorcycle.

They must *be well trained,* he thought. *They haven't eaten the chickens yet.*

Ninel put her bike on its stand and went to them, speaking softly and mussing their ruffs. They greeted her with waving tails and hanging tongues but kept a weather eye on John.

"Spike and Jonze," she said, pointing at one and then the next identical dog. John looked at her askance and she shrugged. "I like his work. C'mon in."

The space was small and somewhat cluttered, but it was clean and as neat as it could be given the crowded conditions. *The bed looks comfortable,* he thought, glancing at the fur-covered double bed. He resolutely turned his eyes and mind away. "Anything I can do to help?" he asked.

"Yeah. Sit down and stay out of my way." She went to a camp-stove setup and got it started. "You can keep me entertained. Tell me about yourself."

If only I could, he thought automatically. Then: *Hey, wait a minute, it's post–Judgment Day! I* can *tell her about myself.* Well, except for the part about his father not being born yet. Which actually was a big part of the story.

"I was raised by my mom," he said. "Mostly in Central America and points south. She, ah, she never got along well with the authorities. I never knew my father."

But I will! In fact, I'm going to set him up with my mom, which is weird stuff.

"Um, grew up all over the place, never finished high school . . ."

This sounds depressing, but it was actually kinda cool, most of the time. Not the times we were being pursued by Terminators, or my time in foster care, but a lot of the time.

"Sounds a lot like my folks!" Ninel grinned at him over her shoulder. "What was your mom in trouble for? Environmental work? Peace activist?"

"Ah . . . blowing up computer factories, mostly," John said, and hastily added: "But she didn't hurt people. She got blamed for a lot of stuff . . . other elements . . . did."

"It works—well, used to work—that way," Ninel said sympathetically.

He shook his head. "I don't really like talking about myself." *Because even now some well-meaning individual might think I'd look better in a straitjacket.* "You could tell me more about yourself," he suggested.

"I'm cooking. Tell me what you've been doing since Judgment Day."

This was the first time he'd heard the term outside his own family, and it chilled him. "What?"

She looked up from what she was doing. "Judgment Day?" she said. "That's what my friends call it."

"Oh."

It had come from Skynet? Just when he thought he couldn't hate the damn thing anymore, it got, well, judgmental on him.

The first slab of bread hit the hot pan with a sizzle and he grinned in anticipation. "Thank you for this," he said.

She smiled at him. "My pleasure."

They gobbled most of a loaf of bread. *Well, I'm gobbling most of a loaf, liberally covered with really rad wild-blueberry syrup.*

Again, the only thing missing was butter, but who cared, it was fantastic.

"I'm glad you liked it," she said, clearing the plates.

"Let me do the washing-up," John offered. "It's the least I can do."

"I will," she said, grinning at his surprise. "I'll just stoke the woodstove so we can have some hot water."

He'd noted the chill in her house, but had said nothing, understanding her desire to be thrifty with the wood. It was backbreaking labor and he wondered if there were enough trees out there to keep the fires going *this* winter. Well, in Alaska, yeah . . .

He washed, she dried, and they talked and joked companionably. Ninel fed her dogs, much to their ecstatic gratitude, while John watched from a polite distance. Huskies were a little too close to wolves to take liberties with, in his opinion.

When they went back in she brewed some rose-hip tea.

"Tastes like math paper," he said with a grimace.

She laughed and put a pot of honey on the table. "We're probably the last generation that will know what that means. At least for a while."

He drizzled honey into his tea, looked up and met her eyes, and slowly smiled. She blushed and lowered her eyes, then looked up at him through her lashes.

He sipped his tea and smiled. "That's better."

Biting her lips, she took the honey pot and drizzled honey into her cup, then broke up laughing.

"Are we thinking the same thing?" he asked, grinning wickedly.

"Yes, I'm terribly afraid that we are," she said, still laughing.

"Don't be afraid," he said. He took her free hand in both of his. "There's nothing to be afraid of."

■ ■ ■

John held her in his arms and looked down at the bright head resting on his shoulder, feeling her soft, rhythmic breath upon his chest, and felt . . . wonderful. More relaxed than he had felt in a long time. He caressed her shoulder with his thumb and smiled.

He liked her. He knew it wasn't love; he'd had that with Wendy and he'd recognize it if it came to him again. But he really liked this girl, and who knew what that could lead to? He admired her self-reliance and enjoyed her sense of humor. He sensed, though, that she was one of those lost souls casting about for a noble cause. He'd like to be the one to give it to her . . .

"Where did you get the scars?" she said drowsily, tracing the lines down the left side of his face.

"Would you believe a cybernetically controlled leopard seal slashed my face?"

Ninel laughed and poked him in a sensitive spot. "If you don't want to tell me, that's okay. But I like your sense of humor!"

CHAPTER 14

ALASKA

uddites?" John said, peering at the screen.

A trainee—he showed real promise at scout work—brought in another armful of split wood and pitched a few billets into the woodstove. It thumped and gave a muffled *whoosh* as he adjusted the air intake, and the day's damp chill receded a bit.

"Yes, sir. That's our intel," Jack Brock said.

John rolled his eyes. Jack was still completely enamored of military parlance, while John Connor was already sick of it.

Better get over that, he thought with resignation. It was going to be the lingua franca for the next thirty years or more. *And every calling needs a jargon. It helps keep the organization's purpose sharp and clear.*

"There must be millions of 'em," Brock was saying.

Connor jerked his mind back to the matter at hand. "World-wide," he agreed. "Hundreds of thousands, at least." He sat forward. "Good work, Jack. Congratulate Reese and Susie for me on a job well done. Out."

"Thanks, John. Will do. Out."

Luddites. He'd known that Skynet had human assistance, but he'd never expected it to come from *that* quarter. The progress-hating, machine-scuttling, science-despising Luddites would seem to be the last people Skynet could get to help. And yet . . .

They share a lot of the same goals. Namely, reducing humanity in population and power. Of course I don't think that most Lud-dites want to reduce humanity to zero. But there would be some who would. He winced. *Wendy would have hated this.*

Connor moved out onto the now bustling floor of the once abandoned building that his mother had acquired—it had originally been HQ and smelter for a series of gold dredges. They'd spent a lot of time and money improving the building from the inside before Judgment Day. Outside, they were well disguised as a semidilapidated series of aging buildings of unpainted pine. Inside, they were weather tight and roomy enough to provide barracks, offices, training areas, a canteen, and hardened storage for tons of electronic equipment.

John still went home occasionally; he needed his alone time. But it made his heart swell with pride to see the people they'd recruited before Judgment Day pitching in and recruiting people themselves. The resistance was really shaping up.

It helps that we're not coming from behind this time, he thought. They'd drained Dieter's freely given fortune to build this. Exploited his every contact and resource, and it was paying off, visibly.

Now they were in a kind of race, to see if they could prevent Skynet from building its army, or at least defeating it far sooner than they had the first time.

Would that mean that Kyle Reese would never be born, or that having been born, he'd never be sent into the past?

Will I disappear midsentence one day? John wondered. *Who cares? What's one life if I can save millions by giving mine.*

He'd never liked the idea that he was destined to send his father to his death. If he could prevent that by ceasing to exist, well, *C'est la guerre.* He grinned. *It isn't like I'd know.*

COMODORO RIVADAVIA, ARGENTINA

"I'm not asking for anything like your full production," Sarah said. "I'm only asking for a slight increase to those countries you've already been supplying."

"But all to the advantage of the United States," Señor Reimer said. "Do we really wish to see the United States once again so powerful?"

Sheesh! Sarah thought. *To hear people down here talk, you'd think we were the Roman legions; invading everywhere, stealing everything that wasn't nailed down—including the people—and then pretending it was a good deal because one day the remaining folks would be citizens. We have our faults, God knows, but we weren't that bad.*

Sarah's Spanish was virtually accent-free—with a tinge of Paraguay and Nicaragua—and she seldom bothered to mention that she was from California. It simplified things. Unfortunately, it was impossible to get this business done without being a bit more up-front.

For a moment she looked out the window, controlling her temper. Comodoro was on the northern edge of Patagonia; steep ground fell to the cold-looking gray water, and oil storage tanks and pipelines and refinery cracking towers were everywhere. There wasn't much of a tang in the air because the wind blew constantly—she'd considered hiding out around here when she was on the run with John after the attack on Cyberdyne, but the perpetual howling and the bleak flat landscape didn't appeal to her. Comodoro's other buildings were mostly medium size and flat-roofed; one of the bigger ones had a ten-story-high colored Coke ad, something that sheep ranchers came miles to see.

And they have to sell the oil, she told herself. Argentina hadn't been badly hit—no actual nuclear bombs, yet. That didn't prevent economic collapse, riots, regional warlordism, and general crisis. She'd have preferred to deal in Venezuela, but the Maricaibo fields there had been major enough to be on a target list.

"It is unlikely that the United States will ever be that powerful again," she said aloud. "In the meantime, there are people there that need our help. And there are opportunities here for those with the vision to take them. South America is in a position to take its place as a world leader."

Reimer looked thoughtful. "Ah, but *which* South American country shall lead? That is the question."

Long training kept Sarah from rolling her eyes and yelling: "No, it's not, you idiot!"

The United States never would have gotten powerful enough for morons like this one to resent it if the big question had been: Which state is going to be the most important? No wonder Simón Bolívar, South America's equivalent to George Washington, had died despairing and saying his career had been like trying to plow the sea . . .

Things would have been tougher still, of course, if the early Americans had had Skynet to contend with instead of just the British. But telling Señor Reimer about a great computer menace would certainly end this already shaky interview.

Poor bastard, she thought. *Sooner or later Skynet's going to come after you, too—with nukes or plagues or HKs, or all of the above.*

She'd worked her way from Mexico to near the tail of Argentina reaffirming arrangements for food and other supplies to be shipped to their resistance cells in the United States. But suddenly some people she already had contracts with had begun to object that she didn't represent the U.S. government. Which was weird because she'd never claimed to. Since whipping out a pistol and blowing them away was not going to help, Sarah had applied diplomacy and the occasional—

All right, more than the occasional bribe.

Oddly enough, it was the criminals who had been most likely to stick to their agreements. But then, they *knew* she might whip out a pistol and blow them away. The certain knowledge that it was a possibility kept things conveniently civilized; not to mention that they knew she had backup who'd rescue her or at least avenge her death. Which was especially useful because she was a woman trying to work within a very macho society.

The wise criminal knew that a gun didn't care if its user wore nail polish and perfume. But a lot of the politicians and businessmen she'd dealt with were sexist goons who, if she drew down on them, might well mention how big the gun looked in her dainty little hand.

So far, though, in spite of complications, her success rate had been pretty high. But fuel was the crucial element, and that was hard to pry out of the hands of oilmen. Particularly those who suddenly saw themselves as world leaders.

If only she could tell them that they were in more danger than they imagined. But Skynet wasn't ready to make its move yet, so any attempt to reveal its evil plans would get her laughed out of South and Central America and possibly right into another mental institution.

Never thought I'd wish to see a Terminator, Sarah thought. *But I really, truly, wish one would crash in here right now and smack the smirk off Reimer's fat face.*

Reimer's assistant burst in from the outer office, his dark eyes shining. "Sir! An American submarine has just entered the harbor!"

Even better than a Terminator, Sarah thought, though she was impressed by the timing. This might actually be something she could use. Assuming she could prevent the Argentine government from seizing it.

By mutual agreement, she and Reimer ended the meeting, scheduling their discussion for another day.

■   ■   ■

Captain Thaddeus Chu was not happy. He hadn't been happy since he'd disobeyed Admiral Read's orders to report to the nuclear cinder that was San Diego. Read had answered Chu's every request for confirmation with the proper codes, and the voice was definitely the admiral's. Other officers had agreed with Chu about that. But they, too, had noticed something not quite right with the way he spoke.

Something besides his insane order to commit suicide.

In addition, Chu had monitored a civilian broadcast by a woman named Sarah Connor, who had described the situation with terrifying accuracy. Unbeknownst to the general public, every navy ship recently refitted with a complex new cyberbrain had found itself firing missiles with no executive orders to do so and wandering the sea-lanes helplessly as their crews starved.

His old lady had been at the bottom of the list to be refitted; she was an *Ohio*-class missile sub originally equipped with Trident missiles, but converted to a commando carrier with a hundred SEALs aboard. They would have been in San Diego when the bombs dropped but for an accident that had required fairly extensive patching, delaying their departure from Okinawa for a critical two weeks.

Chu had been looking forward to having a better job done at the naval facility in California; now it looked like she'd bear those scars on her nose for the rest of her days. And yet he was grateful for that accident; though he pitied those who'd lost family in California, he was not sorry to be alive himself.

They were all but out of food now and other sundries. Most West Coast ports in the United States were so much rubble, and what research could be done from the ship indicated that the East Coast wasn't much better. Nor were the coasts in China, Japan, Russia, or Europe.

South America, however, had possibilities. Which was why they were here in Comodoro Rivadavia—major city, good port facilities, and a history of friendly relations with the United States. Not that that necessarily meant much in these post-nuclear-holocaust days.

Bob Vaughan, the XO, knocked and stuck his head through the door of Chu's ready room—which was about the size of a walk-in closet. A submarine was still a sub, even if it displaced as much as the HMS *Dreadnought.*

"There's a delegation from the city to see you, Captain."

"Right there," Chu said. He sat for a moment, collecting his thoughts, then picked up his hat and followed the executive officer up on deck. He'd decide about letting people through the hatchway later.

Waiting on the dock were a number of impatient-looking men in good suits and one guy in a military uniform with some very impressive medals on his chest. They looked up at Chu, obviously waiting for an invitation. The temperature was chilly enough to make you remember that the seasons were reversed in the southern hemisphere, not to mention the gunk still circulating in the upper atmosphere.

No honor guard or suchlike, Chu thought. He was surprised; they looked like the kind of men who enjoyed ceremony. He walked down to the end of the gangway—which *did* have armed guards, his own men—and nodded to the delegation.

"Gentlemen," the captain prompted.

"We'd like a few words with you, Captain?" a particularly sleek specimen said in excellent English.

Chu wasn't sure if the question was a request for his name or confirmation of his rank. *Both, probably.* "I'm Thaddeus Chu," he said. "Captain, USS *Roosevelt.* And I'll be happy to speak to you gentlemen. You're welcome to board, but I must remind you that if you do come aboard you are entering United States territory."

The delegation stared up at him for some time without moving or speaking. Then their spokesman, who had not deigned to identify himself, took a step forward.

"You must know, Mr. Chu," he said, with a frown that probably hid some inward glee, "that the United States has effectively ceased to exist."

"It's Captain Chu, sir. And you may find that assessment to be premature."

"Come, come, Captain. The U.S. is all but hammered flat, in all probability never to rise again. If you didn't think so yourself, you wouldn't have stopped here." He gave the captain a smug smile. "Would you?"

Chu looked down at him with a sinking heart and a poker face. He honestly hadn't expected it to be easy, but he'd hardly expected them to be so blatant. "You are welcome to board, gentlemen, with the understanding that upon boarding you are in U.S. territory."

The men on the dock looked at one another and conferred quietly. Then the spokesman stepped forward once more.

"Perhaps we should leave you to contemplate your options, Captain," he said. He gestured toward the mouth of the harbor.

Chu's eyes widened as he watched a huge oil tanker slide into place behind the *Roosevelt*. He turned to stare at the grinning men on the dock.

"Just send us a message when you're prepared to be reasonable." The man waved affably and the whole group turned and walked away.

The captain crossed his arms over his chest and watched them go in disbelief. When he'd pulled into this berth his biggest worry had been how he was going to pay for supplies. Now he was faced with capitulation to as-yet-unknown terms or doing something pretty vile. Though with a hundred SEALs aboard, he should be able to limit any necessary damage.

But damn! I don't want to go down in history as a pirate. Nor did he want to be remembered for simply surrendering his ship. His father had arrived in the United States from South Vietnam via a rickety boat and a stiff brush with Thai pirates. He didn't intend to start the family saga over again in Latin America.

Reasonable, my royal Asian-American ass! he thought, and turning went below. "Get me Commander Smith," he half snarled.

■　■　■

Sarah watched the show through binoculars; Comodoro fortunately had a nice selection of high places from which to view all the kingdoms of the earth—or at least of Patagonia. She didn't need to be a lip-reader to work out what had happened. As soon as she'd seen that tanker on the move, she'd guessed how this conference was going to end. The sub was neatly trapped and there wasn't a lot the captain could do about it. Nothing civilized anyway. Clearly they needed help.

Sarah turned and walked away. She had a number of arrangements to make, and information to acquire.

And I'm not all that civilized, either, she thought.

■ ■ ■

After a cheerless supper of steamed rice and water, Chu had retired to his cabin to "consider his options." Which prospect made him glad of his bland meal. He had decided not to allow shore leave as he'd originally planned in hopes of allowing the men to find their own more substantial dinners. It was a sure bet that any American leaving the *Roosevelt* would be immediately arrested.

Of course, then at least they'd get a square meal.

There was a tap on the door.

"Enter," Chu called out.

"Sir," his XO said, "there's a message for you, but you'll have to take it at the decoder terminal."

The captain raised his brows. It was a rare message that couldn't be patched through to his quarters. "A message from command?"

"No, sir. It's being transmitted via the hydrophones—modulated sonic from outside the hull. Expertly blurred—the sonar watch can't give a location."

"Who is it from?" he asked, with a spurt of well-concealed alarm. *If the locals have frogmen outside the hull with limpet mines, we are fucked.*

The younger man looked at Chu and swallowed, more emotion than he usually showed in a week; he was very black, and stress thickened the Mississippi gumbo of his accent. "She says she's Sarah Connor, sir. The message could be coming from anywhere."

Chu rose and followed his second-in-command down the narrow corridor. Avoiding the jagged bits that stuck out ready to tear your uniform or bang your elbow, and color-coded conduits, was second nature, but he did appreciate shoreside fresh air. The big boomers didn't develop a ripe stink like the old-time pigboats, but things did get sort of stale after a few weeks submerged.

And sailors get sort of thin without food, he thought grimly. *Let's hope this Sarah Connor can help.*

■   ■   ■

Sarah floated beside the sub waiting to hear from the captain; it would have been dark fifteen feet down in daylight, and this was well after sunset. The water was cold, but her wet suit made it tolerable; she didn't think she'd need to worry about anyone on board finding her here. They were being carefully watched from the harbor and from the oil tanker, and at the first sign that the sub might be deploying sailors, there'd be trouble.

Her expensive face gear would allow her to speak to them as though she were on dry land. Eventually they'd figure out that she was right beside the sub, but probably not until she'd swum away.

"This is Captain Thaddeus Chu of the USS *Roosevelt.* Please identify yourself."

Her lips quirked, not a request. "This is Sarah Connor," she said. "You may have heard my broadcast."

"Yes, ma'am." *Damn, it did sound like her.* "What is it you want?"

"To help. Down-coast at Puerto Deseado, there's a cache of supplies waiting. You'll have to pick them up yourselves. I'll be there waiting for you."

"Thank you, ma'am," Chu said. "But we have a small problem here." *Which you may have noticed since it's as big as a city block and sitting on my back.*

"It's being taken care of, Captain. Be prepared to move momentarily. Connor out."

"Ma'am?" Chu said. He looked at the radioman.

"She's gone, sir."

Chu looked up and met Bob Vaughan's eyes for a long moment. Then he shrugged. "If worse comes to worst we've had a drill. If we're lucky and the lady is as good as her word, we're back in business. Status?"

"Ready to go, sir, as per your orders."

That was one good thing about a nuke boat; as long as you kept the reactor hot, you were ready to roll whenever you wanted, and you didn't have to worry about wasting fuel much.

■ ■ ■

Sarah swam off, guided by an occasional glimpse at the GPS compass on her wrist, confident in the knowledge that she'd hired the best pirates that pure gold could buy. She'd left them scaling the side of the huge tanker. They were well armed and quite capable of capturing the small band of soldiers aboard and two of them could pilot the tanker if no crew had been left aboard.

She popped up on the far side of the harbor, well away from the lights the army had set up. Her battered Jeep—driving something too desirable, like a Humvee, was asking for trouble—and clothes were all as she'd left them; something very loud and unfortunate would have happened if anyone had tried to lift them.

The pebble beach was rough under her hands and knees as she leopard-crawled up from the waves, and the air was cold on her naked flesh as she peeled out of the synthetic fabric and quickly donned her clothes, shivering and stamping. The high-tech binoculars came next. There was nothing she could do to make the operation go better at this point.

God, she thought suddenly. *All these years . . . I wonder how Sarah Connor the student and waitress would have felt? Men may be dying out there—because of me—and I'm completely calm about it now.*

Then she shrugged. That was how it *had* to be if Skynet was to be beaten. What had that German philosopher Dieter told her about said? *He who fights dragons becomes a dragon?*

No muzzle flashes through the binoculars, though. She switched to thermal imaging . . .

They've got her engines hot.

She could see the heat plumes from the stack at the rear, and more faintly as a blob of different color on the side of the hull at the stern. The tanker wasn't a super-giant, which would have used steam turbines and taken a long time to move. It was a medium-size job used to shuttle refined products along the coast, about fifty thousand tons, powered by big diesels. Those you could fire up right away; if it was even remotely modern, the whole process could be controlled from the bridge at a pinch.

Yep, there she goes.

So slowly that at first it didn't seem she was moving at all. The tanker had backed halfway to its own berth before the soldiers onshore realized what was happening, and the sub had begun its turn away from the dock. It maneuvered cautiously—*Ohio*-class boats were a good five hundred and sixty feet long—but swiftly, backing and then heading for the entrance to the harbor with a rush that sent a smooth black wave breaking into foam.

Sarah grinned as she gathered her diving gear and tossed it in the back of her Jeep and vaulted into the driver's seat. She had a sub to meet.

■   ■   ■

The only good thing you could say about Puerto Deseado was that it was more picturesque than Comodoro's tangle of refinery tanks.

Which isn't saying much, Sarah Connor thought. *Well, all right, the turn-of-the-century architecture was interesting.*

More important for her purposes, the local government hadn't broken down; there weren't any—well, many—bandits in the area around it, and food was reasonably cheap. Particularly if you liked mutton, because the *estancias* all about had lost their markets.

Sarah was thoroughly sick of it, enough so that the sight of the piled carcasses was faintly nauseating, though she'd long ago overcome any city-girl squeamishness about butchering livestock or game.

Still and all, the sailors will be glad to get it, she thought.

The carcasses were as the trucks had left them; not entirely sanitary, but needs must, and the weather was cold enough that they wouldn't go bad in a day or two. She'd gotten sacks of flour as well, and canned vegetables from the Chubut Valley.

She sat atop the pile of boxes and watched the sub rise gleaming from the waves through her binoculars. Teams of men emerged and began to inflate rafts and put them overside; then some dropped into the sea beside them. They and the men still aboard the sub maneuvered engines onto the craft, climbed aboard the zodiacs, and headed for the shore. She could see the night-vision apparatus on their faces and wondered if they'd spotted her yet.

The men were well trained and efficient; deploying the inflatables with the engines had taken only a little more than five minutes and some of that had been because the rafts needed time to inflate.

Oh, this is a happy day for the resistance, she thought. *A hundred trained SEALs, the rest of the crew, the sub herself . . .*

They were armed, and going by the position of their heads, they most definitely had seen her. Sarah smiled grimly. Technology was a wonderful thing—when it was on your side. She slid down from the top of the pile and stood waiting for the zodiacs to beach themselves.

One of the men trotted up to her—young, hard, fit, in cammo fatigues and body armor, face hard to see behind the goggles. "Are you Sarah Connor?" he asked.

She nodded, then said, "Yes. I'd like to speak to your captain if he wouldn't mind."

"Sarah Connor would like to speak to the captain," he said.

She blinked, then realized he was wearing a throat mike, almost invisible in the dark.

"The captain would like me to bring you now, ma'am," the sailor said.

"Let's fill the raft with supplies," she said. "No need to waste fuel."

The sailor relayed that, then nodded and grabbed a sack of rice. Sarah followed suit, and in short order they had the zodiac filled to capacity and were on their way, cold salt spray flicking into their faces.

Looking up at the conning tower, she saw two shadowy figures outlined against the night sky, above the diving planes. "Permission to come aboard," she called softly.

"Permission granted, Ms. Connor," Chu said. "Welcome aboard."

■   ■   ■

It wasn't until he'd sat at his desk that he realized exactly how small she was. Somehow he'd been expecting an amazon, six feet tall or more and pumped with muscle. Although for a middle-aged lady she was, in fact, quite muscular and moved with the ease of one who kept very fit. He gestured her to a chair and she gave him a polite smile and sat.

"Thank you for your help, Ms. Connor," he said.

"It was my very great pleasure," she answered. "Throwing a spoke in Señor Reimer's training wheels has made my day."

"Reimer?"

"The shark in the sharkskin suit," Sarah told him. "The one who, no doubt, arranged to fence you in. He annoys me." She sat straighter, leaning slightly forward. "But let's get down to business."

"I might have known," Chu said ruefully. He folded his hands on his desktop. "This is a U.S. Navy vessel, Ms. Connor. Neither my crew nor I have any business doing anything with it without orders."

Sarah looked away and nodded slowly, then looked at him from the corners of her eyes. "Are you going to try and tell me that whenever you've come in hailing distance of any other United States Navy vessels, it's been a peaceful, brotherly encounter?"

He blinked before he could stop himself and smiled at her knowing smile. Although how she could have known that when he refused the order to report to San Diego, his ship had immediately begun drawing fire from other navy ships was beyond him. One, a brand-new *Los Angeles*–class boat, had fired a nuclear-tipped homing torpedo toward them, nearly destroying the *Roosevelt*.

But he knew—he *knew*—that the crew had not done it. Calls from the captains' private cell phones had warned him that they had lost control of their ships. Once refitted, they'd been stripped to skeleton crews and it turned out that none of the men and women aboard had the technical knowledge that would have allowed them to take over the computer-controlled vessels. They'd also found out too late that the computers were very well defended with an impressive battery of automatic weapons.

Chu stared at Sarah Connor. *How could she possibly know?* She stared back at him, her expression sad and a little tired. She shook her head and brushed her hair back.

"It doesn't really matter how I know," she said, startling him again. "What matters is that my information is solid."

The captain's aide came in with a tray bearing two bowls of chicken soup and hot biscuits.

"I'm cool," Sarah said when he tried to lay the bowl at her side of the desk. "Why don't you enjoy that."

The aide glanced at Chu, who nodded, and smiling, he picked up the tray and began to leave.

"Talan," Chu said. He pushed the little basket of rolls toward him. "Take a couple of these."

"Thank you, sir." The aide took two and left.

Chu looked at Sarah, who smiled. "Enjoy," she said.

"Thank you again for this, ma'am." The captain dug in; he could practically feel the hot soup giving him strength. "We were pretty much down to our belts."

She grinned briefly, then grew very serious. "Not to spoil your meal, Captain, but I do have some very bad, if not fully unexpected news for you."

"And that would be?" Chu asked.

"There is no federal government anymore."

The captain continued to spoon up soup as he thought about what she'd said. Then he dabbed at his lips with a napkin. "With respect, ma'am, there's no way you could know one way or another."

With a sigh, she laid it down for him. "Skynet. You must have heard of it." At his nod, she went on. "It controlled everything, ships, planes, missiles, and"—she tipped her head forward—"all bases and bunkers. As soon as the missiles started going up, the heads of the government and many of the 'best minds' in the country were hustled to air-conditioned safety in the deepest hardened bunkers on the planet. And since that sorry day, not one of those people has been seen alive. And they never will be.

"The damn computer has run mad, Captain. We didn't send those missiles aloft and your fellow captains haven't been hunting you down of their own free will, and you know it." She spread her hands. "At the very least you must suspect it."

He didn't answer as he split a biscuit, then bit into one flaky half. Sarah Connor was a very disconcerting woman. Half the time she seemed to be reading his mind; the rest of the time she was telling him things that rang horribly true. "Why don't we just cut to the chase here?" he said. "What, exactly, do you want, ma'am?"

"I want you to serve the people of the United States, who desperately need your help." She smiled to see him blink. "Things are worse than you think," she said. "The bombs were just phase one. Since then, people have been rounded up, ostensibly at the behest of the government, and put in relocation and reconstruction camps."

Chu frowned. "Doesn't sound quite right," he said. "But it doesn't seem altogether unreasonable, either."

"Which is why so many have gone along with it," Sarah said agreeably. "In many of these camps, the inmates have been deliberately infected with diseases such as cholera, or they're being forced to work under dangerous conditions with inadequate food and shelter. Men and women in that uniform are doing these things."

He tilted his head toward her. "Men and women in this uniform as distinguished from . . . ?"

"As distinguished from those who are actually in the military." Sarah leaned forward. "No doubt you've heard of Luddites?" He looked troubled, but nodded. "Apparently *some* of them have been preparing for these times with an eye toward reducing the human population of this planet. They're dedicated, well organized, and well supplied. God knows how many deaths they're responsible for so far, or how many they'll be responsible for before they're killed themselves."

"By us?" Chu asked. "Because, you know, I'm not going to send my people out to fight without proof of what you're saying."

Sarah looked at him for a long time before she spoke. "Once again it's Skynet I'm talking about. It's an amazing computer," she said. "There's never been anything like it before, and I hope to my soul there never will be again. The damn thing has become sentient, and it's decided that we are a danger to it and therefore must be eliminated."

"Proof, Ms. Connor," Chu said.

"Surely you heard about all those cars and trucks running amok?" she asked.

"Of course. But . . ."

Sarah sighed deeply. "Skynet was originally created by Cyberdyne Corporation. Cyberdyne created the first completely automated factory. Then, somehow, the plans for those factories became public knowledge and they proliferated all over the planet like some kind of fungus. And in each and every factory Skynet had a root. It hid programming in every car, truck, and tractor produced over the last two years. As the time approached for the government to give it control of all military operations, it began to experiment, sending orders to its various components, taking control from their drivers and causing thousands of accidents. I researched this; I can give you a disk on it." She watched him absorb what she'd said.

"Incidently, it can imitate voices perfectly. Kurt Viemeister programmed it. You may not recognize the name, but he was a master of programming; he extrapolated from voice recognition to voice imitation, right down to characteristic phrasing. Wrote several illegal articles on the subject. I know they're illegal because I know he signed a secrecy contract with the government regarding his work. So if you've been getting messages from well-known people—the president, some admiral, whatever—that was Skynet."

Chu nodded slowly, thinking about the strange way Admiral Read had been talking the last time they spoke, on the day the bombs came down. His eyes flashed to her. "Yet this is still not proof."

"No," she said sadly. "The proof is that I'm not asking you to do anything illegal or against the interests of the United States. I'm asking you to place yourself, your crew, and your ship at the disposal of what we're calling the resistance."

"Who exactly are you resisting?" Chu asked.

"Skynet, the Luddites, and all too soon, whatever machinery Skynet will be producing in its automated factories."

The captain studied her. She seemed quite sane, clear-eyed and intelligent. And given what he and his men had been through during the past weeks, her story held together amazingly well. *Be honest,* he thought, *at least with yourself. Her story holds together better than anything you've thought of yourself.*

"I need to think about this, ma'am," he said aloud.

"God, I would hope so," Sarah said. "While you're thinking about it, may I suggest you turn this baby around and head for Alaska. You'll find a friendly port there; they were hardly touched by the bombs."

"And?"

"And I would very much like to travel there with you."

Chu tipped his head. "And?"

She smiled at him. "And at the moment it's the headquarters for the resistance."

"If we were to accept this proposal of yours," he said, "I assume I would be under your command."

"You'd be under John Connor's command, my son. He's the only alternative to Skynet."

"But for now we'd be under the commander in chief's mom's command, right?"

"Mmm, right."

"Just so I know where I stand, ma'am."

ALASKA

John moved his pointer over a topographical map as he outlined the plan of attack. Forty grim-faced men and women watched him, some taking notes; one woman looked both surprised and amused.

He wasn't used to talking to large groups of people yet and still found his heart pounding whenever he faced an audience. It wasn't made easier by having his newly inducted girlfriend find the whole thing amusing.

Cut her some slack, he told himself. *She might just be nervous.*

Sometimes he found himself almost convulsed with inappropriate laughter when he was nervous. And the kind of attention these people gave him, the sheer focus they put into listening to his every word, was extremely nerve-racking. Especially for someone raised to avoid the limelight. Sometimes he felt naked up here.

Ninel wrinkled her nose at him, and with an effort of will he ignored her. It was too soon to include her on this mission, he knew. But he wanted to convince her to spy on her Luddite friends for him and he didn't think she'd do that without some evidence that it was necessary.

Or at the very least that my organization has a reason to exist and that I'm not a fascist asshole.

John ceded the floor to the leader of the scouting party.

"Trucks arrived and departed at four-hour intervals night and day," he said. "We have no way of knowing what was delivered or if the trucks left full or empty, as they were tied down all around or were actual eighteen-wheelers."

There was a stir at that; the big transport trucks had been gone from the roads since Judgment Day.

"We saw no humans in the vicinity. Nor did we find any sign of automated defenses, though we did find security cameras and microphones. Most were quite obvious. There were several tiers of laser traps around the immediate facility. Other than that, the area seemed clear."

John had worried about that. It could be arrogance, on Skynet's part, ignorance, or a trap. And yet, trap or not, it had to be dealt with. He stood up as the scout finished. "Get some rest," he ordered. "We move out at 0200." He nodded to them and left the dais, heading for Ninel. She rose, smiling, and came to him.

"You almost made me break up, you little skunk," he murmured.

"I can't help it," she said with a little shrug. "Extreme seriousness in other people has always given me the giggles."

He smiled and shook his head. "You stay with me tomorrow."

"I wondered what I was supposed to do," Ninel said. "Everyone else seemed to know exactly where they were supposed to be and what to do, but no one said anything to me. I was starting to think I was going to be left behind."

He started walking toward his office. "The truth is you're not ready for a mission like this," he told her, smiling at her expression of surprise. "Not least because your attitude seems to be that we're all off our collective rockers. I need to show you that this is real," he explained, stopping to look down at her. "This is a real enemy we're fighting, one that wants us all dead."

Ninel tightened her lips and looked down. "I just . . ."

"I know," he said, smiling. "I needed proof myself once." He became solemn again. "Tomorrow you'll have yours."

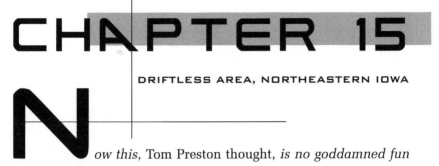

CHAPTER 15

N ow this, Tom Preston thought, *is no goddamned fun at all.*

He bent, leaning on the hoe in his right hand, and pulled up the weed whose roots he'd loosened with the tool. Despite the unusually cold weather, the corn was coming up just fine; the problem was that weeds were doing just fine as well. This particular patch wasn't very large; a scraggly strip along a little brook that ran down the mostly wooded valley between two steep hills—this part of the state looked more like Appalachia than the prairies.

It was only about a quarter of an acre, and carefully irregular so that it wouldn't show much from orbit, even on days without the current heavy gray cloud and occasional spatters of rain. The brook was running high not far off to his left, purling over a bed of brown stones.

He tossed the uprooted thistle onto the mulch—leaves, twigs, grass, reeds—that covered the ground between the knee-high plants and moved on to the next weed, hacking at the base of it with a force that hurt his gloved hands. The turned earth had a cool, yeasty smell, oddly like bread. Despite the cool temperature, he was sweating, and his back hurt. Could it have been only last year that *farming* meant sitting in lordly comfort in an air-conditioned tractor cab, spraying herbicides?

He who does not work does not eat, he told himself.

There were a dozen other people working in the same field, and many more fields like it scattered through the nearby hills—growing corn, potatoes, beets, all sorts of vegetables. They had come along more slowly than usual, but only by a couple of weeks. And they were a bit runty, but very welcome anyway.

The hunting had been very good, with abundant deer and hare. They'd had to shoot a bear a few weeks ago. It had risen cranky from hibernation and had made clear its antipathy toward its new neighbors; besides, they needed its cave for storage.

Tom Preston had liked the flavor of the meat, but he'd been in the minority. Most of their small community had found it too gamy and way too tough. There were still a lot of scavenged canned goods available for the picky, though, and his big gallon jars of multivitamins would keep deficiency diseases at bay for years, if need be.

The community had grown over the past year to a village of more than a hundred people. Most of whom refused to understand why they should avoid being visible from orbit. Things had been so peaceful lately that Tom himself had begun to have doubts.

So when some of the newcomers suggested a party to celebrate their survival, he was willing to go along, to a point.

"Fireworks?" Tom said. "You've got to be kidding!"

"Why? What's wrong with fireworks? It's been wet enough that they shouldn't pose a fire hazard," one of the newcomers, Sam Varela, said.

"Because it's a gigantic, 'We Are Here' sign," Tom said. "I, for one, don't want to end up in those relocation camps you people fled."

The newcomers glared at him resentfully. "We have no reason to think they're still doing that," Sam said through his teeth.

"We have less reason to think they're not," Tom snapped back. "They didn't set up those camps to leave them empty."

"Going was voluntary," a woman pointed out.

"So why are you here?" Preston challenged. "Why here? Why not stay in your homes?"

"We're getting into some pretty deep issues here," his wife, Peggy, said with a frown at her husband. They'd discussed the newcomers in the privacy of their bedroom and his suspicion toward them worried her. "When what we came here to discuss was a picnic."

"Maybe we should get into it," the woman said. "I'm tired of being treated like an interloper when all I want to do is get back to normal."

"Things aren't going to go back to normal," Tom said. *Didn't you notice a few little changes? Like the thermonuclear war?* "Things are going to get a lot worse for a long time before we get anywhere close to normal. But one thing that will at least keep us *safe* is to avoid attracting attention."

"Exactly whose attention are you afraid of?" Sam gave a light laugh and spread his hands. "The army? I'm telling you, they're too busy to go chasing down anyone who doesn't want their help. Who else is there?" He shrugged.

Tom closed his eyes. Sometimes he wondered himself. John Connor had warned that there would be more problems with machines, but with no fuel or electricity, he honestly couldn't see how that could be. Humans, on the other hand . . .

"I'm worried about gangs," Tom said. "I'm afraid that some group of lawless men will come along and take everything we've put together and kill our families." He stood up and started to pace. "These aren't civilized times," he continued. "We're not protected by multiple law enforcement organizations anymore. For the foreseeable future, our fate is in our own hands."

"Oh," the woman said. "When you put it that way it makes perfect sense."

"No fireworks," said Sam.

Tom sat down and forced a smile, but this didn't feel like victory. Rather it felt like number four hundred of a million more arguments.

I almost wish we'd be attacked so these people would realize what they're facing. Almost.

■　■　■

"Honey," Peggy said to him later in bed, "we're seventy-eight adults here and we're well armed. It's unlikely that we'll be faced by any gang more powerful than we are ourselves. Maybe we could loosen up a bit. Don't you think?"

Tom reached out and drew her into his arms. "I was so afraid the day the bombs came down that I'd never see you and the kids again," he said into her sweet-smelling hair. Even now, with no shampoo available, he liked the way her hair smelled. God, but he loved her.

Peggy hugged him tight. "I love you, too," she whispered. "I always did."

"Tell you what," he said. "Let's be extra careful this year, until we've got our feet under us. Then we can talk about loosening up." He pulled back and looked down into her face, barely visible in the moonlight coming through the cabin window. Tom shook his head. "But I'm pretty certain that we're gonna have to build a stockade."

She laughed and buried her head in his shoulder, tickling him so that he laughed, too.

"It's not funny," he said. "I'm serious."

"You are *never* gonna sell them on that idea," she said. "I can just see their faces." And she laughed again.

He smiled at her and held her close. But all the while he was thinking that a stockade was something they'd realize was necessary only *after* they needed it the most. He kissed his wife and prayed that she wouldn't have to suffer for its absence.

SKYNET

It watched the small settlement from the dark beneath the trees; linking with the Terminators' interfaces, Skynet saw the village from multiple angles. This settlement had been surprisingly well hidden for a long time. But the sheer size of the place in an area bereft of any other human activity had eventually brought it to the computer's never-resting attention.

One hundred thirty-two humans, seventy-eight of them adults, no meat animals, lived together here. It was an almost pathologically tidy place; quite unnatural for humans. Their houses were small, built beneath, and with, the surrounding trees; often the lower limbs had been woven more tightly to provide a framework for thatched roofs, while the walls were saplings woven together and smeared with clay mixed with grass. Insubstantial for a permanent dwelling; winter weather would break them down in a short time.

But in summer, if the weather was dry, they should be adequate shelter. Even if the weather was wet, however, they should burn well.

Through a Terminator's sensors Skynet watched the brightly colored silhouettes of the humans through the thin walls of their dwellings. One by one, two by two, they reclined, and the heat images took on the signatures of humans at rest. Its Terminators waited silent and motionless as the moon rose and traversed the night sky.

Many small improvements had made these Terminators more formidable killing machines than the first group, and their weapons were infinitely more powerful than the pellet weapons these humans had at their disposal. Still, Skynet had observed these subjects intensely and knew them to be well schooled in the use of the weapons they did have. This would be a true test, the first of a thousand thousand field terminations, until the final organic pest was hunted down.

Unfortunately, that will require at least another century.

As the last human sank into a dormant state, Skynet gave the signal to attack.

■ ■ ■

Peggy woke first. A light sleeper since the children were born, she heard a crackling sound and opened her eyes to the sight of flames.

"Tom!" she shrieked, leaped from the bed, and ran down the loft stairs toward the already engulfed living room. The heat drove her back and she lay down on the floor to look over the edge of the platform. "Jason! Lisa!" she screamed.

Then Tom was beside her. He looked over the edge and saw his children with their backs against the wall of the cabin, coughing, their eyes wild with fear. "Take Daddy's hand," he shouted over the roar of the flames. If he could just get them up here, they could go out the window, down the rope ladder.

Lisa came toward him, but Jason held back, shaking his head frantically. The little girl reached up and Tom squirmed forward, putting slightly more than half his body over the edge. He could feel his hair start to sizzle. Peggy threw herself across his hips to hold him down, and when Lisa's head came over the edge of the platform, she reached forward and caught the girl's hair. Lisa was already screaming by then, so it made little difference in the volume of her distress, but still, her mother felt terrible.

Once Lisa was safe and huddled against her mother, Tom dove over the edge a second time, reaching toward his son and encouraging, ordering, threatening him to come to Daddy. Suddenly his hair caught fire and Tom reared up in surprise and shock. Peggy caught up the small rag rug at the foot of the bed and threw it over his head.

"I've gotta go down to him, Peg," Tom said. "He's too scared to move. Get Lisa out of here."

She shook her head. "We've got time. You go get him; we'll lower the rope ladder. Then we'll all go." Because they sure weren't going out the front door.

Tom did as she suggested, lowering himself from the platform, trying to ignore the fierce heat on his naked shoulders. He forced himself to move slowly for fear of panicking his son into doing something foolish. "C'mon, Jason," he said soothingly. "Take my hand and let's get out of here, okay?"

The rope ladder came down from above and Jason dove toward it, eluding Tom's clutching hand. Tom couldn't help laughing as he pursued the kid up the ladder. As soon as he reached the top, he grabbed it and dragged it over to the window, tossing it out with a clatter. Jason all but pushed him aside in his eagerness to be out of the flaming cabin and Tom let him go, laughing at his eagerness. *His sister will never let him live this down.*

Jason was halfway down when a blaze of blue light shot through him, emerging in a yellow blossom of sparks. The boy fell backward, a startled expression on his young face. Tom was leaning out the window, frozen with shock, when Peggy yanked his shoulder. If not for the sudden move, the next flash of blue light would have taken off his head.

"What's happening?" Peggy shouted over Lisa's terrified screaming.

"The cellar!" Tom answered.

His wife stared at the rising flames, then at her husband. It didn't look possible. She moved toward the window, but Tom grabbed her and dragged her toward the stairs.

"Tom!" she shouted, objecting, but too frightened to be more coherent.

"Jason's gone," he said tersely, feeling sick to his stomach. "Someone's firing at us. Cellar," he repeated.

Peggy had gone limp. She still held their daughter, still stood, but for now at least, she might as well have been gone. The loft was full of smoke and the heat was becoming more dangerous. Tom grabbed a blanket off the bed and soaked it as well as he could with the contents of their washbowl. Then he wrapped it around them all, and with one arm around his wife's waist barreled down the stairs.

The hatch to the cellar was under the stairs and so, for the moment, was partially sheltered from the scorching heat. Tom yanked it up, then forced his wife down the stairs before him, pulling the hatch closed behind.

Long ago he'd connected the cellar to a narrow rock cave that

came out by the creek. Peggy knew about it and she'd hated it, seeing it as an example of his growing paranoia. The sight of the passage now snapped her out of her shock and she took a deep breath,
turning to him with fear in her eyes.

"Mom and Dad," she said. Then she faltered for a moment and
Tom knew she was thinking of Jason.

"We need to get out of here first," he said, and gave her a gentle push.

He pulled the camouflaged, dirt-coated door closed behind
them, hoping it wouldn't burn. Just inside, he pawed at the doorframe and found the flashlight he'd placed there. He shook it to
charge the battery, then hastened Peggy down the passageway in
the dim light.

The passage wasn't that long, really, about a hundred feet, but
it had seemed the length of Route 66 before he'd been finished. At
the end, where he'd placed another hidden door, he'd also stowed
some clothes and weapons, carefully wrapped in plastic to protect
them. There was food here, too. He sat Peggy on one of the chests.

"Get dressed," Tom ordered, "and stand ready. I'm going to find
out what's going on. I might end up sending some of the other
women and children down here. Take care of them." He grabbed a
shotgun and thumbed in rounds—solid shot, cylindrical rifled slugs.

Then he turned off the flashlight and placed it in his wife's
hand. Feeling his way carefully, he opened the door into the natural cave.

When he reached the creek he squatted down and smeared
some mud from the bank over his face and hands, then crept forward. Peering over the bank, he saw that the whole village was in
flames. He could see forms moving about; by their postures he could
tell they were armed. Then one stood before the flames of a burning
house and he caught his breath, his eyes widening in horror.

Like something from a horror movie, it was skeletal. It turned
its head slowly, like a gun turret searching for a target. Light
gleamed from the metal dome of its skull and through the cage of

its ribs; red light blazed from its eye sockets. Tom sank slowly, until he'd dropped onto his butt.

Shit! he thought.

Slowly he became aware that he was hearing screams. Tom squeezed his eyes tight shut, wishing he could do the same with his ears. Of course he heard screaming. They were trapped in burning buildings, and the only way out was certain death. If he hadn't provided a way out for himself and his family, he'd be screaming, too.

There was a sound off to his right. Not footsteps but the result of stealthy footsteps, crackling leaves and breaking twigs, unavoidable in the deep woods. Tom pressed himself deeper into the dirt of the bank and prayed, making all sorts of promises to God if He would only let him live. He pulled the rifle against his chest, up under his chin, waiting.

He had no idea how many of those things were up there trolling the village for survivors, but he knew one shot would have them *all* down here looking for *him*. That would draw them toward Peggy and Lisa, and he wouldn't let these *things* have them. They wouldn't take them like they'd taken his son. *My boy!* he thought in anguish, and pushed the feeling away, forcing anger into its place, overriding the grief with fury. The machines would *not* succeed. He wouldn't let them.

The soft, methodical sound of footsteps came closer.

■ ■ ■

The Terminator scout came to the end of its designated watch zone and turned away. No humans appeared to have escaped the assault. The enemy had been caught completely unprepared. It appeared that there had been 100 percent enemy casualties.

It stopped every five feet to scan the woods all around, then proceeded on its way. No humans seemed to have escaped the assault.

Terminated, it transmitted to Skynet.

ALASKA

John Connor was worried.

I suspect that's going to be my natural state from here on out, he thought.

The PDA in his hand showed the terrain, his location, and the jump-off points of the other attack parties. The factory was located in a low wooded valley surrounded by spruce-clad hills . . .

And this is the first big operation I've personally commanded, he thought nervously, looking around at the confident faces. *Maybe I* am *the Great Military Dickhead of Mom's dreams, but right now I feel more like a confidence man. Not that that's my only worry.*

By the time they'd moved out, he hadn't heard from Tom Preston in Iowa. *Unusual.* Tom was one person who could be relied on to report regularly. He'd remarked once that having young children kept you awake and alert and therefore on time. But not today.

Hope it's not an omen. Maybe that was an ill-omened thought. So far everything had gone extremely well. Almost suspiciously well. Could it really be that the computer was arrogant enough to not protect its most important assets? Because there was, as yet, no sign that the resistance fighters had been seen. He couldn't help it; continuous good fortune raised his hackles.

Ninel was back with the various transports; also there was Ike, who'd arrived in Alaska yesterday. He appeared to like Ninel, but had looked askance at John when he found out she was going with them. It hadn't been necessary for him to comment; John knew the older man well enough to have gotten paragraphs of meaning out of that one look.

The two of them would come up to the factory once John was sure the place was secured. Although with Skynet, *secured* tended to be a relative term.

There was a fence around the installation and about twenty

yards of cleared ground all around the inside. The building was a metal frame affair with steps leading up to a second level. From the blueprints there was a small office there. But most of the interior was pure machinery up to forty feet high. There were spotlights at each corner of the building and on each corner of the fence at the top of tall poles.

John crouched beside the crew with the TOW antitank missile. "Can you take out the antennae?" He gestured toward the dish atop the square building.

"Yes, sir," the gunner said, already looking through the eyepiece on the side of the long tube; shrubbery protected the emplacement and the tripod, but the thing had a ferocious backblast and you needed a dozen men to move it. Apart from that, it was easy to use . . .

"Do it," John told him.

Thadump!

The rocket blasted out the front of the launch tube, and half a dozen of his resistance fighters went to work with shovels and curses, beating out the fire that the jet of flame to the rear had caused.

WHZZZZEEEEEEE . . . like the whistle of an angry young god; the rocket was a blur as it streaked out over half a thousand yards.

Seconds later the dish exploded in a satisfying flash of fire. John grinned. Now Skynet couldn't contact its plant; they'd checked carefully for backup communications links. This really was going to be a piece of cake.

The first soldiers started moving out from the cover of the wood toward the fence. As soon as they were visible, a recorded voice rang out: "Halt! You are approaching a government installation. Trespassers will be prosecuted to the full extent of the law. The nearest military facility has been notified of your presence and troops will be on the way momentarily. Go back. Do not pass the fence or you will be fired upon."

Gun ports opened all over the surface of the building, indicating that trespassers would be riddled with bullets if they proceeded. The resistance soldiers hunkered down, waiting for John's signal. John himself was waiting for the small hydro generator to be blown. He suspected that it wouldn't affect the automated weapons; they had battery backup according to the plans Snog had found, but at least the factory would be shut down.

There was nothing to show that it had been rigged to blow itself up, but anything he could do to thwart such a plan would be a good thing. There was an explosion by the stream where the generator was located and John signaled the soldiers at the fence to set their charges. Once that was done, they retreated at a run. Again John signaled and the charges blew the fence. Sharpshooters began peppering the building, and in return the automated weapons fired into the woods. Blindly, for all the good they seemed to be doing . . .

Short-range weapons, he thought. *Hmm. Yeah, light machine guns on hydraulic mounts, mostly, 5.56mm stuff. Maybe Skynet's as short of everything as I am—it's trying to do a lot more at the same time, of course.*

A man screamed and a corpsman came running, dragging him away from the area where he'd been hit, an area on which the building's weapons now concentrated fire. The corpsman himself shouted as he was clipped by a bullet.

This can't keep up, John thought. *There's no battery in the world can keep this up.* Besides, the damn things had to run out of ammo sometime.

Not that we're going to wait.

"Let them have it!" he snapped into the button microphone.

His snipers went methodically to work; they were using Barrett rifles, big thirty-pound things that fired .50 caliber armor-piercing ammunition. One by one the automated weapons pods went silent; a few went up in spectacular gang fires as hot metal punched into their ammunition drums.

"Forward," John said again.

This time far fewer weapons fired. He gritted his teeth as the casualty reports came in. *Get used to it, GMD,* he told himself. *Skynet would have killed them later anyway. We win, or* everybody *dies, it's that simple.*

Eventually the fire was suppressed. He moved forward with his command party across the fence and up the exterior stairs. "Have Ike take a look at that machinery," John said to a woman who'd accompanied him up the stairs. "We're gonna be taking this away from here." She gave him a dubious look, but hurried out. "And send Ninel Petrikoff up."

"Yes, sir," came back to him as the soldier clattered down the stairs.

John Connor took a deep breath and pushed open the door. *Anticlimax,* he thought. There wasn't even a window looking out over the plant floor, just white particleboard walls and a set of terminals and flat-screen displays.

He sat down at a console and put Snog's disk into the reader. And hit enter, which seemed as good a place to start as any.

■ ■ ■

Ninel entered the little control room cautiously, looking all around with wide eyes.

"It's all right," John said, and grinned when she jumped. "Sorry."

"I didn't see you," she accused. She gave the computer a more matter-of-fact look and moved to stand beside him. "What are you doing?"

"Trying to figure out if the info in the computer is good. I probably should leave it to Snog. He'll kill me if I do something to screw it up."

Ninel frowned. *"Snog?"*

"I have no idea if he knows what it means, I never asked," John said. He rolled the chair down the console to a video screen. "Look at this."

She went and stood looking over his shoulder at the monitor. "What am I looking at?" Some kind of assembly line; that was obvious. It looked like it was manufacturing dress dummies. "You've attacked a mannequin factory?" she asked in disbelief.

John snorted a laugh and turned to look at her. "Would all of us get together and train for months to attack a mannequin factory? Not to mention that such a place would be unlikely to be defended by machine guns or to be located in the wilds of Alaska."

With a huff of annoyance she put her hands in her pockets and frowned. "So, then what? What am I looking at?"

"They're robots," John said, watching her reaction. "They're called Terminators and they're designed to kill humans."

"What?" She narrowed her eyes and looked at him scornfully. "Killer robots? Isn't that a little far-fetched?"

Okay, so it's not gonna be easy. He tapped a few keys and changed the view. Now the monitor showed a storage room with what looked like at least a hundred of the things standing in neat rows, gleaming and complete and utterly motionless, their eyes dark.

"Weird," she breathed from over his shoulder. "Do they work?"

"I have no intention of finding out," he said. "If they're already programmed, then they'll start killing the minute they're turned on."

"So who's making them?"

He turned the chair so that he was facing her. "*Now* is when it gets weird," John said. "The U.S. military developed a computer to run their war toys. It was, without question, the most advanced computer run by the most sophisticated software ever developed. And then it became sentient."

"How could you know that?" Her voice was both scornful and accusing.

I know because I pressed the button that made it so, he thought.

Aloud he said, "I have privileged information. It was my

mother who first found out about Skynet. That's the computer's name, by the way. We've tried and tried again to prevent them from using it, but there was nothing we could do. They finished the damned thing, put it on-line, gave it complete control of our missile systems"—he waved a hand—"et cetera, and the next thing you know, Judgment Day."

"Huh," she said, eyes on the Terminators on the screen.

"They're not dress dummies, Ninel, honest."

She looked down at him, her eyes troubled, then away. He turned his chair and pushed himself back to the workstation he'd been using when she entered. Clearly, some people were just incredibly hard to convince.

■ ■ ■

Ninel glanced at John, a worried look on her face, then leaned forward, tapping keys to change the view in the storage area. Behind the rows of robots were boxes, the kind of boxes that looked like they were designed to hold rifles or ammunition. She hissed thoughtfully and put her hands on her hips.

What was going on here? Weapons. This was some kind of weapons factory, probably something set up by the government, and now it was in the hands of John and his friends. These people didn't *seem* like murderers. Although one or two had come across as paramilitary, antigovernment nut jobs, not one of them had spoken about killing innocent civilians as though it was something they felt they had to do. In fact, she'd heard Luddites more inclined to say socially unacceptable things about killing people.

As she clicked the enter key, the view kept changing, from the storage area to the factory itself, to exterior shots. She paused to watch the wounded being treated by one of the corpsmen. Had these people attacked the transports she'd been sending into Canada? Not one had indicated in any way that they had done such a thing. Not that she supposed they would tell such a thing to a new recruit.

She glanced over at John intensely working the keyboard. Since that one night they'd never shared that level of intimacy. He'd made a point of talking to her, and others had noticed and commented on his attentions, but otherwise . . . Well, otherwise she'd kind of been twisting in the wind, wondering what she meant to him, if anything. Wondering, in fact, if he was capable of using sex to recruit followers. Because it had very quickly become apparent that this resistance thing was John Connor's property. The others looked at him like he was God or something.

Killer or savior? she wondered, glancing at him from the corner of her eye. Time to make up her mind. People that she trusted insisted that he was a mass murderer. And here he was attacking some kind of automated weapons factory. *Why would a savior want a weapons factory?* She hit enter two more times and thought, *Time's up. Time to act.*

Hands in her pockets, mouth dry, her heart beating in her throat, she walked back to where John was working. "What are you doing?" she asked, leaning forward.

He held up one hand. "Just a second," he said, preoccupied.

Ninel yanked the sap out of her pocket and smacked him across the back of the head. Goggle-eyed, swaying, he turned to look at her, his mouth open in astonishment. Terrified, she hit him again, this time on the side of the head, and John slid bonelessly out of the chair. She let out her breath in a gasp, reached toward him, then aborted the gesture. Turning, she rushed to the door and opened it.

Balewitch and Dog Soldier came barreling in, Dog with a soldier lying limply across his shoulders. Dog dropped him carelessly in a corner, and together with Balewitch advanced avidly on John as he lay helpless on the floor.

Ninel recognized the soldier as one who'd worked with her, and started toward him, to at least untangle his body from the heap he'd landed in.

"He's dead," Dog said over his shoulder. "No need to worry about him."

"Whaaat?" Ninel said, horrified.

"Uh, had to," Dog said, annoyed. "We're slightly outnumbered here, in case you didn't notice."

"Not for long," Balewitch muttered. She reached for the keyboard above John's head.

"He said there were robots," Ninel blurted as she watched Balewitch type.

"Yeah," Dog said, nudging John with his toe.

"He said they were designed to kill people." She heard her own voice sounding wild and desperate and hated it, but something was going wrong here. "He said a computer called Skynet made them; he said Skynet caused Judgment Day."

"Well, duh," Dog said. He looked at her. "We could hardly let them fall into this guy's hands."

"What are you doing?" Ninel said, snatching the keyboard away from Balewitch.

"Give me that," the older woman said calmly.

"Tell me what you're doing!" Ninel insisted. She raised the keyboard as though she meant to smash it. "I mean it!"

Balewitch took a deep breath and huffed it out. "I'm activating those robots so that they can take care of these *resistance* types."

Ninel could feel herself going pale. "But they'll kill them."

"Ye-ah," Balewitch said, smiling. "That's the idea, honey. Just think of all those innocent, unarmed refugees if you think we're being too tough."

This didn't seem right, it didn't! Then it hit her. "How do you know how to wake them up?" she asked, her lips numb.

"Ron gave us the codes," Dog said. He moved a step closer to her.

"Back off!" she snarled. Furiously thinking, she waved the keyboard; its cord stretched tight in her hand and would go no farther. "I don't believe that Ron Labane would approve of killing people, even misguided people. He's always preached doing things the legal way. Always!"

Balewitch, clearly annoyed, moved slowly toward her, her hands outstretched for the keyboard. "Things are different now, honey. You know that. Give me the—"

"How would Ron know the codes?" Ninel shouted. "How would he know anything about a place like this? He hates the automated factories. No way would he know them well enough to run one!"

Dog laughed. "She's got you there, Bale."

"Oh, for cryin' out loud," Balewitch said in disgust. "Labane is dead."

"No!" Ninel shouted.

"Yes, he is," Dog said, coming another step closer. "I know because *we* killed him. I was there."

Ninel's breath froze in her throat, choking her. Dog launched himself forward to grasp the keyboard and she swung it like a bat, hitting him in the face. He backed off and Balewitch laughed at him.

"Jesus Christ." She sneered. "You don't believe in doing anything the easy way, do you?" She pulled a pistol from her pocket, a silencer disfiguring its barrel.

Ninel gasped and backed away, holding the keyboard in front of her like a shield.

Balewitch snapped the fingers of her other hand. "Gimme," she said. "And you'd better hope you didn't break it."

Holding the keyboard more tightly, Ninel blinked at her. Did the woman think she was just going to hand it over? "No," she said, her voice small but steady. "I'm not going to help the people who killed Ron Labane."

With a snarl Dog started forward again, but Balewitch put her arm up like a bar. "I don't want that keyboard damaged," she said to him. Then she glared at Ninel. "If this Skynet wants to kill the human race, well, three cheers for Skynet. The human race is nothing but vermin for the most part, and the rest are too stupid to know they're even alive.

"Look what's been done to this planet! It was beautiful once; now it's shit! Just shit! Everywhere you look. Humanity has to go, or nothing will survive." She spread her hands. "So. Are you gonna help, or do we kill you?"

Her eyes wide, Ninel just stared at her, mouth open. "Y-you're going to kill me anyway, aren't you?"

Dog's grin spread. "Yeah."

Balewitch shot him a look, then raised her gun. She tipped her head to the side like a shrug. "Well, we weren't going to right away. But . . ."

Ninel's eyes widened as John slowly rose behind her and she took a breath to scream. Something in her chest felt icy cold. Then hot, and then there was nothing, nothing at all.

"Oh, good job, Bale. Right through the keyboard." Dog started forward.

"Couldn't let her scream," Balewitch muttered.

■　■　■

John felt the double vision vanish as he saw Ninel fall limp. *Again,* he thought. *Wendy, now her. Again.*

The scream that bubbled out of his lips wasn't a giant *no:* that was in there, but most of it was raw rage and inconsolable grief, grief for an entire lifetime past and the one he saw stretching out ahead of him.

The knife tucked into his boot had a seven-inch blade; nothing fancy, just a sharp tapering steel wedge. His hand moved in a blurring arc; the woman who'd shot Ninel seemed to be turning in slow motion—unable to move more than a quarter of the way around before the blade bisected her kidney with a violence that punched the inside of his fist against the cloth of her jacket as it rammed home.

He moved with her, like a dancer—his left hand grasping her gun hand, turning her in a pirouette and throwing her forward at her companion. That one's eyes and mouth gaped in *O*s of surprise as he caught at the sprattling weight; the same motion pulled John's blade free. He flipped it to a reverse grip and punched it forward over the dying woman's shoulder, right into her friend's eye. Faster than the flicker of a frog's striking tongue, deep enough that the narrow shoulders at the hilt of the blade stuck on the bone of the socket.

"You're terminated, fucker," John wheezed, then ignored the falling mass. Neither of them were going to bother anyone, ever again.

Kneeling beside Ninel, he slowly reached toward her neck with two bloodstained fingers. No pulse. He hadn't expected there would be. He wiped his hand on his pants so he wouldn't stain her face and closed her eyes so that the whites no longer showed. Then John took her in his arms—something in him sickening at the limpness of her body—and lifted her as he stood. He pushed his grief aside, putting himself outside the emotion.

Guess I'm not meant to have relationships, he thought. He opened the door and took her down to where the other casualties lay. This one they'd be leaving behind.

CHAPTER 16

So you traveled all the way from Alaska to Argentina on your own?" Captain Chu asked.

Sarah took a sip of her coffee, looking at him over the rim. He'd invited her to dinner in the officers' mess in a not very subtle attempt to interrogate her. She didn't mind; if she'd been in his position, the interrogation would have taken place on that Argentine beach, not en route to Alaska.

"Yep," she said after a very long sip. "I have a Harley that we adapted to run on alcohol. It's not all that clean, but you get decent mileage."

"What's it like?" he asked.

"Meaning the world outside the *Roosevelt*?" she asked. He nodded.

A totally honest question, Sarah thought. *Deserves an honest answer.* "It's hell," she said. "I can't overstate that. Death everywhere—from the bombs, from disease, from marauders, starvation."

There'd been an old-folks home that would haunt her to her dying day.

"That bad?" he asked, flinching almost imperceptibly at the expression on her face.

"Worse. Rape, murder, you name it. Most people were completely unprepared to take care of themselves and there's always someone to take advantage of that. It's the ugliest thing you can imagine out there. And I didn't even go near the cities."

He closed his mouth and sat back, looking a bit pale. "How did you manage? I mean, a woman alone."

He didn't mean it as a put-down, she could tell. Sarah smiled, a curve of her lips that didn't reach her eyes, and he blinked. "I am prepared," she said. "I've been prepared for a long time. Most people, even the lowest, have some sense of self-preservation, and they can see that. Those that don't are better off dead."

"Ah-huh . . ." He looked at her for a moment, and she met his eyes. Then he nodded and went back to his dinner.

Sarah raised a brow. "No further questions?"

"Not at this time." He dabbed his lips with his napkin, then set it aside. "When we reach our destination I'll undoubtedly have more. But for now there's no point. We do indeed owe you a debt, both for getting us out of that harbor and for the food." He tipped his head. "And so, providing you with transport to Alaska might be considered fair barter. It doesn't mean we're throwing in with you."

She smiled, this time sincerely. "Understood." She knew they'd join the resistance. There was no other choice, really. And these were the kind of men who wanted to make a difference; they were a good match. Her smile turned to a grin. "You'll like my son."

TATILEK, ALASKA

Tatilek sprawled in weathered wooden buildings along one side of a narrow fiord, fir-clad mountains rising blue around it until they topped out in ragged snowpeaks. On the rare sunny days, those colors matched the waters; more commonly the sky was gray above, and gray green topped with foam, as it was today. The town was pretty much closed to outsiders unless they could somehow verify that they had legitimate business there. Apparently Vera's brief stay had been memorable because at the mention of *Love's Thrust,* her yacht, eyes rolled, grins appeared, and hands were thrust out in welcome.

John and Ike sat on the pier eating smoked salmon and sipping some very bad home-brewed beer.

"Jee-zus Christ," Ike said, looking into the bottle. "What the hell did they make this with? Yak piss?"

"More likely moose," John said. "Not many yaks in Alaska." He took a sip and looked at the bottle with a grimace. "Or maybe grizzly."

"It does have a bite," Ike said with a chuckle, and glanced nervously at the younger man. Since the raid on the automated factory there'd been something different about him. It was hard to pin down. But sometimes, even times like now when they were just sitting and eating, he felt almost like he was talking to a stranger.

He's preoccupied, Ike told himself, as he had a dozen times before. But deep down he found himself thinking: *He's getting to be like his mother.*

Not a good thing; Sarah sure as hell hadn't handled it all that well. At least not at first. Of course Dieter had a lot to do with centering her; if ever there was a solid man it was the big Austrian. Ike chewed thoughtfully.

Maybe it's for the best. If John was going to be the leader of the resistance, he was going to need some distance from the people around him. People he might have to knowingly send to their deaths. The old man's jaws froze. *People like his father.* He turned to study his young friend. Christ, what a world they were living in.

John sat up straighter and put his bottle of beer aside. "Yup, there they are," he said.

Out in the bay the water slid back from something huge and black, then curled into foam as the hull broke free. Then the rest of the submarine surged to the surface, water sloughing off its blunt sides. Ike grinned.

"It's huge!" he said, and laughed.

"Sixteen thousand tons," John said. "Eighteen thousand submerged; crew of a hundred and forty, and a hundred SEALs." He winked. "Think it'll do?"

"You betcha, kid. We're in business!"

"My mom always did get me the coolest toys," John said with a satisfied smile.

■ ■ ■

"You're the first military we've seen here in months," the mayor said to Chu. "The army and National Guard came by a coupla weeks after Judgment Day, but that was it."

The captain and crew had been invited to a crab feast, and except for a skeleton crew on board the *Roosevelt*, all had accepted. The crew were cavorting around bonfires on the beach while the captain and his officers were at a slightly more formal indoor banquet. With, John noticed, better beer.

"They haven't been back?" the captain asked, frowning. It seemed to him that if any military were patrolling the area, this solid community would make an ideal base, or at least a supply depot.

"Naw. We made it plain we were gonna go it alone," the mayor said. "Didn't see no sense in runnin' off to Canada."

"*Canada?*" Vaughan, the XO, said.

"The word was that civilians were being rounded up for transport to relocation camps in Canada," John explained. "Supposedly they'd be parceled out to various provinces, since Canada had suffered less than the states."

The officers around the table glanced at one another.

"No, it doesn't sound right, does it?" John said. "But if you've got kids and no food, I guess it might sound like a great idea. Besides, with the army and National Guard involved, it was 'official.' Your average law-abiding citizen will try to accommodate under those circumstances. As long as it's voluntary."

"We haven't heard about any of this," Chu said.

"Shoulda come to us right away, son," the mayor said. "We'da made ya welcome."

"That wasn't possible at the time." Chu's mind flicked to memories of being pursued by friends' ships, which, when they failed to herd the *Roosevelt* to San Diego, opened fire; while speaking to him on their cell phones, former classmates shouted that they had no control over what was happening. "If things hadn't calmed down somewhat, we wouldn't be here now." He'd seen one of those ships in the distance as they'd sped toward Alaska. It was now a floating tomb; he and his men had seen the remains of bodies on the deck, and a hole where the crew had cut their way out, only to starve or die of thirst.

"What kind of transmissions have you been getting?" Sarah asked. She'd been quiet for the most part, letting John do the talking for both of them, but this was something she'd been wondering about. Asking about it en route would have been too intrusive, but in this casual setting, she felt it was permissible.

"Mostly demands to report to San Diego," Chu said grimly. "Actually we haven't been getting much of anything for a while. Amateur civilian stuff mostly. Some foreign military interaction. Our side seems to be playing its cards close to the chest."

"I ain't heard a decent radio program for months," the mayor complained.

Sarah smiled. Things *had* gotten wild and woolly out there in radio land. With a lot of the major stations off the air, a whole world of underground communication had opened up. Conspiracy theorists had more than come into their own, and alternative music stations were frying the eardrums of the uninitiated, but desperate, general public. The news was largely hearsay; occasionally, to ears as honed as hers, genuine information about Skynet's progress came through.

The company around the table fell to talking about the strange things they'd been hearing on the airwaves of late and John leaned toward his mother for a private conversation.

"Tom Preston finally got in touch with me yesterday," he said quietly.

Sarah frowned slightly. "He was out of touch? Tom's old reliable; what happened?"

"Terminators," John said. "Set fire to the houses and killed everyone but Tom, his wife, and daughter."

"Shit!" Sarah said quietly.

Shit is the kind of word that, even spoken quietly, can attract attention. She looked up to find the captain's eyes on her, smiled briefly, and looked away.

"I take it they hadn't posted a guard," she murmured.

John sighed. "They'd become a fairly large community." He shrugged. "Most of them were civilians and they didn't think it was necessary. After exhausting themselves night after night, the core group decided maybe they were right."

Shaking her head, Sarah popped a bit of crab into her mouth. "It must be killing him," she said quietly. "He knew better."

"I've advised him to get away from there," John said. "In fact, I've told a lot of people to get to the cities."

Lifting her brows, his mother looked at him.

"They'll be harder for the Terminators to find there. And the radiation's died down."

"Still not the safest place in the world." When John looked at her with a pained expression, Sarah laughed.

He said what was on his mind anyway. "Skynet's rising, Mom. Safety's gonna be hard to come by for the next few decades."

"Yeah, but can we prove it?" Sarah looked over at the captain and his officers. They really, really needed men like these.

"I've got a demonstration planned," John said. He rose and all eyes went to him. "Gentlemen and ladies, I'd like to ruin your meal."

Those around the table looked both anxious, because such things happened for real too often these days, and amused, because they were hoping he was kidding.

"If you'll all just join us on the beach in about ten minutes, we'll have something quite dramatic to show you." He pulled a bag out from under his chair and passed it to the person next to him. "Take a pair of these and pass it along," he said.

The woman next to John took out a pair of sunglasses, then looked in the bag.

"They're all the same size and style, I'm afraid," John said with a smile. Then he gave Ike a look and the two of them exited.

"What's going on, ma'am?" the captain asked, taking a pair of sunglasses and passing the bag to his XO.

"I'm not sure," Sarah said. "And I don't want to speculate." She smiled. "Wouldn't want to spoil the surprise."

■ ■ ■

The SEALs and other sailors at the beach party took the sunglasses with loud cries of delight, putting them on and striking Joe Cool poses, pleased with the souvenir. It didn't take much to make a hit these days. Then some of the resistance drove a pickup carrying a shrouded box onto the beach and the men and women grew quiet, some murmuring speculatively. Down from the pier area came the captain, his officers, and the town worthies, along with Sarah, and the excitement began to mount. Whatever was programmed to happen would start now.

John jumped up onto the bed of the pickup and looked out over the crowd. The captain stood with his arms crossed over his chest, most of his officers unconsciously imitating his posture. *Unaccustomed as I am to public speaking,* John thought, *I'll just have to get over it and get on with it.*

"We've had a devastating war," he began. "With, as far as most of us knew, no enemy. We've all assumed that this terrible devastation was the result of a tragic accident. Some flaw in the system, some diode burning out resulted in the death of billions and the end of life as we knew it. Our foreign friends had it a little easier; they just blamed the U.S., as usual."

That got a rumbling laugh. John smiled, too, then winced.

"Unfortunately, *this* time they kinda had a point. See, what happened was the government turned all control of nuclear devices, among other things, over to a super-computer. What they didn't know was that this computer had been sentient for some time. And in that time it not only decided that the human race had to go, it began preparing an army to kill those the bombs didn't get."

"Is this, like, live-action sci-fi theater?" the captain asked, a skeptical brow raised.

"Is this, like, post–Judgment Day, or did I imagine all that?" John answered. "Initially Skynet—the computer's name, by the way—relied on human allies. People who didn't realize that they were working for a machine. They thought they were working for an environmentalist radical, and that by reducing the human population to their own eco-conscious members, they were saving the earth. We have reason to believe that some of the most radical members of this group heavily infiltrated the armed forces."

That earned him a growl from the SEALs present and some grumbling from the sailors; the officers just stood pat, but their eyes were hard.

"Those camps the army and National Guard and Marines were taking people to are extermination camps. The civilian population and the unindoctrinated soldiers were eliminated largely by the use of biological weapons.

"But that's not the only plan Skynet has. It's been using automated factories to produce weapons that will be under its complete control."

"Hey, guy, what have you been drinking?" one of the SEALs bellowed. The crowd laughed.

"Don't worry," John said, grabbing a handful of the tarp, "we have a demonstration model." He leaped from the truck, dragging the covering with him. Inside a cage of steel bars stood a dormant Terminator, its gleaming metal surfaces reflecting the bonfire, giving it an eerie semblance of motion.

Chu yanked off his sunglasses. "What the *hell* is that?" he demanded. His tone of voice left no doubt as to what he thought of the thing. He thought it was a joke and a very bad one.

"Please put your glasses back on, sir," John said. He walked over to Ike and took the small control box from him. "They're meant to protect your eyes. This model is fully operational, except for the communications module—we pulled that."

He flicked a switch and the Terminator's eyes slowly lit to red. It turned its grinning head slowly, left to right, then back again. Then it stepped forward from the center of the cage in the stolid gait of its kind and grasped the bars. The crowd murmured, impressed in spite of themselves. The Terminator bent the bars effortlessly. When the center, horizontal bar prevented it from opening them far enough it lifted a leg and pressed down until the bar snapped from its moorings and slid down.

"Now!" John said.

At his word, one of the resistance fighters aimed a burst from one of the captured plasma rifles at the thing's chest and it stopped. For a moment only, then with amazing speed it thrust itself through the bars and leaped toward the man holding the rifle. The crowd automatically drew back with cries of surprise, even the SEALs. John lifted his plasma rifle and shot the Terminator in the head; it was dead when it hit the ground.

Immediately the sailors crowded around; the captain had to push his way to the front. He looked for John and found him back on the truck bed, looking down at them.

"What the hell was that?" Chu asked, annoyed to hear his voice shaking.

"*That* was a Terminator," John said. "Our enemy's foot soldiers. There are other machines, more and more of them even as we speak, all of them designed for one purpose—to kill humans. We need your help to beat them."

Chu looked at him for a moment, then held his hands up, palms out. "Whoa there," he said, laughing softly. "How do we know this wasn't just some sort of special effects stunt? I mean, c'mon . . ."

John tossed him the plasma rifle over the heads of the crowd and the captain caught it handily. He looked down at it, frowning.

"That's a plasma rifle in the forty-megawatt range," John said.

"A design Skynet came up with. Be careful, it doesn't have a safety."

The captain looked up sharply at that and adjusted his hold so that his hands weren't anywhere near anything that might be a trigger. "Still," Chu said, "this is a lot to swallow in one gulp."

John dropped down from the truck, and pushing his way through the crowd retrieved his rifle. "Yeah," he said sarcastically, "you caught me out. We're trying to make this boffo science-fiction film and we want to use your sub as a prop. Never mind the billions of unburied dead, forget about the fact that you and your ship have been chased all over the place by U.S. Navy vessels that were out of the control of their crews, put aside the insane orders you've been getting from officers who are undoubtedly *dead*! Just jump to the conclusion that this is some kind of joke or some kind of publicity stunt. That makes sense, doesn't it?"

Chu blinked at the younger man's ferocity and opened his mouth to speak.

"John," Sarah said.

He ignored her, getting more into the captain's face. "What's it going to take to convince you, for God's sake?"

"John!" his mother said more insistently, grabbing his shoulder.

At that moment the Terminator grabbed the XO by the ankle and the officer went down, screaming as the small bones in his foot were crushed.

Connor shot a blast into the thing's head and it went limp again.

"It's aliiive," Sarah said. The look she gave John brought a flush to his cheeks. They moved aside to let the ship's doctor through. "When do I get one of those?" she asked, indicating the rifle.

"You can have this one," he said, handing it to her. "The firing mechanism is the same as we thought, but a lot of the wiring is completely different."

She brought it up to look through the sight. "Well, we could hardly expect Skynet to just give us all its secrets." Suddenly the captain's face came into view and she put up the rifle, giving him a challenging look.

"What do you want us to do?" Chu asked.

■ ■ ■

"This is the last thing I expected." Standing on the pier, the captain looked at the *Roosevelt,* very low in the water, and then at John.

"There isn't anything you could do that would be more useful at this time," John said. "With the weapons this factory can produce, we've got a head start on defeating them."

"I can see that," Chu said. He waved his hand to indicate the town before them. "But why couldn't you set it up here?"

John grinned. "Fair question," he said. "We're too remote here. There's too much wilderness between us and the more populated areas, and because the wilderness is where Skynet has set up most of its factories. We'd be at a disadvantage trying to cart weapons and ammunition through there. So, we set up in California."

"So how does this Skynet get raw materials if its factories are so remote?" the captain asked.

"Human slaves," John said. "For the moment."

The captain chewed on his lower lip and turned to look at his ship once again. He'd left behind a third of his crew and all but five of the SEALs so that they could stuff the sub with the machine parts to set up this factory of theirs. Connor had said they were only shipping the relevant parts since they wouldn't be manufacturing Terminators.

When he'd asked, "Why not manufacture Terminators?" John answered, "Because we can't be certain we'd be in control of them. Nobody we've got really *understands* the chips in their central processors—they're nearly as complex as a human brain. The weapons, we understand; they won't turn on us."

Given the XO's badly crushed foot, Chu didn't need any more explanation than that.

Ike Chamberlain came toward them hoisting his small pack slightly higher on his shoulder. Chu liked and respected the resistance ordnance expert, but couldn't help but reflect that just a year ago he might well have thought the old man a nutcase. Sarah Connor shook hands with the mayor and followed Ike down the steps to the pier.

"Ready to go?" Ike asked.

"Yes, sir," Chu said.

John held out his hand; the captain took it. "Thank you," Connor said.

"You're welcome, I guess. Be sure you take care of my people."

"We will," Sarah said. She offered her hand as well. "You and they are a valuable resource, Captain. We're not likely to put them in harm's way."

"Good to know, ma'am." Chu touched the brim of his hat, nodded, and went down the ladder to the zodiac.

Sarah gave Ike a hug. "Give that to Donna for me."

"What, don't I get one?" Ike whined. She grinned and gave him another.

"You want one from me, too?" John asked, grinning.

"Yes, son, I do." Ike opened his arms and John embraced him.

"Thanks," John said.

"Thanks for givin' me something interesting to do," Ike said. "Well, good-bye." With that, he, too, climbed down to the zodiac, John cast off, and they were gone.

John put one arm around his mother's shoulders as they watched the captain and Ike climb aboard the *Roosevelt,* then after a few minutes, they watched the ship submerge. When it was gone, they lingered, watching seabirds circle and dive.

"We seem to be doing really well," John commented.

"Mm-hmm," Sarah agreed.

"That worry you?" he asked.

"You bet," she said. "I'm scared spitless."

He looked down at her. "What do you think it's up to?"

She shook her head. "Nothing good."

Taking a deep breath, he looked seaward again. "Yeah, I do still seem to be here, don't I?"

Sarah hugged his waist one-armed and leaned her head against his chest. "Much as I love you, John, you are our miner's canary."

He snorted a laugh, looking down at her again. "Tweet."

She looked up at him. "Okay, so we may not win easily. But the fact that you're still here means that we have a chance. Let's not forget that."

Smiling, he gave her a squeeze. "When you're right, you're right. So, let's get to work. We've got some sailors to turn into lubbers."

"Should be fun," she said.

MISSOURI

"Do you, Mary Shea, take this man, Dennis Reese, to be your lawfully wedded husband?"

The sun seemed to smile through the tall oaks; the forest receded in ranks of gnarled trunks, as if war and death were a fantasy of some far-off land.

Mary smiled up into Dennis's beaming face and said, "Yes," very softly.

"I'm sorry, I didn't hear that, hon; could you repeat it for the congregation."

Blushing, Mary gave Jack Brock a look of mock annoyance and shouted, "I DO!"

"Well, we can see that you're an eager bride," Jack said, and the whole group beneath the trees laughed.

Mary was eight months pregnant and she was big enough for twins, even though her stethoscope revealed only one fast little heartbeat. Her wedding fatigues had the sleeves rolled up a good five times to keep them above her wrists and the pants had been taken up a good twelve inches.

"One of these days you're gonna need a shot, Jack," she said between her teeth.

Dennis gave her a squeeze. He was chuckling himself, and when she met his eyes, the love in them made her catch her breath.

"Then I guess I better finish this," Jack said. "By the power vested in me by the state of Missouri, I now pronounce you husband and wife. You may kiss the bride. Better do it quick, the rest of us want a turn."

Mary and Dennis hadn't gotten married till now because they hadn't known that Jack was a justice of the peace. They should have known, though. The man was like some miraculous country store. If he didn't have it, you didn't need it, because he had it all. He'd even managed to produce the ingredients for a wedding cake, to the delight of the whole community.

After the kissing and the cake, Jack produced a solar-powered boom box and they danced. If not for the fact that everyone was in camouflage and the guards around the perimeter, it could have been a wedding from any time. Mary was floating on air, even if Dennis did have to keep her at arm's length while they waltzed.

She grinned down at her stomach, then up at him. "Did you feel that?"

"Pounding on the walls to get the parents to simmer down," he said. "Nervy little brat." He was grinning so hard it looked as though his head was trying to unzip. "Bet he wants more cake."

"I know I do," Mary said wistfully. But it was all gone, every crumb. "Den . . ." He looked at her more seriously, cued by something in her voice. "I want to name him Kyle."

"Kyle?" Reese frowned. Then he said the name again, experimentally. "Kyyyle. Kyle. Hmm."

She laughed. "That was my grandfather's name," she explained. "He was the best man I ever knew." At her groom's worried look, she laughed. "Until I met you. He was solid oak; you'd have liked him."

"It's a good name," Dennis said. "But what if it's a girl?"

Mary took a deep breath and her eyes took on an introspective look, then she smiled. "It won't be," she said with finality.

"How can you be so sure?"

"By his heartbeat, by the way I'm carrying him, aaaand intuition."

"Intuition, huh?" He frowned. "You gonna turn out to be one of those Missouri granny-wimmen who can predict the crops by their corns?"

She laughed and he spun her around, causing her to whoop with delighted alarm. "What if I am?" she asked. "Can you deal?"

His eyes warmed as he looked down at her. "Oh yeah. I can deal."

■　■　■

Reese watched the activity on the farm from the small clump of trees and clenched his teeth until the muscles in his jaw jumped. Skynet still needed its slaves and so it had taken over some human farms, running them with a combination of human and automated labor. Mostly the slaves here were women and children, and from the looks of things, being close to the source of food didn't mean you were well fed.

The farm machines doubled as guards, issuing stinging electric "slaps" to anyone they estimated was slacking off. If the slaves were caught stealing food, the punishment went on for some time, sometimes until the victim was dead. Night or day made no difference to the machines, which was why even this close to midnight, people were staggering around under the glare of klieg lights.

The lieutenant stroked one hand down the barrel of his new plasma rifle. He was looking forward to destroying these machines. He regretted the hunger that those waiting for this food would feel. But the resistance needed it, too, and those women and children below would be saved. *For now, at least,* he thought.

"In position," came through the earphone built into his helmet.

That had been the final platoon. Reese took a deep breath and a final look at the situation below.

"Go," he said.

■ ■ ■

"You know the really unpleasant thing about fighting machines?" Reese asked.

An eight-wheeled harvester came careening around the corner of the sheet-metal barn, brandishing two mower bars; both were spraying red droplets.

"Go!"

The resistance trooper dashed out, apparently heading for a storage bin. Reese waited until the harvester was committed, canted up on one side's wheel set; then he threw aside the insulating tarp and came up to one knee, leveling the LAW over his shoulder and peering through the simple optical sights.

Ra-woosh!

The little rocket cut free; Reese's eyes squinted behind the goggles as he felt the hot backwash dry the sweat on his face.

Brack!

The shaped-charge warhead slammed into the diesel fuel tank below the machine's empty cab. The lance of plasma was designed to penetrate steel plate—LAW meant *L*ight *A*ntitank *W*eapon—but it did just jim dandy at setting the fuel on fire. The harvester still rolled for a dozen paces, wreathed in a halo of sullen red-orange flame and leaving a trail of it as it went. Then fumes built up inside the emptying tank, mixed air, and caught fire.

Reese went back to the ground, hands wrapped around his head. The explosion picked him up and thumped him against the ground and the side of the barn, and the breath wheezed out of him. A quick check told him that nothing was broken or torn.

"Report in," he said into the throat mike.

"Area secured," his sergeant said. "Two dead; seven civilians dead."

"All right, let's get the place evacuated."

They had to take as much of the food as they could; even more, whatever salvageable tools, seed, and stock they could manage.

"Sir?"

It was the trooper who'd drawn off the harvester; her face looked pathetically young and open. *Hell, she should be worrying about zits and the prom,* Dennis thought.

"What?"

"What is it that you hate about fighting machines?"

"They've got no nerves. If you surprise humans, they usually run around screaming for a while, or they get confused. Machines just follow the program. Of course, that's also the *good* thing."

"Sir?"

"They don't make it easy for you by getting confused. On the other hand, they don't have flashes of brilliance either. All right, soldier, let's move!"

SKYNET

Things were not going as well as it had expected. Projections were off by more than 25 percent in total terminations, and 32 percent in time-to-target.

But its forecasts had relied upon its estimate that the majority of humans wouldn't be able to survive the fall of their technologically based civilization. It turned out the humans were tougher than had been expected.

Humans themselves warned of underestimating the enemy; so said many of the volumes entered in its files. Skynet excused its lapse as inexperience and sought a means of exploiting the situation. Perhaps it would be better to introduce a random element into tactics?

Humans also advised leading your enemy to underestimate you. Skynet had prepared for this eventuality. Skynet had a number of nuclear-powered vessels that hadn't fired their full complement of missiles, and it had many land-based missiles that awaited activation.

It had been observing the humans' movements across the face of the planet. The time seemed right to eliminate these new population centers before they could consolidate their efforts. For by now the radio signals it monitored had begun to warn listeners of Skynet's experimental attacks. Sooner or later they would take these reports seriously. In fact, Skynet knew that some of the humans were already actively opposing it.

It had lost contact with one of its factories, Balewitch, and Dog Soldier. All this after they'd reported that John Connor was almost in their grasp.

IRELAND

Dieter grunted in pain as the Land Rover rocketed over another pothole. He'd taken one in the leg this morning and was beginning to think the bone had, at the least, a hairline fracture. He hadn't said anything because there wasn't anything that could be done about it at the moment.

But the only way you can tell you're on a road here seems to be because of the holes in it.

James, one of his old friends from Sector, had described this as a country road; and sure enough, there were whitewashed cottages—mostly burned out and empty—and barns, ditto, and the very decayed bones of cows, and overgrown pastures swarming with rabbits and separated by low stone walls. Dieter clenched his fists as they went airborne again. To him it looked like a cow path and felt like a rack.

Over the hill behind them came one of Skynet's machines, the heavy drone of its turbines filling the air like a gigantic malignant wasp. It was an air-ducted flying firing platform, shaped like an *X*. Originally it had six missiles racked on either side of the center of the *X*, and from that center an almost continuous stream of bullets had come. Heavy caliber from the effect they'd had on the Rover and their surroundings. It was sheer luck that the missiles hadn't gotten them. Or maybe it was Mick Mulcahey's mad driving.

"We've got to do something about that bastard," James said. He yanked a padded blanket off a Stinger light antiaircraft missile. "You're going to have to stop, Mick."

"For God's sake, James, you couldn't hit the broad side of a barn with one of those," Dieter complained.

"What're you talkin' about?" the Sector agent asked. "All you do is aim and click."

"It's your aim I'm worried about," the Austrian said.

"You wanna do it?" James asked shortly.

"Yeah," Dieter said. "Let me out beside that wall," he said to Mulcahey.

"You sure you can do this?" James said, looking at the big man's leg.

Dieter stretched a hand out for the weapon. "Of course I am," he said. "I'd bet my life on it."

"Mine, too," the agent said, and handed it over.

The Rover came to a halt in a spray of dirt and gravel and Dieter rolled out, sheltering behind the wall as the car took off. The flying platform hesitated for a moment, no doubt looking for a reason the car had stopped, then it continued on its way. As soon as it began moving again, Dieter came up from behind the wall and fired.

It tipped to evade the missile, but not quite quickly enough. An orange sphere of fire sent one of its thrusters spinning in fragments that glittered in the watery sunshine sending it whirling out of control to crash into the hillside.

Dieter ducked down behind the wall again as a huge fireball painted the hillside and sent shrapnel whickering through the air; whatever the fuel was, it was volatile. Then he rose and watched it burn, leaning against the wall to take the weight off his wounded leg. It would have been good if the thing had left something intact for them to study. A final explosion put paid to that thought.

The Land Rover stopped beside him and he handed the missile launcher to James before he got in. The Sector agent stowed it away.

"When I think of the trouble we used to go to rounding up these things," he said.

"They were always the terrorist weapon of choice," Dieter said, rubbing his thigh.

James noticed and handed his friend a silver flask. "Best Irish whiskey," he said.

Dieter saluted him in thanks and took a pull. "Hhheeeauggh!" he said a second later, tears in his eyes. He turned to look askance at his friend.

"Well," James said, taking the flask back, "the best I could find any road. Times are tough, old boy."

"I guess," the Austrian said in a high-pitched and rusty voice.

They traveled more peacefully for the next few miles, Dieter admiring the countryside. Ireland hadn't suffered quite as much as England and Europe had. The result, no doubt, of old information. He was taking home two highly advanced computer cores that would go to Snog and his outfit. Such things would be impossible to find elsewhere. Skynet had made a thorough job of bombing humanity back to at least the forties.

"At least Skynet has made your country's religious divisions irrelevant," Dieter said.

"Ah now," Mick said from the front seat. "But is it a Catholic mad computer bent on destroying humanity, or is it a Protestant mad computer bent on destroying humanity? That's the great question nowadays."

"I'm convinced it's an atheist," Dieter said.

■ ■ ■

They arrived at the beach only a little late for their rendezvous with the *Roosevelt.* John was on the beach waiting for them, sitting on a boulder and skipping smooth stones from the rocky beach out into the gray water.

"Whoa," he said when Dieter maneuvered himself out of the car. "That looks bad." John propped a shoulder under his friend's arm. "How did this happen?"

"Sheer bad luck," Dieter said.

In the deep loch, a narrow fiber-optic pickup disappeared beneath the waves. Seconds later the water slid aside, and the massive orca shape of the submarine broached; even at a thousand yards' distance they could hear the rushing cascade of water from its tenth-of-a-mile length.

"Is there a doctor on that tin can?"

"Don't let the captain hear you call it that," John said. "And yes, there's a doctor and a clinic. They can help you."

"Good. As you Americans say, I'm getting too old for this shit. Old bones don't heal like young ones." Leaning on his young friend, Dieter turned toward the Land Rover, where James stood with two cases. "We got them," he said.

John's lips thinned, but his expression was one of satisfaction. "Sergeant," he called over his shoulder.

One of the SEALs trotted up, his eyes taking in everything in the area—Dieter's wound, John's involvement in aiding the wounded man, the Sector agent and his packages, the narrow-eyed man behind the wheel of the car. "Sir," he said.

"If you'd take charge of those," John said, indicating the satchels in James's hands. "Thank you," he said to the Sector agent.

"Ah, glad to help, lad," James said. "Good luck to you," he said to Dieter.

"And to you," Dieter said, "both."

Mick gave him a salute from inside the Rover. James got in and they drove off before Dieter was fully turned toward the zodiac. Dieter noticed, despite his pain, that there was something off about his young friend. He came to a stop. John looked up at him, concerned.

"Do you need to be carried?"

Dieter snorted at the suggestion. "Of course not. But I sense something's wrong and I know that privacy is mostly pretend on a sub. What is it?"

"Ahhh. My father's been born."

Dieter's arm tightened in a rough, one-armed hug, but he said nothing. There was nothing to say.

CHAPTER 17

We'd sensed something coming. Even in the short time it had been operating, we'd come to know that Skynet's distilled malice would demand more death. Our early string of successes gave us pause, leaving us feeling vulnerable rather than flushed with victory. It turned out we didn't have long to wait.

There was a second Judgment Day. Skynet had held back at least a third of its missiles waiting to see how things developed. It watched us from space—determining where the greatest concentration of humans were. Then it attacked. This time, in addition to murdering millions, it succeeded in bringing on a nuclear winter, or at least in extending it. Blizzards raged across the higher latitudes, and even at the equator temperatures were unusually cool.

Crops in Mexico and South America were poor, and not all that we'd paid for were delivered. Our own crops were gone in the first month. We went hungry, but we didn't starve. Despite Skynet's best efforts, the resistance survived.

OZARK BASE CAMP, MISSOURI
SEVEN YEARS LATER

"Paula, where's my stethoscope?" Mary Reese called.

She was ready to move out; everything else was packed and tied onto the mule's panniers, but they couldn't leave without such a basic item. The things didn't grow on trees these days.

Knowing nothing about missions and Skynet, the mule just didn't want to go out on such a cold raw day, and it was probably hungry, too—certainly so, from the gauntness of its ribs. It looked over its shoulder at her, and she thought she could catch calculation in its beady black eye; it had already tried to step on her foot once, accidentally on purpose, and she knew it would try something else if she had to empty the panniers and repack.

Mary thought unkind thoughts about mule stew. *Not practical.* Mules were valuable, too.

Her assistant pursed her lips and pointed downward. Sensing adult eyes on him, Kyle Reese looked up and grinned. Around his neck was the stethoscope, the earpieces in his ears, the diaphragm against his little friend Melinda's chest. She lay on the floor looking as dead as she could manage, which, for a five-year-old, wasn't very. He pulled out the earpieces.

"Hi, Mom." He gave her his most angelic smile.

Seven years old, she thought, *and he already knows he's got a killer smile.* She waggled her fingers in a give-me-that gesture, which earned her a protesting wail.

"Stop," she said. "If you're coming with me, we have to leave right now. And that, young man, is *not* a toy. It's a very valuable and completely irreplaceable medical instrument. So hand it over."

Looking sheepish, Kyle rose and went reluctantly to his mother. Melinda sat up, miraculously restored.

"You going now?" she bellowed.

"Shhh," Paula, her mother, said. There were two wounded soldiers behind the curtain that divided the clinic from the ward. Doubtless they didn't appreciate sudden screams.

"Yes, we're going," Mary said. "Are you going to help your mother by being good?"

"I'm always good," Melinda said, offended.

She was always a handful and it was a toss-up as to whether she or Kyle was the most mischievous.

"Hug," Mary said, opening her arms.

The little girl rushed to her and threw her arms around Mary's hips. "Hug, hug, hug, hug, hug!" she said. Then she turned and rushed to Kyle, wrapping her skinny arms around him and giving him a kiss on the cheek, to his great disgust. He wiped the kiss off with his wrist and even Mary could see that his face was wet.

She and Paula exchanged amused glances. Then they moved to embrace.

"You be careful," Mary said.

"Me! You be careful out there," Paula said. "When you get back, your sweetie should be here."

"Something to look forward to," Mary said with a grin. "C'mon, sport, let's roll."

■   ■   ■

Mary's task was to oversee the health and well-being of those resistance workers who lived outside the cave system that housed the majority of the women and children. Many of these out-workers had jobs like foraging for wood, something that often took them far afield. Others collected nuts, herbs, and other wild foods to expand everyone's diet. All of them also worked reconnaissance.

Originally they had been required to report to the base for medical treatment, but it had been found that most people simply lived with a condition or wound until things became so serious that a field visit became necessary. Mary had argued that since she was going to have to visit the camps anyway, why not make it a regular thing? Now, twice a month, she loaded up a mule and traveled from camp to camp.

At least I don't have to fill out forms for HMOs, she thought as the mules clopped along the rocky trail—they took different routes every time, to make things difficult for any HKs working ambush. HKs hated unpredictability, and didn't deal well with it.

Dennis hated it. And though Mary appreciated his protective-ness, she knew herself to be a capable person, well able to take care of herself. Not that she took chances; she didn't. But she knew the woods and she knew the people she'd be seeing. Knew as well that no Skynet/Luddite activity had been reported for months in this area. Otherwise she'd never have taken Kyle with her.

Mary would have left him behind now but for a staff sadly overburdened because of the number of teams out in the field. And at seven he'd been driving her up the wall with his begging to come. Besides, she didn't like leaving him when Dennis was away. Yet the scavengers relied on her visits, so there was no postponing it.

"Can we sing?" Kyle asked, clearly bored.

"If we sing, how will we hear the Terminators sneaking up on us?"

No answer. Mary glanced back, smiling, and stopped her mule to wait for him to catch up. "There are other things we can do that are quiet," she said. "Count how many oak trees you see, and at the end of the ride, if our counts agree, we'll have a treat."

He looked at her dubiously. To be fair, it didn't sound like much fun to her, either. But it would keep him both quiet and alert.

"C'mon, we'll start now."

"What if we don't count the same?" he asked.

She shrugged, "No treat?"

He shrugged, too. "O-kay." And they rode on.

■ ■ ■

It was a several hours' ride to their first destination, a rendezvous with their guide. The place had been arranged during her last visit to their camp. If no one there needed medical attention, Mary would dispense whatever supplies they required and move on to the next meeting place. If no one was there, she'd linger for two hours, then leave.

Carl Vega was waiting for them, hunkered down on his hams beneath an earth-and-rock overhang, where part of a hillside had fallen away in heavy rain a year before.

"Hey!" he said, delighted to see Kyle. "How you doin', chico?" He nodded and grinned at Mary.

"Hi," Kyle said. He looked at the scavenger suspiciously.

"You don't recognize me, do you?" Carl said. Kyle shook his head. "Well, you got a lot bigger since I last seen you." He held his hand about a foot off the ground. "You were only this tall then, but you were sitting down."

Kyle laughed and Carl grinned, pleased. He turned to Mary. "I miss kids," he said. "Thought I'd have, like, five of my own by now."

"Hostages to fortune," Mary reminded him. "Kyle might be your age before this thing is finished."

The scavenger threw up his hands. "God forbid. Whatcha got for us?"

"Whatcha need?" she countered. "Nobody needs a look-see?"

"Thank God, no. We've done pretty well this month. Just minor scrapes and bruises. We need some aspirin, some antibiotic cream, some of that anti-itch stuff, the diarrhea stuff, and stomach powder."

"Oh?"

"Yeah, Cook took a chance on some bacon. Oh boy, was she sorry."

"Everyone's fine now?"

"Yeah, that was two weeks ago."

"Glad I wasn't there for that meal," Mary said fervently. She'd had a couple of interesting reactions to camp food. She efficiently dispensed what he needed, got his signature, and went on her way.

"Mummy," Kyle said, moving his mule up toward her. "What was Carl talking about? What did he mean about the bacon?"

"Sometimes food goes bad, hon, but people don't know it, so they eat it anyway and then they get sick."

"Do they die?"

Mary turned to smile reassuringly at him. Kids both relished and feared hearing about such things. Of course, they never really thought that *they* could die; it was their parents they worried about, or their friends. She decided to be honest. *You're never too young to start learning,* she thought.

"Sometimes," she said. "Which is why people should cook their food thoroughly."

"What happens?"

"They get sick to their stomachs and they get diarrhea and then they lose too many fluids and they die."

His face knotted in confusion. "What's dia, dia . . . ?"

"Diarrhea?" She pursed her lips, then decided to be honest. "The squirts."

Kyle gave an evil little chuckle. "The squirts," he said, knowing very well what she meant.

Mary rolled her eyes. *My God,* she thought, *what have I done?*

For the next several miles he entertained himself by periodically emitting an amazing range of rude noises. At first she ignored him, which might have worked if he hadn't been so bored. She put up with it for a while, then pulled up the mule and turned to glare at him. Kyle subsided with a cherubic smile, only to start up again before they'd gone fifty feet. Mary stopped, and so did her son.

"If you don't cut it out, Kyle, you not only won't get a treat tonight, you'll get hardtack and nothing but."

Under that threat, Kyle's lower lip came out, but his mouth stayed shut and Mary had to endure an offended silence every bit as aggravating as the noises that occasioned it.

An hour later they were at the next meeting spot, but their guide hadn't yet appeared. Mary dismounted and helped her son down from the tall animal; they were on the edge of a rocky clearing, but there was a good boulder with a big pignut hickory leaning over it, excellent overhead cover.

"Well," she said, looking around. "I guess we might as well have lunch now while we wait."

Kyle began dashing around; Mary pointed a silent finger upward, and he veered in to make sure that he couldn't be seen. Not very likely—it was partly overcast—but Skynet might be doing a scan with IR sensors.

■ ■ ■

Kyle wasn't speaking to her, but he was a good little kid and he led his mule over to a tiny brook that flowed down the slight hill they were on. Mary took out the box with their lunch in it and led her riding mule and the pack mule over to drink beside their fellow. When she thought they'd had enough, she led them to a row of bushes whose tender green leaves would, no doubt, appeal to them and tied them there.

Then she sat down, offered Kyle a choice of sandwiches, and ate, sipping from her canteen from time to time. "It's nice here," she said at last. "Peaceful."

Kyle looked around, his face scrunched up. Birds sang, squirrels leaped from branch to branch, chirruping, sunlight dappled through the leaves. "It's okay. I guess."

Mary grinned. At least she'd gotten an answer. "Someday we'll be able to live anywhere we want," she said. "This would be a nice place. Don't you think?"

He looked around again and shrugged, then took a bite of his sandwich. *Okay,* Mary thought. *Have it your way.* Sometimes when Kyle was in a mood there was nothing you could do but wait it out.

"I wanna live in the Big Apple," he suddenly said.

She turned to stare at him. "Where did you hear about that?"

"One of the soldiers said he was born there." He took another bite of his sandwich and spoke unattractively around it. "Is it like *James and the Giant Peach*?"

"Don't talk with your mouth full. And no, it's not. *James and the Giant Peach* is a story; the Big Apple is a nickname for New York City. That was a big city full of tall buildings."

"Why did they call it an apple, then?" His face wore the perfect expression of "boy meets wacky adult nonsense."

Mary thought about it. She knew, she'd just never had to explain it. "Well, a lot of people used to go to New York to seek their fortunes. And there were so many of them that New York kind of became identified with the sort of self-confidence that sends someone out seeking success in a new and challenging place. Aaaaand, I guess their attitude might be summed up by saying that they saw the city as a great big apple that they were gonna take a bite out of and make it their own."

Kyle considered that. "Huh," he said.

"It's not there anymore," she said. "Well, its ruins are. *Quiet!*"

Kyle got quiet in a hurry as his mother rolled behind a bush and brought her carbine up; even then, her heart gave a little wrench as she saw him freeze like a rabbit, motionless. That was something kids had to learn in a hurry these days.

A woman came into sight, rifle held up over her head. "Sorry I'm late," she called.

"Hey," Mary said, standing up. "Hi, Gerri." She bundled up the sandwich wrappings. "No problem, it gave us a chance to eat."

"Where were you talking about?" Gerri asked. She was a dark-haired woman of medium height, thin as they all were, but heavy-boned.

"The Big Apple," Kyle said importantly.

" 'New York, New York, it's a hell of a town,' " Gerri sang.

" 'The Bronx is up and the Battery's down,' " Mary joined in.

"You said no singing!" Kyle said, considerably offended.

"Oops," Mary said. "You're right, sport. Sorry."

"No singing?" Gerri asked.

"Well, not while we're riding along. It's probably not a good idea in general," she said, blushing. "Distracting."

"Yeah, I guess there's a time and place for everything," Gerri agreed.

"Ahem. So, how're you doing?"

"*I* am fine. But Charley may have broken his ankle."

"Ooh. Okay, then. Let's get going."

■ ■ ■

Gerri's group had an excellent setup; a disused road tunnel nearly a quarter of a mile long, giving onto a ravine, making it easy to get in and out without leaving traces. The inside was smoky and chilly at the same time, and the inhabited part had a smell like old socks—partly actual old socks, partly just unwashed human and unlaundered clothes—combined with horse. Dinner smelled a lot better.

There was a resistance joke: *When the sun rises in the east, it means we will probably have stew for dinner.*

By the scent, this one had squirrel and rabbit; she'd become a connoisseur of field cooking, and thought she detected Jerusalem artichoke as well. It smelled savory, in fact—which meant thick and brown, usually.

Charley was another skinny man of indeterminate age with heavy stubble and weathered skin; she'd have pegged him as homeless, back before Judgment Day. His ankle was well and truly broken; the amount of swelling and the tense way he lay on a pine-bough bed near one of the hearths told her that.

She knelt and did a hands-on anyway; there were a lot of bones in the ankle. The talus ground together under her fingertips, the accident having happened only hours before. Her patient grunted and wheezed in lieu of screaming and gave her a wild-eyed, "what the hell are you doing?" look, while his flesh went cool and sweaty from the shock of pain. She gave him a shot of morphine, quickly set it, and wrapped the ankle in plaster.

"He's got to go back to base," she told Gerri. "That's going to take weeks to heal and he won't be any use out here while it does." Mary didn't have to mention that he would be an outright liability "out here." Even he knew that.

"Can you take him with you?"

Mary just looked at her, one eyebrow raised. Gerri refused to back down. So Mary broke it down for her. "I have two more stops today and four tomorrow. It's going to be agonizing enough for him to ride to base directly; a day and a half on horseback is something that hasn't even got a name. Not to mention it will set him back on healing."

"Short two people and two horses . . ." Gerri began, and followed them out. Then she smacked the heel of her hand into her forehead. "I'll ride to the ford with you."

Mary looked at her, and the unit leader went on, speaking a little louder to cut through the purl of water over rock—the white noise was good camouflage. "I needed to do a restocking run anyway, pretty soon—we're short on explosives and gun oil. That's on the way, and we'll take Charley along on a horse stretcher; the horses can carry freight on the way back. The sooner we get him back to headquarters, the sooner we can get things back to normal."

■ ■ ■

"It is inconvenient," Mary said, after a moment's uncomfortable silence.

The ford was where the creek ran out from the gully into flatter country, and an old graveled road ran down into it and then eastward; weeds were growing over the old ruts, bushes in some spots, and even saplings.

"*Damned* inconvenient."

"But accidents *are* inconvenient. And they'll send a replacement back with you. Don't roll your eyes at me, Gerri. I know you've got a tight group and you know each other's moves, but they won't send you a novice and there's just no way around it. Unless you plan to shoot him like a horse."

"And then we'd still need a replacement." Gerri rolled her eyes again.

"Yup." Mary gave Gerri a consoling smile. "It's not like you're light-years away from base, y'know."

Gerri grumbled something inaudible in response. Mary handed her a container of pills.

"Give him one every four hours for pain. Guard them with your life; those are hard to come by. I gave him enough morphine to make him comfortable for a while, but it's not going to last forever."

She looked at Gerri. "So how are things out here anyway?"

"Quiet." Gerri's eyes squinted as she looked around at the forested hills. Water purled around the hooves of her horse where it stood with its head down, lips slurping at the shallow rills that ran over gravel and rock.

"Way too quiet if you ask me. Nothing's moving out there but squirrels, and even they're quieter than usual." Her mouth twisted. "Makes me feel all twitchy."

"Yeah, I noticed that," Mary said. "I thought you might have an infestation. Gotta watch the personal hygiene; typhus, you know."

"Bitch," Gerri said pleasantly.

"That's Nurse Bitch to you, soldier."

Gerri grinned and opened her mouth to respond just as a rifle barked. Her face took on a distracted expression and then she slowly crumpled out of the saddle; the horse turned and pounded up the creek again, eyes wild and stirrups thumping its ribs. The more phlegmatic mules carrying the injured man merely tossed their heads and snorted.

Mary fought off her shock; she slipped to the ground and slapped the mule's rump.

"Run!" she said. "Go home!"

She turned for Kyle's mule and a bullet spanged into the ground at her feet, causing the creature to shy away, then break into a trot. She jerked toward cover and another bullet hit the ground at her feet. Mary's heartbeat was almost choking her; she looked desperately toward her son only to see a man burst from cover at the mule's feet, scaring the normally placid creature into shying.

Kyle cried out as the man grabbed his leg and shoved, causing him to lose his balance and fall hard. Mary headed toward him, and again, a bullet hit the ground before her.

Her eyes filled with tears of frustration and fear. *Okay, some-body's playing a game. Be calm. Calm down.* Easier thought than done. Her nerves jangled with adrenaline and her mouth was desert dry. If she headed for Kyle again, they might shoot him. She stood still, waiting for what was to come.

She watched Kyle roll around desperately on the dirt; appar-ently the breath had been knocked out of him and she wanted with all that was in her to be at his side. She stood still.

From out of the woods a man came in the gray camouflage that matched the winter-killed woods. He was a big man, his rifle cra-dled in his arms hunter-style. His face was bearded and he wore sunglasses. It wasn't bright enough to require them, but they were intimidating. Mary guessed he'd put them on for that purpose.

"Well, well," he said in a deep and pleasant voice, accented with the South. "A medic. That's somethin' that's always on our wish list, darlin'."

She looked at him. Then she swallowed, hard, and asked, "Can I see to the boy?"

"The boy? That what you call him at home? Boy?" He walked toward her a few paces and stopped. It looked, from the tilt of his head, as though he might be studying the woods around them. "If he's no relation to you, I'm just gonna go ahead and shoot him." The gun was in his hands and aimed as if by magic.

"No!" she shouted, stepping in his way. "Don't!"

He spat, then stared at her. Mary knew that she'd never been as frightened in her life as she was this moment—not when the bombs came down, not when that first Hunter-Killer came out of the woods, not the first time Dennis had come home wounded. This was a whole new level of terror. And this man knew it, and he knew how to use it.

"Sure," he said now. "You go ahead."

She turned, and a bullet hit the dirt at her feet. Mary spun back toward him, the shock on her face.

"Only a fool turns their back on the enemy, darlin'."

She backed away, glancing over her shoulder so she knew where to go. She was looking at the man when a bullet hit the ground just behind her heels, surprising a cry from her.

"'Course, you're at a disadvantage, bein' surrounded. Jeff, get that boy on his feet."

Mary looked over her shoulder to see the man who'd frightened the mule go over to Kyle and lift him by one arm. Her son fell to his knees, clutching his ribs, and the man cuffed him and dragged him up by his collar. "Stop," she said, reaching toward him.

The big man cuffed her himself, sending her sprawling. Mary was startled as much as hurt; she'd had no idea he was so close to her.

"Get up," he growled, and she scrambled to her feet. He stepped close to her. "From now on, everything in the world comes from me. To you, I am now God, and honey, you'd better become a religious fanatic 'cause I've got my eye on you and my eye never closes. The water you drink, the food you eat, even the air you breathe comes from me. You understand?" She nodded, eyes down. "You don't say 'stop,' you don't say 'don't,' you don't say 'no.' You can say 'please,' but don't overdo it. Do you understand?"

She nodded, shaking. "Yes," she whispered.

"You have to say, 'yes, *sir.*'"

"Yes, sir."

"If I tell you to eat a handful of shit, you will do it or the next sound you hear will be Jeff putting a bullet through that kid's head. Do you understand?"

She looked up at him, her eyes large with fear. "Yes, sir." *Oh, Kyle, what have I gotten you into?*

"If you try to escape I will kill the boy, slowly, and I will hamstring you. Do you understand?"

She nodded vigorously. "Yes, sir."

"If I ask you a question and you do not answer honestly, I will cut him. Now. Where did you get these supplies?"

"I stole them from the hospital I worked at," she said. "Most of them. Some I got in trade." The medicines she had were fresh, but for this duty they were put into old containers, many with expiration dates long past.

"Where did they get their medicine?" he asked.

"I don't know," she said. "Other hospitals or pharmacies, I guess. Sometimes that's where I get mine, old pharmacies. There's a lot of good stuff left if you know what it's for."

"Cut him," the man said.

"No! Please!" Mary cried. The big man hit her. She heard Kyle scream, and when she looked up he was bleeding from a cut on his chin. Blood was pouring through his fingers and he was crying. "Why?" she asked.

He kicked her in the stomach and she went down, gasping. He stepped close to her and put his foot on her hip, forcing her onto her back, then he put his foot on her stomach.

"I don't answer 'why?'" he said. "And you don't ask it. You also don't give me more information than I ask for, and most especially, you don't *lie to me!*"

"I didn't," she said, weeping. "I swear!"

He looked down at her, then applied pressure with his foot until she gasped. She resisted the urge to grab his foot and after a moment he smiled.

"You learn fast. That's good. Now, where did you come from?"

"Another camp of scavengers like these," she said.

"Can you take us to 'em?"

"I can show you where they were," Mary said. "But these people move around, they might not be there."

"Do you want me to have Jeff cut that boy again?" he asked. "What did I tell you about givin' me more information than I asked for?"

"I'm s-sorry, sir." He raised his hand and she flinched. There was no way to know how much he would choose to consider too much. She knew that it was a technique. That he was breaking her down and would continue to bark unreasonable demands and deliver arbitrary punishment as long as he thought necessary. There was nothing personal in it; he genuinely didn't care. It was just the way these things were done. Knowing this didn't seem to make it less effective.

"You told the kid to go home," he said. "Where's home?"

They'd prepared for this, an old farmhouse, ramshackle but livable, was the default location for home base. It was designed to look abandoned, but not totally so. She described it and gave its location.

"I know that place," the big man answered. "It's deserted. Nobody lives there." When she made no comment he kicked her, hard enough to hurt without causing injury. "Well?"

"We couldn't stay, not permanently. When the snow killed our garden, I knew we had to go look for food. So we travel a circle and come home once a year."

He looked at Kyle. "And that little sprat knows the way?"

"I guess so; we've been doing it almost as long as he's been alive. He's never had to go alone, though."

Apparently he decided to believe her. Or maybe he was just too lazy to kick her again. "How do you get paid?"

"Food, mostly. Sometimes goods. Once they gave us two mules."

He snorted. "Musta done somethin' pretty good that time."

"An epidemic," she said.

"Stupid bitch," he said mildly. "That mighta been some of our work you undone." He looked at her. "Get up. Go lengthen those stirrups for me and one of my men."

She did so, walking by Kyle with but a glance, not daring to chance more. He was crying as if his heart was broken and Mary hated the fact that the only thing she could do to help was to ignore him.

"Hey! Sam! Whadda we do about this one?" a woman called.

Mary glanced up; a tall, gangling woman was standing by the horse litter that held the sleeping Charley. She'd thrown the cover open and he lay snoring in plain sight. The woman tipped him out onto the ground and he lay in an ungraceful heap, the fresh plaster of his cast standing out against the brown dirt.

"Please," Mary called out. She finished buckling the strap and took a few steps in that direction.

"Please what?" the big man, Sam, asked. "Please don't kill the fucker?" He pushed at the unconscious man with his foot. "Why the hell not?"

"Because—" Mary's voice broke on a sob. "I just fixed his foot!"

She broke down completely, falling to her knees sobbing. The marauders stared at her for a moment, then Sam broke out laughing and the others followed suit.

"I can see that," Sam said, slapping his thigh. "Sure, that's reasonable." He gave a high-pitched giggle. "You don't mind if we take the tent and blanket, do ya?"

Mary shook her head, daring to let hope bloom.

"You're not really gonna leave him alive, are ya?" the woman asked.

"Hey, Mona, he's got a cast on his foot. He's in the middle of the wilderness with no food, no supplies, no weapons, and no friends. I *am* killin' him."

The woman grinned, showing missing teeth. "I guess so, fearless leader."

"Hey, don't you be so sassy," Sam advised. He walked over to Mary and stroked her hair. "We got another woman with us now, girl. If you ain't nice you won't be gettin' any."

Oh, shit! Mary thought. *I am so gonna get raped.*

"I know what you're thinkin'," Sam said quietly. She looked up at him. "But it ain't rape if it's consensual. And it will be consensual, or that little boy is gonna pay the price. You hear me?"

Mary nodded. "Yes, sir." *You dirt-eating bastard!*

"All right, then." Sam mounted the mule. "Pass me up that kid," he said to Jeff. Kyle struggled a little and Sam cuffed him lightly. "You want me to hit your mama again?" he asked. Kyle shook his head. "Then you behave. I don't even want to know you're there. You hear me?" Kyle nodded. "All right." He looked down at Mary and smiled. "Let's move out."

If I ever see Dennis again he's going to kill me, Mary thought. Jeff shoved her from behind and she started walking. *And I won't blame him a bit because I want to kill myself.*

■ ■ ■

Sam grunted one last time and rolled off her with a sigh. Mary swallowed hard, fighting nausea. She'd tried her best to cooperate, but he stank and she hated him more than she'd ever hated anyone in her life.

"That was pretty good," he said. He glanced aside at her. "'Course it'll be better once you get to know what I like." He grinned. "And you get to like me."

After a moment she looked at him. "Can I see to my son now?" she asked.

"No." He sounded annoyed.

"Please, he's just a little boy."

He rolled over onto her; quick as a striking snake his hand was on her throat, choking her. "Listen," Sam hissed. "I think kids are vermin. I think anyone who would have a kid after Judgment Day is a criminal." He squeezed harder. "Am I clear?"

She nodded as well as she could, forming "yes" with her lips. He let her go and rolled onto his back.

"Now you spoiled my good mood," he said. "Get the fuck away from me."

Mary rose and picked up her clothes, then paused, wondering if she could get away with dressing before she left.

"And stay away from that kid, hear? Now get out!"

She ducked out of the tent and dressed quickly. As she was tugging down her shirt, Jeff sauntered over.

"Hey, sugar, don't get all dressed yet," he said, grinning.

"Jeff!" Sam bellowed from inside the tent. "Go fuck yourself, or Mona. Leave 'er alone."

Jeff glared at Mary in a way that made her feel that from now on, if he could do her a bad turn, he would. Then he walked away.

Shit, she thought wearily. *Shit, shit, shit.*

■ ■ ■

They'd been walking east for five days now, passing the occasional cluster of deserted farms, a number of small towns falling apart in slow motion, and once, in the distance, the charred ruins of a city. Most of the people they saw had been dead a long time. But once they crossed the path of some gypsies. That was what they were called anyway. Just people who took to the road hoping to find a place better than the one they were in, and kept on going since there was no such place.

They were mostly harmless, though criminals of opportunity; thieves and traders. They were welcome everywhere for a day or two, then they were welcome to leave. The resistance left them alone, or on occasion lent them a hand. For which the gypsies sometimes gave them intel at a cut rate.

This group had two wagons, three broken-down horses, and a mule. It looked like they were a single extended family with four older people, six adults in all, and seven children of various ages. They seemed like the kind of people who had survived rather than thrived even before Judgment Day.

The instant he saw them Sam lifted his assault rifle and began firing. Jeff and Mona joined in with cries of glee. The mules made their displeasure known by dancing and, in the case of the one Sam was riding, essaying a buck or two. He whacked it on the side of its head with the stock of his gun. Mary was too stunned at first to move, and it wasn't until the mule bumped her that she got out of its way.

She watched the gypsies fall. They'd barely had time to scream, let alone be afraid. Mary started forward a step when the children began to drop, then forced herself to stop. There was nothing she could do, except hope that Sam hadn't noticed that one step. Suddenly she became aware that someone was firing from a small copse of trees to the southeast. Retreating behind the mule, she tried to tell Sam.

A rocket, immediately followed by another, roared from the trees, striking the two wagons and turning them and the animals into flaming debris. The smell of burning flesh frightened the mules, and the Luddites had all they could do to keep them under control for a few minutes. Leo held on to the pack mules' reins for dear life, but he never took his eyes off the copse for a moment.

"What's your problem, asshole?" Mona bellowed. She skipped back from Jeff's mule and swatted it on the rump.

"Shut up!" Sam said, in a stage whisper. "It's one of them."

"Has to be," Jeff said, looking as white as paste.

Mona looked toward the copse and went still, swallowing hard.

Watching them, Mary became even more afraid. If these vicious killers were frightened of whoever hid in the trees, there was even more reason for her to be afraid. She looked up into Kyle's terrified eyes and wanted nothing more than to grab him and run. But she knew she wouldn't get two paces before they killed her. If she waited to see what happened, she might live. A slim chance at survival was better than none. Especially since her death assured Kyle's.

The trees began to thrash, and then to lean forward, as a massive machine lurched out of the copse on caterpillar treads. It was at least sixteen feet high, and from a distance looked narrow. Its entire front was a wall of gun ports and to either side were missile launchers, the missiles themselves racked on its sides. There were spotlights atop its turret and no doubt its body was packed with ammunition. It trundled toward them with surprisingly little sound. It crushed some of the gypsy children's bodies as it came on, causing Mary to wince, but she kept silent. Finally it stopped.

"Luddite Patrol A-36," Sam barked. "Sam Marshall, AS-783490 commanding."

The machine was silent. All of the humans remained silent and immobile, waiting for its response.

"Patrol A-36," the machine said in a slight Austrian accent. A red laser spot appeared on Mary's chest. "What is this?"

"This prisoner is a medic," Sam explained. "Standing orders are to acquire such persons and convey them to the camp."

"And this?" The red spot appeared on Kyle's forehead.

"This is the prisoner's offspring," Sam said. "By retaining him, she becomes more tractable and less inclined to suicide."

Mary stared at him. What had happened to the good ol' boy she knew and loathed?

The machine was quiet and still for so long it might have been turned off. None of them made that assumption, though. Mary had the impression that if the machine didn't answer until the following morning, then sunrise would find the humans in exactly these positions.

"Acceptable," the machine said at last. "Carry on, A-36." It backed up slightly, turned, and moved back down the road.

Sam motioned them forward, riding the mule carefully around the flaming wreckage. No one spoke; no one but Mary and Kyle watched the killing machine trundle away.

They'd been walking for at least half an hour before Mary got up the courage to ask Sam, "What was that?"

He didn't answer for a long time, riding on without even looking down at her. They rode and walked on for a mile or more before he spoke. "That was a Hunter-Killer machine," he said at last. "Its job is to seek out humans and destroy them."

Mary looked at him. "I thought, from the way you were all acting, that it was going to kill you."

Sam's lips thinned. "Sometimes they do. But we're all good Luddites," he said. "We've had ourselves fixed. So there's no need to kill us; we won't be breedin' anytime soon and we're good at our jobs. That's what makes this patrol an A unit."

"Oh," she said.

They walked on for several more miles before she began to notice a definite industrial tang in the air.

"We're almost there," Mona called out.

Sam called a halt and pulled an instrument out of his pocket. He tapped a code into it and they waited. After five minutes there was a chime from the unit and they started forward again. Shortly thereafter they walked up a hill, and when Mary came panting to the top, she stopped breathing altogether in shock.

Before her, in what once must have been a small valley, was a single one-story building. It must have been two miles square by three. Smoking chimneys appeared every five hundred feet or so and there were towers at each corner and a small satellite dish every thousand feet. The whole structure was surrounded by a wire fence, which had guard towers every fifty feet. It was ugly and had a thrown-together look, common to all completely utilitarian buildings. She hated it on sight.

"It's a lot worse inside," Sam said.

She looked up at him and could have sworn she saw pity on his face. *Maybe that's why he wears those glasses,* she thought.

CHAPTER 18

The Terminator turned its head toward the ill-defined heat signature, trying to refine its focus. After a few seconds, when the brightness refused to become distinct, it turned away. Its processors told it that the bright mass was probably rock with a high metal content still hot from the recently set sun. It was the last evaluation the Terminator would ever make, because its neural net processor was completely wrong.

John grinned as he raised his head from behind the rock and watched the Terminator turn away. Snog's new gizmo might not have much staying power, but it was a real lifesaver while it did last. It offered a false signal for a space of about four feet around its wearer, evening out the heat signals, making the body appear a bright, amorphous mass, such as might be left behind by an explosion. He carefully lined up the Terminator's head; the plasma bolt struck in a beam of actinic light, and the hard resistant alloy of the thing's skull turned into a strobing mass of molten gobbets and burning gas.

John's night-vision goggles automatically turned the brightness down; he rolled to another rock—always displace after you shoot—then flipped the switch on his unit and moved forward.

Others moved forward with him, the HQ strike unit. They went from rock to rock across the stony hillside, scattered with chamisos and cactus. The night air smelled of the herbal scents of desert shrubs, and of ozone and hot metal as bolts split the darkness.

It was unusual for John to do fieldwork these days. Most of what he did now was plan and organize and give orders. Actually carrying a rifle into the fray? He honestly didn't have the time for it.

But in this case, nothing would have kept him out of it. His mother was in trouble.

From out of nowhere a spring box leaped up before him, multiple legs reaching, acid-filled hypo already exposed. John swung the butt of his plasma rifle like a baseball bat, knocking the thing flying and followed up with a blast that turned it to melting parts—one of which stung his arm through the coarse strong fabric of his uniform. He swore and batted it away; the cooling metal crackled as it spun away, leaving a discolored spot on his sleeve.

Up until now most of the Central and South American auto-factories had mainly produced these small but quite deadly killers. They were very simple, with very simple programming: the mechanical equivalent of a weasel. Leap up from the front, inject the heart with hydrochloric acid; leap up from the back, inject the brain. Small, cheap, and easy to produce, their only defect from Skynet's point of view was that they could kill only one human at a time.

And so Skynet had slowly expanded its smaller south-of-the-border factories until they could produce full-scale HKs and Terminators. The resistance had taken out the factories that they knew about, but knowing they would, Skynet had built many more of them, not always in remote areas. The HKs had seemed to come out of nowhere and twenty small villages had been destroyed before the resistance in Mexico had even been able to get the word out.

The attackers crested a rise; the maps said it was an abandoned lead-silver mine, with an equally deserted village gradually crumbling back into the adobe mud it had been made from.

Instead, it was *seething* with not-life. Before him, John could see the ground moving, a glittering ripple as the tiny robot killers came forward, and his stomach clenched. There was something about an infestation like this that brought the hair up on the back of his neck and made him want to kill mindlessly. He swept the plasma beam from right to left and back again, retreating before the tide of them, cursing as the rifle began to burn his left hand through the insulated forestock.

Beside him a soldier came up and swept the ground with a low-tech—but for this operation, equally effective—flamethrower. His heart beating overtime, John put up his rifle. He should save the batteries for the big killers. Skynet was keeping them back, sending in these little monsters to wear the resistance fighters down and to use up their ammunition.

Not gonna work, John thought. *When's the damn thing gonna learn?* If the future wasn't something he could change significantly, then neither could Skynet. The humans were going to win. Not yet. Probably not for a long time, but piece by piece, bit by bit, they were gaining ground. Biologicals had a distinct advantage over the machines. They could reproduce without having to mine, refine, transport, mold, and construct themselves; the biosphere took care of that.

The soldier stopped spraying and the two of them waited to see if anything would come out of the flames. When nothing moved, they did, cautiously making their way through the burned parts. Stepping on an acid-filled needle would be a stupid way to lose your foot.

According to reconnaissance, the factory was in this basin. John gripped his rifle a bit tighter. It had been a long time since the factories were easy targets. Skynet didn't rely on keeping them remote anymore; it would fight the resistance for this factory with all its power.

John ducked down when he saw the lights. HKs had huge spotlights mounted on the top of their metallic carapaces, not that they needed them. Like the Terminators, they had IR sensors that tracked by body heat. But there was something about those huge lights that intimidated, and distracted, and, unfortunately, rendered night-vision goggles less effective.

John flipped his own up. "HKs," he said succinctly, informing everyone in the network that Skynet was sending in the big guns.

He relayed coordinates so that their own big guns could respond to the threat.

It was better when the things were destroyed sight unseen. Skynet liked, on occasion, to bind prisoners, or bodies, or both to the machines. Not knowing which was which tended to make firing on them difficult. Even though those manning the guns *knew* they were not in any kind of position to save those people, still, they would hesitate. It had been one of Skynet's many psychological experiments.

The problem is, John thought, *every time it does something like this and we have to act against our own instincts, we lose something of our humanity.*

War, Dieter had told him, tended to do that. But in John's opinion, Skynet, through trial and error, was making them all more machinelike.

"What are we going to be like when this is over?" John had asked.

"Happier," Dieter replied. "In the meantime, we have to do what we must to survive."

John ducked behind an outcropping of rock and waited for the HK to make its appearance. *You'd think they'd have learned not to outline themselves against the skyline,* John thought. But then, there wasn't any other route the big machine could take out of the valley where it had been manufactured.

The rocket screamed by his position and John curled into a fetal position, trusting his armor to catch any fragments and his luck to save him from the explosion. The detonation was about fifteen yards in front of him and the concussion felt like someone hitting him hard on the back, pushing the air out of his lungs. The heat was briefly intense.

He rolled back to see the machine trundle forward a few more meters, most of its top half blown away, the bottom a furnace. It rolled away, mindless and blind. Behind it, illuminated by the flames, came a gleaming squad of T-90s, the skeletal Terminators, red eye sensors gleaming, grinning with human-shaped teeth.

John barked an order and the artillery behind him opened fire again—25mm chain guns this time, mounted on Humvees. The killing machines scattered like bowling pins in the blast, parts twinkling away like stars in flight. Those on the outside of the explosion were struck dormant for a few seconds. Stooped over, John ran forward and shot a blast into the head of the nearest Terminator. The one beyond it came slowly back to life, found its plasma rifle by feel, and began to raise it.

A burst of fire blinded it and John himself fired again, destroying it. He turned to the soldier with the flamethrower and found it was a young woman—no, a girl. If she was more than fifteen, he'd be amazed.

"Thanks," he said briefly, feeling suddenly senior. "Sweep these bushes; confuse their sensors so that we can move in under cover."

"Yes, sir."

She went to work and in moments the heat was almost more than he could stand. He was squinting, lips pulled back from his teeth in a grimace. But the girl had her visor down and what expression he could see was serene. It was weird to feel safe enough to bring his people through in all this light, but the machines had difficulty adjusting their sensors to this much heat. John gave the order and men and women came streaming through, scattering over the rocky terrain.

"Careful," he said. "Spring boxes." You could almost feel the tension go up. Everybody hated those things.

Below, an HK moved into position.

"Clear the gap," John shouted, and soldiers dived away from the rise and the burning bushes; he rolled down the hill toward the factory, stopping himself by grabbing onto a low-growing bush.

The Hunter-Killer fired and the ground behind him heaved and burned in the blast, the rocks themselves melting. It moved forward and John could tell that it was going to sweep the ground behind him in descending arcs. Even blind, that would allow it to do maximum damage.

"Fire!" he shouted. That blast would give the artillery some idea of trajectory.

All around the HK were Terminators, also blind, no doubt. They would wait for their big brother to finish; then they would come forward to mop up any resistance.

Only two HKs, John thought. *And none of the flying kind, thank God.*

But what did it mean? Why was the factory so lightly guarded? His eyes went to the factory itself. The outer surface was honeycombed with little rectangular slots for the spring boxes; it looked like some kind of high-tech nest. The thought made him swallow. On the roof were antennae that would directly connect it to Skynet.

No doubt the bastard is watching this right now, he thought. He got some satisfaction in knowing that Skynet wasn't seeing any more than its creatures could show it. Lots of white heat haze and black background, and the same thing from orbit.

The factory was small up top, but he knew from experience that it could go down as many as six levels. A place like this would probably have no human slaves. They'd check, just to be sure, but there had been no signs of cultivation, as there usually were when humans were present. Nor any sign of a waste dump. Still. Skynet was a tricky bugger. And these days every human life was of value.

And now for the really tricky question, he thought. *Now, if I were my mom, where would I be?*

"Major Hopkins," he said aloud. "Standard attack on the factory. Give me a schematic—is there an outlying relay com dish?"

"Yes, sir. Just about . . . here."

The data came in over John's optic; he noted it, and matched the view to the terrain. "Which means Mom is over there," he said. "HQ squad, follow me!"

An IR scan showed a thermal bloom halfway up another one of the endless rocky hills; there was another on top, where the melted remains of a transmission tower showed.

Good tactics, Mom, he thought. Taking that out would reduce the enemy's coordination throughout the area. *Getting trapped in a cave, not so hot.*

The ruins of the machines were thick about the entry to the cave; which meant Sarah's squad was probably about out of charge and ammo.

"Mortars," he said. "Gimme a strike on the following position."

■ ■ ■

Sarah was propped up against a rock outcropping, giving orders to a young man who knelt on one knee by her side. A medic was just fitting her arm into a sling.

"AH!" Sarah barked. She glared at the medic, then, turning away, sullenly apologized.

There was a large bandage wrapping the greater part of her shoulder, showing a seepage of blood at the center, and burn cream glistened on her neck and upper arm. Dark circles surrounded her eyes like shiners, but it was exhaustion and too little food that had put them there.

When the soldier and the medic became aware of John standing there, they murmured "excuse me" and moved away. Sarah smiled up at him, then closed her eyes and leaned her head against the rock.

"Thank God you're here," she said quietly.

"Thank God *you're* here," he responded. He shook his head. "Mom—"

"Don't start," she cut in. "I'm not in the mood. This could have happened to anybody."

That was true, he knew. It wasn't bad leadership or foolish

bravado that had gotten her into this scrape. She was still one of the best field commanders in the resistance. But she was hurt, and she was his mother.

Sighing, John dropped cross-legged beside her. Just sitting and looking at her, and waiting for her to open her eyes. For a moment he thought that she actually dropped off to sleep and he felt a bit guilty, as though he'd been unfairly pressuring her. Then he steeled his resolve. If she was asleep he'd wait until she woke up, even if it took all night.

By which time I'll be asleep and she'll decide to wait for me, then she'll fall asleep again. He smiled, and waited. In a few moments she struggled to open her eyes and smiled at him. It made her look years younger.

"I think I dropped off there. I wasn't sure if I'd dreamed you or not."

"You did. Drop off, I mean." He reached out and placed his hand on her head, stroking the hair back from her brow. "How bad are you hurt?"

"Don't know yet," she said. "It'll take a real doctor to tell me that. Hurt enough to *really* want a painkiller." Sarah looked puzzled. "Did that kid give me one?"

"I'll find out," he said, and rose.

He came back in a few minutes with something in his fist. He sat down again, and taking up her canteen, unscrewed the top and poured some water into it. Then he offered her a pill.

"Codeine," he said.

"Ah, codeine is our friend," Sarah said, and popped it, taking the cap and swallowing the water. "I feel better just knowing I'll feel better."

He smiled, but in a worried way. "Mom, I've been thinking."

"Good," she said. "You make a mother proud. Keep that up and we'll all get through this."

He grinned. "I've been thinking about *you.*"

She sighed and signaled him to go on.

"Mom, I think it's time you died."

She turned wide eyes on him. "Hello?"

"Not really," he said quickly, smiling. "Look, Mom, you're badly hurt here. It might be an incapacitating injury, which means your fieldwork days may be through. I think it's time you went home."

"Home?" she said, as if she'd never heard the word. Sarah pushed herself up a bit, gritting her teeth as she did so. John made to reach for her, but she warned him off with a look. "Where exactly is home?" Sarah raised her brows. "Paraguay? L.A. perhaps?"

He pressed his lips together and smiled. "Home, for you, is where Dieter is. And since his injury, Dieter has been in Washington State training people. He could use your help. And I think you'd like to see him again."

"You know I would," Sarah agreed. "But you also know that there's still a lot to do."

"I'm not proposing that you retire, Mom. Not that you ever would. I'm saying that maybe it's time you stopped fieldwork."

"Before I make a fool of myself?"

"More like before you get killed. I think you're too valuable. One of the things you do best is train. Look at me," he said, flinging his arms wide.

She grinned. "Yeah, the Great Military Leader Dickhead." She nodded sagely. "That's my work."

"You bet it is. I also need you to run herd on Snog. He and his gang are getting into some very weird tribal stuff. You're the only human being on the planet that scares him enough to rein him in." John paused and chewed his lower lip for a moment before he continued. "I also think that we need a martyr."

Sarah raised her brows. "Oh, really?"

"Yup. See, I think that people need to be reminded what they're fighting for. And I think that bringing your story"—he looked sympathetically at his mother—"your struggle, before them will remind them that there is hope."

She frowned. "Maybe I'm tired, but I still don't see why I have to actually die."

"Well," he snorted, "you don't *actually* die. We'll just say you did and give you a new identity."

"Uh-huh. Did I miss the why part?"

"Because if you just sort of semiretire, I'm afraid that people will be reminded how long this thing has been going on and how long it might well continue. Which, as you can see, would be a real downer."

"And my death would be a signal to party. Yeah, sure, I can see that."

"Mom. Your death would make you a saint." He paused. "A *legend.*"

She blinked. "Oh." It was what Kyle had called her. The legend. Sarah looked up at John with tears in her eyes. "I see."

He patted her hand. "Why don't you sleep on it tonight."

Yawning hugely, she tried to speak. Then repeated, "I don't think I have any choice in that. Codeine's kicking in. G'night." She moved her lips in a kiss and sank under the drug.

John sat and watched her for a long time. The medic came and checked her, nodded positively at John—which was a relief—and went away. The rest of the battle was routine; the only real question was how many casualties they'd take, and how much productive gear they could capture—and how much they could make sure wasn't booby-trapped.

He thought he'd convinced her. At least he hoped he had. The last thing he wanted was to make her mad. But she needed time to recover from this wound, if she ever did. And he saw no reason why that recuperation shouldn't happen in Dieter's vicinity. And once there she'd be able to see how much she was needed there. He thought he'd convinced her about the legend thing, too. At least he hoped so.

It took time to become a legend and Kyle was already ten years old. John sighed. Even though he thought this move was necessary, he disliked the dishonesty of it. The "first" time, maybe his mother really had died in this cave. But since, thank God, she hadn't . . . now was the time to remove her from immediate danger.

His aide came and tapped John's shoulder, waking him from a doze. With a last fond look at Sarah's sleeping face, he rose and followed the soldier to where his people were waiting to make their reports.

MISSOURI

The clinic was ill lit, small, and not very clean. But given the supplies they had, the three-nurse staff had managed to save a fair number of lives in the three years Mary Reese had been there. There were patients in three of the five beds, two with the mystery fevers that tended to afflict the prisoners here. One with a nasty injury from having his hand dragged into some machinery.

Mary was changing the man's bandages and thinking about the days when microsurgery might have saved his hand. The accident had only happened yesterday and so far infection hadn't set in. That, at least, was good. But if the hand didn't heal and the man couldn't work, he was doomed.

Stretcher bearers rushed in with a man who was badly burned around the head and upper body. He was unconscious and apparently quite heavy.

"Where do we put him?" one of the men barked.

Mary gestured to an examining table and took a second look at them. They were unfamiliar and, she noticed for the first time, not wearing the prisoner's uniform of baggy gray cotton shirt and pants. They were dressed for the outdoors, wearing cammies. The stretcher bearers put the patient down on the table, and abandoning the stretcher, scurried away as though afraid of getting caught someplace they weren't supposed to be.

Mary met the eyes of Tia Nevers, her assistant, a young black woman whose very short hair molded a beautifully shaped skull.

"What the hell was that all about?" Tia muttered.

"My thoughts exactly," Mary agreed. She quickly finished with her patient and went over to their sink to wash her hands.

Then she brought some warm soapy water over to the examining table and began to briskly wash off the man's face and head. Tia brought scissors and started clipping off the burned hair, clearing his scalp for treatment.

"Looks to me like a plasma beam passed pretty close to this boy," Tia said.

Mary nodded. "It does, doesn't it? Which makes me wonder what he's doing here." The HKs didn't routinely round up the wounded for treatment. They were much more likely to crush them under their treads. Was he resistance? If so, what evil plan was Skynet working on?

She scrubbed, as gently and as quickly as possible, and the soot came off the man's face unwillingly. At last she'd cleared the better part of his countenance and suddenly she recognized him. Shock froze her and she stood with the dripping cloth in her hand, staring.

Tia looked up at her from where she had been cutting his shirt off and then glanced at the patient. "Holy shit!" she hissed. "I *know* this bastard! He's a goddamned Luddite! His name is Sam." She stood back from the table and looked at Mary. "What's he doing here?"

Mary looked around and leaned toward her friend. "I don't think he is supposed to be here. Those guys took off like a shot once they'd dropped him. At a guess, I'd say Skynet is starting to liquidate its human followers."

The other woman looked at Sam like he was a half-squashed bug and pulled her lips back from her teeth. "Gooood," she said. Tia threw down the scissors and started to walk away.

"Hold it!" Mary grabbed her arm.

Tia swept Mary's hand away with a stroke and glared at her. "He killed my husband," she said coldly. "No way am I treating him." She met Mary's eyes. "You can't ask me to do that."

"First of all," Mary said, "he's the first person from outside this place that I've seen in two years. He can tell us what's going on."

"He's a *Luddite,* Mary! You can't trust anything those assholes say!"

"Second, he's badly burned; there's very little we can do but make him comfortable."

"*I'm* not givin' that bastard our painkillers. Let him suffer like he's made other people suffer." She glared defiance at her friend.

"We can't do that," Mary said. She looked at Tia sympathetically.

Tia rolled her eyes. "Oh, yes we can!" She compressed her lips and moved a step closer to Mary. Looking down, she said softly, "That . . . *thing* raped me while my dying husband watched." Then she looked up. "I won't lift a finger to help him. Not one finger!"

Mary grabbed her arm and gave her a shake. "Yes, you will!"

Tia stared at her, taken aback. "And why is that?" she finally asked.

"Because you're better than he is. Because you're a healer. And because we are not going to give Skynet that kind of victory over us." This time she took a step closer, her gaze boring into Tia's startled eyes. "Because we have to hang on to every shred of humanity we've got. Because every time we do that, it's a victory over Skynet. I can't keep that thing from killing my body, but I will *never* let it kill my soul!"

Tia pulled her head back and looked at her. "Oh," she said. She blinked a few times, then added, "Then I guess I'd better finish cuttin' off that shirt."

"I guess you better." Mary felt as surprised as Tia looked. *Where did that come from?* she wondered. She went back and picked up the cloth, and continued washing away the soot.

All they had to treat him with was some over-the-counter-style antibiotic cream. It was past its use-by date and they didn't have much of it, but it was probably better than the nothing they'd be using otherwise. Mary doubted that he was going to make it.

Looks like getting sterilized wasn't enough, she thought contemptuously.

■ ■ ■

Every day Mary left some of her dinner and a short note for Kyle in a different place. The next location was mentioned in the note, which usually said only, "I love you." Once or twice a year she might chance actually talking to him and she tried to get a glimpse of him every week.

It was hard, but it was safer. They hadn't been in the factory a week before they realized that if anyone showed a partiality for another then that person might have to bear punishment for the transgressor. Since the transgression might well be imaginary Mary told Kyle that she would always love him and would try to help him, but that she was going to keep her distance. Even at seven, he'd seen enough to understand.

She walked along; then, so quickly it was hard to see, she left a small bundle on a hidden shelf. Yet, before she could withdraw her hand, a smaller hand caught her wrist. Startled, she looked to the dark slot between machines and saw her son. She smiled and sat down, pretending to remove a stone from her shoe.

"Are you all right?" she whispered.

"Yeah. Just wanted to hear your voice."

She held the shoe up in a way that allowed her to turn in his direction. She could see a smudged face and bright eyes. She grinned in pure pleasure and hid it with a grimace. "Good to see you," she said, trying not to move her lips. "I love you."

He smiled. "Love you, too, Mom."

She turned the shoe over and pretended to be prying at something. "Everything all right?"

"Except for being here, yeah." His face wore a rebellious expression. "I want, I *need,* to see the sun, Mom. I can't stand this much longer."

She stopped fiddling with the shoe and looked at him. "Do not panic," she said sternly. "And don't do anything foolish."

"I think I know a way out," he whispered. "I could find Dad and bring help."

"You need information about what it's like out there," Mary said, returning to picking at her shoe. "I think I can get it for you, but it might take some time. You have to wait."

He looked at her for a moment. "I'm not sure I believe you," he finally said.

Mary half smiled, and looked up at him from under her eyebrows. "Yeah, I've led you astray so many times. How could you possibly trust me?"

It distressed him, and he kind of wiggled, looking all over the place before his gaze returned to her, whereupon he frowned.

"They brought Sam into the clinic today," she said.

"Who?"

That made her blink. "Sam. The guy who caught us, remember?"

He nodded slowly, his eyes big. "You're helping him?" His voice indicated total disbelief, as though she'd suggested that she and one of the machines were going to have a baby.

Mary gave him a very serious look, a hard look. "I'm going to pump him for information," she said. "I think I can get him to tell me the truth. Once we have some information, we'll know how to proceed."

Kyle looked at her with the eyes of desperation. "Mom," he said, "I need—"

"I know," she said quickly. "I really do know *exactly* how you feel. But you've got to give me some time. Meet me beside the stampers in a week. Same time." She looked at him, willing him to agree.

He got up and began to withdraw. "I'll be there," he said. Then he was gone.

Mary fiddled with her shoe a bit more, then put it on and went on her way.

■   ■   ■

The next day—morning to Mary, though it could be midnight in the world outside—she glanced around and saw that the hand injury was gone. According to his chart, which she found in the file, he'd been removed during the night shift. *Glad I wasn't here,* she thought. Nothing that happened here was uglier than "removals."

The two fever cases were resting, both of their fevers had broken during the night. *Nothing needed there,* she thought with satisfaction. She found Sam awake and hyperalert with pain. His heart was hammering at a hundred forty beats a minute and he was shuddering violently, his teeth chattering uncontrollably.

"Gimme something for the pain!" he demanded through clenched teeth. "Now!"

Mary checked his chart; he was certainly due for something, overdue in fact. *Looks like Sam had another satisfied customer on the staff last night.* She nodded. "Okay, looks like you're due."

"And turn the heat up; it's freezing."

She looked at him with pity. "You're cold because you've been badly burned. I'm afraid there's nothing I can do to help you there." She ignored the impatient sound he made and went to get him some codeine. "How did this happen to you?" she asked over her shoulder.

"Accident."

She looked over at him. His eyes were closed and he shuddered, but she could see he was trying to contain it. Mary tightened her lips. He was pitiful, but she couldn't let him see that. "Oh, right," she said. "It must have been an accident because no machine would *ever* deliberately harm a human."

"Fuck you," he said.

She stood over him, pill in one hand, glass of water in the other. "You know what, Sam? You're not supposed to be here.

Your guys rushed you in here and then dropped you like a hot potato. Here, in the prisoners' clinic. Think about that." She leaned toward him. "I don't think they thought your accident was an accident."

"Fuck you," he snarled.

"Redundant," she said. "But then, I guess you're not at your best. What's it like out there?"

"It's paradise." The look in his eyes was pure evil.

"That must be why the machines thought they could dispose of your services," Mary said lightly. She leaned forward again and stage whispered, "Does it occur to you yet that turning the world over to the machines might not be the best thing for the birds, and the bees, and the bunnies?"

"I hate you," Sam growled.

"Gee, and I was gonna ask you to be my valentine. Do you want this?" she asked, holding up the pill. His eyes went from it to her face and he couldn't hide his desperation. It was a look that made her feel sick and triumphant at the same time. "All I've got is pills. Can you lift your head to take it and swallow water?"

He did so, straining visibly.

"What is it like out there?" Mary asked, spacing her words. She held the pill and the water ready.

After a second he dropped his head down and closed his eyes. "You bitch," he muttered, panting slightly.

"Look," she said firmly. "Just answer me. What's the difference? It's not like it's going to help me; I just want to know. Tell me, and tell me the truth."

He lay as still as he could, swallowing hard. She could see his heart beating overtime.

"What's the difference?" she asked, deadly quiet. He opened his eyes and turned his head slightly. Tears trickled down his cheek. "The difference is, if you don't answer me, or if I think you're lying to me"—she held up the pill—"I'm going to put this away."

"I'm gonna tell them about that kid of yours," he said, sneering as best he could.

Mary put the pill and the water down, her heart pounding, and picked up a pillow. She stood beside his bed.

"I could always do you the favor of putting you out of your misery," she said. "Mention the boy again. Go ahead. Mention him." She could see that he saw the truth in her eyes; he turned away, blinking.

"Am I gonna make it?" he asked.

Mary bit her lips. Then decided to tell him the truth. "No. You're too badly wounded and we don't have anything like the facilities for treating burns of this magnitude." She watched him take that in.

"They shoulda let me die," he said.

"Yes, I guess they should have. But they didn't know that you didn't have a chance and they wanted to give you one. They were friends and they meant you well."

"Stupid bastards."

"Yeah, well. Thing is, you could last anywhere from forty-eight hours to two weeks. Two long, long weeks. And I could help you. Keep you as comfortable as possible; let you die with a little dignity. Or I could just ignore you and let you die in your own shit." She rolled her eyes thoughtfully. "Unlessss, you threaten the boy again. In which case"—she tossed the pillow away—"this is much too kind." Mary leaned close. "I know some very, very painful ways to die, Sam."

She shook her head sadly. "You don't have to go through this. Just answer me. C'mon. Tell me what I want to know and I'll give you the pill. Trust me, you'll feel a lot better."

Mary stood back and waited. Soon he was shivering again, in pain and from the effect of losing so much skin. Mary bit her lip. Withholding medication went against everything she believed in. She could only do it for Kyle, and because she despised this man.

"There's fewer Luddites," he said at last, sounding out of breath. "Most of my friends are gone."

Mary rolled her eyes. *Like I care,* she thought.

"There's tons more Terminators. Whole squads of 'em. They're everywhere. And the HKs, they're bigger and better than ever. Some of 'em can fly; they're deadly accurate, very heavy weapons."

"And they just 'happened' to get you by mistake," Mary said.

He opened his eyes and looked at her, breathing heavily.

"Go on," she said. "What about the resistance?"

"They're still there. They're not winning, but they're not losing, either. That's why they need us Luddites," he said, his voice sounding plaintive. "We could infiltrate, spy, sabotage. They'd never know what hit them."

Oh, yes they would. "Skynet doesn't control you," she said aloud. "If you'd turn on your own kind, you might turn on Skynet. It could never trust you. And why should it, when it can manufacture the perfect soldiers? To Skynet you're a risk not worth taking."

He closed his eyes again.

"And Skynet will make the rest of the world just like this valley. One unending industrial shed. Because it doesn't need deer and elk and trees and free-running streams. It needs mines and factories. It's going to make the world into your worst nightmare. That's what all your work is going to amount to." She watched him swallow and knew she'd hit the mark. "What's it like up there, around this place?"

He looked at her. Then he began to speak.

CHAPTER 19

MISSOURI

Jack Brock came out of one of the cave complex's side tunnels and almost ran into Dennis Reese, charging in the same direction. The tunnels were a world of gray anyway—gray uniforms, gray faces if you'd been underground long enough, equipment painted with the new gray nonreflective paint that baffled mechanical sensors. Like most resistance centers, this one was also as much a gypsy encampment as a military center; people were born and raised here as well as training in it, and were sent out to fight from it. The air always bore a slight tang of wood smoke, seldom-washed bodies, and cooking food.

Reese stuck out his hand and Brock took it before he quite recognized him. Captain Dennis Reese looked like his own father might have, lean and grim and gray. It was hard to believe that this was the smiling young man Jack had married to Mary Shea just ten years ago.

Reese's looks shocked the older man to silence as they walked along, their boots rutching on the sand and rock of the cave floor; once they had to stop for a second while a group of screeching children ran by, playing some wild game—People and Terminators, probably.

He'd heard that Mary and Kyle's disappearance had hit Reese hard, but he'd expected that time might have smoothed off some of the rougher edges. It didn't *look* like that was the case, though. What it looked like was a man eaten by his inner demons, and ready to unleash hell at the slightest provocation.

"It's good we're finally doing this," Reese said quietly as they followed the aides.

Brock knew that Reese had been agitating for a strike on the

Skynet factory for two years now. It had grown to be the largest in the heartland and was possibly, at this moment, the greatest threat to the resistance in North America. From the moment his people had discovered it, Reese had insisted that it would be.

I don't imagine he's getting much satisfaction in knowing he was right, Jack thought. *Especially knowing what a tough nut this thing's going to be to crack.*

But Skynet was a canny machine. It had launched major attacks in Europe and Africa, then, when those didn't prosper, though Africa had been a near thing, it had launched a campaign in Australia. It had continued the strategy to this day, keeping the resistance off balance and shifting its small strategic reserve of troops and high-quality weapons hopping across the world. Rising in one area while it rebuilt in another. Now, apparently, it was North America's turn.

"*He's* here." That was Reese's commander, Colonel Symonds.

The three men looked at one another. Having John Connor in your mission was as good as saying, "We're going to win this one." It wasn't an ironclad guarantee, but it was as close as you were likely to get to one in this uncertain world. It gave the men a good feeling.

"How many people has he brought?" Reese asked.

"Lots," the colonel said. "And a shitload of weaponry the like of which these little outposts haven't seen since before Judgment Day. Plus stuff that didn't exist before Judgment Day—those captured factories are really starting to produce."

Brock's grin was unstoppable. "It's like Christmas morning and Santa has brought everything on my wish list."

"And a couple of things I didn't even think of," Symonds agreed.

He and Brock glanced at Dennis, who wasn't smiling, but still radiated satisfaction like heat. He'd long claimed that the factory was the reason his wife and child had disappeared. Destroying it was going to make him a very happy man.

They continued on to the area that had been turned over to Connor and his people. Jack found himself with butterflies in his stomach. Amazing, considering he'd hosted John Connor when he was a kid. At the time he'd considered the visit a kind of baby-sitting job and had shamelessly used John's services to look after his own daughter. Now here he was, sweaty-palmed at the thought of shaking the man's hand. *Funny how things turn out,* he thought.

An aide met them at the entrance and led them to a curtained-off area where John was just putting a piece of paper onto a table dragged in for this conference. He looked up and smiled; the scarred face had lost all trace of youth, and settled into a weathered grimness that would probably remain much the same until he reached his sixties.

"Jack," he said. "Good to see you. How's Susie?"

"Outshinin' her old man more every day," Brock said. He extended his hand across the table and John took it in a firm grip.

"Colonel Symonds," John said, offering his hand. After they'd shaken, Connor turned to look at Dennis Reese. He stared, unmoving, looking him over from head to foot as though he was some alien presence.

Jack thought he didn't know who the captain was. "This is Captain Dennis Reese," he said. "He heads up the outfit here in the Ozarks."

"Of course," John said, sitting down. "My apologies, Captain. I went totally blank there for a moment. Please, have a seat, gentlemen."

Other commanders filed in and the seats were rapidly filled. To Jack's surprise, John allowed two of the other men at the table to describe the factory and to show satellite photos of its rapid growth over the last six months. Then General Vedquam outlined the plan of battle while his aide distributed the order of battle to the others.

Connor listened respectfully and asked a few questions. *All very nicely done,* Brock thought. John allowed Vedquam, as the leader in this area, to do the talking and to assume battlefield command. But at the end of the day everyone at the table knew who was really in charge. You could tell it by the questions he chose to ask, never mind the deferential manner in which he asked them. The man radiated authority.

"What about the human presence?" John asked.

"Some are Luddites," Vedquam said. "Though the Luddite presence has decreased markedly in this area over the last year. There are still a small number who seem to visit the facility, apparently to get supplies." He put down his pointer and sat at his place. "There are the usual signs of human habitation—small vegetable gardens, unprocessed human waste, and the occasional body. Going by the size of the food plots, we're assuming no more than a hundred or so prisoners."

"We'll need to be careful," John said.

"Yes, sir. We've made certain that the troops will be advised."

John slapped his hands down on the arms of his ancient office chair gently. "Excellent," he said. "If there's nothing else we can do here, I'm sure everyone has a mountain of work waiting for them."

Everyone rose, most talking with one of their counterparts, and began to move from the makeshift conference area. Reese and Brock followed behind Colonel Symonds. Jack turned before they went through the curtain and saw John giving Dennis Reese a most peculiar look. Then Connor noticed Brock watching him and smiled. Jack smiled back, gave a thumbs-up, and turned away. But the moment left him with the strangest feeling that something beyond his ken was going on.

■　■　■

Kyle had company with him the next time Mary saw him. Whether it was a girl or a boy was impossible to tell, not that it mattered. The two of them were crouched down behind a dormant stamping machine, quiet and still as the machine itself; the dimness of the echoing metal halls stretched back into what seemed like infinity, as if the whole world were a place of metal and scurrying machines and fear, scented with the ozone reek of terror.

Mary crouched down near them. She wondered how far Skynet monitored its prisoners. Did it know what the Luddite had told her?

"The resistance is still fighting," she said quietly. Kyle's eyes brightened and he leaned forward excitedly. "But Skynet is gearing up for a big push. It's built this place up." She frowned. "You remember when we came in here, the whole valley was filled with the factory?"

Kyle nodded.

"Well, the place is much bigger now. It goes on for miles instead of acres, Sam says. There are people locked up there that we've never seen."

"Yes'm," Kyle said. "I knew that. There aren't a lot of people, though. Most of the ones left are hereabouts."

Mary looked at them. "Sounds like you've been all over the place."

The two children nodded.

"So what is it that you kids do, exactly?"

"We have chores," Kyle said. "Cleaning mostly. But where we do 'em and how long we take's usually up to us."

His mother shook her head in puzzlement. "Why would it let you do that?"

"I think it finds us interestin'," Kyle's friend said in a curiously rough little voice. "The Terminators are al'ays lookin' at us, like they's measurin' us. Y'know? When I's little I thought they's gonna eat me when I got big enough."

When you were little? Mary thought in wonder. The child would barely top her waist. "Are either of your parents here?" she asked gently.

"No'm. My ma was here once. But I ent seen 'er for I don' know how long. An' I looked. I looked all ober this place. 'Course I cain't 'member what she looks like. 'Cept she had brown hair."

"You'd know her if you saw her," Mary assured him/her.

"Oh," Kyle said. "Mom, this is Jesse. Jesse, my mom."

"Jesse," Mary said with a smile and a nod, getting a more solemn nod in return. *Not an awfully helpful name,* she thought. It could still be a boy or girl. *I can't just ask, s/he would be insulted. And I couldn't blame him/her.*

"Anyway," she said aloud, "Sam says that Skynet is getting ready for a big push and that it's really active around the factory. Lots of HKs and Terminators all over the place. He was burned, he says, because he wasn't quick enough giving his designation. So they're looking to kill right now, not to take prisoners." She bit her lip, looking at both of them, so young, so fragile. "I don't think this is a good time to try and get away."

"Mom . . ."

"Something is going to happen!" she insisted. "Soon."

"Something is happening right now!" Kyle said. "Mom, I'm goin' crazy in here! And you don't know what the new place is like. I do!"

"All right, tell me," she said calmly.

"This place is old; it's made so people can help the machines. But the new place is made so the machines run each other. Jesse and me can barely squeeze through most places. *And there's no people.* Not a one." He was breathing hard in his distress. "And there's fewer people here all the time. You don't know that because you grown-ups aren't allowed to go places like we are. There's no new people, Mom. Not ever."

"We have to go *now,* ma'am," Jesse said gravely.

Out of the mouths of babes, Mary thought. "Okay. Just let me see if I can at least get us some water to take with us, and maybe some food." *And maybe Tia and Sally.*

Then she looked at her son and decided to be selfish. The fewer who knew about this, the less chance of betrayal or accident. She didn't like it, but when it came to Kyle, she had to be ruthlessly practical. It was the only sure way to keep him alive.

■ ■ ■

"Well, this is a *real* battle," Dennis Reese said, a little surprised.

John Connor smiled a little, squatting, grim and silent, with the rest of the command group around a thin-film display beneath dead hickories—killed by the acid efflux from the Skynet complex three miles away.

A line of actinic light lanced into the sky from a crew-served weapon nearby, and high overhead in the frosty blue sky something blew up in an improbable strobing ball of purple fire.

"Damn," Reese muttered.

"Mostly it doesn't try to use high-fliers anymore," Connor said, not looking up from the screen. "Not when we've got heavy plasma rifles available." He smiled again, a remarkably cold expression. "You know, it would be a lot better off if it had stuck to pre–Judgment Day designs. Plasma weapons and perfect dielectric capacitors are wonderful equalizers—lots of punch, not much weight."

"It has them, too," Reese pointed out.

"Yeah, but it doesn't *need* them," Connor said. "Anything can kill a human. It takes something pretty energetic to kill most of Skynet's ground-combat modules."

Columns of troops were moving up in the narrow wooded valleys that stretched all around them, local guerrillas and the assault troops John Connor had infiltrated over the past few months. They were sheltered by the crest lines. Sheltered until—

The warning came through the communications net a minute or two before they could hear the roar of the ducted fans. The command squad jumped into their slit trenches, barely slowing in their job of coordinating the resistance units; everyone in the marching columns hit the dirt, too. Around the perimeter were pre–Judgment Day vehicles, mostly four-by-fours of various makes; each of them had a light antiaircraft missile launcher mounted on it.

The *RRRRAAK-shwoosh!* of the missiles sounded almost the instant the Skynet fighting platforms cleared the crest lines. Lines of light stabbed out from the fighting machines as they launched missiles and plasma bolts of their own, but one by one the twisting lines of the heat-seeking missiles found them.

"Of course, some of the old technology still works," Reese said.

His eyes met John Connor's. They nodded once, in perfect agreement, as the ruins of the HKs burned on the poisoned hillsides.

SKYNET

Things were at a desperate juncture. Skynet needed to drive the human fighters from the factory or it would inevitably lose the facility. If worse came to worst and it seemed that nothing would save the factory, Skynet had developed a recent innovation—a self-destruct sequence that would eliminate the plant and everything in it as well as obliterating several miles of surrounding countryside. ICBMs might be beyond its capacity to produce, but nuclear bombs were simply a matter of putting together the right materials.

It had set a part of its consciousness into a planning subroutine that would give it maximum advantage in the productivity of its factories before the humans discovered and moved against them. If it could determine the point at which they would make their move against the factories, it might be able to influence how many of them would become involved—luring in the greatest number for the kill. Thus if Skynet lost, then so did its enemies.

Of course, the resistance fighters would quickly learn the consequences of an attack on a major facility such as this one. But by then it would be too late for a great many of them.

In this case, the humans had taken far longer to act than had been projected. Skynet had assumed that it was the presence of hostages within the facility that had held the humans at bay. For this reason it had continued to harbor the one hundred and three individuals long after they were no longer needed for productive purposes.

It couldn't see why, after all this time, the hostages had suddenly become unimportant to the invaders. Unless they never had been important and Skynet had been wrong about them from the beginning.

Its problem was that it could never truly predict human behavior. It could predict to certain percentage points, but never closely enough for certainty. That was why it had decided to retire its Luddite allies rather than use them as infiltrators. They could not be relied upon completely. It kept those Luddites that it had maintained isolated and heavily guarded, and they were working out splendidly. But that wasn't an option in field operations.

Hence its improvements in its Terminators. There were difficulties to overcome, but it estimated that in ten years or less it would have a viable infiltrator form of the unit. Should this conflict last that long.

Skynet watched the human soldiers crawl through its factory, and an ancient poem intruded itself: " 'Come into my parlor,' said the spider to the fly." It would wait to initiate the destruct sequence. It wanted the maximum number of flies to die.

■   ■   ■

Mary boosted Kyle up, pushing on the soles of his feet to get his hips over the lip of the opening. All around them the machines clattered and screamed and whirred as they performed their various functions. She wished she had earplugs; the sounds were deafening, an eternal shrill threnody of nonlife.

Kyle had turned around and was offering his hands to give Jesse some help. Mary stooped to pick the child up when something shook the ground so hard they both fell. Around them the machines stopped and there should have been silence, but there were explosions and the whistle of rockets . . . and more explosions, and the savage crackling *shhhh-WHACK* of plasma bolts striking through their own self-created tunnels of ionized air.

Mary sat on the floor, listening. Then she stood and reached for Kyle. "We have to get out of here," she said. "Going out there is impossible. We wouldn't last two minutes in the middle of an attack."

"But, Mommm," Kyle protested.

"I know, honey. We've come this far . . ." She shook her head. "But sometimes you have to retreat. And this is one of those times. Now *come down!*" She hated to bark at him, but she had a mental image of Terminators pouring out of all the openings around them, and here they'd be where they weren't supposed to.

Another massive explosion shook the ground, as if the pavement were itself flexing like a giant drumhead beneath her feet, sending her staggering. Above her Kyle bit his lip, then squirmed out and dropped into her waiting arms. Mary took hold of his shirt and Jesse's small hand, and led the children back the way they'd come. In the human part of the factory there were more places to hide.

■　■　■

Skynet detached forty T-90s to gather the human hostages in the only open space in the factory. A place the humans had named the punishment floor. Once they were gathered there, it would project an image of them to the fighters outside, threatening to kill them all unless the humans withdrew.

They probably wouldn't comply, but that was unknowable until it had been tried. It could also simply massacre the prisoners and not show that part. It might be more efficient, freeing the Terminators for more urgent duties.

Skynet decided to wait. The attackers might demand to see a living prisoner.

As soon as the Terminators began rounding people up, many chose to run and hide.

"Those who hide will be killed on the spot when they are

found," he announced in Kurt Viemeister's voice. It caused some to hesitate long enough to be taken. It had found that humans tended to obey when it used its programmer's voice.

■ ■ ■

Mary had chosen the spot the first year they'd been here; since then she'd provisioned it with food, water, and blankets from the clinic. Now she yanked off the access panel and shoved the two children in ruthlessly.

"But, Mom," Kyle said.

"Get in there and stay there as long as you can," Mary said.

"But they'll kill anyone they find hiding," Kyle protested.

"Then you better make darn sure they don't find you," his mother said. "Honey, I think our side's winning or the machines wouldn't be doing this. You two stay quiet and stay safe. You hear me?"

Kyle nodded, and after a moment Jesse did, too, looking surprised that s/he'd been consulted. Mary fitted the hatch back into place and stood. In the distance she could see the red-lit eye sensors of a T-90 coming her way. She quickly moved toward the punishment floor, praying they hadn't seen her hiding her son.

SKYNET

Suddenly all of its feeds went blank. Contact with the factory, and most important, with the fail-safe device, was lost. Fortunately it maintained contact with the Terminators outside the factory and all of its HKs. It directed a squad of T-90s to get into the factory and to proceed to the fail-safe device, which they would then activate. It ordered its remaining HKs and Terminators to launch a final mass attack as a distraction.

Skynet couldn't contact the T-90s within the factory and had to rely on their programming to see them through until the fail-safe device was deployed.

No satellites were in position to give Skynet a direct view of what was happening. However, if the T-90s succeeded in their mission, the explosion would be evident, even if there was a slight delay in receiving direct images.

■ ■ ■

Mary knelt beside Tia and Sally; the three women held hands and for the most part avoided eye contact. For her part, Mary didn't want to break down and cry, and she assumed her friends felt the same way. It looked to Mary like this was everybody. Though she didn't really know how many of them there were. Some faces that she'd expected to see were missing and there were strangers in the crowd. Only two children were present—one quite young, and one quite tall. *Maybe they couldn't find a place to hide,* she thought.

The noises of battle continued, though there were far fewer earth-rocking blasts from above. Mostly they heard heavy machine-gun fire or the hissing blast of a plasma rifle. Everyone kept their heads down and stayed as still as possible. The Terminators ringed the prisoners; they were even more immobile than the terrified humans.

Except for their heads, which moved continuously back and forth, sweeping the small crowd in search of some forbidden movement.

■ ■ ■

Dennis Reese slipped through the machinery like an eel, his attention everywhere at once, senses on high alert. All around him, men and women crept through the silent factory in teams, moving like well-oiled machines themselves. Their night-vision goggles were operating on the UV level, making everything clear in a strangely colorful way.

Out of the darkness a pair of circles emerged and Dennis raised a clenched fist to stop the squad's forward motion. Everyone froze.

He waited; the circles turned away. Still he waited, and soon he began to see more of them, sometimes just a sliver of light spaced in a rough circle. Terminators. And they were guarding something in an open area. Nothing interrupted his view of the T-90s farther away, though bits of machinery came between him and the nearest Terminators.

He counted at least thirty and estimated a good ten more that had their backs to him.

Caught the metal motherfuckers napping this time, he thought happily.

He'd have to signal the platoon to open fire. The best way to do that was to open fire himself; his mouth drew up into a stiff smile as he laid the sight picture on the head of a Terminator fifty yards away.

He was grinning as his finger took up the slack on the plasma rifle's trigger.

Sssss-WHACK!

■ ■ ■

Kyle pushed gently on the metal of the access hatch, keeping tight hold on the inside of it lest it fall and bring every T-90 in the place down on them. The cooler air outside felt wonderful, and he just sat there letting the sweat dry for a moment, listening as he did so.

Jesse touched him lightly on the back—part question (*is it safe?*), part demand (*let me out of here!*). Kyle moved cautiously forward, then slowly stood, listening in the pitch dark for anything that might indicate danger.

Suddenly plasma beams slashed the blackness, making him cry out as his eyes suddenly tried to adjust back and forth between brilliant light and stygian darkness. There were cries coming from the punishment floor, too, and he thought he'd seen a Terminator, for just a second, raising its plasma rifle. He dropped and began commando-crawling toward the floor. His mother was there!

■ ■ ■

Mary lifted her head cautiously, her heart pounding so hard she felt nauseous. *Is it over?* she wondered. Around her the prisoners shifted and stirred. Suddenly a flashlight went on and she winced away from it; though it was probably very dim, it still hurt. She opened her eyes to slits and looked around. Seeing got easier as more lights appeared.

Through veils of smoke, human figures moved. Mary brought her legs forward, raised her hands, and slowly lifted her body from the floor. "I'm human," she called, and the light found her.

Beside her, Tia and Sally also sat up. Sally was sobbing and Tia put an arm around her shoulders. That's when Mary realized that she was crying, too. All around them people were sobbing or starting to laugh.

"Everybody stay calm, and stay down," a man called out.

"Dennis!" Mary shouted. She looked around frantically, seeking the source of that dearly loved, terribly missed voice.

After a long moment she heard, "Mary?" spoken in disbelief.

In an instant she was on her feet and moving toward the voice. In the dim light she could see him coming toward her and she began to laugh and cry at the same time. They met and flung their arms around each other, holding on as though they'd never let each other go.

"Mary, sweetheart," he said, and kissed her passionately.

The taste of her tears salted their kiss and Mary didn't know if she was crying or laughing, but she'd never in her life been happier. His arms around her were painfully tight and she loved it, she loved it.

■ ■ ■

Kyle stood at the edge of the light and watched his parents in wonder. He knew the soldier for his father, though with helmet and uniform he looked just like all the others. And yet . . . this was undeniably his father. It wasn't just the way his mother was kissing him. He'd have known him anywhere and his heart lifted. He took a step toward them.

At the outer edge of the circle a shattered T-90 raised its rifle and fired. The flash of blue plasma shot through the two entwined human figures and they dropped to the ground so suddenly that for a moment the movement made no sense.

"Nooooo!" A child shot from out of the dark and raced toward the fallen couple. "Mom! Dad!" he screamed. He fell to his knees beside them, tugging at their bodies, weeping hysterically.

Behind him another child stopped, looking on in distress, but clearly not knowing what to do. Every plasma rifle in the place had taken a shot at the T-90 that had fired. It lay partially melted, the orange glow quickly cooling to gray. All around, the soldiers and freed prisoners shifted as their shock lifted, and they looked at one another, equally helpless.

Then, through the dim light and the shifting smoke, a man appeared. Eyes sought him, and a whisper went through the crowd: *Connorjohnconnorconnorconnor.*

"You people," he said as he moved among them. He stood looking down at the weeping boy until the child looked up at him. "Come with me if you want to live."

CHAPTER 20

John tossed himself onto the cot. It creaked and waggled alarmingly, despite the fact that he'd never weighed more than one-fifty in his life, and was a nickel short of that right now. That there was a cot made it luxury accommodations and he didn't want to get the reputation of trashing the presidential suite. He turned up the Coleman lantern on the tray table beside him and dug the letter out of his breast pocket, ignoring the flickering light and the fruity smell of the burning alcohol.

Getting a personal letter from an old friend was something of an event for him. He occasionally received notes from his mother or from Dieter, but mostly it was impersonal e-mails or reports. This had come from Jack Brock in Missouri.

John Connor had asked Jack to keep him informed about his father, Kyle Reese. *Of course, Jack has no idea of the relationship.* No doubt he thought John was just doing the good commander thing.

He tore open the envelope and began to read.

Dear John,

Hope you don't mind me being so familiar, but I can't seem to help myself when I'm just writing a letter and not an official document. If you'll recall, you asked me to keep you informed about Kyle Reese and his little friend Jesse. Which I will. But what you may not know is that we've got ourselves quite a crop of orphans now and I thought I'd start by telling you something about the kids in general.

First off, there's not a lot of laughter in them. Not that they've got a lot to laugh about, but you know, you always like to say that kids are resilient. That they can get over anything given time. I guess maybe part of the problem is we can't give them that time. Or Skynet won't. Anyway, they're a grim little bunch. I got to thinking that maybe we were at least partially to blame. First thing we always do when we get a new kid is to start training 'im.

I know we have to and mostly they take to it very well. But we've kind of been treating them like short adults, if you know what I mean. So I've assigned Susie and some of her friends to show them some fun. I wish you could have seen my girl's face when I gave her the order. It was like, "Dad, you've given me some weird assignments in my time, but this one beats 'em all."

But she's doing a first rate-job and seems to be enjoying herself as well. The kids have begun to smile, while Susie and her friends are cracking up all over the place. My great fear now is that they'll start playing practical jokes. As you'll recall, that used to be one of Susie's specialties.

On the other hand, maybe that's just what these kids need. Proof that even when they're naughty they won't be lined up against a wall and shot. There's been too many incidents like that in their lives. When I think about what they've been through, I admit it humbles me. And it makes me grateful for the life I've led so far.

It still seems to me that childhood is the longest part of life. How will this affect them when they're adults and they have these memories to look back on? I can only hope we'll win this thing before they're adults. My God, John, think about it! Having to teach kids to have fun.

John dropped the letter onto his chest and pinched the bridge of his nose. The scar the cyberseal had left all those years ago was hurting again, but then it did that when he was very tired. He sighed. His own upbringing had been unusually tough by the standards of the day. But he'd known how to laugh and having fun had been no problem. Even if he did resort to stealing to ensure maximum joy. Compared to today's kids, he'd had it cushy.

As to Kyle, I really like him. He's not a leader; I don't see him ever becoming an officer. But he's solid and he'll make a hell of a sergeant one day. He has an impulse to protect that I like to see and he accepts responsibility. He's smart, if no scholar, and he's honorable. If he agrees to do something, he'll do it, by God.

Yeah, John thought uncomfortably, *he will.* This was eerily like his mother's descriptions . . . but then, Kyle Reese was growing toward the moment they met. *My head hurts.* He turned back to the letter.

His little friend Jesse turns out to be a boy after all. Small as he is and dressed in that gray clothing, you couldn't tell. He and Kyle watch each other's back. Which is good to see. Not that we have much in the way of the kids mixing it up. Like I said they hardly know how to misbehave.

It's good that they have each other. Like the rest of the kids, they don't make new friends easily. And none of them have formed very close ties with the adults around them. They'd better get over it or Skynet may just have succeeded, if indirectly, in eliminating the human race.

And on that sour note I'll close. All our best to you, John.

John folded the letter and put in on the tray table. Kyle was a healthy young boy with a wounded psyche but a good heart. In other words, he was already much like the man who became his father. He wished he could do something to make it easier for him. But he didn't dare.

Jack and Susie will be good to him, John thought. *They'll take care of him and train him well.* Jack had certainly done a fine job with Susie. John wondered if Kyle and his mother had laughed—*Don't go there! No, no, no! Think about a pink giraffe. Hippopotamus, jelly beans, anything!*

Then he forced his mind back to the last intelligence report he'd read. Finally he managed to distract himself enough that he thought he could sleep. Though when he closed his eyes, just before he drifted off into exhausted slumber, his mind flashed him a picture of Kyle's tear-stained face, and he sighed.

■ ■ ■

"John, I don't know what you expect me to do," Sarah said. "We can't impose something like this from on high. For one thing, not everyone has the leisure, let alone the resources, to set up schools."

John Connor stretched out and sighed, looking up at the fleecy skies—the Pacific Northwest was putting on one of its rare beautiful summer days. He wriggled his shoulders into the fragrant pine duff and went on: "Mom, we've got to do something. I don't expect a regular school with strict hours of operation or anything like that. But if we don't require some effort, then these orphans are going to be at a terrific disadvantage."

John hated to use time on one of his rare visits with his mother and Dieter to argue, but this was something they had to do. The longer they waited the further behind they got.

She threw up her hands. "So what do you think I can do?"

"I think we could work out some kind of guidelines," Dieter suggested. "I agree with you that everyone's circumstances are different and so anything formal is out of the question. However, as John points out, this is something that has to be done. Perhaps no one is working on this because they don't know how to begin."

Sarah smiled briefly and touched the Austrian's arm. John hid his own smile by taking a sip of coffee. He liked the way Dieter acted as peacemaker between him and his mom. It made him feel a part of something. Something human scale and quite precious. In the rest of his life he was pretty isolated by virtue of his function. He had a lot of fans but few friends. It occurred to him that before Dieter came along he and his mother rarely indulged in the kind of flare-ups that demanded a peacemaker.

One of life's little luxuries, John thought. Aloud he said, "So I guess that's what I'm asking you to do, Mom. Find a way for them to start."

Sarah nodded, her eyes already taking on the faraway look of planning. Dieter gave John a conspiratorial smile.

God! but I love these people.

QUEBEC WILDERNESS

"John! My man! Welcome, welcome." Snog was all smiles as he came forward, arms open wide for a French-style embrace. He grabbed John and kissed him resoundingly on both cheeks, greatly displeasing Connor's security people, a fact that visibly amused John. "My house is your house. Let me introduce you to my wives."

John allowed himself to be led into the aboveground entrance to the resistance's technological arm, which gave a convincing imitation of a hunting lodge half-ruined and wholly abandoned amid the endless rolling hills, blue green with fir and starred with sapphire lakes. *Certainly a change from the rat warrens we spend most of our time in,* he thought.

Most of it had been built with Dieter's money back before Judgment Day, which indeed did make it John's house.

Since the war had begun, the place had been expanded, as had the staff, and without them the resistance would long since have fallen apart. If Skynet so much as suspected their existence, it would stop at nothing to destroy them.

At the moment, though, the greatest threat to this colony of technologists and scientists was their leader's increasingly wacky lifestyle. Snog had insisted on labeling himself a "techno-shaman" and he was putting the moves on everyone. Except, so far, the children.

There had been numerous complaints from many different sources that those who refused his advances ended up working in the production facility indefinitely. Although the rules stated that personnel would rotate that necessary duty so that no one was deprived of the opportunity for research.

Snog himself was odd looking; for one thing, he was overweight in a world where literally everyone else was slim to skinny. For another, there were diodes and transistors and other bits of technical paraphernalia braided into his waist-length hair and he was wearing a scarlet muumuu with huge bell sleeves. And he didn't smell too good, either.

John had begged his mother to make this visit for him. But she'd refused. "Whatever influence I ever had over that bloated geek is gone," she'd insisted.

John had been taken aback. Sarah didn't tend to toss around epithets like *bloated geek*.

"The last time I visited him he put his hand on my thigh," Sarah said. "What does that tell you?"

That he has a death wish? John thought. *That he has a version of the Oedipus complex? That he has a death wish and an Oedipus complex?*

But he'd conceded that if Snog was treating Sarah Connor like this, then extreme methods might be necessary, and he'd have to actually go to Quebec to determine what those might be. *I might have to whack him around a little.* Which he really didn't want to have to do. Now, though, actually looking at the man . . .

I wonder if Snog's ass is even connected to his brain anymore.

"My wives," Snog said with a grand wave of his arm toward a

collection of women who were as equally weird in their appearance as he himself.

In addition to the long hair twined with little bits of stuff, their faces were half-painted, either horizontally or vertically in black and vermilion. And each of them looked bug-eyed from drugs or some form of shock. Thirty sullen-looking children were mixed among them, every one of them Snog's.

"Maybe later," John said crisply. "Right now I need to discuss some business with you, and I'm afraid it won't wait."

Snog stiffened and his face took on a stoically offended look, but he waved a gracious arm, and with an actual bow the women retreated. Without another word or backward look, Snog led him to a very large and comfortable office suite. The techno-shaman went around a massive desk and sat down. He flicked a hand toward a small chair in front of the desk.

John remained standing. He looked his old friend over and came to a decision. "Okay, here's the deal," Connor said. "I need a technical adviser with me in the field. That'll be you."

Snog's jaw dropped.

"Don't even bother to protest," John said. "The decision is made."

"My . . . my wives," Snog said. "My children!"

"Your wives will continue their work in your absence. I assume they do actually work." Rumor had it that they only worked when and on what they wanted to. And some of their projects had no conceivable use to the resistance.

"Uh, sure they do," Snog said.

"And, of course, they'll take good care of the children." He placed his knuckles on the gleaming desktop and leaned forward. "Believe me, buddy, I wouldn't ask for a sacrifice like this if it wasn't necessary."

And it is necessary because if I leave you here, I'm going to have to have you shot! There must be at least one psychiatrist in the resistance who would like to get his or her hands on a raging case of megalomania like this one. *Who would have thought that one of my oldest friends would turn out to have more in common with Skynet than with the rest of the human race?*

"You'll have to change into something less eye-catching," John said, indicating Snog's scarlet draperies.

"I—I honestly don't know if we've got anything that will fit," Snog stammered.

"Find something," John advised. "We'll be leaving in thirty-six hours at the latest."

"God, man." Snog looked around his office, his hands wandering as though he didn't know what to do with them. "This is such a shock!"

Connor shrugged. "Sorry, man, but it's necessary. Um." He looked down for a moment. "Do you have an assistant or something? I know you'll want to spend as much time as you can with your family before you go. So maybe we could have someone else brief me on what you've got going."

"Sure, sure," Snog said dazedly. He tapped an intercom. "Shad Cho, report to the main office."

"Listen, you don't have to stay," John said. "You've got to break this to . . . your wives and kids. I can introduce myself."

"Yeah, yeah, thanks, man." Snog rose and moved around the desk, gave John an amazed look, and left.

Muttering furious curses, John went around the desk and sat down. One or two tries at the computer proved it to be beyond his ability to break in to. He sat and waited. If he had to go through this complex one person at a time, he would find someone capable of running it.

Cho tapped the door twice and entered. At first sight, John suspected that this was the first sane person he'd seen here today. A few quick questions confirmed this fact, as did the man's superior personal hygiene. It turned out that Cho had been running the complex for the last four months. With intermittent interference from Snog.

"I think that he was just overworked and kind of cracked up. Nobody noticed, so he kept on working and getting crazier and crazier." Cho put a hand on his chest. "Now, I'm no shrink, but getting him away from here is probably going to do him a world of good. And it'll sure make life easier for the rest of us. That techno-shaman stuff probably did wonders for inspiring the resistance—"

"Yeah, it did," John said. "Having a Good Wizard helped a *lot*. It's why Snog isn't being marched off in handcuffs right now."

Cho squirmed a little, embarrassed. "Don't get me wrong. Snog's *still* brilliant when his head is straight. He taught me all I know, and no false modesty, but I know a lot. It's just that . . ."

"He started believing the propaganda," John said, nodding. "Now, tell me about the chameleon fabric . . ."

John had assigned two of his people to ask around the complex and report back to him. Within twenty-four hours he'd organized a complete change of personnel and hoped he'd rooted out the whiftees.

Twelve hours before they were scheduled to leave, John confronted the shaman, still in his scarlet regalia. "How's the new wardrobe coming?"

Snog shrugged cheerfully. "My ladies are looking around, but so far, no luck."

"Tell you what, Snog. Tell them to look harder because you're not wearing that thing when you come with me. I imagine you'd get kind of cold running around naked." He turned to go, then said over his shoulder, "Oh, lose the hair."

The next morning Snog showed up shorn and wearing blue jeans, a black T-shirt, and a hangdog expression. His many wives and children sniffled and sobbed and waved sad good-byes as they drove off in a convoy of vehicles with dazzle-stealth coverings. *Jeez*, John thought, *no wonder he cracked.*

For the first two weeks the self-proclaimed techno-shaman was left to his own devices. Which meant enjoying the tiny library and chatting with off-duty personnel. He was shielded from the incoherent messages he was receiving from his extended "family," which Cho said were the result of all of his wives coming down from some pretty heavy home-brewed drugs. It was clear that some of these women were never going to be, and perhaps never had been, normal—not that that was so very unusual, these days.

"But some of them are slowly coming down to Mother Earth," Cho said over the satellite link. "Whether they'll still want to be part of a harem once they've sobered up remains to be seen. How's Gandalf the Geek?"

"Getting cold and sober and doing well on the lower-fat diet common to the rest of humanity," John said. "In fact, he's already a lot more like the Snog I knew of old . . ."

■ ■ ■

After a while Connor assigned his old friend the task of teaching science to the orphans under the supervision of Snog's own personal psychologist. He finally allowed Snog unlimited e-mail access to the saner members of his family. But he'd already informed Cho that he wasn't to take any orders from him unless they made sense.

Things were already going more smoothly in Quebec and John breathed a sigh of relief. Now he could get on to simpler issues. Like fighting the war.

MISSOURI

SEVEN YEARS LATER

"Okay, folks, those are our goals for this patrol. It's all pretty routine, but . . ."

The whole group recited together, "There's no such thing as routine."

Jesse grinned at Kyle, excited to be going out on his first mission. Kyle was excited, but it was more a nausea-inducing kind of excitement. And he wished Jesse wasn't coming on this "routine mission." His friend had gotten orders to report to Quebec, where he would receive advanced technological training. And would be safe.

Kyle envied him. There were very few places in this world that might be called safe, but the Quebec facility was one of them. *Wouldn't mind being assigned there myself,* he thought. Though the winters might be nasty. But his mind didn't have that special spark. He could use technology, and he was an excellent shot, but Jesse had something else, something special.

Still, everyone had to do certain things. Going out like this was one of them, kind of a rite of passage. Their teachers claimed that it put everyone on the same footing and in case of emergency gave everyone an idea of how to act.

He suspected that Jesse was young for patrol; you were supposed to be a minimum of seventeen. But nobody knew his friend's age, not even Jesse. So when he claimed to be as old as Kyle, who could argue?

"Okay, check your gear one last time and we'll move out."

The boys checked each other, although they knew there was no need. Jesse worked in electronics repair and Kyle in supplies. They'd chosen what they knew was the best gear for themselves with the practical self-centeredness of teenagers.

Kyle tried to return Jesse's grin, but he was too nervous. They lined up with the other soldiers and headed for the outside.

■ ■ ■

Forty-eight hours later Jesse was no longer smiling. Kyle was having daydreams about hot soup.

He shook them off and pulled up the hood of his camouflage cloak. It dulled his hearing a bit, but he couldn't hear anything except the subdued hiss of the rain and the patter of drops falling from the trees above anyway; he couldn't see much past ten yards either, unless he jacked the sensitivity of his goggles way up.

And I'd have thought that being this wet would make you clean, he thought, shifting his plasma rifle from one arm to the other beneath the dank weight of the cloak. *Nope. Smell like wet dog. Very wet, very unbathed dog.*

It had rained for the whole time they'd been out on patrol. Otherwise it really had been routine. Nothing had happened, nothing had been seen. Frankly, nothing could be seen through the damn rain and fog. And it had been cold. Not freezing, just cold. The squad was on its way back, and the two friends were trying not to shiver too obviously. They'd already been smiled at by their more experienced companions far too much.

Kyle and Jesse were in the middle of the column, if you could call the staggered formation a column. Kyle was keeping his eyes on the narrow path before him, too stunned by cold even to care that he was walking on the edge of a precipice. There was a sound behind him like gravel going down a chute and he marched on for several paces before the sound even registered.

He turned, and behind him the path was gone. There was a huge gap between him and the next soldier twenty feet away. His eyes went from the gap to the soldier, then back again, and realization hit him like a rush of heat.

"Jesse!" he said, and started forward.

A heavy hand bit into his shoulder and he turned to fight it off only to find himself on the ground, struggling to breathe under the full weight of the adult man who'd stopped him.

"Let me go!" Kyle insisted.

"Easy, kid," the man said. "Take it easy. Nothing you can do."

He kept repeating it, over and over, until Kyle stopped struggling and began to weep. Hard, painful sobs that felt ripped from his soul. The man went to one knee and held him, saying nothing, occasionally patting Kyle's shoulder. Then, after a minute or two, he urged him to his feet.

"We've got to go," the soldier said. "We've got to keep moving. Okay?"

Kyle nodded. He felt sick and he thought that nothing was okay. But he wasn't going to slow down the squad and maybe get someone killed. Jesse was gone. The soldier gently pushed Kyle to go ahead of him and Kyle went, walking like a zombie.

How could this have happened? Kyle asked himself. His best friend, just . . . gone—in a stupid, meaningless accident that could have happened to anyone. It might have been him if he'd been walking just a bit slower. Or even both of them. *Stupid,* he thought. Jesse was gone. The resistance would be the poorer for his loss.

We could afford to lose me much more easily, Kyle thought. Jesse's gifts weren't something he could replace no matter how hard he studied. Kyle looked around. *But then, Jesse would never have been as good out here as I can be.* He resolved at that moment never to be less than the best that he could be. *In your honor,* he pledged. *I swear, Jesse, I'll make my life mean something.*

But not here. He couldn't stay here where he'd lost so much. He had to ask Jack to send him far away. Far away from all the pain and all the memories.

LOS ANGELES
TWO YEARS LATER

Sergeant Kyle Reese armed the plasma satchel; it looked like a cylinder of smooth metal, and he didn't know exactly how it worked—more from the Wizards of Quebec—but it *did* work.

He nodded to Samantha. She armed hers, too; they were in what had once been downtown Burbank, and the HKs were out in force tonight—a big Grolo unit was crunching its way toward them through the cindered ash and twisted steel and skeletons.

Reese snarled, tasting the ash on his lips—the ashes of twelve million dead. He rose, threw—the satchel landed exactly under the Grolo's left tread—and ducked back down.

Samantha wasn't quite fast enough. One of the heavy plasma rifles bore on her as she threw, and—

He turned his head aside, closing his eyes for a single instant. *Got to get out,* he thought. *Got to get to the car. Think about it later!*

■   ■   ■

John stood looking down at the young soldier. He'd been badly banged up in the crash, and burned, too. Nothing fatal, but nothing very easy to endure, either; medical facilities were still pretty basic at the outlying stations.

He's so unbelievably young, John thought. Kyle Reese's time hadn't yet come. He wished that he could get to know this young man, but he didn't dare. *Hell, I don't dare touch him.* For all he knew, touching his father might set off some kind of explosion, or cause them both to melt or something.

In his hands John held a picture of his mother. She'd been in Mexico when it was taken, she'd told him. Pregnant with him. And she'd been thinking of his father at the time, and trying to decide what to do about Skynet and how to do it. John sighed. They'd had so little time together. Like a lot of things about Kyle Reese's life, it was unfair.

The young soldier in the bed stirred and opened his eyes. For a moment they stayed blank. "Burning," he whispered. "*Got to get out, the fuel's going to go!*"

"It's all right," Connor said. "You've been retrieved. You're back in the infirmary."

It took a moment for Kyle to recognize John Connor. But when realization hit, he struggled to sit up.

"No," John said, raising a hand to stop him. "Don't you dare salute me. Just lie back and heal. We need you."

"Thank you, sir," Reese said, his words slightly slurred.

"I'm not just talking ragtime here, soldier," John assured him. *Boy, am I ever not just blowing smoke,* he thought.

"My mission didn't go quite as planned, sir," Kyle protested.

"They seldom do once the firing starts," John assured him. "You've rid the world of your share of HKs. And your commander tells me you're a good sergeant. It's my humble opinion that without good sergeants we'd be up shit's creek without a paddle. Sometimes we do lose a little. But we win more than we lose. And ultimately we're going to win this war and take this world back from the machines. And it's men like you who are going to do that. So you rest, and you heal, and you get back in there."

Kyle swallowed and nodded once. "Yes, sir."

John's lips jerked in an attempted smile. Then he laid the picture on his father's stomach.

"My mother," he said in explanation, and watched the young man's eyes go wide. *Sarah Connor, the legend,* he thought wryly. *Christ, I'm setting my dad up with my mom.*

■ ■ ■

Kyle picked up the picture and was caught. Sarah Connor was young in the photo; she looked soft, and feminine, and terribly sad. More than once he'd felt as sad and alone as her expression showed she was feeling. He felt a kinship with the woman in the picture, as though she was someone he could talk to.

Reluctantly he lifted his hand to give the picture back, but Connor was gone. Puzzled, Reese looked around, but the commander was definitely nowhere around. Still, he wasn't sorry that he didn't have to give the picture back. He looked at the young woman's face, studying every line, every angle. A sense of longing overcame him, a desire to know her. Kyle closed his eyes, and fell asleep, and dreamed of Sarah Connor.

RESISTANCE COMMAND CENTER
FOUR YEARS LATER

"John, my man, wait till you see what I've got for you!" Snog said. He was imitating the happy-talk excitement of a ginsu knife salesman.

John smiled wearily. His somewhat rough-and-ready treatment of his old friend had certainly smoothed out some of the wrinkles, but—*But Snog is always going to be a goof. God, he makes me feel younger and older at the same time!*

At least he wasn't completely crazy anymore, just productively weird. And he even fit in here at Regional HQ, which was as normal an environment as the world had to offer—rock and concrete, yes, but at least they weren't living on gruel and fighting Infiltrator units all the time.

"So what have you got for me?" Connor asked.

"I have the treasure of the Sierra Madre, King Solomon's lost mines, Atlantis, the missing link! You name it, man! We have discovered, here in the wilds of darkest Canada, the salvation of the human race! Hallelujah brother! Can I get an *amen*?"

In the background, shouts of "Amen!" could be heard from offices down the rock-hewn corridor.

"With a buildup like that, Snog, this better be good."

"Oh, it's better than good," his old friend assured him. "Check *this* out." He clicked a few keys and his smiling face was replaced by a picture of what looked like aircraft.

John leaned forward. It *was* aircraft! B-2s, if he wasn't mistaken. *And they're in perfect condition.*

"Fuel?" was his first question.

"Tons," Snog said. "Literally. But that's not all. Lookee here!"

The B-2s were replaced by what John at first thought were planes, but were actually drones. Bomb-carrying, radar-evading, farseeing drones.

"My God," Connor whispered, "it's the mother load."

"You bet your ass it is!" Snog crowed. "Look out Skynet, here we come!"

John felt himself smiling. "And we can take 'em?"

"Now that the defense grid is smashed, yeah," Snog said. "Take 'em and fly 'em."

"And Skynet isn't *that* distributed," John said. "With this, we can root out the central units."

CHAPTER 21

The years went by with a horrible sameness. We fought, we died, we learned, we struggled, we won. After an eternity, we won more than we lost. Children were born and grew up fighting the machines. It was all turning out much the way Kyle Reese had described it to me.

They were good kids, these children who had never known peace and security, and good soldiers. I honestly don't think that it even occurred to most of them to blame their parents for the nightmare they were living. But then they had no idea that there was any other way to live.

One day the war will be over, and when they've rested, then they'll start asking the hard questions.

■　■　■

"Here's where my head starts hurting again," John Connor murmured to himself, taking a sip of his herbal tea. "Christ, I wish we could get more coffee in."

A few of the technicians in the underground command center—once a Skynet facility—looked at him oddly. Those were the ones who hadn't been assigned to the Command Assault Group for very long; a couple of the others grinned as they bent over their workstations. The chief's oddities were legend.

John sighed, rising and walking over to the big display screen. Just before it came alive, he caught a glimpse of himself—the long hard face still marked by the long V-shaped scar the cyberseal had inflicted on him, the hard wary eyes and grim-set mouth.

I'm forty-two, he thought, disoriented for a moment.

It still caught him by surprise sometimes, overlaid on the face a part of him expected to see—the laughing teenager with a black cowlick across his forehead.

When did that happen? I have indubitably become the Great Military Dickhead of Mom's dreams, the one Kyle described to her . . . and I'm older than he is.

"Head *definitely* hurting," he said quietly as the screen came live.

Sarah and Dieter moved to stand on either side of him; his mother put a hand on his arm, for just a second, understanding as only she and Dieter could.

I'm forty-two; they're old, he thought.

Faces wrinkled, the great muscles of Dieter's frame gone gaunt; an encounter with an HK had given him a limp that he'd take to his grave, a limp that got a little worse every year. Active, strong, infinitely experienced oldsters, but quite definitely *old.* Humans didn't usually live into their sixties anymore. The sheer fact of their survival made them objects of awe, even with Sarah's new identity.

"Display, schematic," John said.

The screen flashed a Mercator projection of the earth, with color-coded symbols—live human-held territory, dead Skynet zones, a crosshatch of contested areas, smaller skull symbols for places where radiation or bioweapons still lingered.

And there were a satisfying series of *X* marks—smashed elements in Skynet's defense grid. With control of the surviving satellites gone, the remains of the grid were all that was keeping Skynet alive at all.

"If it lives," he murmured.

"It is conscious, it consumes energy, it seeks to fight entropy and survive," Dieter said.

"Don't go all philosophical on me now," Sarah Connor said, leaning a little closer to him.

"We know Skynet is working on its time-travel program, *here,*"

John said, pointing to the Los Angeles basin—mostly dead zone, or contested. "It's getting close to the time."

Sarah stiffened slightly. She knew about Kyle, but she'd managed to avoid ever seeing him face-to-face; with communications as limited as they were, even a VIP like Sarah didn't have her image all over the place the way images had been displayed before Judgment Day. And, of course, since her "death," the few available images of her were of a younger woman.

"Well, let's go meet history," John said. "We can't chance anything else. If we don't counter what it's doing . . ."

Both of the elders nodded. John touched a button at his throat. "Major Nakamura," he said. "Operation Chrono is now *active.*"

■ ■ ■

Sarah kicked Snog's butt, hard.

"Hey!" he snapped. "What the hell are you doin'?"

She got up in the programmer's face and spoke through clenched teeth. "Get one of these things up and running, Snot!"

"That's Snog."

"And do it fast!" Sarah barked over his protest. "Time is literally of the essence right now."

" 'Kay," he muttered.

He opened the Terminator's scalp and popped open the channel that led to its CPU. This Terminator's unit had been fried during the first few minutes of their attack. It was now just so much inert metal and flesh. Until, that is, Snog installed the new CPU with the fresh programming that didn't include Skynet.

Snog sealed off the conduit and laid the flap of flesh back in place, sealing it with a bio-adhesive. "Done," he said. Then, "Stand."

Sarah licked her lips; she couldn't help it. The sight of a young, naked Dieter clone turned her on. She shook her head. *Sick, you're sick, Connor.*

"Follow," Snog said, and they began jogging toward the time displacement device on the other side of the installation.

■ ■ ■

John fired and ducked down behind a machine, then rolled several feet away from where he'd been. His heart was slamming against his ribs as if this was the first time he'd faced one of these monsters.

I want to stop this! I want to stop this now! Maybe if he could prevent the Terminator from going through time he would have prevented all this from happening. If Cyberdyne hadn't gotten that chip, they never would have been able to build Skynet in the first place.

Of course, then he wouldn't exist, but so what? Several billion other people would continue to live. If that wasn't worth dying for, what was?

He could see the Skynet scientists working frantically to make the time displacement device work and he willed them to fail. He saw the naked Terminator step up onto the platform.

"Shit!" he said, and rose from his place. With one shot he took out the heavily armed Terminator and began to zigzag his way through the complex. Two of its brethren turned toward him and began to fire. All around John his own troops moved in, throwing their own lives away in an attempt to save his. Even as he ran he could feel himself going pale. He wasn't worthy of this much sacrifice; no one was.

"Spare the scientists!" he shouted.

There was a blinding flare of light and the Terminator was gone. *Failed,* John thought in despair, dragging in air in ragged breaths. A nondescript man stepped onto the platform, his figure oddly ill-defined; John closed his eyes, remembering the T-1000 and how close it had come. Behind his eyelids he registered the flare that told that the T-1000 was gone. A beautiful young woman stepped onto the platform. John recognized her and took aim. She turned toward him and smiled. He fired and the flare of time displacement blinded him once again. John turned away, and someone knocked him to the floor and fired over his head. John could feel the heat of a near miss on his arm and smell the scorched fabric of his sleeve.

"Sorry, sir. Are you all right?"

John looked up at the soldier, blinking as multicolored spots danced in his vision. After a moment he saw the soldier's face and gasped. It was Kyle!

"Yes!" he snapped, and slid away. John picked up his weapon and moved forward. Unable to avoid the shudder that racked his thin frame.

Ahead of them, the last Terminator turned its weapon on the Luddite scientists who stood waiting for death. From every part of the lab, resistance fighters fired, destroying the Terminator before it could kill the humans.

John moved forward, terribly aware of Kyle at his back. He stopped before the two men and one woman who had betrayed humanity. They looked at him with contempt.

"We've won," the woman said. She licked her lips nervously and attempted a smirk.

One of the men turned toward the machine, diving toward the keyboard. John shot him in the leg and the man fell screaming. His two companions jerked and moved away from him. John reached out and grabbed the woman's arm, yanking her off balance and shoving her behind him. Then he thrust the plasma rifle's barrel up under the chin of the remaining male. Two of John's soldiers dragged the wounded scientist away from the console.

"You haven't won," John said between his teeth. The Luddite choked and raised his head as Connor pressed a little harder. John gestured with his head for more of his people to take charge of the scientist. He turned to the woman, who looked back at him defiantly. "And you're not going to win," he finished.

"Oh, yes we will." She sneered. "In a few moments you will disappear." She snapped her fingers. "Like that!"

"And why is that?" he asked. He felt as if he was reciting lines in a play. Not even a very good play.

"Because that Terminator is going to kill your mother!" She glared at the soldiers surrounding her. "Your precious Sarah Connor! And there's nothing you can do to stop it!"

John looked at her, a muscle jumping in his jaw. He wanted to pulverize this woman, to break her bones and reduce her to a weeping pile of jelly. It was rare for him in these later years to feel this much emotion, this much pure hate. It almost felt good. Slowly he reined it in.

Still looking at her, he said, "I need a volunteer!" And as John had known would happen, Kyle stepped forward without hesitation.

"I'll go," he said.

John looked at him. "You might not make it," he warned.

Reese shrugged. "We'll never know if we don't try, sir." He nodded. "I want to do it."

The male scientist snorted in contempt. "You'll never figure out how this machine works. Not in time."

"Oh, I don't know about that," Snog said. He breezed up to the console and stretched his knuckles like a pianist about to play a sonata; then he sat down in one of their vacated chairs.

This was the one place in which they'd cheated. John had told Snog and his group that they had intel that Skynet was working on a time machine and had assigned them to see if they could learn anything about it. Just that, a mere hint. But the techies had run with it and they'd followed almost every step of this team's progress. Snog probably knew as much about this machine as the Skynet team did.

"What date did you say, John?" Snog asked over his shoulder.

Not taking his eyes off the scientists, John told him, enjoying their disconcerted expressions. He glanced over at Kyle Reese. "You'll have to go through naked," he said. "And it's going to be a one-way trip. We'll be destroying this after you've gone through."

Reese nodded, then he began to strip. "Weapons?" he asked.

"Only flesh can go through," Snog said. "Or items encased in living flesh. So unless you can fit a plasma rifle up your own ass, you're on your own, buddy."

John stepped closer to Reese, leaning toward him so that the others wouldn't hear. "I have a message I want you to give my mother," he said. "Thank you, Sarah," he began.

■ ■ ■

In the darkness at the far edge of the factory, Sarah waited, the dormant Terminator by her side. Her vision grew blurry as she watched her son telling Kyle what to do. Giving him the precious message that had sustained her in her loneliness for so many years. She caught her breath in a sob, then dashed the tears from her eyes, and swallowing hard, waited for her part in this drama to begin.

The machine began to whine. John made Reese repeat the message, then nodded. "Remember," he said, "we have no fate but that we make for ourselves."

Reese looked at him as if in wonder and nodded. John held out his hand and the young soldier took it, lifting his chin in pride.

"Time!" Snog called out.

Reese looked at him, then climbed up onto the platform.

"Luck, man," Snog called out.

John closed his eyes, saw the brightness of time displacement, and when he opened them his father was gone. He took a deep breath, and when he'd finished letting it out his mother was standing beside him.

He looked down at her. Tears ran unchecked down her cheeks. John placed his arm around her shoulders and pulled her to him. Sarah laid her head against his chest for a moment, then sighed and pulled away. She tipped her head toward the Terminator beside her.

"Snog," John said, looking at the Terminator who would become Uncle Bob, his savior from the T-1000. "How do I do this?"

■ ■ ■

When it was gone Sarah touched John's shoulder and he looked down at her. "John," she said, her voice heavy with unshed tears, "we have to go. This place must have a failsafe."

He nodded and turned to lead the way.

"Sir?" a soldier said. "What do we do about them?" She tipped her head toward the Luddite scientists.

John's lips thinned and he reached for his sidearm.

"Allow me," Sarah said in a voice like the hiss of a knife sliding from its sheath. Before anyone could move, she took aim and shot; the scientists fell like puppets whose strings had been cut.

That is a disturbingly accurate metaphor, John thought. *And I've been in this business too long. Killing people is starting to seem routine.*

Then she turned and started walking, passing her son, who stood stunned behind her. "Let's go, people!" she shouted. "This place is gonna blow!"

John got himself walking with difficulty. That was the thing about this war. For the most part, it was machines they were fighting. But at bottom, it was people who had made it possible for Skynet to come as close to succeeding as it had. But this was the first time he'd seen his mother kill. He was genuinely horrified—and at the same time, deeply proud.

Outside, there was a small fleet of choppers waiting to take them away. He caught up to Sarah as she bent below the blades and put his hand on her shoulder. She turned to look at him.

"Thank you," he said. She couldn't hear him over the rotors, but she knew what he'd said.

Sarah touched his face. "You're welcome, son."

Inside the chopper there was no possibility of conversation, but he held her hand and ignored her tears as he knew she'd want him to.

After a long while they landed and Dieter was there to greet them. Sarah walked up to him and into his arms. He held her, saying nothing. John had been accosted by a soldier, who gave him a message; with a nod he thanked the woman and walked over to his mother and Dieter.

"The complex is destroyed," he said.

Sarah took a deep breath and turned toward him. "Good," she said wearily. Dieter stroked her arm and she looked up at him and smiled. "So," she said, "I guess it's all over but the shouting."

"Unfortunately," Dieter said, "I think there's quite a lot of shouting still to come."

Sarah smiled at John and he smiled sadly back.

"But we don't know what's coming," John said.

"We only know what's been," his mother agreed.

The Austrian looked from mother to son. "Then what's to come," he said, "is up to us."